Cover Design by Manoj Vijayan,
Marketing Edge Designs.Com

i

A Prophet

Without Honor

A Novel of Alternative History

by Joseph Wurtenbaugh

Acknowledgments

I wish to acknowledge with special thanks the services of Heather Flynn, who brought to the task of copyreading both an astonishingly acute professional acumen and the type of personal commitment that cannot be purchased with mere money.

My thanks also to Oliver Jarvis, for a thorough and professional proofreading;

To Ann Bilodeau, for another reading of scrupulous accuracy and strict attention to detail;

To my friends Scott Edwards, Kassandra Edwards, Mark Lawrence, and Karen Lawrence, for their initial reading of the manuscript and insightful comments; and, above all,

To my wife, Nina Zipkin-Berry, whose enthusiasm and belief in this book never wavered through a number of uncertain years, and without whom it would never have been completed.

Table of Contents

Historical Note

In March of 1936, Adolf Hitler undertook the first overt military aggression of the Third Reich, ordering the German army to reoccupy and 'remilitarize' the Rhineland, the Western part of Germany. The reoccupation was in breach of both the Versailles and Locarno Treaties, which had defined the area as a demilitarized zone, one in which no troops were to be stationed.

It was a daring undertaking. The general staff of the German army, the Wehrmacht, was strongly opposed to the operation. At that time, the rearmament of Germany had barely begun. The German military was still enfeebled. It could easily have been routed by even a small contingent of French or British forces. For that reason, the Wehrmacht insisted on precautionary orders to the troops to retreat immediately back to the frontier of the demilitarized zone at the least sign of opposition from the Western powers.

But the British and French did not know of this Order.

So no opposition occurred, and no retreat. The military venture was a complete triumph. Hitler went on to one spectacular diplomatic success after another in the latter half of the 30's, and from there, on to the catastrophe that engulfed the entire world. At the time, the Rhineland reoccupation seemed only one more incident in the ceaseless ebb and flow of European national politics. Only in retrospect did it become apparent that the West missed its best – possibly its only – opportunity to halt the Nazi momentum without significant human cost. Contemporary historians now view the remilitarization of the Rhineland as one of the great watersheds of Twentieth Century history. If the Allies had met the Nazi bluff with the slightest show of force, the balloon of Nazi pretension and 'the Man of Destiny' would have been punctured, perhaps decisively, and with negligible bloodshed – perhaps none at all.

Thus the small cause, thus the large effect – a breath of wind, or not, and the hurricane is born, or not. If the British and French had only known of the orders to retreat . . . that they could have opposed the German force with complete safety . . . but they did not know. So, they did nothing . . . and the main chance was lost.

If they had only known of the Order . . . everything would be different.

Preludes

Excerpt from: A History of Europe in the Twentieth Century
Giacomo Benedetti
Houghton, Mifflin (1957)

Can the course of history be changed by the actions of a single individual?

To ask the question is to answer it. Of course not! Heroes and villains are for children's fables, not scientific historians. If we are to do history seriously, we must do away with all such Romantic delusions.

The controversy that surrounds the role of Leutnant Karl von Haydenreich with respect to the Rhineland Affair and the Wehrmacht Putsch of 1936 is thus completely misplaced. The force of history is what doomed Adolf Hitler and the Third Reich. Had his demise not been caused by that group of men, it would have been another, soon enough.

Excerpt from: A History of Germany in the Twentieth Century
Josef Behrens
Alfred A Knopf (1964)

Everyone knows that the National Socialist regime – the so called 'Third Reich' – collapsed with dramatic speed in March of 1936. In short order, the Rhineland Affair led to the Wehrmacht Putsch of 1936.

But how? And why? And who?

It is in this context that the arguments concerning Karl von Haydenreich begin.

Excerpt from: Destiny Betrayed - A Chronicle of Treason
Harald Quandt
Franz Eher Nachfolger Gmbh (1952)

Karl von Haydenreich was the most monstrous traitor in German history. All alone, he brought about the collapse of the Third Reich. On that sad day, the German nation lost its last, best chance for glory.

4

Excerpt from: Memoirs
The Right Honourable Eric Phipps
Houghton, Mifflin (1946)

. . . [I]t is impossible for anyone who experienced the change in mood in Berlin in March 1936 to believe that event was a tragedy for anyone.

-

Excerpt from: My Name is Ike - Reflections on Fifty Years of Service as Soldier and Statesman
Senator Dwight D. Eisenhower
Random House (1986)

. . . [K]arl was my godson. I have mourned him all the days of my life. Those three weeks in March 1936 might have been the making of me as a public man, but sometimes I wish to God they had never happened. . .

-

Excerpt from: Service to the State - in War and Peace
Major General Werner von Blomberg
Reichswehr Press (1949)

I have no personal knowledge of the guilt or innocence of Karl von Haydenreich, despite the continual assertions to the contrary by my enemies.

Was he a traitor or not? It is hard to believe he could have played so central a part of these events without some deliberate choice.

-

Excerpt from: A Twentieth Century Life
Albert Sommerville
Houghton, Mifflin (1959)

Karl von Haydenreich was the best friend I ever had in my life, from our school days in Uppingham. True, he had an unaccountable sympathy for the Yid, an absurdly blind eye to the cunning and malice of that race.

But he would never have behaved dishonorably to anyone on any matter, large or small. Of this I am certain . . .

-

Excerpt from: Interview
Adolph Breslau
Der Spiegel, March 31, 1961

Karl von Haydenreich, the savior of Germany? The savior of German Jews? The von Haydenreich family was the most profoundly anti-Semitic family in all Bavaria. Karl himself gave financial support to the Nazis throughout his life.

5

His father was the ruin of my Aunt Rosamunde. The son's actions resulted in the torture and murder of my father.

I pray to God we be saved from any more saviors of that kind . . .

-

Excerpt from: Interview
Kurt Weill
New York Herald, June 4, 1949

I don't know anything about what sort of soldier Karl became or what took place at the Chancellery. I only knew him at the Hochschule.

But, God! How he could play the saxophone! He was born to that instrument. He should have stuck to it.

-

Excerpt from: A Twentieth Century Life
Albert Sommerville
Houghton, Mifflin (1959)

. . . [I] am often asked about Karl's widow, what she knows and what she might have said to me.

Elizabeth Whittingham and I are bound together by mutual admiration and a profound mutual grief. Our political differences are trifling in comparison. Our barbed exchanges in Parliament are as often as not the prelude to the sharing of a glass of wine, or a convivial dinner with her family and whomever I am married to at the time.

But she has never discussed March 1936 with me. She never will, with me or anyone. Historians must look elsewhere . . .

-

Excerpt from: Preface
My Name is Ike - Reflections on Fifty Years of Service as Soldier and Statesman
Senator Dwight D. Eisenhower
Random House (1986)

. . . These memoirs will be published on March 31, 1986, the fiftieth anniversary of the date of the Wehrmacht Putsch. I regretted frustrating all my contemporaries, but about Karl, and all that happened, I could only speak comfortably from beyond the grave. With luck, enough time has passed that the uproar has subsided. Even now, I would have preferred silence. But history must be served.

If all has gone according to plan, my friend Kurt von Hammerstein's memoirs will appear this same day, as well as the publication of Karl's journals . . .

-

Excerpt from: Preface
A General Speaks - the Autobiography of Kurt von Hammerstein Equord
Major General Kurt von Hammerstein Equord
Reichswehr Press (1986)

... [B]y agreement with Senator Eisenhower and Mrs. Whittingham, these memoirs of mine will appear posthumously on March 31, 1986, the fiftieth anniversary of the date of the Wehrmacht Putsch. Like Senator Eisenhower, I, too, would have preferred silence . . .

-

Excerpt from: Preface
The Journals of Karl von Haydenreich, 1922 - 1936
Alfred A Knopf (1986)

The long-awaited publication of the journals of Karl von Haydenreich, kept between 1922 and 1936, will finally occur on March 31, 1986, the same day as the publication of the memoirs of Senator Dwight D. Eisenhower and Major-General Kurt von Hammerstein Equord. This extraordinary triple event reflects an agreement made by the principals nearly forty years ago, in January of 1947.

The publishers express their gratitude to the author's widow, the Rt. Honorable Elizabeth Whittingham (MP, QC), for making the material available. Mrs. Whittingham has provided no comment on the contents, and wishes to make it known that she will not respond to any inquiries, either professional or personal, concerning those same contents, or any of the events of March 1936 . . .

-

Excerpt from: My Name is Ike - Reflections on Fifty Years of Service as Soldier and Statesman
Senator Dwight D. Eisenhower
Random House (1986)

To understand anything about Karl, you must understand his relation to his stepmother. He admired his father, but he adored his stepmother.

-

Excerpt from: Destiny Betrayed - A Chronicle of Treason
Harald Quandt
Franz Eher Nachfolger Gmbh (1952)

... [I]t is only necessary to add that he was corrupted by his stepmother from an early age . . .

-

7

Excerpt from: A Twentieth Century Life
Albert Sommerville
Houghton, Mifflin (1959)

     . . . [T]here is no question that his character, his beliefs, his values, were shaped largely by his stepmother. This may not have been altogether to the good. She was, after all, a Yid.

       -

Excerpt from: A General Speaks - the Autobiography of Kurt von Hammerstein
Equord
Major General Kurt von Hammerstein Equord
Reichswehr Press (1986)

     . . . Leutnant von Haydenreich very rarely spoke of his parentage, but when he did, it was always with respect for his father, unlimited affection for his stepmother . . .

Mummi

Excerpt from: A History of Germany in the Twentieth Century
Josef Behrens
Alfred A Knopf (1964)

Between 1880 and 1914, the late summer was a busy time for that vast military machine known as the German Army. It was then that what were known as the Kaiser Maneuvers took place, vast field exercises in various open fields in Germany, beginning in late July with brigade and division maneuvers, and working up to full field corps by September. These had a serious military purpose, but were conducted in a deliberately light spirit. Military bands performed music for German villages that was not otherwise available to them. Many older men recalled their first experiences with the Maneuvers (at ages 16 and 17) as their first adventures away from home, something of a lark, the way boys from other nations went to summer camp.

Senior officers and others, of course, could expect to be away from their homes for extended periods during the Maneuvers, no matter how pressing personal commitments might be.

1910

-

September 1, 1910
Neustrelitz am Schliersee
Bavarian Alps

Captain Heinrich-Werner Mertz von Haydenreich
First Royal Field Artillery Brigade
First Royal Bavarian Division
First Royal Bavarian Corps
At Kaiser Maneuvers, near a field near Berlin

CAPTAIN STOP LOTTIE BEGAN LABOR TONIGHT STOP HAVE
SUMMONED DOCTOR FIEDLER STOP BIRTH IMMINENT STOP
FRAULEIN ROSAMUNDE BRESLAU

-

September 2, 1910
Neustrelitz am Schliersee
Bavarian Alps

Captain Heinrich-Werner Mertz von Haydenreich
First Royal Field Artillery Brigade
First Royal Bavarian Division
First Royal Bavarian Corps
At Kaiser Maneuvers, near a field near Berlin

My dear Captain,

It is with the greatest pleasure I write to inform you of the birth
yesternight of your first son, to be christened (as I am informed) Werner-
Karl Mertz von Haydenreich. The labor of Frau von Haydenreich began
unexpectedly on the morning of September 1st. I was summoned to the
castle during dinner and came as quickly as I could, arriving at about 8
p.m. Labor was already far advanced and proceeded in the normal manner
until shortly after midnight, when she was delivered of a healthy baby boy.

Mother and son are both doing well. There was perhaps more
blood loss than I would have liked, but I am confident in her full recovery.

Again, my congratulations.

Sincerely,

Dr. Leonard Fiedler

-

September 2, 1910
Neustrelitz am Schliersee
Bavarian Alps

Captain Heinrich-Werner Mertz von Haydenreich
First Royal Field Artillery Brigade
First Royal Bavarian Division
First Royal Bavarian Corps
At Kaiser Maneuvers, near a field near Berlin

```
CAPTAIN VON HAYDENREICH STOP COME AT ONCE STOP
CHARLOTTE IN TERRIBLE DANGER STOP PAY NO ATTENTION
TO FIEDLER STOP COME HOME PLEASE STOP ROSAMUNDE
BRESLAU
```

September 4, 1910
Neustrelitz am Schliersee
Bavarian Alps

Captain Heinrich-Werner Mertz von Haydenreich
First Royal Field Artillery Brigade
First Royal Bavarian Division
First Royal Bavarian Corps
At Kaiser Maneuvers, near a field near Berlin

My dear Captain von Haydenreich,

Forgive the tears that stain this page, but I can't stop weeping like a child! I would rather choke to death on these words than put them on paper – your beautiful wife, my best of all friends, Lottie, is dead, DEAD!!! She died early this morning of blood loss and other complications – Fiedler has given reasons, but I don't trust his explanations – what matters is that your wonderful wife, and my lovely friend, is gone forever!

I am doing my best to provide comfort to poor little Magdalena – such a wonderful little girl – but she doesn't understand what has happened to her mother – how could she? What does one say to a three-year-old? Only yesterday she was so radiant with joy at the birth of her baby brother! Oh, your son is fine, and doing well. I should have begun with that. I have sent for a wet nurse from the village.

And now I find myself overwhelmed again – tears smear the ink – forgive me, Captain von Haydenreich – I have made a fine mess of this letter, but it would be useless to begin again, as the same thing would

12

happen. I will write when I have regained my composure. I am so very, very devastated – God have mercy!!

Sincerely,

Fraulein Rosamunde Breslau

-

September 5, 1910
Neustrelitz am Schliersee
Bavarian Alps

Captain Heinrich-Werner Mertz von Haydenreich
First Royal Field Artillery Brigade
First Royal Bavarian Division
First Royal Bavarian Corps
At Kaiser Maneuvers, near a field near Berlin

Dear Captain von Haydenreich,

Once again, I must implore your forgiveness for assuming an unpardonable familiarity with you. But I don't understand why I haven't heard from you – surely messages of this importance must be delivered even during maneuvers – something must have gone terribly wrong – I hope no misfortune has befallen you. In any case, someone must inform you of these awful events – I wish it were anyone but me – I think it best to continue as if you had received my telegrams and letters. I am myself today, and I think capable of acquainting you with all the details of this nightmare. (I still pray I will awake and find it was only that, only a horrible dream!)

I arrived on the 24th as we had planned. Lottie looked wonderful. I thought at first that the plan of having her confinement take place at the family estate had worked to perfection. She glowed with health and energy. She was so happy! She was certain she was going to present you with a son. We spent a few happy days together and made plans to fill the time before and after the birth. Lottie looked forward to you and me renewing our old acquaintance and once again becoming friends.

On Thursday, during the afternoon, Lottie suddenly began to experience spasms. These were of the most painful and intense kind. We did not know what to make of this, because her time was not due for nearly three weeks. I became extremely concerned. She was in such distress, even agony! When these continued past dinner, we sent for Dr. Fiedler.

He did not arrive until nearly ten. He was in the company of a midwife, a Frau Achterkirchen. By that time, Lottie was in the full throes

13

of what even I could see was true labor. I know this to be extremely painful, but that is woman's lot. Still, it seemed to me that there was far more distress than I thought was normal. Fiedler seemed kindly enough, and well-intentioned, but very much a country doctor. Frau Achterkirchen seemed no more than competent. I wished then that Lottie had gone to Munich.

But it seemed to go well enough, and so quickly! I thought at the time this was a godsend. Your son Karl emerged into the world at about 12:20 a.m., praise all. Truth be told, he came on his own accord, without my assistance, or Dr. Fiedler's, or barely his mother's, for he was obviously a strong healthy boy with an appetite to live. He is doing quite well, and the only sunshine in this whole world of night. Of course, he does not know yet he will never know his wonder of a mother – and now I have succeeded in undoing myself again.

I am resuming a little while later, with my tears dried, and will try not to make a fool of myself again. It was at the moment of rejoicing at Karl's birth, when all seemed best, that all became worst. There was too much bleeding – I was sure of it – I was also certain that the afterbirth had not been completely discharged. Fiedler disagreed with me, though it seemed to me he was uneasy. He and the midwife stopped the bleeding with a combination of hot and cold compresses, and said all was well. Lottie had fallen asleep, but not the sound sleep of a happy mother – something deeper and more ominous – I could not make Fiedler and his helper understand. They kept saying this was normal, when I knew it was not. But then they left.

I made up my bed in my best friend's room, determined to be with her when she awoke. But, oh, Captain, she never did – at least, not entirely. She continued in that troubled unsleep all the night and the next day. We sent for Fiedler, but he did not come. That was when I sent the telegram, for I knew then something was terribly wrong! But we waited and prayed, and hoped her own strong constitution would see her through safely. I stayed with her the whole long day, hoping and praying.

I barely took my eyes off her. But that evening, about eight o'clock, I looked over and was horrified to see her bed sopping with blood. Something must have given way within her womb. I screamed for Frau Schallert, who came running with the nearest housemaid. We did what we could, but with the amount of blood and her feebleness, we worked without

14

hope. At the last moment, Lottie seemed to wake. For a moment, she was herself. She smiled at me – Oh, God this is an unendurable memory! Then she squeezed my hand – I am certain she was thinking of you, Captain, though I could not tell you why!! But she was too weak to say anything. A moment later she was with God, and my heart was breaking – I must stop again.

Fiedler came later that night. He looked as guilty and ashamed as he should – for we found the remains of the afterbirth in Lottie's bed, so I was right all along. But I was too exhausted and devastated to remonstrate with him. He said he would write to your father, but did not mention you. From what Lottie told me, that sounds typical.

So I console myself by consoling your daughter Magdalena, who now has a child's awareness of what has happened. She sits in my lap by the hour and I distract her with stories, and thus distract myself. I try to keep from weeping – meanwhile, there cannot be a sweeter baby than your new son Karl, a little angel – and now with an angel for a mother – I'm sure she watches over him!

There I go again. I don't understand why you have not come or even answered! You must not have received my letters and telegrams. But how can that be?

Sincerely,

Fraulein Rosamunde Breslau

P.S. I have re-read this letter and hardly recognize the woman who wrote it. Had we resumed our friendship under the circumstances we originally planned, I hope you would have encountered a woman with a certain poise and delicacy of manner, instead of the giddy girl you remembered. But I am –

There I go – as if my vanity mattered!! At such a desolate time – I would start again, but this is the fourth try – every time my foolish heart fails me!

Please return home quickly!

R.

-

September 7, 1910
Kaiser Maneuvers, field near Berlin

Captain Heinrich-Werner Mertz von Haydenreich
First Royal Field Artillery Brigade

15

First Royal Bavarian Division
First Royal Bavarian Corps
At Kaiser Maneuvers, near a field near Berlin

My esteemed Captain,

Enclosed in the attached dispatch bag find (a) a telegram and letter from Dr. Leonard Fiedler, and (b) two telegrams and two letters from a Fraulein Rosamunde Breslau. I have learned this day that this correspondence was withheld from you at the direction of your father under his authority as unit commander. I have forwarded them to you with all possible dispatch.

You are granted leave from the Kaiser Maneuvers, effective immediately, to attend to these family matters. My staff and I express our sincere and utmost sympathy for your loss. Divisional flags will be flown at half-mast for the next three weeks.

My heartfelt condolences,
Rupprecht Maria Luitpold Ferdinand
Commander, Royal Bavarian Army

[Added by hand]
P.S. Heinz, the behavior of your father is inexcusable. My sincerest condolences.

Rupprecht

-

September 7, 1910
Kaiser Maneuvers, field near Berlin

FRAULEIN BRESLAU STOP JUST RECEIVED COMMUNICATIONS DELAYED IN TRANSIT STOP AM PROCEEDING AT ONCE TO SCHLIERSEE STOP EXPECT TO ARRIVE BY THE 9TH STOP ETERNAL THANKS FOR WHAT YOU HAVE DONE STOP HEINRICH VON HAYDENREICH

-

September 7, 1910
Kaiser Maneuvers, field near Berlin

Captain Heinz Haydenreich
Neustrelitz am Schliersee

Little Brother,

I'd like to begin this letter with one of those expressions of epigrammatic wit for which I am so renowned (some would say notorious), but I am too devastated to think of any epigrams worthy of my reputation. In a different situation, the knowledge that I am no longer burdened with the duty of producing an heir to the house of Haydenreich would be cause for shouts to the highest heaven. But, Heinz, the loss of Charlotte causes me too much anguish to think of doing any shouting, except to shout for more wine, and enough to blot out the sun. If I was forced to choose a woman, Lottie would have been the one I chose; and, as God is my witness, I might even have come to love her. I can only imagine the grief of an unrepentant heterosexual such as yourself. If there is anything I can do, please, please, please call on me.

Father's absurd behavior is the talk of the encampment. Once again, in his determination to out-Junker the Junkers, he makes a prodigious ass of himself. I hear he is to be summoned before the Prince to account for himself. How you will deal with this outrage is for you to decide, but you will have my sympathy and support no matter what action you choose to take.

With a heart aching with grief,

Willy

P.S. You won both personal and divisional commendations, delivered to me in your absence by Rupprecht himself. I'm sure they mean as little to you as have the all others. Father will be as pleased and frustrated as he always is. I will send them along to you.

W.

September 8, 1910
Kaiser Maneuvers,
Staff headquarters, Royal Bavarian Army

Captain Heinrich-Werner Mertz von Haydenreich
First Royal Field Artillery Brigade
First Royal Bavarian Division
First Royal Bavarian Corps
Neustrelitz am Schliersee

My son,

I am directed by Crown Prince Rupprecht to offer explanations to you for the withholding of mail and telegrams during the last week. We both know no explanations are necessary. My fear was that knowledge of the developments at Neustrelitz would cause you to request leave to abandon your post at the Maneuvers. (Perhaps if the messages had come from a reputable source, I would have thought differently of the matter, but Fiedler did not send any message indicating an emergency.) This would be still another blemish on your record and the Haydenreich name. It would constitute still another impediment to your advancement. I know you understood my reasons. There was no reason for complaint to Prince Rupprecht.

Most confinements go smoothly. I am deeply regretful this one did not, and express my profound sympathy. Let me at the same time congratulate you on the birth of your son, who will one day inherit the name and estates of the Haydenreichs. He comes into the world with the sad burden of Siegfried, as the cause of his mother's death. Perhaps he will be a true German hero.

I am looking forward to meeting my grandson.

With profound sympathy,
Oberstleutnant Wilhelm-Werner Mertz von Haydenreich
Staff Officer
First Royal Bavarian Division
First Royal Bavarian Corps

-

September 10, 1910
Neustrelitz am Schliersee
Bavarian Alps

Oberstleutnant Wilhelm-Werner Mertz von Haydenreich
Staff Officer
First Royal Bavarian Division
First Royal Bavarian Corps

Father,

I am too much afflicted with grief, my time too beset with labor, to leave any room for your complaints.

Your letter was characteristically silent about your granddaughter Magdalena, who I know for a certainty does not exist in your view of the world. Even so, I will tell you she begins to realize that her mother is gone forever, a sight that breaks the heart of those who do love her. As for 'reputable sources', please, no more of that eternally wearisome and

18

disagreeable issue. It is in fact our great good fortune that Fraulein Breslau, who – as disreputable as you may perceive her to be, in the blindness of your bigotry – I will remind you was Lottie's best friend in life, was here. Magdalena spends most of her time in the Fraulein's arms and appears to find some consolation there. I fully approve of this.

You did not ask when the funeral will take place, which is just as well, for you would not be welcome at it.

Your grandson is indeed healthy and lusty and a delight to all of us. Please do not ask when you will see him, for I have no idea when that will be.

You must know I did not bring this sordid matter to the attention of Prince Rupprecht. You have only yourself to blame for his lowered opinion of you.

I did find time to make a rough estimate of the condition of our finances. I am confident we will be able to continue yours and Willy's stipends as before. Do not trouble me with any more letters.

As ever,

Heinrich-Werner Mertz von Haydenreich

-

September 10, 1910
Neustrelitz am Schliersee
Bavarian Alps

Captain Wilhelm-Werner Mertz von Haydenreich II
First Royal Heavy Cavalry Brigade
First Royal Bavarian Division
First Royal Bavarian Corps

Dear Willy,

It is my regret far more than yours that your famous wit has failed you, for I could use a bit of it about now. Everyone does their best to put a brave face on things, but Neustrelitz feels as desolate as the third act of *Tristan*. My newborn son is a wonder, but we are reminded with each cry that he will never know his mother – and what to say to my darling little girl Lena?

Fortunately, Fraulein Rosamunde Breslau arrived the Wednesday before. I am not sure you remember her. I met her five years ago in Munich, during the weeks I spent there reorganizing the family's finances. She was Lottie's best friend. The two of them (the 'light princess' and the

19

'dark princess', as they were known) made a striking impression in certain Munich social circles. For a while, we were a lively threesome in Munich in those same circles, until my feelings for Lottie became profound and a formal courtship began. After that, I saw much less of the 'dark princess'.

Fraulein Breslau had already earned my gratitude for her forthright letter about Lottie's death. She had come to attend the birth and stay with Lottie afterward, but now she bustles about with unlimited energy and accomplishes much that is presently beyond me. The funeral is set for next Saturday. Thanks to her efforts, it will be well-organized and a proper farewell to Lottie. Her activity makes possible the private moments I need, in which I can throw off the stoic mask and give vent to my own grief – for I have loved Lottie as I never have, and never will, love another. There are times when I must be alone, when I cannot endure the company of another being. Fraulein Breslau has a blessed sensitivity to this.

At other times, I find consolation in small mercies. God be praised for taking Frau von Eisen these three years. How that worthy woman would have endured the loss of her only child – the thought is unbearable. But perhaps she and Lottie are happy together in Paradise. I wish my own faith extended so far.

One practical note I must include – I intend to adhere to the schedule I had made for the surveys and creditors meetings next year. Our fortunes continue to prosper. We are going to be able to continue your stipend and Father's at the same rate (if he can avoid too many champagne and caviar dinners with Frau Brehmer), and possibly even raise them. I know this is trifling good news at this time, but I thought I would share it.

I believe in my heart that life holds nothing more for me. I will live beyond this, because I must, for Lena and my new son Karl. Thank you for your generosity of spirit.

Your little brother,

Heinz

P.S. Please do not ask for any special leave to attend the funeral. Father has created scandal enough about this. Lottie knew, and I know, how much you cared for her. A better time will come.

H.

-

Excerpt from: A Twentieth Century Life
Albert Sommerville
Houghton, Mifflin (1959)

I realized the moment I exited the station I was in one of the most beautiful places on earth – the lake with its deep placid blue, the sky above with light fleecy clouds, and everywhere the smell of pine scent . . . Looking down over all is the mansion, a castle really, with a magnificent medieval grandeur, where Karl was born and where the family lived.

-

Excerpt from: My Name is Ike - Reflections on Fifty Years of Service as
Soldier and Statesman
Senator Dwight D. Eisenhower
Random House (1986)

. . . [I]'d formed a view in my mind's eye from what Heinz had said, but in no way did it prepare me for the reality. As God is my witness, Neustrelitz is the most beautiful place in the world. A crystal blue lake meets a cloudless blue sky, framed by the most picturesque mountains and pine forests imaginable.

-

September 23, 1910
Neustrelitz am Schliersee
Bavarian Alps

Dear Captain von Haydenreich,

I am addressing this note to you because words would in all probability fail me should we meet directly.

I give you the humblest of all apologies for the incident this afternoon. Once again, the fullness of my heart overwhelms me and I embarrass myself. I am truly, truly sorry and hope you can forgive me.

With the most profound and sincere remorse,
Fraulein Rosamunde Breslau

-

September 23, 1910
Neustrelitz am Schliersee
Bavarian Alps

Dearest Fraulein Breslau,

I regret that I cannot offer you forgiveness for your behavior, for the prosaic reason that there is nothing to forgive. You did not offend

21

anybody or ruin anything. The purity and nobility of your spirit shone through every tear you shed. Your conduct commanded admiration and respect of the other guests, rather than disapproval. It bespoke the sincerity and immensity of your grieving for Lottie, which touched everyone.

I have replied in writing because I sensed you preferred the veil of words to a personal meeting. However, I have some matters of utmost personal importance to discuss with you. If it is not inconvenient, could we plan to meet for luncheon at 1:30 tomorrow?

With the most profound and sincere respect,

Captain Heinrich Mertz von Haydenreich

-

September 25, 1910
Neustrelitz am Schliersee
Bavarian Alps

Captain Wilhelm-Werner Mertz von Haydenreich
First Royal Heavy Cavalry Brigade
First Royal Bavarian Division
First Royal Bavarian Corps

Dear Willy,

It is Sunday evening, two days since my beloved Charlotte was laid to her eternal rest, and time now to assemble my thoughts and convey them to you.

But first let me describe to you Lottie's funeral. It was in all ways a success, assuming that word has any meaning in connection with such an event. For this, all credit goes to Fraulein Breslau. The events began at 11:00 at St. Sixtus. We first had to endure a sermon by Monsignor Bergren, that was as dull and pointless as they all are, but mercifully brief. This was followed by a procession to the family plot. This made a striking impression – Fraulein Breslau had somehow persuaded the von Knabens to provide their Percherons for the occasion. They made a splendid appearance in their black drapes, which Fraulein Breslau also managed to procure from somewhere.

Ah, Willy, it was a day of such aching beauty – if we did have to exile our worthy dead from this vale of tears, what a magnificent site we chose for them! I will not break my heart again by describing the interment. But the funeral feast after that was held outdoors, on the strip just outside the plot, a suggestion of Fraulein Breslau's. Frau Schallert

22

brought out the platters from the castle. It proved to be an ideal setting. The effect was perfection. I even wondered for a moment if I might one day be happy again.

The dramatic moment came a bit later. After food and drink, the persons in the assembly were asked to share vivid recollections of Lottie. This was still another suggestion of Fraulein Breslau, and a very good one. Rather than tepid, and usually very poor poems and declarations, we heard a series of vivid and often very humorous anecdotes concerning my wonderful, beloved wife. The gathering became lively, even festive. That may shock you, but I felt that Lottie was with us then, brought back from the dead for a moment by this gaiety – for she loved gaiety. The denouement came, however, with Fraulein Breslau herself. She had prepared in great earnest for the occasion, and had a number of accounts of adventures she had shared with Lottie in school and later at Munich social occasions, all quite innocent, and some very amusing.

But in the midst of a reminiscence about our wedding, of a sudden she caught herself, began to stammer, and then to weep openly – and copiously, buckets of tears. She fell into the arms of the bewildered Monsignor, who passed her over to me. Between sobs on my shoulder, she informed me that she had just then realized that the route to the family plot was the same as our wedding procession, and had been unable to stem the flood of tears. This caused others in the assembly to recollect their grief and return to mourning. My own eyes flooded. But these emotions were so natural and even inevitable that they did not undercut the previous high spirits, but augmented them, like a good baseline in a piano score. The result was that the day was all I could have wished for as a farewell to my beloved. Authentic laughter and authentic tears, and how my Lottie would have approved of both!

I am in receipt of a completely unnecessary letter of apology from Fraulein Breslau. I really did not know her all that well in Munich, simply as a gay companion. She is an interesting personality – dignified and highly intelligent, but possessed of extremely powerful emotions, which she does her best to control, not entirely with success. However, when her feelings do overcome her, the result is actions and gestures of such a sincere and authentic nature that they are always appropriate and often noble. Though all observers are touched by this, she herself is mortified and then apologizes quite needlessly for such conduct. She has been a very valuable, even essential, member of the household at this trying time.

But there is more, and also concerning Fraulein Breslau. I arranged a luncheon meeting to speak with her about possibly extending her stay through Christmas, as Lena has become inordinately attached to her and the separation would not be good so soon after the loss of her mother. When I made this proposal, Fraulein Breslau informed me somewhat shyly that she also had given thought to the matter. Subject to my consent, she hoped to stay as long as necessary to secure the children's well-being. She mentioned that she had surveyed the huntsman's cottage, the one near the lake, that has been vacant since we reduced our household. She believed it could be furnished in a way that would meet all the needs of a woman of her station, and that the separate quarters would also address any question of social decorum.

Still more. She had ascertained that there was a definite need for an instructress at the Miesbach Gymnasium, in English and French, in both of which she is fluent. Then – she is that sort of woman – there were tears again, that she did her best to stem. She told me that she had fallen in love with Lena and little Karl and could not bear to leave them, that I would be making her the most blessed of women if I permitted her to stay. She expressed these thoughts as she always does, interrupting herself with constant apologies for her temerity, her tears, the love she expressed for children who are not hers, etc., etc. She is really the most amazingly diffident woman for a person with such a good heart!

However, so far from being annoyed, I find these qualities profoundly endearing. I had an impulse to take her in my arms and kiss away her tears – an impulse, I assure you, composed entirely of tenderness and sympathy and no baser element. (The voice of the carnal devil is quite still at this moment; I doubt I shall ever hear it again.) Instead, I politely ignored both her tears and apologies, took her hand, thanked her for her love and concern for my children, and at once accepted her offer. I did insist on seeing to the appointments in the cottage myself, as I am quite sure she would be hesitant in requesting all she needs. Her tears disappeared, she became quite cheerful, and we discussed the particulars in some detail over lunch.

You need hardly remind me that this is an extremely irregular living arrangement. Yet it seems to me practicable in the short term, indeed, perhaps the only practicable one. I am too numb with grief to undertake the task of obtaining a suitable governess, even if one were available on such short notice. Rosamunde Breslau is older than any governess would be, wiser, and extremely intelligent. Already there is a strong bond of love between her, Lena, and baby Karl. The prolongation of her stay seems to fit all needs, as odd as it might seem to live in this manner.

As for the rest, I have applied to the Prince for transfer to the reserves, which application I believe is certain to be granted. I am slightly closer to forty than thirty now, and have given active service enough. This news you can share with Father. He will be as angry as the devil, but this is an anger to which I am quite accustomed. I must prepare for the creditors' meeting, which I believe will go quite well. But this will require time and travel, another reason I am grateful to Fraulein Breslau – or Rosamunde, to name her as the others in the house do.

With that, adieu, older brother. When next we see each other, we shall find a time for your own personal farewell to Lottie, as I promised.

Your affectionate younger brother,

Heinz

-

December 26, 1910
Karlsfeld
Munich, in the district of Dachau

Fraulein Rosamunde Breslau
Neustrelitz am Schliersee

My dearest sister,

I hope this letter finds you well and in good health. However, you should know that your prolonged absence from Karlsfeld has become a subject of considerable discussion amongst your family. In fact, we talked of little else during our Christmas feast. A decision was reached that I should write to you on behalf of all, to express our reservations we all share about the irregularity of your situation.

Your decision to prolong your stay at Neustrelitz after the shocking death of Frau Haydenreich was, I think, received sympathetically by all of us. You are to be commended for undertaking a work of the most profound Christian charity in the giving of comfort to a family so grievously afflicted. The prolongation of your visit for these reasons was not cause for any anxiety.

However, your stay has now extended ten weeks. You also tell us that you have accepted a position as assistant schoolmistress in the gymnasium in Miesbach. There seems to be no end to this visit of yours. Are you planning an indefinite stay?

We cannot approve of such an arrangement. You *do* have a family in Karlsfeld, Rosamunde, to which you belong and to whom you owe the proper duty. There is, in addition, the question of propriety. Although I know you well enough to be certain you have not compromised your honor, the fact is that you are sharing a house, no matter how large, with a widower in his early middle years. No matter how virtuous your conduct in reality, scandal based on mere appearances is sure to arise, and no less odious for its falsity. You must not allow your reputation to be sullied in this way.

I implore you to pay your respects to Herr Haydenreich as soon as convenient, and make plans to return to your family's bosom at once. On these matters, your entire family is in agreement. I convey this advice to you on behalf of all of us, with your best interests at heart.

Your affectionate brother,

Fritz

-

December 29, 1910
Neustrelitz am Schliersee
Bavarian Alps

Herr Frederick Breslau
Breslau and Breslau
Munich, Germany

My brother,

I considered whether I should wait to answer your letter until my anger had cooled, but decided instead to reply while my indignation was still high. How completely you have misjudged the situation! But this is hardly the first time. Besides, I know Mama well enough to know that she does not share these sentiments. Since Papa died, she is simply too intimidated by you and the others to speak her mind.

I remain here because I am needed here, and useful. That is enough reason to stay. Do you think I would ever abandon my poor Lottie's motherless children while they are in need of love?!! And they are so easy to love – Magdalena – her smile was missing for so long, but now it greets me like the sunrise when first I see her in the morning – I share baby Karl's joy as the world begins to unfold before him, in all its splendor – these moments are treasures to me!

You may inform whatever wagging tongues you meet that I have separate quarters from the main house, in a cottage between the manse and the lake, that Herr von Haydenreich has furnished in a simple, comfortable manner. We do not share living quarters. This man's heart belongs to one woman and one woman alone, my poor friend Lottie. Every day he visits her grave. Every day, he sheds his own quiet tears there. There is nothing between us but friendship and respect. He has no sense of me as a woman, no feeling at all for me in that way. That is completely apparent to everyone, and to me especially.

I remain at Neustrelitz because I love and am loved by these children, and find a warmth completely missing from my life at Karlsfeld. Let that be my answer to the family. I hope you will convey that to all of them, with my sincere respect and affection. Please express my undying gratitude for all their concern for my happiness and honor.

With sincere gratitude for your concern about my virtue,

Rosamunde

P.S. Gossip indeed! Does anyone seriously think that this man would take a Jewess for his mistress? Heinrich-Werner Mertz von Haydenreich?

Whose father and brother are among the most prominent anti-Semites in all of Europe?

R.

1911

-

February 11, 1911
Munich, Bavaria

Captain Heinrich-Werner Mertz von Haydenreich
Neustrelitz am Schliersee

My son Heinrich,

... [Y]ou propose to resign from the army? You have three times
now won mention from His Imperial Majesty in the Annual Maneuvers –
how can you throw away this jewel of renown as if it were a pebble you
found stuck in your shoe? Your behavior is incomprehensible. Once again
you besmirch the Haydenreich name, with no thought of the generations
who bestowed their lives and honor to secure its nobility.

But these decisions merely cause me shame. Others fill me with
disgust and horror. Am I to understand that my grandson is now in the care
of a Hebrew woman? Not only Jewish but a member of the Breslau family,
who – as you know better than I – were the instruments of our family ruin?
I had hoped you regretted the part you played in that fiasco – evidently not!
That you would ever allow your son to come under the influence of such a
person is beyond all understanding.

I will not set foot on the estates at Neustrelitz until you have
revised all these arrangements. Please consider your family honor.

Your Father,

Oberstleutnant Wilhelm-Werner Mertz von Haydenreich
Staff Officer
First Royal Bavarian Division
First Royal Bavarian Corps

-

February 12, 1911
Neustrelitz am Schliersee

Oberstleutnant Wilhelm-Werner Mertz von Haydenreich
Munich, Bavaria

Dearest Father,

With respect to yours of the 11th, I regret I must correct your
understanding of certain historical facts. What brought our family to the
brink of ruin was the epic mismanagement of the estate over 150 years by a
number of heads of the Haydenreich family, you yourself being the last

and possibly the worst. What has permitted us to salvage something of the ruin is the forbearance of our creditors. The most, not the least, generous among them was the firm of Breslau and Breslau, and in particular, the late Adolph Breslau, which you now repay by casually slandering his daughter. You owe a debt of gratitude to them and him, rather than your curses.

As far as the influence of Fraulein Breslau, if as a result of such influence Karl avoids joining the ranks of the spendthrifts, gamblers, alcoholics, adulterers, and ordinary fools who have adorned our family tree over the last few generations, I will be eternally grateful to the Fraulein. If she were to have such a sublime influence on my baby boy, I would be indifferent to whether she was Jewish, or a Hindu priestess, or danced bare-skinned around a totem in the manner of a Red Indian. I would be forever grateful for such influence.

Your son,
Heinrich
-

March 9, 1911
Neustrelitz am Schliersee

Captain Heinrich-Werner Mertz von Haydenreich
At the offices of Bayer, Leverkusen, Westphalia

Dear Heinz,

Vexed am I, exceedingly wroth am I, to have missed you on the rather unexpected grant of leave that suddenly fell my way. Off on family business, so I am told. I do hope this letter finds its way to you, so you will know forthwith of my displeasure!

My first meeting with my little nephew – and what a wonder he is! Quite a bold young man, for when I smiled at him, at our first meeting, he smiled fearlessly back at me, and even took my finger in his little fist! He has already begun to push around on his hands, looking for adventure – a born cavalry officer! With Lena, I make jokes, and she laughs and puts her hands to her mouth. Fraulein Breslau is teaching her to read. Soon she will be as pretty as was her mother.

Ah, Fraulein Breslau! As you requested, I left my 'ignoble prejudices' at the door, though I am at a loss to know why calling a thing by its proper name is an ignoble act. A Jew is, after all, a Jew. But I could see why you trust her. The house observes a respectable mourning, yet everyone bustles about as always. The Fraulein seems able to resolve any domestic problem with a smile and a nod, and everything goes smoothly.

Then she is off on her bicycle to her classes at Miesbach. She is both a Jew and the New Woman, two reasons I should despise her. Yet I found myself liking her.

Not without her womanly attributes, either, despite her mourning garb. Even a man of different inclinations can see that there are some delectable roundnesses there, particularly when she pedals her bicycle! I am surprised you have not taken her to bed. I know you mourn still, but a man is still a man, little brother, and you must begin to live again. The voice of the carnal demon, as you style it, will not be silent forever. Be again the Heinrich of your university days! You could do worse than to fill your days with an attractive Jewess, while you look for someone suitable.

Your older, wiser brother,

Willy

-

March 25th, 1911
Munich, Bavaria

Fraulein Rosamunde Breslau
Neustrelitz am Schliersee

My dearest sister,

You have now been residing at the home of Heinrich Haydenreich for over six months. How long do you intend to continue with this highly irregular situation? The same people who once extolled your Christian sympathy for your dear departed friend now cluck their tongues at your behavior and suggest scandal.

Mama encloses her own letter.

Your loving but concerned brother,

Fritz

-

March 25th, 1911
Munich, Bavaria
(Enclosed letter)

My wondrous daughter,

. . . [D]oes my only daughter believe I am so blind to the secret desires of her heart as to not know the true reason she lingers on at

30

Neustrelitz? I remember you and Charlotte and Heinrich in Munich vividly! Six years ago, now, but it seems like yesterday.

I write to assure you I am not at all of your brother's mind. Perhaps nothing is ever to come of all this. Perhaps a time will come to reconcile yourself to that fact. But for now, I believe you should remain where you are, and find out if your heart knows best.

Your loving,

Mama

-

March 25th, 1911
Neustrelitz am Schliersee

Herr Frederick Breslau
Breslau and Breslau
Munich, Germany

My always officious brother,

Must I remind you again that advice of the type you proffer so unctuously is both discourteous and exasperating?

I have been treated with respect by every member of this household. In any case, for reasons of my own, I shall not remain here much longer. Captain von Haydenreich is completely absorbed by his love for his children and his grief for Lottie. They fill the entire horizon of his sky. He has no eyes for anything else, or anyone else. It is apparent I have done all I can here. There is no real place for me. I must get about my own life.

At the end of school term, I intend to inform the headmaster at Miesbach that I will not be returning in the fall. As soon thereafter as a suitable governess can be found for these two angels, I shall be wending my way back to Munich. My dull, commonplace life beckons me return.

So you see, my dear brother, there was no need for your officious and infuriating interference.

Your sister,

Rosamunde

-

April 11th, 1911
Munich, Bavaria
Headquarters, First Artillery Brigade
First Royal Bavarian Division

Fraulein Rosamunde Breslau
Neustrelitz am Schliersee

Dear Rosamunde,

I hope you will forgive me for the familiar salutation. Regular formality seems to me almost discourteous in view of the confidences we exchanged at lakeside during the last evening of my stay. You managed as superb an Easter as you had a Christmas. But the most striking and memorable event of all was the tête-à-tête we shared at the lake, after all the guests and children had departed. I should have recollected your insight and humor, the pleasure of your company, from our happy days in Munich. But like so much else, it was lost to me.

I had forgotten, too, there could be so much joy, so much simple pleasure in being in the company of a woman of lively intelligence. In those moments by the lake, you seemed to personify the Spring, and the warmth that dispels the winter's chill. The evening was beautiful, as were the mountains and the lake, with the full moon overhead. But I do not believe I could or would have perceived the full magnificence of that scene without you present.

My duties at the brigade should lessen as my replacement gains understanding of his responsibilities. I look forward to a much longer leave in mid-June, and the opportunity to renew our conversation where we left it Sunday evening. I also wish to discuss an arrangement by which you could honorably extend your stay at Neustrelitz. You would be sorely missed by everyone – and I mean particularly myself – should you deprive us of your warmth and companionship any time in the near future.

I will be back in two months. I look forward to enjoying the pleasure of your company again, perhaps in the same circumstances.

Yours, respectfully,

Heinrich

-

April 18th, 1911
Neustrelitz am Schliersee

Herr Frederick Breslau
Breslau and Breslau
Munich, Germany

My meddlesome brother,

I am writing to inform you that I have changed my mind!

32

I have informed the headmaster at Miesbach that I will be returning for term next fall, as he had so courteously requested. You may put this change of heart down to the frailty that is woman, or, as Maestro Verdi would say*, La donna è mobile*, for I have no intention of furnishing you with any other explanation.

Please convey these sentiments to the family, with my love. But I have no intention of ending my visit at any time soon.

Firm in these resolutions,

Rosamunde

-

June 3rd, 1911
Munich, Bavaria
Headquarters, First Royal Heavy Cavalry Brigade
First Royal Bavarian Division
First Royal Bavarian Corps

Captain Heinrich-Werner Mertz von Haydenreich
Headquarters, First Royal Field Artillery Brigade
First Royal Bavarian Division
First Royal Bavarian Corps

My dear little brother,

I will spare you the usual barracks gossip. Rumor travels on the wings of the wind in my circles. Recently I heard a rumor concerning you, about which I must speak. It seems you were overheard at headquarters expressing admiration for Fraulein Breslau in terms of such warmth and familiarity that they could only signify the deepest personal affection.

Bedding her is one thing, my brother. God bless the chase and the conquest! But it is quite another thing to take a woman of her race into the innermost places of your heart. You press a viper to your bosom when you do so. I am sure Fraulein Breslau has many commendable virtues. But I am also certain the Jewess possesses a guile well beyond the ken of a naïve Bavarian nobleman.

Please be watchful, Heinz. I am afraid your better sense has been overwhelmed by grief and gratitude.

Your ever-vigilant brother,

Willy

-

July 14th, 1911
Neustrelitz am Schliersee

Captain Heinrich-Werner Mertz von Haydenreich
Headquarters, First Royal Field Artillery Brigade
First Royal Bavarian Division
First Royal Bavarian Corps

Dear Captain Haydenreich,

I have the most wonderful news for you – and yet my hand trembles and my heart quakes as I write!

Your precocious son Karl has spoken his first word – this morning, as I came to greet him, he looked at me and clearly said 'mama'! I could only pick him up and hug him – also, he knows his sister's name and day by day does his baby best to produce it. He truly is a bright boy, to be doing such things at just over nine months old!

But even as I picked him up and hugged him, I felt the most frightful guilt overwhelm me – for it is Lottie who is his mother, Lottie who deserved this word, Lottie who should have received Karl's radiant smile. I long to be Karl's mother, but I am not – you deserved to be here when he spoke – this delight, this wonder . . . it is not something I have earned or merited. I felt like a thief in the night. Do you see me in such a light, Captain? A thief? I would not blame you if you did – sometimes I wonder if I belong anywhere.

But that is the news. Please write me and tell me you forgive me!

Rosamunde

P.S. As I reread what I have written, I see so much foolishness. But it is my third attempt, so I will post it anyway – you must be made aware of this wonderful news, however I play the fool.

Doubts torment me – that moment by the lake this last time – what you must think of me – if only I could relive it – But no, NO!! I don't think I would pull away from your arms if I relived it a thousand times! I did not want you to think I am unfeeling – and of course, you know now I am not.

But what you must think – are you worried your children are not in the care of a virtuous woman? And now your son has called me mama – How can I ever face you?

Please write to me when you can – I must appear such a goose in your eyes – I conduct myself so calmly with others, but with you I am always awhirl in agonies of uncertainty. Please write. Please!

R.

July 16th, 1911
Munich, Bavaria
Headquarters, First Royal Field Artillery Brigade

Fraulein Rosamunde Breslau
Neustrelitz am Schliersee

Dearest Rosamunde,

You have indeed sent me wonderful news. But there was no reason why your hand should shake and your heart tremble at informing me of such an event. That Karl regards you as a mother comforts me. It delights Lottie in Paradise; my own heart is certain of this. If my son could not feel the touch of his own mother's hand, I can think of no one better or worthier to take her place than yourself, Rosamunde. You have been all a mother could possibly be to him. The warmth of your love will accompany him all his life.

I too have not forgotten that moment by the lake. In fact, I have thought of little else since. I think of the soft fullness of your body in my arms, the sweetness of your breath, the way your lips yielded to mine. I did not feel I was holding a fallen woman, only a desirable woman. Such sudden awakenings happen in the world – there is no reason for self-reproach by either of us. You yourself had required I live again. Such incidents are one of the expressions of renewed life. I have not forgotten Lottie – I never will – but neither will I forget again that I am a man, and alive.

My dear Rosamunde, it bothers me that you even think like this. Of course I have not lost respect for you. I burn with impatience to return to Neustrelitz, to my children and to you – to hold my baby in my arms, and to meet with you once again at our special place. I have begun making plans. I have commissioned a portrait of Lottie, to be painted from our wedding photograph. Upon completion, it will hang in a place of honor, above the fireplace, framed in black.

But beyond that, our mourning will be done when the year of mourning is completed. Lena should have the bright, gay colors a girl of that age likes so much – and Karl, too, should be bedecked in infant finery! As for you, my dear Rosamunde, you deserve a holiday more than anyone. I have taken rooms at the Excelsior Muenchen (on separate floors) and obtained opera tickets for the premiere of *Girl of the Golden West*, the new

Puccini work. Please do me the favor of accepting my hospitality on this occasion, Rosamunde, offered on the most honorable terms. It would please me if you would put your hair up for that occasion; I would like to see it in that style. Perhaps at that time we can discuss an arrangement by which you could stay on with the family that has come to have such affection for you.

My replacement Gernreich at last shows some competence at his new position, so I can finally quit active service honorably. I will be returning home in the last week of August. Soon enough, we will be at our special place.

Affectionately,

Heinz

P.S. Why do you address me formally as 'Captain'? Had we not agreed, 'Heinz and Rosamunde'?

H.

-

September 4th, 1911
Excelsior Muenchen

Dear Heinz,

I do not know how to face you – or what you want of me – or anything – I am confused beyond endurance – I do not know what to think!!

But now you know everything – my heart is open to you now – so I will confess my shame wholly. I have loved you since first I saw you. When you chose Lottie, and began to bestow all your attention on her, I felt my heart would break.

I don't regret losing my honor to you or to be numbered among your conquests – for a long time now, I have longed to be in your arms and (I will say it!) in your bed – but now my heart seizes with anguish – am I to be your mistress while you court another? Has this been your plan all along? Will you be done with me, then, and I am to lose both you and the children I have come to love so much?! Do I mean so little to you, that you use me in this way? Oh, but I must accept this fate, because my heart is yours, has always been yours – you know that full well now – perhaps you always did.

And I worry, too, that my embraces disappointed you, for I am not Lottie. Oh, God! What have I done???

36

Why have you done this to me? After what we have said to each other? When you spoke of an arrangement, I had hoped – what any woman would hope! Is this all that you meant? My seduction?!! Did you plan everything?!? When you asked me to put my hair up, was it so you could take it down, while I trembled, resistless, at your touch??

I am so confused – my heart is breaking – please come to me if you have any heart!

Your troubled,
Rosamunde
-

September 4th, 1911
Excelsior Muenchen

My darling Rosamunde,

Calm yourself. Don't send any more notes. I have been in the process of preparing a long letter to you which will explain my behavior, and also make certain proposals that I believe will please you very much.

H.
-

September 4th, 1911
Excelsior Muenchen

My darling Rosamunde,

I don't wish you to remain in suspense during the reading of this letter. This is a proposal of marriage.

During the last year, I have fallen in love with you. If you would do me the honor of becoming my wife, I would be the happiest of men. But before I receive your answer, I must discuss certain facts with you, not the least of which is my behavior last night.

The first of these is Lottie. I am concerned, my darling, that you will make constant comparisons in that way that you do, and become either guilty or jealous. Let me anticipate. I loved Lottie during the time I had with her, until she was gathered to God. I love you now, during the time I have been blessed to have with you. As each single human being is different and unique, and as times are different, and unique, so is each love different and unique. That was then, this is now. There is nothing to compare nor even a basis of comparison. So do not trouble yourself in this manner.

37

The second is the Haydenreich family, and in particular the open anti-Semitism of my father, brother, and the rest. This must at the least give you pause, and make you wonder about my own attitudes. To be candid, this prejudice has always been a disease in my family. It has taken particularly virulent form in the last generation, due to a modest musical talent that also runs in my family, and our association with a certain composer. I am referring, of course, to Wagner. My father possesses a good enough tenor to have been a member of the Gibichung chorus at the first *Gotterdammerung* at Bayreuth. I have first and second cousins who were also participants, in the orchestra and chorus. (I myself performed in the boy's chorus in *Parsifal* when I was 12.) Their admiration for the composer's art has unfortunately led them into acceptance of other aspects of Wagner's thought and, regrettably, his ugly and repulsive sayings about Jews.

(Ah! I have just received your note, much as I expected. 'Disappointed with your embraces'? My poor darling! I'll get to that.)

My love, these have never been my views and never will be. I have lived in the world long enough to believe that virtues and vices occur in men as they will, and without relation to their race or station. Wagner's music is sublime. But his ideas about life off the stage seem to me a joke, and a dangerous joke at that. Even if I had not fallen in love with you, I would find these views obnoxious and repulsive. I do my best to respect my father, and my brother has always been my best companion. But they embarrass me in this way.

I am sure you have heard of the other scandals that beset the Haydenreich family, as we have for many years provided rich fodder for the street gossips of Munich and elsewhere. I regret to tell you that whatever you have heard, particularly the worst, is as likely as not to be true. But it is not my family, but myself, Heinrich Haydenreich, who makes this proposal – and I pray with all my strength that you will consider me simply as myself, as a man, as unworthy and vice-ridden though that man may be – and that you can find enough forgiveness in your beautiful soul to forgive those all-too-human weaknesses, accept my suit, and make me the happiest of men.

Finally, about last night.

We have had a peculiar courtship, my darling. My heart opened to you as I saw the way baby Karl smiled at you and cuddled in your arms, the manner in which you led Lena out of her natural grief and back to the gaiety that is a young child's right, and the strength you lent me in my own despair. I came to care for you profoundly while I was still living in the city of the dead, before I regained my appreciation of you as a desirable woman. (It is annoying that Willy, who has no inclination for this aspect of womanhood, saw how attractive you are before I did. You were always a princess, from when I first knew you. I should have remembered that earlier.)

I became aware, too, of your diffidence, of the perpetual concern in your angel's heart that your good works are not good enough, that you have failed those around you in some way, even as you bless them with the richness of your love. If I were to have simply made a proposal before last night, you would always wonder how much of my love was a simple regard for you as the best of all stepmothers, and whether I cared at all for you as a woman. You would never cease comparing yourself to Lottie and others, and doubting my love, no matter how great my ardor.

I had my own doubts of similar kind. Though I had come to love you in all respects, I wondered how much regard you had for me as a man, and whether the satisfactions of the nursery and kitchen were sufficient for you – there are such women. Were I to propose formally, these anxieties would remain with me, with you.

Is it possible to seduce a woman honorably? For this is one time when it seemed to me the consummation must precede the formality, if love were truly to know itself. You are quite right that when I asked you to put your hair up, it was with the eager hope that it would come down – and come down it did, in a black, lustrous cascade I could not forget in multiple eternities. Nor can I forget how it fell over the ivory white of your bosom, or the firm roundness of your breast – nor the desire that replaced your timidity, once you had been convinced that what must be, must be, and accepted your fate. It was a night of splendors, and reminded me anew how much I detest celibacy.

And it resolved all doubts of mine, and I hope, any of yours.

You need have no concern about the adequacy of your embraces, my love. You would be the most excellent of all mistresses, as you have been the most excellent of all stepmothers, the most excellent of all companions, and the most excellent of all counselors. But what I wish is that you be the most excellent of all wives.

So, with heart in mouth, and trembling hand, I ask you, Rosamunde Breslau, to become my wife. We are neither of us children who need the consent of our families, so I believe you can make your answer as your own heart sees fit. I will await your answer this evening, at dinner at the Husar, where I will escort you at 8:00. I have reserved private rooms for us.

There I will discover whether you will make me the happiest of men, or whether I must proceed through life bereft of your love. In either case, my own love and esteem for you, my wonderful Rosamunde, will continue unabated.

I will see you this evening.

Love,

Heinz

-

September 4th, 1911
Excelsior Muenchen

My beloved Heinz,

I have received your note. As you request, I will wait until our dinner this evening to give you my formal reply. But you know what it will be!

You were so open with me, I shall be honest with you. Last night was the best night of my life! A relatively inexperienced woman could not wish for a better lover, at once so bold and so tender – this morning, when I wrote, it was with the great fear that I would never again feel you possess me in that way – the thought was unendurable. Perhaps later on, such an event might happen at our special place at the lakeside? Where first we opened our hearts to one another? With the same splendid moon overhead?

I will give you my answer tonight. But when we return to Neustrelitz, you will have the key to my cottage, so you know that no way is barred to you. For, from this day forward, I am Yours, and you may take what belongs to you when it pleases you to do so.

Today is the happiest day of my life!!

With all my heart and love,

Yours, completely

Rosamunde

-

40

September 8th, 1911
Munich, Bavaria

Fraulein Rosamunde Breslau
Neustrelitz am Schliersee

     My demented sister,

     This morning our mother presented me with news so horrifying my hair literally stood on end. She informed me that Heinrich Haydenreich had proposed marriage to you, and that you had accepted.

     My dear sister, you cannot do this. You will make the Breslau family the laughing-stock of every respectable bourgeois family in Munich. Not only is the Haydenreich family a pack of jackals, you have chosen the worst of the worst. I was witness to the reorganization of that family's finances in '06. If only you could have seen the callous way in which Heinrich Haydenreich cut out his father and older brother, and claimed management of the family estate for himself, you would have been appalled! You would have seen him for the merciless usurper he actually is. Entrusting your future to a man like that?

     And what of yourself? You are born to Munich, my sister. Do you remember the life you led here? There are no art galleries in Neustrelitz to delight you. Klee and Klimt do not exhibit their paintings there. The latest of Strauss operas are not performed. There are no elegant dinners – Munich is the most cosmopolitan city in Europe, after Paris, and you were a part of all of it.

     And now you propose to immure yourself in this little village in the country?! With this beast of a man? You will go mad with regret, if you are not mad already.

     Please come to your senses at once.

             Your concerned brother,

                 Fritz

                 -

September 9th, 1911
Munich, Bavaria
Headquarters, First Royal Heavy Cavalry Brigade
First Royal Bavarian Division

Heinrich-Werner Mertz von Haydenreich
Neustrelitz am Schliersee

     Dear Heinz,

Father and I have discussed the contents of the letters you sent us on September 5th. He is too upset and enraged to address you, so I am writing on behalf of us both.

Heinz, you cannot do this. You cannot pollute the Haydenreich name and blood with this alien, Jewish strain. I mean nothing against Fraulein Breslau – she seems a fine person, and a woman who any man might prize. But even in a barrel of sourly rotten apples, there may be one that is fresh and edible. That does not mean the others are not rotten. At bottom, she is a Jew, and brings with her all the vices of her race. Have you considered that, should she bear you children, they will take their place in the family succession? Jews! In the Haydenreich family and estate!! This must not be, Heinz.

I can only implore you, on behalf of myself, of Father, of our poor deceased Mother, of Lena, of Karl, of all our noble ancestors, and of your lost, beloved Lottie, to come to your senses and to not do this horrific, unnatural act. Heed the advice of all your family, and all Germany, in this matter.

Willy

-

September 25th, 1911
Munich, Bavaria

My wondrous daughter,

My first thought, on receiving your letter and the copy of your brother's of the 8th enclosed, was to journey to you personally. But then I thought something in writing, that you could keep by you and renew, might be better. Your brother has not behaved kindly in this matter, or well.

The truth is this, as I learnt it from your father. By 1906 the von Haydenreich estate was in danger of financial ruin, by reason of the mismanagement of the von Haydenreich patriarchs. The last – Heinrich's father – was as bad as the others. Worse - the Oberstleutnant refused to take any responsibility for his own foolishness. This was not helpful. Finally, Prince Rupprecht ordered him to Munich, and the bankers to do their best, since a family as venerable and once respected as the von Haydenreichs could not be allowed to fail. The father complied, but continued to make the worst impression, blaming his creditors, the bankers, and everyone else for the crisis he had brought on himself. The older son, his namesake, is bright, but frivolous, and too intimidated by his father to be of any use. It was left to the younger son, Heinrich, your intended, to demonstrate he inherited his mother's brains, not his father's, and rescue the situation. (A shame the cholera carried Elsa off in '98 – you would have had a great friend in your mother-in-law!) He consulted with his own advisers, used his own sound judgment, and proposed a well-considered plan that would resolve the situation with prudent management over time. This involved selling off some minor properties, and substantially reducing the household. Both his proposal and Heinrich himself made a most powerful, favorable impression on everyone in the banking community. Your father told me this.

Unfortunately, the father, Wilhelm, refused to understand the necessity, let alone the wisdom, of Heinrich's plan. He flew into a rage, finding a conspiracy in all this good sense, into which conspiracy (he concluded) Heinrich had entered. It was obvious to all that the financial arrangements would not succeed if it were left to the father to implement them – he could not be trusted to follow through. The Prince intervened again – he was well acquainted with Heinrich and had the same extremely high opinion of him as the others. The elder von Haydenreich was forced to give over control and management of the estates to his younger son. He then took up residence in Munich with his mistress, from whence he continues to fulminate that he has been usurped and Heinrich betrayed him. But that is not true – were it not for Heinrich, he would have lost all. In fact, Heinrich's plan came off quite well, and he has even brought the family from the edge of ruin to a modest prosperity – he is a very intelligent investor. The father owes him nothing but gratitude, and I believe he knows this in his heart of hearts. But of course, he will never express this thought aloud.

That is the truth. Heinrich became manager of the family properties *faute de mieux*, and not as the result of any wish of his own. It is my belief that he does not relish the role of family savior. In his heart of hearts, I think he would much prefer his freedom, for he is a man of great capability and lively curiosity. But he shouldered the burden without protest, and discharges it without complaint. Your brother, of course, knows all this, but chose to put the matter in the worst possible light. I can only put this down to his intense dislike of the von Haydenreich family and Heinrich. You must know he had his eye on Charlotte, before Heinrich began his courtship.

This is the whole story, and the true story. But there is more you should know. That time that Heinrich spent rescuing his family's future was also when he kept company with you and Lottie and the others of your set. What lively times you had! However, it was also apparent that Heinrich was in a serious search for a wife. Your father and I had to consider what our attitude would be if his eye fell on you. Your father's opinion of Heinrich von Haydenreich could not have been higher – he would have welcomed him as a son-in-law without reservation. However, we would likely have opposed the match because (in our opinion) you were still a bit too giddy to assume the responsibilities of marriage. I knew how smitten you were with Heinrich even then, my wondrous daughter – a mother always knows. You might console yourself that it is my belief that his choice fell on Lottie back then in part because she was a touch readier than you were at that time. Of course, he did also fall in love with her.

The time is certainly right for you now. I welcome this joyful news with all my heart. Your father would have rejoiced as well. I believe your brother's attitudes reflect an ancient jealousy and bitterness, that he would do well to put aside. I shall speak to him.

Love,

Mama

-

September 10th, 1911
Neustrelitz am Schliersee

Captain Wilhelm-Werner Mertz von Haydenreich
First Royal Heavy Cavalry Brigade
First Royal Bavarian Division
First Royal Bavarian Corps

Dear Willy,

You are my beloved brother, the fondest companion of my life. I will always have the highest affection for you. But for God's sake, do not address me again in this manner about my Rosamunde.

I will confirm your worst fears. I plan a marriage with my beloved in all the aspects of marriage. If God wills it, we will have children – and if they are blessed with their mother's warmth of heart, breadth of mind, and depth of spirit, what children they will be! Of course, they will stand in the line of succession to the Haydenreich estate – why should they not? So far from being in any way embarrassed by this intention, I take pride in it. I proclaim it.

You will be amused to know that the head of the Breslau family is as horrified by these plans as you are. Rosamunde came to me in tears with a letter from her brother that set forth the most bizarre slanders of me personally. But I care not a fig for their opinions, or yours. I will have this woman to wife, and that is all. It is high time you gave up this view of German Jews. You are echoing Father, I know, and I understand the loyalty of a son to his parent. But he is at his worst in this manner, mimicking the worst of the Junkers he admires so extravagantly, and the composer Wagner at his worst. There is no Jewish question, or should not be one, in any case.

I have not forgotten Lottie, nor ever will. From the Paradise where she now resides, I know she blesses this marriage. Join her in the blessing and congratulate me in my happiness. I will never lose my love for you, but please don't test it in this way.

You are, of course, invited to the wedding – October 25th, after the banns have been read. Please attend, if you can manage to arrange leave. Your approval is important to both me and my bride.

Your loving brother,

Heinz

P.S. The portrait of Lottie I commissioned last spring has been delivered. It is all I could have wished. It is our intention – mine and Rosamunde's – to hang it in a formal ceremony, on the same day as our wedding – for we both loved Lottie. Thus do we twin the two events, and conjoin love, death, and rebirth. I could not express to you my complex feelings any more simply than this.

H.

-

Parish Records, St. Sixtus
Miesbach, Bavaria
October 25th, 1911

Certification of Marriage

Groom: Captain Heinrich-Werner Mertz von Haydenreich
Bride: Rosamunde Breslau
In Attendance: Frau Johanna Rosenberg-Breslau, various servant

members of the Haydenreich household. No other members of either family present.

[Added by hand;] *Marriage rite performed under compulsion. That I should live to see the day when a von Haydenreich is married to a Jew!*

-

November 1, 1911
Munich, Bavaria

Captain Heinrich-Werner Mertz von Haydenreich
First Royal Field Artillery Brigade
First Royal Bavarian Division
First Royal Bavarian Corps
Neustrelitz am Schliersee

My dear friend Heinz,

Let me extend both personal and Royal congratulations to you on the splendid marriage you have made. I am familiar with the Breslau family, who have done great service to the State, and with Rosamunde herself, who epitomizes charm and virtue.

It is therefore with the deepest regret that I must request a service of you. The Kaiser has convened a military conference in Berlin to discuss the role that aircraft may play in military planning and campaigns of the future. Young Gernreich is capable, as you promised, but only that – he is no Heinrich von Haydenreich! I will not be able to participate in the conference meaningfully without your wisdom and insights. Although you are no longer in active service as a commissioned officer, your insight and acumen must remain available to the State in these and other sensitive matters.

I regret this intrusion into your domestic arrangements. You have my word that I will not call on you without good cause. But these are perilous times for Bavaria, Germany, and all of Europe. A man of your capability cannot be idle and indifferent to events.

Again, congratulations on your wedding. My best wishes to you and your new bride.

With sincere affection,
Prince Rupprecht Maria Luitpold Ferdinand

-

46

Excerpt from: A Twentieth Century Life
Albert Sommerville
Houghton, Mifflin (1959)

I think I will break the chronological narrative and simply summarize what I learned over time about Karl's family – not so much from Karl himself, but during innumerable vacations at Neustrelitz. His stepmother was named Rosamunde, whom he always called 'Mummi'. That was his garbled attempt at her name when he was a small child. It became his name for her all his life. His natural mother, Charlotte, was venerated throughout the town as an elegant, gracious woman by those few of the older townspeople who remembered her. But there was something a bit distant and impersonal in those memories. On the other hand, Rosamunde von Haydenreich – 'Mummi' – was an active presence, beloved universally. Everyone adored her.

The first time I visited her grave, in 1927, fresh flowers adorned it, years after her death. Three decades later, fresh flowers are still placed daily on her grave and her mother's.

As the story was told to me, the townspeople were initially wary of her because of her Yiddishness – an understandable caution. The marriage was scorned, and the bride shunned. But 'Mummi' (as I shall call her) rode her bicycle to her classes every day, and greeted everyone she knew, friend or foe, as a warm friend. At the gymnasium, her natural sympathy, so different in affect from the general sternness of German schoolmasters, endeared her to both the students and in short order, to their families.

Then, a few months after her own wedding, some conflict with the local church calendar left a bride and groom in considerable distress, without a place to wed. 'Mummi' found out about this, and in all innocence, volunteered the Lakeside Chapel in the manse. This caused a considerable stir, as the von Haydenreich family had never before been so generous with its holdings. There was worry that her husband, who was engaged elsewhere on the Prince's business at the time, would disavow her offer when he learned of it. But upon hearing of the matter, Karl's father endorsed her gesture and reproved himself for not having done the same much earlier. (This was in fact the first use of a place that has become one of the most popular locales for weddings in all Bavaria.)

47

This one deed made her immensely popular. Thereafter she became increasingly involved in the lives of the townspeople. She was quick to assist and even – most uncharacteristic for a Yid – to lend money without any expectation of repayment. Once she even paid for the passage to America of a young man down on his luck. Heinrich found out about it, so the story goes, and became exasperated that she had paid with her own money. He reimbursed her, and required she use his funds thereafter. There were countless similar tales – anyone who heard the mention of her name had one of his own. She might as well have been the patron saint of the town.

Since she was a Jewess, one would naturally wonder whether some shrewd connivance of disinheritance lay behind all this. Perhaps there was some cunning plan that simply did not come to fruition. But perhaps not. 'Mummi' seems to have been a person of exceptional kindness and vigor. There are such people, even among the Yids.

1913

-_-

Frau Johanna Breslau
Munich, Bavaria

My dearest Mama,

. . . [T]hank you for sending me the Klimt catalog, Mama. Also, do send me all you can about the Strauss premiere. How I wish I could be there!

Time sometimes goes so slowly here. I have my lessons at Miesbach, of course. But Lena and Karl are my great joy – to see them grow in grace and beauty daily! English and French for them as well – how could it not be? But Yiddish is our fun language. (The very sounds of the syllables make Karl giggle.) I find purpose, too, among my townspeople. Since the chapel was opened to the first wedding, there are many others, and baptisms, and so on. I attend always. There is so much need here – so much that can be done with a kind act, or a good word, sometimes more. I was always sure they had good hearts underneath, even in those first awful months. Now that at least some know that not all Jews are the Devil's workmen, it is much better. Every so often now some kind neighbor leaves flowers on our doorstep. I blush at this expression of gratitude I know I don't deserve. But it pleases me anyway!

(While I am thinking of it, please tell Fritz to stop pestering me for accountings of the moneys I have provided my neighbors. They are embarrassingly small sums for a Breslau, less than two weeks of my personal income in total, but so important to my friends. I have no intention of asking for repayment. Money is scarce here, and much better lent in turn to someone in need than used to repay a rich city girl.)

But sometimes time does go so slowly – when Heinz is gone. Then – Mama – I must confess to you – questions and doubts besiege me. Lottie's ghost – he met us both at the same time – but he chose her. She has given him two beautiful children – so far, I have not provided one. Her portrait is magnificent, and lovely, and hangs (as it should) over the fireplace in the main room. Would he do the same for me? If I were taken from him? Who would he choose? I do what I think is right and best – but

49

is it truly 'right' and 'best'? Do I fall short?

I know you would call me a 'goose' if you were here. So, too, would the real Lottie, if she could speak to me. So, too, will Heinz, when he is once more with me, and I am once more in his arms. All doubts vanish then. So, too, when I am with the two angels God and Lottie entrusted to me, I am blessed with joy! And I know – I KNOW – that when at last I present Heinz with our child, I will be fully at home here – the ghosts and doubts gone, forever!

Do not mistake me, Mama, the trade I made for love is one I would make a hundred times over, and then a hundred times again. I know I am among the most fortunate of women!

But there is no life without misgivings and questions. These are my questions and misgivings – on the days when Heinz is gone – on the days when the clock ticks so, so slowly.

Your loving daughter,

Rosamunde

-

December 3, 1913
Neustrelitz am Schliersee

Oberstleutnant Wilhelm-Werner Mertz von Haydenreich
Munich, Bavaria

Dear Father,

I am too wearily familiar with your bent for dramatic gestures to be other than amused by them. As you well know, you are more than welcome to visit here for the holiday. The granddaughter who barely remembers you, and the grandson whom you have never met, grow curious as to what this strange person often mentioned as their grandfather truly looks like. If, however, a precondition of your visit is that 'that woman' remove herself from these estates, it is for the best that you remain in Munich. 'That woman' is my beloved wife Rosamunde, the adored stepmother of your grandchildren, and 'these estates' are the home that she has chosen to bless with her presence.

My wife, the city woman, the Jewish outsider, has won more loyalty to the Haydenreich family in two years than the rest of us accomplished in three centuries. Nowadays, on those occasions when I am home and wander into the village (too rare!), I find caps tipped with genuine good will and respect – attitudes not shown to the masters of this household for – how many centuries?

And despite this, Rosamunde remains diffident and anxious, haunted by the recollections of Lottie all about her, and the comparisons she is certain that everyone makes. I reassure her constantly, but she is the type of person who wonders regardless. Thus, I am ill-disposed to permit you to pay us a visit, indulge yourself in some flamboyant act of disapproving insult, and thoroughly dismay my lovely wife.

It seems to me best for all that you celebrate the holidays in Munich in worthier company than you find with me and my 'Hebrew' wife.

I respond to your other complaint. I think the Prince and God both know that my gratitude to him is unmeasurable, and my loyalty to him absolute. However, the plain fact is that he has entrusted me with so many missions and duties that I have to some degree become *de facto* an ambassador without portfolio. In the past two years, I have seldom spent two consecutive weeks in Neustrelitz and have often been gone for weeks, even months, at a time. It was for these reasons I advised the Prince that I will be resigning all positions on the date of my fortieth birthday, twenty months from now – August 1914, if you have forgotten. Rupprecht has accepted these decisions, not without reluctance, I am flattered to write.

I can only hope and pray that you too will accept these decisions, and Rosamunde, and all the blessings she has brought to this household. It is my fervent prayer that God will see fit to bless our union with children, and that you will ultimately accept these, too, as your own worthy grandchildren. The prejudice with which you are cursed blinds you to all of this happiness, but someday, I pray, you will see these matters as they are.

In the meantime, my best wishes for a happy Christmas and all other blessings. My respects to Frau Brehmer.

Your dutiful son,

Heinrich

-

December 29, 1913
Munich, Bavaria
Headquarters, First Royal Heavy Cavalry Brigade
First Royal Bavarian Division

Oberstleutnant Wilhelm-Werner Mertz von Haydenreich
Munich, Bavaria

Dear Father,

. . . [S]he is a kind and loving mother, I will grant her that. Both Lena and Karl adore her.

But there is no sign of a proper German education. Both children jabber like magpies in French and English, as well as German, and speak of stories of other lands. When you hear little Karl gibbering away in Yiddish, it is enough to make your skin crawl. . .

Your son,
Wilhelm II

1914

—

February 9, 1914
Neustrelitz am Schliersee

Captain Heinrich-Werner Mertz von Haydenreich
Envoi to Prince Rupprecht Maria Luitpold Ferdinand, Crown Prince of Bavaria
Berlin, Prussia

My beloved Heinz,

Please forgive me for interrupting such an important conference, but I must tell you that my fondest hopes have been realized – I do in fact carry our child, who will greet us in this world sometime in July (if I am not too excited to count correctly!) God could not have blessed us more – I am happier than I have ever been!!

I promise you on my heart and soul that when our baby arrives, he will not displace Lena and Karl in my affection – for you know I love those two as if they were my own two, flesh of my flesh – and one of my own will only make me care for them more!

And please tell me that a dark young von Haydenreich, taking his place among the blond gods and goddesses that abound in your family, will be warm and welcome in your heart – I know in this worry that I am the most foolish of foolish women, for I know that you, too, have longed for God to bless our union so – but even so, please – when you have time – write to me, and tell me I am a foolish woman, and our baby will be as dear to you as these others are. I will press it to my bosom and all my doubts will disappear like morning mist!

'He', 'his' – what premature pronouns – for I would welcome a daughter with a full heart, but I hope for a son, so that the survival of the Haydenreich name is that much more certain.

I am so happy!! Your foolish wife adores you, my wonderful husband!!

Praying all blessings upon you,
Your Rosamunde

March 9, 1914
Neustrelitz am Schliersee

Captain Heinrich-Werner Mertz von Haydenreich
Envoi to Prince Rupprecht Maria Luitpold
Ferdinand, Crown Prince of Bavaria
St. Petersburg, Russia

CAPTAIN VON HAYDENREICH STOP LAST NIGHT MIDNIGHT
FRAU HAYDENREICH SUFFERED A MISCARRIAGE STOP FRAU
HAYDENREICH IN NO DANGER, BUT DISTRAUGHT STOP
LETTER WITH DETAILS FOLLOWS STOP RETURN HOME
ADVISABLE AS SOON AS POSSIBLE STOP FRAU HILDEGARDE
SCHALLERT

March 9, 1914
Neustrelitz am Schliersee

Captain Heinrich-Werner Mertz von Haydenreich
Envoi to Prince Rupprecht Maria Luitpold Ferdinand, Crown Prince of
Bavaria
St. Petersburg, Russia

Dear Captain,

Before writing anything else, let me assure you first that Frau von Haydenreich is recovering quite well, and her health in no way endangered. She is a strong, vital woman, and attended now by a number of the women in the village. Some of the men, too, have paid calls – for, as you know, she has made herself much beloved of all here. Everyone shares in her sorrow.

Let me now tell you what happened. This sadness came with no or very little warning. Frau von Haydenreich had gone about her business as usual, meeting her French and English classes at the gymnasium, and tutoring Karl and Lena in the afternoon. She complained mildly of indigestion, but this seemed of small import, and she had a reasonable dinner. About an hour afterward, though, she was seized with a violent cramp, a blood flow began, and in a few moments, the pregnancy had come to an end. The child was examined in the aftermath and seemed well-formed. There is no accounting for this happening.

Frau Rosamunde is a courageous woman, and greets her friends bravely. She intends to meet her classes two days from now. In terms of her condition, there is no reason why she should not. But I know when she

54

is alone, she weeps without ceasing. She is so much loved, everyone offers consolation. But only you can bring to her the true comfort she needs. She is burdened not only by her own sorrow, but also by the worry that she has disappointed you. That is not so; the God who sees even the sparrow's fall, wills some things so, some things not. This is one He willed not. Frau von Haydenreich knows this, she accepts the truth. But she will not believe it in her heart of hearts until she hears you say it and knows you mean it.

I know the meetings in St. Petersburg are important. I beg a thousand pardons for burdening you with this tragedy. But as soon as you are able, you should plan your return. Your wife will be disconsolate until you do.

Respectfully,
Frau Hildegarde Schallert

-

April 11, 1914
Neustrelitz am Schliersee

His Royal Highness, Rupprecht Maria Luitpold Ferdinand
Crown Prince of Bavaria, Duke of Bavaria, of Franconia and in Swabia,
Count Palatine of the Rhine
Munich, Bavaria

My friend Rupprecht,

My formal resignation from service to the Crown you will have received in a separate letter in appropriate style. I know it comes as no surprise. Some time ago, I made you aware of my belief that, in the words of the French philosopher, the time has come to grow my own garden. All I have done is advance this decision by a few months. My domestic situation requires this action, in my opinion.

I remain your comrade, and your friendship remains precious to me. Of course, I will be at your service in the unlikely event of war or national crisis.

Your friend and obedient servant,
Heinz

-

June 22, 1914
Neustrelitz am Schliersee

Monsieur Rene de Monterose
Societe de Construction des Batignolles
Paris, France

Dear Monsieur Monterose,

Allow me to introduce myself. I am Heinrich von Haydenreich, the manager and partial heir apparent to the von Haydenreich estates. My family owns several properties in the Bavarian Alps, about an hour or so by rail from Munich. I would like to arrange a meeting with you at your earliest convenience to discuss certain ideas I have for the development of these holdings.

Very truly yours,
Heinrich von Haydenreich

-

June 22, 1914
Neustrelitz am Schliersee
Note left with jewelry case at breakfast table

My love,

My thought was to present you with this gift on the anniversary of the day I first took you in my arms as a woman, three years ago. But that is two days from now. As it happens, I prefer to celebrate the first truly happy day you have had in two months. Even little Karl noticed.

Besides, today is Midsummer's Day, the longest and brightest of the year.

I can only share, not fully comprehend, your sorrow. But I know a time comes, my Rosamunde, when it is necessary to look forward, not back. Let's walk with our children – for they are yours more than anyone's – this afternoon, out into the sunshine, and down to the lake. Perhaps we will have a picnic.

I am done with service to the Prince. My business is in good order. I have some thoughts for how the estate may be developed that will enable me to remain home, with you. You are indirectly the inspiration for these, the time when you lived in the cottage. I have this day written to the director of the Batignolles civil engineering firm to see how these might be realized.

Walk down to the lake on this Midsummer's Day, with me and your children. It is a day to give up all the sorrow of the past. It is a day to walk into the sunshine.

Nothing but sunshine lies ahead of us.

Walk with me.

With all my heart,
Heinz

1915

-

Excerpt from: A General Speaks - the Autobiography of Kurt von Hammerstein Equord
Major General Kurt von Hammerstein Equord
Reichswehr Press (1986)

I met Karl's father, Heinrich von Haydenreich, on only one occasion during the Great War. It was one of those chance encounters that for some reason one recollects for many years.

It was June of 1915. We had been summoned to some staff meeting or other, and were at mess for luncheon. Von Haydenreich was at our same table. Everyone knew everyone, so I was aware that he commanded a division of the Second Bavarian Reserve regiment, and that he had distinguished himself in the early fighting at Ypres. I knew, too, that he had left both the military and the service of the Bavarian Prince before the War broke out, but had been recalled when the officers' ranks were decimated in the first months of the War. He was a citizen-soldier. These are often the best kind.

What I recall is that we were engaged in some conversation, when suddenly von Haydenreich smiled, in a way that had nothing to do with what we were saying. I asked him his thoughts.

'*I just recollected,*' he said, '*that it was exactly a year ago today that I spoke to my wife of perpetual sunlight and the happiness that lay ahead of us.*' He shook his head. Beyond him lay the wreckage of the battlefield, a sea of mud which the perpetual rain was splattering, endless fields of broken, ruined weapons, and the barbed wire and trenches that seemed to stretch on to infinity.

'*Those were possibly the most foolish words I ever spoke in my life.*'

We all had to agree, and laugh.

-

August 7, 1915
Neustrelitz am Schliersee

Frau Johanna Breslau
Munich, Bavaria
[by hand]

My dearest Mama,

. . . [A] cramp in the night, then a torrent of blood. I have miscarried again.

I must summon up the courage to write Heinz. Cold fear stays my hand – suppose it is the last letter he ever reads from me! Why cannot I give him the children Lottie gave him?

Your loving daughter,

Rosamunde

1916

October 7, 1916
Neustrelitz am Schliersee

Frau Johanna Breslau
Munich, Bavaria

My dearest Mama,

Karl has discovered a new kind of music. He heard a gramophone record of a song called *Alexander's Ragtime Band* by the American composer Berlin. It is certainly very different than Mozart or Beethoven, but quite lively! He insists on hearing more of this. Could you scour the neighbors for anyone who has records of other songs by this composer? Or more recordings by American Negroes? 'Jazz', as they call it?

Also, if you can find any more stories by the American author Aleichem – I have adapted them for the children and they both want to hear more. Lena dotes on Tevye the milkman. There is nothing in the house but the Grimm Brothers and the like. These do not seem to me suitable for wartime. Any children's books of any kind will do, except the sternly moralistic.

I will be sending you a food parcel with Joseph, a farmer in whom I have a particular trust. I do not have to tell you to be discrete in how you use it . . .

Your loving daughter,

Rosamunde

Excerpt from: My Name is Ike - Reflections on Fifty Years of Service as Soldier and Statesman
Senator Dwight D. Eisenhower
Random House (1986)

. . . [H]einz and I didn't talk too much about the War during that first long week in Paris. He was too modest, I was too shy. But one night it did come up.

He told me that by the spring of 1916 he was completely disillusioned by the War. He couldn't remember why it had started, or what anyone was fighting for. He had seen scores, hundreds, of good men

60

mowed down by machine guns like wheat by a scythe, and he was frustrated and angry.

'*If I was frustrated and angry, it was evident that hundreds of thousands of other men were frustrated and angry,*' he said. '*I knew then that nothing afterward was going to be the same. I didn't know how the world would be different, but I knew it would not be the same.*

'*As for me, I was living a waking nightmare. All I wanted to do was get home to my children and wife, and make good on the promises I'd made to her. But of course, that was all anyone wanted.*'

-

December 30, 1916
Neustrelitz am Schliersee

Frau Johanna Breslau
Munich, Bavaria

My dearest Mama,

The Christmas leave is over, and my Heinz is gone, back to the front. Fourteen days, and all glorious, but I don't think my husband was able to free himself from the War for even a moment. He was impatient and restless throughout. In his heart of hearts, he wanted to make everything right in the fourteen days. He wanted to restore in a mere fortnight all the time lost. Of course, he knows this is not possible, but when does the heart ever listen?

I will not be shy with you, Mama. When we were alone, we spent most of our time as man and woman. Partly this was simply a man taking a soldier's pleasure in his wife. But there was also an urgency in his manner I have never known. He wants to give me the child I crave, to make our lives here complete. This was the impatience of which I wrote. Often in other times, I would lie on his shoulder and warm myself in the comfort of his protection. But now it seemed more often he lay in my arms, and I was the comforter. (Was it comfort enough? Was there something I could have done that I did not do? Lottie's ghost again – it is never far off these days – we have had so little time together!)

In the dead of night, he speaks in a flat voice of things he cannot say to the household, and of course not to the children – endless rain and mud, horrible barbed wire, the bodies of the poor soldiers spread across the battlegrounds like fallen leaves – and rats grown big as cats, Mama, feeding – oh, I will not write the words! I shudder when he tells me of such stuff – but not just because it is so terrible – but who will mend the men who have seen such things? Their hearts and minds? Is there medicine enough in the world? I shiver when I think of this. What will come after this awful war?

But the most horrible story Heinz told me about the War was not about rats. At the first Christmas, in 1914, as the bells tolled, the soldiers, as one, all put down their guns, and mixed with each other! They sang carols and toasted each other, British and German alike – for they are all ordinary men and have no wish either to be killers or to be killed. They made their peace, and then the officers and generals made them return to their lines and begin the fight again! Can you believe such a thing? When Heinz related this, I almost burst into tears!

I felt my blood run cold – suppose Karl grew up to be the type of man who could do such a thing? Or Lena the sort of woman who would applaud him!?!? Oh, Mama, if the children raised in my care came to that end, I would rather never have been born – I said this to Heinz aloud, then became fearful I had said too much. But fortunately, he agreed with me completely. It was he who comforted me that time.

What monsters this war is creating!

Your loving daughter,

Rosamunde

P.S. Willy II is coming on leave in two weeks. I know he does not approve of me, but I will do my best.

R.

1917

-

January 31, 1917
Somewhere on the Western Front

Oberstleutnant Heinrich-Werner Mertz von Haydenreich
Commanding Officer, Second Division
16th Bavarian Reserve Regiment

Little brother,

That wife of yours! I am in receipt of a parcel, in which I find a useful woolen scarf, hand-knit, and a note written in a tone of warmth one would use to address an oldest and best friend. Also, other scarves for my adjutant and aide. They all bless her name.

Ah, Heinz, I hardly know what to think. She is a good person, your Rosamunde, Jew or not. It is a happy house, even in war. But what am I to say about a niece who greets me in Yiddish from time to time? Or a nephew who listens to caterwauling jazz by the hour? Or that the two of them seem to know as much French and English as they do German? Tales of Red Indians and Chinese nightingales – what a commotion! What happened to a decent German upbringing in a respectable household? This is a real concern, my brother. Enough can sometimes be too much. Lena and Karl are German children, after all, and not Jews of no nation. You must address this.

But little Lena is a beauty, so true a miniature of her mother it breaks your heart. Karl is lively and everywhere. The best hours I have had in years were cavorting with him in the snow. I miss them all, and – yes – the scarf-giver, too.

Your poor, concerned brother,

Willy

P.S. The rumor is you have declined another offer to transfer to Staff. Father will be beside himself.

W.

-

February 3, 1917
Neustrelitz am Schliersee

Frau Johanna Breslau
Munich, Bavaria
[by hand]

My dearest Mama,

. . . [T]here will be no child this time, I learned yesterday. Perhaps it is just as well, in a time of war. But I must live with my ghost a while longer.

Willy II returned to his regiment Thursday. It was not the worst visit. He was polite enough, and I even think he likes me. But I know he disapproves . . .

Your loving daughter,
Rosamunde

-

March 15, 1917
Somewhere on the Western Front

Oberst Wilhelm-Werner Mertz von Haydenreich
First Royal Heavy Cavalry Brigade
First Royal Bavarian Division
First Royal Bavarian Corps
[by hand]

My older fool of a brother,

Do you really believe you are so subtle? Do you think your looks to heaven, your heavy sighs, your small shakes of the head, go unnoticed? And has it occurred to you that – instead of writing to me of what good feeling you have for my wife. . . you might say something directly to her??

Even more than most women, my Rosamunde acts directly from her heart. I told her of the Christmas truce. The story horrified her. She believes this endless war is upon us because we Germans have become too German, the British too British, the French too French, and so on. She does not want Lottie and Karl, and of course our own children, when we have them, to join that number. There you have your explanation for the French, English, Yiddish, and stories that do not always center on wickedness and end with red-hot shoes or pokers.

Before you condemn this as a woman's foolish softness, I have come around to her point of view. I fully approve of my Rosamunde's universalism (to give it a name.) So you are raising an eyebrow at me, too, when you raise one at her. We are going to be coming home to a different world, a different Germany than the one we left, Willy. There are too many angry men, too many grieving women – too much blood, too many tears, for anything to be left unchanged. Does anybody even remember why this war began? Or what is the great reason why so much human misery had to be inflicted? I surely don't. The people will demand answers, and there are none to give. I hope the Kaiser is aware of the storm that is certain to break when all is done.

We will not be the same Germans we were, and it is best that the children be educated to be prepared for that. This is my thinking, so do not blame my Rosamunde for it. In any case, you could have been kinder to someone you basically like (if only you would admit it), who likes you, and whom I love and admire without reservation. So please do a little better in the future – or try, anyway.

As for the rest, Father is already aware of my decision, and the uproar has already occurred. It seems I have missed another chance to pose for General Staff photographs in my steel helmet. But though I will do my duty as I have sworn to do, and as a German officer, I will not spend one day longer in the service of the Kaiser than duty requires. My interests lie elsewhere. If ever again we are together, I will discuss these thoughts with you.

Your younger, but wiser brother,
Heinz

1918

-

April 13, 1918
Neustrelitz am Schliersee
Note enclosed in letter from Rosamunde Haydenreich to Heinrich von
Haydenreich, dated April 20, 1918

Frau Rosamunde von Haydenreich
Neustrelitz am Schliersee

      Frau Haydenreich,

      As you requested, I spent an hour with young Karl. I am delighted
to express my own agreement with your opinion, that Karl has indeed
inherited the musical gift that runs in the von Haydenreich family. I began
by playing scales. After one hearing, he was able to provide the next note
in sequence, even in minor keys. He had no difficulty in distinguishing
tones of higher and lower pitch, and placing them in order. I noticed he
relished the exercise.

      I next sang some simple songs, beginning with little ditties four
bars long, then progressing to comparatively complex melodies as long as
16 bars. Karl was able to repeat these flawlessly, usually after just one
hearing. Again, his pleasure in this activity was apparent.

      I do not think it is too early for him to begin musical studies. The
theory will be on the piano, but he expressed interest in learning to play the
clarinet and flute. I am sure Herr Alterman from the village band will be
happy to give him basic instruction on those instruments. Karl mentioned
the saxophone, but there are none at hand just now.

      After all the many kindnesses you have bestowed on myself and
my parishioners, it would give me the greatest pleasure to tender some
small measure of repayment in this manner.
                     Yours in Christ,

                Father Martin Kugler
                Pastor, St. Sixtus Parish

-

September 15, 1918
Somewhere on the Western Front

Oberst Heinrich-Werner Mertz von Haydenreich
Commanding Officer, Second Division
16th Bavarian Reserve Regiment

Little brother,

Ave, frater, ego moriturus te saluto. This useless scrap of Latin is at last useful. Hope I got it right.

The last letter of my life is what I mean.

About an hour ago, a damned British shell struck the battery, splinters flew everywhere, and several straight into my belly. Only five minutes before relief – I was gathering my kit. A minute before, a minute later, no harm. So the Norns sever the thread. The doctor tries to reassure, but I have seen enough belly wounds to know he's an ass and a liar. A day, maybe two, then the long, endless night. For now, morphine quiets all. But I will have no more. Too many brave men. I must make haste. Thus the scrawl.

Amend. Amends. One thinks of amends at this time. So many – not an honorable life. But first that wife of yours, don't know why. Sticks with me. Priceless pearl, priceless. Showed me nothing but kindness. You said so. Me? A churl. Wish I'd sent that letter. Wish I'd signed it. Too much the coward. Tell her how sorry I am, Heinz. Then take her to bed, and make a baby. Be a worthier heir than I ever was. Good woman. Lottie, too, both of them.

Jew, German? What difference does it make in the eternal night? Say this to Rosamunde. God! Now I feel it fully. Morphine is a dream of paradise – the poets are right. You have to try it, little brother, hopefully in circumstances less dire. But it won't last long.

Father loves me because I remind him of himself. He admires and fears you because you remind him of Mama. Relieved to turn the responsibility over to you. It's all bluster. He worships the Prussians because they aren't Bavarian. As angry as he becomes at your refusals, he respects you for them. Try to be good to the old boy. He knows you are the better man.

Ah! The pain begins to return. I will not take more of the elixir. Too many brave men in need. There is little time. Remember the Christmas Eve I was nine, and you were seven? We found fox tracks at the edge of the forest and decided to track them. We went deep into the dark, dark forest. The moon came out, full and silver, over the snow. The woods

67

became dense, and spooky. Then we heard a great owl, and thought of Hansel and Gretel, and became afraid and ran home. Mama had hot punch, and Father was too proud of our bravery to scold. The last holiday we were all together. Happiest day of my life.

Waiting on the other side – Mama, Lottie, all of us. This time we will find the fox. Everything different. Everyone together.

Always cared for you, little brother. Did not always make that plain. More amends. Live and be happy.

Farewell.

Willy

[Appended by another hand]

My darling Rosamunde,

I would not think in this wilderness of death I could feel such grief, but I do. My brother was not the worthiest of men, but I loved him, as he did me. I cannot believe he is gone. I could not imagine a world without him in it. Now I must live in one. Thank God I still have you.

I remember the Christmas Eve of which he wrote. It was indeed a very happy day. But I have known happier ones. For many of those, I thank you, and the way you have blessed my life. I am a very lucky man. I love you always, my precious Rosamunde.

With all my heart,

Heinz

P.S. I will have the remains shipped to Neustrelitz. Please have them interred as soon as possible, with as little formality as possible. A prayer and a blessing from Father Kugler will do for now. He should be buried on the prime site, as a Count, as befits the man who would have succeeded Father. We will have a more suitable memorial when – if – this war ever ends.

H.

-

November 12, 1918
Neustrelitz am Schliersee

Oberst Heinrich-Werner Mertz von Haydenreich
Commanding Officer, Second Division
16th Bavarian Reserve Regiment
Somewhere on the Western Front

My beloved husband,

Your letter shattered the entire household. Frau Schallert took to her apartment in tears, as did most of the servants. Everybody loved Willy. The house always seemed to sparkle with electricity when he was home. Everyone was devastated.

But I must tell you of the children. They were both distraught, but in different ways. Lena wished to shut herself up in her room. I permitted this, but sent for Father Kugler, to speak to her of the life beyond. Karl wandered aimlessly up and down the halls, as if he could find his uncle if he looked long and hard enough. I did not think the consolations of religion would be helpful there. For a while I was lost.

Then I thought to read the part of Willy's letter where he reminisced about looking for the fox in the snow. We have had an early snowfall, and on that night a full moon, so the woods looked much as they must have on that long-ago Christmas Eve, with the snow on the trees glowing in the moonlight and the stars glittering in the sky above the dark lake. I told Karl we should do what you two had done that night, and look for fox tracks. He perked up at once at the prospect of adventure.

The forest was lovely and mysterious. I wished to say something to him about the people we love never really leaving us, but did not know how to start. I hoped and prayed for an omen. Then – God be praised – all at once a huge snowy owl took wing! We could see it, first white, and then black against the moon. It hooted softly as it flew off. *Perhaps that was the very spirit of Uncle Willy,* I was able to say, *perhaps come to remind us he will never be that far away from us.* I said the people who love us never truly leave, that they are always present, just different in shape and form – that his mother still watches over him, and Willy, and many others – and I saw Karl smile for the first time since the news. *Maybe he has become a wild wolf in the wind,* Karl said. We had recently read of a story in which he learned of this tale of the life beyond, which is told by the American Red Indians. He decided he wanted to be a wolf himself. (The sweetest little boys always want to be the most fearsome beasts!) We walked on, and by and by he was a bit like the happy boy he has always been.

Then to Lena. Father Kugler had done his best, but I could see she was still in torment. I thanked Father, and sent him home. I brought Lena out under Lottie's portrait, and took her onto my lap. She had always felt her mother's presence in that beautiful picture. I told her soon enough there would be a portrait of Willy and he, too, will be with her. With that, her

69

sorrow became open, and she wept unashamedly in my lap, while I smoothed her hair and did what I could. She is such a lovely, gentle girl, Heinz, who has known too much death already! But finally, she found herself and finally went to sleep. Lena is much more religious than Karl, and she will find some consolation there. I will try my best to see that it is sufficient.

And me? When I had done all I could for these two innocents, then only did I take my own turn, out of sight of the world. I wept as if my heart would break, because it had. I re-read Willy's letter, again and then again, and each time tears flowed more freely. I always knew at heart he liked me – I liked him – I know we would have become fast friends, if only God had granted time. I could not stop crying, but knew I had to, for the others. Heinz, I want to name our first son after him – Wilhelm von Haydenreich III. You must oblige me in this.

And I wonder – perhaps the owl was indeed Willy's spirit, come back to remind us he will never really leave – I am not so sure I don't believe this myself. And I most surely do not believe in endless night – and I don't think Willy believed it, either.

I want you with me, my husband, more than ever. I want to hear your voice and feel the softness of your caress. I want to lay my head on your shoulder and feel your arm about me, the only true comfort I have in this life. I want to take down my hair for you, as I do when we are alone, and be completely yours again! I ache for you, for your being, for your presence, simply to be in the same room with you. Please, oh, please, come home soon.

I am aware of the Armistice. All the bells in the province were proclaiming it yesterday. I rejoice for everyone else. But for me, there will be no end to war until I know you are safe, and we will be together again. The War will not be over until you are home, and with me

With eternal love,
Your Rosamunde

-

November 18, 1918
Sanatorium
Beelitz-Heilstatten

Frau Rosamunde von Haydenreich
Neustrelitz am Schliersee

My beloved Rosamunde,

This is the fourth letter I have written you since October 13th. I haven't received any letter from you in two months. I don't know whether you will receive this letter, or who will read it before. Therefore, I will concentrate on the facts, my love. You know what is written in my heart well enough already.

To begin with the most important, I was gassed on the night of October 13th. Then, while at the hospital, I became extremely ill with the new influenza. I have recovered, too, from that, and am convalescing at a residenz I have taken in Pasewalk, in Pomerania. I am still too feeble to travel at present, but I will be recovered in a fortnight or so. Then I will make my way to my soul's content.

Let me tell you what happened. On the night of October 13th, my regiment were near Comines, a Belgian town near the French border, and guarding a ford on the Lys River. We came under heavy attack from British artillery. There were also reports of gas attacks. I knew there were wounded in front of me. But I also knew that they could expect no real help from their comrades. The Army had been collapsing day by day since August. I took it upon myself to lead a rescue party to the front lines, looking for wounded. I did find several, and we returned to safety.

The shellfire missed me, and I thought I had escaped harm. But while I was escorting three messengers back to headquarters, near a village called Werwick, I became aware that I had been exposed to mustard gas, and for a considerable period of time. This pernicious stuff takes a long time to make its effects felt, so it was not until afternoon the next day I became aware of how great the exposure was. Red blisters began to form on my skin, my throat became dry, I began to cough uncontrollably. I knew I had to go to the hospital.

(There is comedy even at the direst times. One of the regimental messengers, Hitler, an Austrian, who had experienced far less exposure to the gas than I, became convinced the gas would make him blind. The physicians, and some of the soldiers who had experience with the stuff, tried to reassure him. But he would not listen and became so distraught that he DID go blind! But this was purely his mental reaction. So he was removed to the hospital to be treated for war fatigue in the same ambulance that conveyed me here.)

71

In fact, attacks of this gas are very uncomfortable, but rarely fatal. Yet I thought for a time I might be the exception. For several days, my throat remained dry and sore. Each breath was labored, and I wondered if each would be my last. Death holds no terror for me, my love – its only torment was that I would never see you again. That thought was agony.

But after a few days I began to recover. Breath continued to be short, but not so labored as before. I knew the worst of the gas was behind.

But this was not the end of it. There has been a new disease with us since the spring – the influenza, as it is called. It rippled through the troops at the Marne. Ludendorff blamed it for the failure of the offensive. (Ludendorff always blames everyone but himself.) We had been spared it in the 16th, but in the hospital, among men already sick and enfeebled, of course it would appear. I thought I was experiencing some secondary effect of the gas, and wondered how that could be. Then the doctors told me I had caught the influenza, and I was ordered to bed.

Then it was upon me – several days of high fever. On the worst day, I was not certain whether I was alive or dead. But ultimately, I was one of the fortunate ones. The fever broke, and I was alive. I would live. It was the longing to hold you again in my arms that saved me. I am sure of that.

But even this was not the end. After the influenza came a bout of pneumonia. The conditions at the hospital were indescribable, with the wounded, the sick and dying overflowing the beds and litters crowding the corridors. I thought again the end had come. But that fever broke, too. However, I was too weak to walk more than ten paces. I could not stay in the hospital, with so many brave men in need. I had myself discharged, temporarily, to the residenz in Pasewalk, from which I write these lines.

The discharge was temporary in theory, but I knew it was permanent as a practical matter. The War was ending. The loyalty of the Army is doubtful – in any case, its fighting spirit is gone. I was still in the hospital when the Armistice came. Thank God! Even in a hospital, amid the sick and dying, joy was all but universal. (Then occurred the second act of the comedy. The Austrian Hitler, the messenger, the one who believed himself blind, having recovered his sight in the mental ward, was so distraught at the news of peace that he became blind again! And took to his bed, weeping – he apparently is the one man who wishes the War to continue, and believes in the cause – too cut off from himself to realize

72

how much he himself has been damaged by it. Poor devil – I laugh, but not without sympathy.)

So here I am. I know your heart, my Rosamunde. I am sure your first thought is to fly to me and give care. But you must not do this. I am beyond the worst of the illness now, and time alone will restore me to full strength. The owner of the residenz lost two sons in the War and cares for me as if I were one of them – not as well as you would, my love, but well enough.

But most of all, travel is too dangerous. Not only has the Army collapsed, but Germany around it. The abdication of the Kaiser leaves everyone in shock, not knowing what to do or what is coming next. There are reports of mutinies and officers taken captive. There are Bolshevik bands and monarchist gangs. Everything is in turmoil and chaos. Men of violence are everywhere, and the authorities cannot be trusted to contain them. So please remain at Neustrelitz, where it is safe. Do not tax me with additional worries on your behalf.

Home is where you are, and home is heaven. I am so sick and weary of all of this. I will make my way to you as soon as I possibly can. That is my solemn promise. Until then . . .

With all my heart and all my love,

your Heinz

-

November 26, 1918
Neustrelitz am Schliersee

Oberst Heinrich-Werner von Haydenreich
Sanatorium
Beelitz-Heilstatten

My beloved Heinz,

My heart near stopped when I beheld your handwriting on the letter. At first, my hands trembled too much to open it – I could only press it against my breast and thank God – simply to know you are alive! Four months without a word – every night I had gone to bed with a desperate prayer – now I knew that God had heard me! I tried to keep from weeping, for I cry too much, like a foolish child. But I could not help myself. Then I summoned Frau Schallert, and she was as much a child as I, as we wept in each other's arms. She has gone to the village, and I told the children. So much rejoicing, so much happiness!

73

Then to read of your gassing, and these dreadful illnesses, and to understand all you have endured – there are not tears enough to weep for that – this dreadful, dreadful war! Your directions to me press on me heavily, my husband. I long to fly to you, and to nurse you myself, as a good wife should. I will do as you ask in this, but it weighs heavily on me. I want more than anything to be with you!

I wish you could see the children. Lena has grown up so much this last year. Now she stands on the edge of early womanhood, in all the radiant beauty of innocence. Karl has been taking lessons on clarinet and flute – already, in just a few months, he gets a wonderful sound from them! He likes to play along to the American jazz records, and it seems to me he is already accomplished – you will be so proud of him when you hear for yourself.

Please let me come as soon as you are confident travel is safe. To be with you again, to be by your side – this is heaven to me!

But mostly, I thank God you are alive!

Yours forever,

Your Rosamunde

P.S. It was the fourth letter you wrote that reached me. You were right to write so many.

I am Yours.

R.

-

November 27, 1918
Neustrelitz am Schliersee

Frau Johanna Breslau
Munich, Bavaria
[by hand]

My dearest Mama,

. . . [s]o I will do as I am bidden, because I know Heinz is right, travel is dangerous, and I am a dutiful wife. But I long to be with him! And, Mama, I ask myself – would a different wife do different? Would a stronger, braver woman simply take the reins in her hand and go to him? Would Lottie?

Perhaps this is truly the desire of Heinz's heart, that I find the courage to ignore his directions. Do you think so? Have I failed him, in what he desires most?

Your loving daughter,
Rosamunde

-

November 29th, 1918
Munich, Bavaria

Frau Rosamunde Breslau-Haydenreich
Neustrelitz am Schliersee

My wondrous daughter,

All those who love you (and I include Heinz) continue to be amazed by your habitual self-doubt. (If you could but hear the way your courier Josef talks of you, and the countless acts of grace he mentions. But the habit of kindness is so deeply ingrained in you, you give it no thought.)

Of course, Heinz has no secret desire of the heart. He has given you sensible and good direction, no doubt to his own considerable frustration. These ARE difficult times. A loving husband takes good care of his wife. These doubts, these worries, these gnawing fears – they are the product of war and separation. They will vanish like moonshadow the moment you are back in his arms and – a mother may write it – his bed. Give the matter no more thought.

Your loving mother,
Mama

November 29, 1918
Sanatorium
Beelitz-Heilstatten

Frau Rosamunde von Haydenreich
Neustrelitz am Schliersee

My darling Rosamunde,

I just received your letters of November 12 and November 26. I all but shed my own tears at the sight of them.

I continue to make progress on my recovery, though not quite as quickly as I had hoped. Before, I could barely pace across the room – perhaps a half dozen steps – before I had to return to bed. Today I negotiated two rounds around the courtyard, and then sat and remained there for most of the morning. Before, I slept restlessly, with strange dreams. Each morning I awoke, not entirely certain where I was or when. Usually I had some notion that Willy was still alive and near, that I was

75

back at Neustrelitz as a boy, or in barracks, or some such, and it would be a few moments before these day phantoms vanished. But that, too, is now quickly passing, and my sleep is sounder with each passing night.

I am determined to be with you at Neustrelitz by Christmastime. I am certain I will be strong enough for the trip. I miss you every instant, my beloved, but not as a nurse. What I miss is your dark hair cascading down when you let it loose. I will not write more in a letter that may be read by others. I know you perceive my meaning. (In my mind's eye, I can see you blush, which only inflames me more.)

But I must continue to forbid you this same journey, and pray that you will respect me on this. The chaos I feared is upon us and no end in sight. Fearsome chaos all about the cities. Food riots now, Bolsheviks, brigands – the Kaiser has flown and nothing and no one to replace him. It is not clear whether the Army is friend or foe to the mass of German people. The roads are thronged with deserters making their way home. Some of the units that remain are now governed by soldiers' councils instead of officers, and model themselves after the Bolsheviks. Others name themselves 'Freikorps' and fight the first kind. There are constant battles. Every morning, dozens of corpses are fished out of the rivers and canals.

For now, stay in Neustrelitz – please do this. You will at least be able to feed yourselves while all these matters sort themselves out – and I will be better, I promise you. When I have regained my strength, I will make my way home – to you, and by Christmas. I will count the days, the minutes, the seconds, until my eyes feast on you again.

Your loving husband,

Heinz

-

December 1, 1918
Sanatorium
Beelitz-Heilstatten

Frau Rosamunde von Haydenreich
Neustrelitz am Schliersee

Dear Frau von Haydenreich,

It is with the most profound regret that I must inform you of my professional opinion that your husband, Oberst Heinrich von Haydenreich, is not yet fit for travel. He is not in fact yet fit for discharge from this hospital. Although he has made some progress, his constitution remains extremely enfeebled and his health a matter of grave concern. Walking more than a few dozen yards exhausts him. His sleep has improved, but he still often wakes disoriented and confused.

This is not a matter of a small infirmity. Oberst von Haydenreich suffered gravely from the gassing and illnesses, and remains with an extremely weakened constitution.

I am addressing you because the Oberst is insistent on returning home to you for the Christmas holiday. I cannot emphasize too much how extremely imprudent such a journey would be, in midwinter, with travel conditions uncertain and a considerable portion of the travel likely to be in unheated compartments. I have to add, in truth, that recovery is likely to be a matter of months, not weeks. But for his own good, he must come to terms with the realities of his condition.

I am writing to you to urge you to add your own pleadings to the advice I am giving him. Your husband's impatience may do him grave harm. I would rather Oberst von Haydenreich make all the progress possible before release, rather than leave prematurely and experience an immediate collapse . . .

Respectfully,

Dr. Friedrich Rosenbaum

Chief of Staff

-

December 26, 1918
Neustrelitz am Schliersee

Oberst Heinrich-Werner von Haydenreich
Sanatorium
Beelitz-Heilstatten

My beloved husband,

. . . Mama was with us, the first visit she was able to make in two years. She shares your view of the State. She is very concerned about the new regime in Munich. I had the Midnight Mass said for Willy. You would have been heartened to see the grief displayed throughout the church. His high spirits, his wit, his adventurousness – these touched more people than you could possibly have imagined

. . . [S]o our first Christmas after the War was all a Christmas could be, my husband – except for your absence. The children missed you,

77

the household missed you, and I missed you until my bones ached. I remembered the Christmases we used to have. I longed for your voice, your touch, the glow of your eyes. The table will always be bare until you are once more at its head.

But I am grateful to the bottom of my heart you paid attention to Dr. Rosenbaum's advice. I would not trade days or weeks with you, for years with you . . .

Yours forever,
Your Rosamunde

1919

-

Excerpt from: A History of Germany in the Twentieth Century
Josef Behrens
Alfred A Knopf (1964)

. . . [T]he first part of the year 1919 can lay claim to being the most turbulent period in modern German history, even more so than 1848. There were mutinies in the Navy and some elements of the Army. Food riots occurred in Berlin and other major cities. Two different Socialist parties fought for control of the government, a moderate faction led by Friedrich Ebert and a far more radical group, known as the Spartacists, headed by Karl Liebknecht and Rosa Luxemburg. In January, the Spartacists called for a general strike in Berlin, that had to be put down by the loyal troops in the Army.

In Munich, an actual Socialist state was proclaimed by Kurt Eisner in November 1918 – 'Red Munich', as it came to be known. From its earliest days, it was an epicenter of strife and violence. . .

-

January 9th, 1919
Sanatorium
Beelitz-Heilstratten

Frau Rosamunde von Haydenreich
Neustrelitz am Schliersee

My beloved Rosamunde,

Today I was able to negotiate a walk of two city blocks before I was forced to sit and rest for a while. To think that I must regard this paltry effort as an accomplishment!

My patience with this endless recuperation is coming to an end. I informed Dr. Rosenbaum that I will not endure this confinement much longer . . .

Your loving husband,
Heinz

-

February 10th, 1919
Sanatorium
Beelitz-Heilstratten

Monsieur Rene de Monterose
Societe de Construction des Batignolles
Paris, France

My dear Monsieur Monterose.

. . . [Y]ou may recall proposals I sent to you in May 1914, for
certain developments I believe could be profitably built at the estates I
manage in Neustrelitz. If not, they are certainly on file.

Our discussions were unfortunately interrupted by the War. But
my calculations remain viable, and – if anything – have become even more
interesting, in view of the expanded railway network and increased use of
the motorcar that has occurred in the intervening years.

I would like to renew our conversation, concerning the exciting
potential for Neustrelitz. Domestic matters in the aftermath of the War
continue to detain me, but I could present myself at your offices any time
at your convenience after the first of April . . .

Very truly yours,

Heinrich von Haydenreich

-

February 10th, 1919
Sanatorium
Beelitz-Heilstratten

Frau Rosamunde von Haydenreich
Neustrelitz am Schliersee

My beloved Rosamunde,

Today was a decisive day. I took another of the obnoxiously short
walks that are my custom in the mornings. It seemed to me that I had made
no progress in more than a month. Enough is enough!

I confronted Dr. Rosenbaum with my frustration at this endless
convalescence. He acknowledged, as I knew he must, that I have already
made the essence of the substantial progress I can expect to make. But he
insisted that the marginal betterment still possible was important to firm
health. I informed him that the time spent separate from you, the children,
and my actual life had become intolerable. I therefore announced my intent
to depart that very day, or as soon as might be practicable.

When the doctor realized that I was firm in this resolve, he bade
me sit down and gave more practical advice. If I were to leave, he implored
me not to return to Neustrelitz, where the severity of the winter could do

me no good. Instead, he suggested I consider convalescing in a warmer climate, such as Italy, for a time. The idea at first startled me, then took hold of my imagination as few ideas ever have. You have not been away from Munich and Neustrelitz for four long years. The children have never seen any other part of the world.

So – my idea. I propose to remove you, the children, and myself, to Italy, for the remainder of the year. It makes little sense for me to journey to Neustrelitz, where the Alpine winter poses a risk of a relapse. Far better for you three to come to Berlin, where I will have taken rooms. From there we will go to Paris, where I have some business to discuss with Societe de Construction des Batignolles, a civil engineering firm. We may be there a week, perhaps longer – in any case, long enough for a proper visit. Then we will go on to Italy, most probably to the Tuscan region near Florence.

These ideas strike me as at once so sensible, and so exciting, that I am somewhat wary of them. I wonder if in my enthusiasm I have overlooked something, but for the life of me, I do not perceive any flaw. If you are in agreement, as I expect you will be, cable me at the Hotel Adlon, to which I will be moving before the end of the day, and I will begin looking for a suitable residence in Berlin and Tuscany. I would expect to greet you in a fortnight, or perhaps a little later if some matter in Neustrelitz detains you. (My spirit sings just to write such words!)

One last thing, that I would wish you to keep to yourself. Prepare yourself and the children for a trip of significant duration, some months, perhaps even years. I am not at all sure that the revolutionary ferment in Germany has run its course. Matters are settled enough for the trip to be safe, with the Spartacists scattered. But the Bolsheviks and the Red Socialists are not done. I doubt that we Germans will go the route of the French Revolution or the bloody Russians. But we will not be returning to Bavaria until conditions are once again normal. We must hope for the best, but prepare for the worst.

Your husband and ardent lover,

Heinz

-

February 17th, 1919
Neustrelitz am Schliersee

Oberst Heinrich-Werner von Haydenreich
Hotel Adlon
Berlin, Germany

WONDERFUL PLAN STOP WILL BEGIN PREPARATIONS
IMMEDIATELY STOP DELAY NECESSARY TO MARCH 10TH
STOP KARL HAS FIRST CONCERT STOP LETTER FOLLOWS
STOP LOVE YOUR ROSAMUNDE

-

February 17, 1919
Neustrelitz am Schliersee

Oberst Heinrich-Werner von Haydenreich
Hotel Adlon
Berlin, Germany

My beloved husband,

. . . Paris! And then Tuscany!!! In your company! I am the most
blessed of women! I will begin preparations as soon as I am finished
writing.

I mentioned a concert in the cable. Ten days from now, a concert
will be given in the Church by the school orchestra, with the addition of
some others, in which the Mozart C Minor Mass is to be performed. It will
be Karl's first concert! He will be playing second clarinet – he has already
made such astonishing progress. I am certain you would not want him to
miss this. Also, a fortnight will give me time to leave my French and
English classes at the Gymnasium in good order. My heart will break
leaving them, but a wife should be with her husband – everyone
understands this.

What wonderful plans! I will be with you in a month!! I am
bursting with joy!!

Eternally and completely Yours,
Your Rosamunde

-

March 4th, 1919
Neustrelitz am Schliersee

Oberst Heinrich-Werner von Haydenreich
Hotel Adlon
Berlin, Germany

DEPARTING NEUSTRELITZ TOMORROW STOP STOPOVER
MUNICH WITH MAMA STOP EXPECT ARRIVAL BERLIN MARCH
6 STOP LOVE ALWAYS YOUR ROSAMUNDE

March 7th, 1919
Munich, Bavaria

Oberst Heinrich-Werner von Haydenreich
Hotel Adlon
Berlin, Germany

LENA KARL FEVERISH STOP BELIEVE INFLUENZA STOP
MUST DELAY TRIP TO BERLIN UNTIL RECOVERY STOP VERY
WORRIED STOP WILL PROVIDE FURTHER NEWS ROSAMUNDE

March 10, 1919
Munich, Bavaria

Oberst Heinrich-Werner von Haydenreich
Hotel Adlon
Berlin, Germany

LENA LIKELY PNEUMONIA STOP EXTREMELY CRITICAL STOP
KARL VERY ILL BUT NOT IN CRISIS STOP ROSAMUNDE

March 12, 1919
Munich, Bavaria

Oberst Heinrich-Werner von Haydenreich
Hotel Adlon
Berlin, Germany

NO EASY WORDS STOP YOUR DAUGHTER LENA DIED 4 PM
THIS AFTERNOON STOP MY DAUGHTER YOUR WIFE
ROSAMUNDE DIED 10 PM STOP AGONIES OF GRIEF STOP
KARL RECOVERING STOP COME QUICKLY STOP FRAU
JOHANNA BRESLAU

March 12, 1919
Munich, Bavaria
*Note of same date, recovered from the sickbed of Rosamunde Breslau
von Haydenreich*

My husband,

Lena died in my arms four hours ago. I mopped her brow, I looked into her eyes. One second she was there, the next she was gone, our precious daughter was gone! Gone!!!! Grief beyond enduring! I do not want to take another breath, think another thought, feel another heartbeat. I wish I were dead and with my little girl!

I feel the same fever steal over me. Maybe this is just a wish, for I so wish I too were dead – but I know this is cowardly and so I will try to live, my husband, I promise, for you, for Karl – I so wish you were here – I could find my special place on your shoulder and weep for the rest of my life!! And then just die!! Lena's face is before me everywhere! I wish I were dead! I wish Lena were alive and I was dead!!

But now I am sure it is the fever – if I am wrong, I will destroy this note. But I am not wrong. So soon perhaps I will be with Lena – and Lottie, too. Dear God, how will I face her??! When I could not save her daughter?? It is the influenza. I am sure of it. Lena had the slightest agitation in her nose when we left. I should have known – I should have guessed!

Heinz, my husband, I would marry you a thousand times, and a thousand times again – I am so glad for the years we had – you made me the happiest woman in the world! I wish I could say that aloud to you!

So you will meet Lottie and me together now, in that place without sadness. Which one of us will you choose? For I have always wondered – oh, what a terrible thing to write!! Too late to change or write another – can you _ever_ forgive me?

Loving you eternally,
R.

A Letter From A Child Become Man

1932

—

August 8, 1932
Regimental barracks
Dresden, Germany

Frau Margaret Golsing
Grunwalder Strasse 16
Munich, Germany

    Dearest Frau Golsing,

    My many thanks for the vibrant memories you shared with the table last night, of my mother Charlotte, my stepmother Rosamunde, and my father. You held the entire company spellbound. But you knew I would be the one most affected, as indeed I was. It may be only my conceit, but my impression was that you hoped to draw me out, and hear my own store of recollection.

    I did not mean to disappoint you. But the truth is my memories of those days are tangled and perplexed to the point of confusion. It is difficult for me to sort them out, even in quiet moments, let alone at a lively dinner party. Yet I do not want to frustrate you. Moreover, the time has come for me to reconcile them, with my wedding imminent, and to satisfy your natural curiosity. A prospective mother-in-law deserves no less.

    So I will give you the truth as best I remember it, and as best I understand it.

    I was not even nine years old in the spring of 1919. The War had barely touched us, in our little village of Neustrelitz. I had only vague and scattered memories of my father. He seemed to enjoy Lena's company more than mine. I knew my Uncle Willy better, and liked him more – a wild wolf in the forest, or a great owl, black before the moon. That is how Mummi (as I have always called her) asked me to remember him. He played with me and took me out in the snow. I knew he had been killed, but I do not believe I fully grasped what that meant. But I knew who he was. My father? He was no more than a collection of kinescope images who flitted in for a few days and then was gone. I doubt I would have felt actual grief if he had been lost. I did not know him at all.

Mummi was everything to me. She was the bedrock of my life, the one who kissed away my childish hurts, made me laugh, taught me my letters, and laid the foundation for my English and French (and of course, Yiddish). She was everywhere during the War, comforting afflicted families, organizing food and clothing collections, making the resources of the castle available for weddings, funerals, and all manner of village celebrations. She was the woman I loved as mother. I know she did not give me birth, and I respect and honor my mother Charlotte. But it was Mummi who laid hands on my life.

We set out from Neustrelitz that spring to join my father in Berlin, and then go on to Paris. But we all fell ill. I was too young and sick myself to be aware how much Mummi had endangered herself nursing Lena and me. Then I was recovering. I heard whisperings outside my door. Suddenly my father entered the room. I had not even known he had arrived. He sat down on my bed, and in a quiet way told me what had happened – that my sister had died, that Mummi was gone from me forever. I do not remember now how exactly I behaved at that moment. My recollection is that I was too numb for tears, that the immensity of the event was too great. But perhaps I did shed some.

As for my sister Lena, I almost can't bear to write of her. She did not even have the chance to have a friend such as you were to my mother and Mummi. Had she lived, she would have rivaled yours and my Elizabeth in grace and beauty.

I did not understand my father's grief then or later. Truth be told, in my childish way, I resented it. It was I who had lived with Lena and Mummi – not him, I who had shared my life with them – not him, he who had been so long away from our home. Neither then nor later did I attempt to understand his sorrow. Instead, I resented him.

In the next days, a terrific row broke out as to where Mummi should be buried. My father won the argument, largely because Grandma sided with him, which is why she lies at rest at Neustrelitz. He took me home for the funeral ceremonies for my sister, mother, and uncle (which had been delayed until his return). Then, after a short but decent time, we went off to Paris as we four had planned. But now it was only we two. (*Do what you had planned*, I remember Grandma saying, *this is too much sadness for such a small boy*.) My resentment grew through all this. Of course, my father knew how I felt about him. But he did not chide me. Instead, with his characteristic wisdom, he waited for me to grow up enough to understand him as he truly was. But that day never dawned, not while he was alive.

Until the day of his death, I mistook the weary, dispassionate man, whom I learned to respect (if not love) for the man himself. I misinterpreted the profound sadness that engulfed him as a distant, philosophical detachment. The reality (I now know) was that when Mummi and Lena died, the larger part of his soul died with them. I have little doubt now that he further ruined his health and shortened his life considerably, in his haste to rejoin us. It was only after his death, when I went through his papers, that I reached even a glimmering of the truth – that he had been the man you knew in Munich, a man of vigor and passion, that he and Mummi had shared extravagant hopes and dreams – that they had been committed, extremely amorous lovers (some of their letters made me blush like a schoolgirl), with huge plans for life. All of this was a foreign country to me until after he was gone, when it was much, much too late.

My father left me several letters at his death, about my mother Charlotte, about Mummi, and one for me, with his last advice on how I should live my life. There is wisdom in it, I believe, and I do my best to heed it. I am enclosing all three. I know you will find them interesting, and – with respect to the advice – reassuring about the choice your daughter Elizabeth has made of me as husband.

I found one more item that I was not sure that I was ever meant to see. It was a note in Mummi's hand, the last one she ever wrote, written while she knew she was dying (but hoped she was not). I found it on my father's bedside table. He must have retrieved it from her death bed in Munich. He apparently kept it beside him always. Frau Golsing, I cannot enclose this note. It is a holy relic to me. I will show it to you when next you come to Neustrelitz. It remains there, with my father's most personal and sacred effects.

That is what I remember. But having written all of this to you . . . I remain perplexed and confused. I have learned over time that three extraordinary people formed my being. My sister had the same blessings as I did. Yet she is gone, and I alone remain. There must be a reason for this. I do not mean anything so prosaic or dangerous as a destiny. My friend Albert laughs at such notions, and he is right. Just . . . a reason – only that – and after that, my thoughts and emotions are too muddled to express in plain words.

But I do believe, too, that whatever reason there may be, is bound up in my love for Elizabeth. I hope you find that, too, reassuring.

88

I hope all this explains my hesitancy and silence last evening. I did not wish to frustrate you.

Your son-in-law to be,

Karl

P.S. You will observe, when you see it, that Mummi's last note is tear-stained. I never saw my father shed tears, not once in his life. But he must have wept often over that note. I learned more about my father's true character from those tear stains than all the rest.

K.

Unlikely Friend

Paris, 1919
Excerpt from: My Name is Ike - Reflections on Fifty Years of Service as
Soldier and Statesman
Senator Dwight D. Eisenhower
Random House (1986)

. . . [T]here I was in Paris in 1919, where I surely did not want to be. I wanted to go home, like everybody else. But when you've more or less blackmailed your way into a combat command in the Great War, there is a price that must be paid. When the Armistice came, just about all the Americans went home within a few months. But a few had to stick around to do basic administration with the sick and wounded, and help out at the Peace Conference – and since I'd begged and borrowed my way over to France, I got tagged with the duty. I didn't like it. I'd have much rather gone home to Mamie and my children. You have to be a damn fool to prefer Kansas to Paris, I guess, but I was that kind of damn fool back then.

But fate has a way of evening things out. Because I stayed, I made probably the best friend of my entire life – certainly, the most significant. The friend I mean is Heinrich von Haydenreich. I would never have met him if I hadn't been forced to stay on in Paris. I would never have become a godfather to his son Karl.

Ultimately, that changed everything.

April 14, 1919
Neustrelitz am Schliersee

Monsieur Rene de Monterose
Societe de Construction des Batignolles
Paris, France

Dear Monsieur,I must express my deep appreciation for the sincere condolences extended by you and your firm to my household. Both my son Karl and I are deeply grateful in a time of the most profound grief.

. . .[I]t is all the more important that we press forward with the realization of these plans. My own health is uncertain and my son is not yet ten. If the meetings we postponed could be rescheduled for early June, I would be again deeply grateful. I will be in the company of my son Karl, if you can assist me in making suitable arrangements . . .

Sincerely,

Heinrich von Haydenreich

-

Excerpt from: My Name is Ike - Reflections on Fifty Years of Service as
Soldier and Statesman
Senator Dwight D. Eisenhower
Random House (1986)

I wasn't on duty the night I met Heinz von Haydenreich. It was a Friday night in July, I forget the exact date. I was on my own. I'd heard a little about some of the new stuff going on in Paris – art and music, Picasso, those guys, and I decided I'd try to find out a little about it. (Not my cup of tea, I found out.) I went over to Montmartre for dinner, to a cafe I'd heard about, La Rotonde. It was a nice night, fairly hot. I expected it would be crowded. But my God! Nothing like it was.

It turned out there was a jazz musician, Sidney Bechet, going to play that night. He'd been doing concerts in London, but he came over to Paris to play, just for a week or two. He already had a huge following. Finding a seat, even for one, was really tough. But Americans were popular in France right then, so the head waiter said he'd do what he could. After a minute, he was back and asked if I was OK sharing a table with a man and his son. I said sure.

And that's how I met Heinz and Karl. They were sitting quietly at a front table. Heinz had a pallor to him that marked him at once as a man who was not well. His clothes were well made, but seemed too large for him. He looked like he'd lost a great deal of weight in the recent past. Karl was average height and build for his age, but so serious. He nodded politely at me, but didn't smile. I liked them both at first sight, though I couldn't tell you why.

Then Bechet took the stage and began to play his clarinet. Heinz just listened, but Karl was transformed. His face glowed. His hands came up above the table, and he began to finger an imaginary clarinet of his own, playing along with Bechet, oblivious to all else. I managed to catch Bechet's eye as he looked out over the crowd, and nodded toward the boy playing the imaginary woodwind. Bechet grinned ear to ear as he noticed, and continued playing. Heinz noticed all this and nodded his thanks.

A couple of minutes after the set was over, a waiter appeared, with a note. It was from Sidney Bechet himself, inviting Karl to come to a rehearsal at the restaurant the next day. Karl lit up like a light bulb. Heinz, who had barely moved during the set pieces, leaned forward and thanked me in a soft, courteous voice. Then, only then, did we introduce ourselves.

That's how the best and most unlikely friendship of my life began. Why a Bavarian nobleman and a Kansas dirt-kicker should hit it off, I couldn't tell you. But there are people with whom you feel an instant rapport, as if you've known them all your life, and who can tell you why? Anyway, that's how it was with Heinz and me.

We walked back to their hotel. They'd come to Paris, I learned, because Heinz had some business with a French civil engineering firm, but also to get away from Bavaria for a little while. I got the impression that there was a long, sad story left untold, but I didn't press for it. Heinz said a little more about the engineering project. I didn't know it then, but he was describing the origin of the famous Neustrelitz resort.

-

July 9, 1919
Paris, France

Herr Heinrich von Haydenreich
% Hotel de Crillon
10 Place de Concorde
Paris, France

My dear Monsieur von Haydenreich,

. . . [W]e can confirm that your abstract proposal, of concentric half-circles of rows of cabins of various size, from single units ('bungalows', as the British would say) to substantial villas, with a small hotel and restaurant at the center, each providing the patron of whatever means of an unobstructed view of lake or mountain, is feasible within a reasonable variance of the cost you originally estimated.

A contract for the undertaking is being prepared and will be available for execution on the morrow. Before proceeding, however, I would advise you that your proposal has generated considerable excitement in these offices. Our own accountants have made their own assessment of the profitability of the 'Neustrelitz Resort' (if I may be so bold). Our firm is willing to waive a substantial portion of the engineering and architectural fees in consideration for a profit participation in the project . . .

Not to mince words, what I am proposing is a joint venture of some sort . . .

Sincerely,

Msr. Armand de Riviere

General Manager

-

***Excerpt from: My Name is Ike - Reflections on Fifty Years of Service as
Soldier and Statesman
Senator Dwight D. Eisenhower
Random House (1986)***

The plan had been for Heinz to participate in the business meetings in the mornings, while the hotel concierge found amusements for Karl. Then the father would rejoin his son in the afternoon for more extended tours and sightseeing. But it was obvious after knowing them only a few moments that the plan would not work. The walk to the hotel was a short one, less than an hour, but Heinz could hardly maintain the pace that Karl and I set, which was not at all brisk. He needed to rest every few hundred yards. Keeping up with a vigorous young boy for even an afternoon, let alone a series of afternoons, was out of the question.

So, on the spur of the moment, I volunteered to escort Karl. Heinz looked at me a bit askance, understandably. But I suggested that the next day, after the Bechet rehearsal, we go back to the American Embassy, where Heinz could meet persons who could vouch for me. I had some leave coming, but mostly there was that burgeoning rapport – plus I had become curious about what the story of the pair actually was. I did not forget my duty entirely – I had already gleaned enough to know that Heinz was a man of significance in Germany. I figured his views on the future of Germany might be useful to State.

The next day Heinz bid his son *auf wiedersehen* at noon, and went back to the hotel for the nap he needed. Karl and I were off. That's how it went for the next week. Karl didn't warm to me instantly, but I left him space, and waited, and in a day or two we were good friends. He was still a sad, serious little boy – but occasionally his eyes would brighten, and every once in a while, something would make him laugh with delight – just not as often as the other

95

children. It was good for me, too. I saw a lot of Paris I would never have visited otherwise.

He frequently mentioned someone he called 'Mummi'. *'Mummi told me about this, or Mummi would have liked to see that.'* When I congratulated him on the quality of his French, which was every bit as good as his English, he said that Mummi had taught him. I formed the impression that Mummi, whoever she was, was a woman who had been pretty gosh darn important to him, and that she wasn't around any longer. I was afraid to ask more.

The only time I saw him cry was at a puppet show at the Champs Elyssees. It was a typical Punch-and-Judy affair, and pretty funny, even to me. But I looked, and there was Karl, with tears cascading down his cheeks. I asked what upset him, and he answered, *'Lena. Lena loved puppets. Lena should be here. Not me.'* I could only smooth his hair and put my hand on his shoulder. I didn't find out who Lena was, until I met Heinz back at the hotel. Lena was the name of his big sister, short for Magdalena, deceased only three months before. I began to get a glimmer of the story and how sad it really was.

At the end of every day, I took Karl back to the hotel, and the three of us would have dinner. These were good nights. Heinz made an impression on me like few men I have ever met. There was a regality in his manner, in everything he said and did. He never said anything to me about his pedigree. It was a hotel clerk who tipped me off that he was the head of one of the oldest Bavarian noble families. But I think I would have known that, even if no one had ever told me anything.

He really didn't give a damn anymore about business or politics. All that had ceased to matter to him. But a few shreds and patches came through. He had originally thought that he and Karl might be gone from Bavaria for some time, due to the threat of revolution. But now he was planning a fairly quick return. A reaction had set in. Though he despised the right wingers as much as the would-be revolutionaries, he knew they were no threat to him. He held out little hope for the new government. He felt that it had made a fatal mistake in not forcing the German Army to join in the surrender. It had even permitted the Army to march in good order through Berlin after the Armistice, in the manner of victorious troops. In any case, he doubted the German people were ready for that form of government. He hoped somehow the new Republic would evolve into a British-style constitutional monarchy.

This wasn't much, but I did write it up in a report, which I doubt anyone has ever read. (It would have been better if someone had.) I just wrote it to justify my time. His own story was what really interested me. But he didn't talk at all about himself, and he said nothing about the story.

It was only on the last night that he finally opened up. I think that was probably because it was the last night. Karl had gone to bed, worn out by the day.

'*We have become friends, I think,*' he said.

'*Yes,*' I answered, '*we have. But the funny thing is I really don't know very much about you. I know a little from Karl. Can you tell me a little more?*'

Heinz thought about this a second, paused a moment, then put down his drink.

'*Actually, I want to tell you much more,*' he said. Then he began to speak, and he told me a longer, sadder story than I would ever have guessed. He told me a little about his circumstances, his estrangement from his father, and how he came to be the manager of the family estates. But then he talked of the people he'd lost, his brother, the women he'd loved and married, and the daughter who had gladdened his eyes.

Heinz spoke matter-of-factly about all this. He was the type who coped with the grief by distancing himself from it. He had a fire-under-ice quality that I've always admired. I knew, I could sense, that my friend was an intensely passionate man. But it was rarely, if ever, on open display. Willy, Lottie, Lena – he spoke of all of them with a detached sadness in a quiet, measured voice, with a calmness that only emphasized how much he ached with loss.

His composure only broke when he began to speak of his second wife, Rosamunde, Karl's 'Mummi'. She had come to attend his first wife, Charlotte, at childbirth, he said, and never left. He had fallen in love with her without warning. It turned out she had loved him from afar for a long time. So they married, and she gave up a sophisticated urban life to be with him and his children. She was a city girl, but her sheer goodness and decency had won over a village that had been prepared to despise her. (Only then did he mention, casually, that she was Jewish.) In his eyes, she was deserving of much, much more than he had been able to give in his years of service to the Bavarian crown. He had been on the verge of making everything right when the War came.

It was at that point that his reserve failed him. He was suddenly lost for words, choking with emotion. I waited. '*I never did make it right,*' he said at last. '*And Rosamunde left me a letter at the end. She never appreciated herself.*

97

Her last words to me were an apology. She died believing she had failed me.'
He stopped again. '*Damnation!*' he suddenly exclaimed and slammed his hand
full force down on the table, so hard that everyone in the room turned to look.
For a moment, the fire had melted the ice. I saw then the full dimensions of the
man he had been before the War savaged him. In that moment, he was a man at
infuriated war with all the powers in the universe. Abruptly, he stood up,
seething, so angry and frustrated he could not sit still, left the table, and strode
to the other side of the room and back again, while I waited. When he sat back
down, he was himself again.

'*My apologies, Ike,*' Heinz said. '*I should not burden you with my
failures.*'

'*I'm glad you did,*' I answered, and meant it. '*It's no burden.*'

'*I have a favor to ask of you, Ike,*' he continued. Then he told me what
his business in Paris was – the development of a major resort at Neustrelitz.
The idea had come to him from the cabin that he had furnished to accommodate
Rosamunde during her first days there. His original thought was to develop a
business that would permit him to remain with his wife and build a life with
her. But the War intervened.

'*I don't care for myself anymore,*' he said, '*but Karl is very young. The
practical point is that the resort I plan can be managed by others –
professional hoteliers. I don't know how long I have left to live – don't interrupt
me – so I go forward with the plan to secure his future.*'

'*But this is not sufficient,*' he continued. '*Karl will need friends —
guidance. When I am gone, there will be only his grandfather, who is old
himself, and not a wise man, and perhaps not even a good one. So, I ask you
this favor . . . take care of my son, Ike. Think of him. Do not forget him.*'

'*Karl's a wonderful boy,*' I answered, '*and it would be my pleasure to
serve as a sort of – sort of –*'

'*Godfather.*'

'*Yes. Godfather to him. But I will be going home in just a few weeks,
Heinz. Back to Kansas, or wherever the US Army sends me. I don't know what I
can do.*'

'*We will not lose touch,*' Heinz said emphatically, and I knew we
would not. '*What I ask is simply that you be mindful of him – aware of him.
That's all. So that, in the worst case, he is not completely alone.*'

'*Of course,*' I answered. I understood him and what he wanted, and I
made the promise willingly.

'*Thank you,*' he said sincerely, '*thank you. Now let me toast my newest and most unlikely friend, the American major from Kansas, with a glass of champagne, and then . . . farewell. I must apologize for my fatigue, but it is a fact with which I must cope. So . . .*'

We raised our glasses to each other, met each other's eye, and then . . . Heinrich von Haydenreich went through the door, back into the hotel lobby. He was the man who changed my life more than any other I ever met. But that was the last time in my life I ever saw him.

We never did lose touch, for the rest of his life. We exchanged letters every few months and particularly at Christmas. I took the duty he impressed on me about Karl as seriously as any promise I ever made in my life. When the time came, I did do what I could for him.

Which turned out to be not nearly enough.

Youngest Member

1922

-

September 1, 1922
Neustrelitz am Schliersee
Bavarian Alps

From the Journals of Karl von Haydenreich (published 1986):

My name is Karl von Haydenreich. I am twelve years old today. At my birthday party, I received this journal from Frau Schallert, our housekeeper. From this day forward I shall keep a journal. And to this journal I make the following vow:

I shall always be truthful, my journal, no matter how poor a figure I may cut. For there is nothing to be gained by lying to myself.

That done, what shall be the first entry? I suppose I should describe myself as I am.

Name: As I have written, I am Karl von Haydenreich.

Age: Today was my twelfth birthday.

Height and weight: I am 1.58 meters tall and weigh 56 kilos. I am the second shortest boy in school, which I don't like at all. Papa is sure I will grow to at least his height (1.84 meters). My Uncle Willy, who was killed in the War, was 1.9 meters. He towered over me like a giant when I was a little boy. I hope I grow as tall.

Friends: My best friend is Paul Kruger. We listen to jazz together.

Hobbies: I love music. I love all music, but I prefer American jazz most of all. Papa sometimes rolls his eyes when he overhears it, but I think secretly he rather likes it. I play two instruments, the flute and clarinet. Father Kugler teaches me music, and requires me join in his small orchestra, his chamber group, and the church choir. From him, I learn the music of Mozart, Haydn, and Beethoven. He also teaches me music theory. He tells me I am very gifted, but I still like American jazz best of all.

Most of all I want to play the saxophone. There is none in the village, so I thought it would have to wait. But today I received a large package from my grandfather, who lives in Munich and whom I have never met. It was a saxophone, of the most beautiful tone and finish! I tried it out and it sounded wonderful. But Papa said I could not play it during the party, nor begin tonight while others try to sleep. So I must wait until tomorrow. I am writing this journal instead.

Where I live: I live in Neustrelitz am Schliersee, with Papa, Frau Schallert, and other servants, in the family home of the Haydenreichs, which we have owned for 300 years. It is now a resort where people come for holiday in both summer and winter. Someday I will own it myself, for I am the only living heir of the family.

Papa and I are the only members of our family who live here. It is just us two. My mother, my stepmother Mummi, my sister Lena, and my Uncle Willy are all buried at the gravesite near our house. Papa visits the place nearly every day, but he has forbidden me to visit, except on church feasts. He says I must learn to look forward, not back. But I miss them all terribly, especially Mummi. Father Kugler says I will meet them all again in Heaven if I am virtuous and good. I will try to be that good. He says their leaving this world is all part of God's plan, which is not for man to know.

I try to believe that. Yet I wonder why it is that they were all called away, and Papa nearly, and I alone left to remember them all.

When I am grown, I will live somewhere else.

-

Excerpt from: A History of Germany in the Twentieth Century
Josef Behrens
Alfred A Knopf (1964)

. . .[T]he transformation of Munich, from the most open, cosmopolitan city in Europe before the War, to the focal point of ultranational politics it became in the '20s, was the result of a natural historical process. Munich before the War had attracted more than its fair share of political cranks and visionaries. When the socialist Kurt Eisner managed to seize power temporarily after the abdication of the Kaiser, these elements surged forth and created a government so revolutionary, bizarre, and at odds with the standards of traditional German society, that it terrified the ordinary citizens of the City. When the inevitable reaction arose, and destroyed Eisner and his colleagues, it

103

was welcomed with a profound relief and enthusiasm. The considerable, very troubling excesses of the Rightists were ignored or rationalized.

The result was that Munich became a feverish cesspool of the most reactionary political elements in German society . . .

-

Excerpt from: *A General Speaks - the Autobiography of Kurt von Hammerstein Equord*
Major General Kurt von Hammerstein Equord
Reichswehr Press (1986)

It has been widely surmised that I had a relationship with Karl Haydenreich and his father Heinrich before Karl became a cadet. But the one and only time I did meet Heinrich von Haydenreich was at a military conference in 1915, where he made the joke I recounted in an earlier chapter. I did not meet him after the War, nor did I visit the famous resort he founded until long after his death – 1938, in fact.

I did hear about him from time to time, in the way Army officers keep up with news of each other. I know for a fact that von Seekt invited him to join the rump Reichswehr permitted by the Versailles Treaty. Haydenreich had exactly the breadth of mind and scope von Seekt desired for the new Army. But Haydenreich's health forced him to decline, which was probably his natural inclination in any case. By that time, he was apparently fully occupied by his plans for the Neustrelitz resort.

I heard also that his refusal caused the further widening of the rift between father and son. It was common knowledge that the son was a far more capable man than the father. His disinterest in the military honors that the father desperately craved was a source of continual friction between them. The older Haydenreich also regarded the resort development (by which the family, in practical fact, secured its fortune) as a desecration of the family estates.

And, of course, their political views could not have been more at odds . . .

-

Excerpt from: *Destiny Betrayed - A Chronicle of Treason*
Harald Quandt
Franz Eher Nachfolger Gmbh (1952)

Karl von Haydenreich's treachery did not end with the German nation. His family were among the earliest and most enthusiastic supporters of the National Socialist Party. When he betrayed the Fuhrer, he betrayed not only the

Party, but the nation, his own family, and, most of all, himself and his sacred honor.

-

September 15, 1922
Munich, Bavaria

Oberst Heinrich-Werner Mertz von Haydenreich
Neustrelitz am Schliersee

Dear Heinrich,

I learned of Karl's interest in playing the saxophone from a Frau Johanna Breslau, the mother of your second wife. You permit your son to visit her, even though I never have his company. Karl told her of his interest in the instrument. Frau Breslau sent me a courteous note, suggesting that I might make a gift of a saxophone for Karl's twelfth birthday and thereby make an impression on the boy. I am grateful to her.

Frau Breslau also tells me Karl is curious about me. I wish to see him. I must ask you, then, Heinrich, how long you intend to keep me from my grandson's life – forever? I cannot believe I raised such a cruel and unnatural son. My grandson is the only family I have left – you would deny me this ordinary consolation of a man's last years? I know the boy is old enough to travel by train to Munich on holiday and the occasional feast – as he does to the apartments of Frau Breslau. This is all I ask, the same sort of visit he pays her.

I never meant to insult you or this Rosamunde. I know there are good Jews. There are many good Jews. Frau Breslau has sent me the most courteous and gentle letter. I am sure that her daughter was also a courteous and honorable woman, and a worthy wife to you. Willy tried from time to time to make me see her so. I should have listened to him. I am so sorry that I did not. With a German succession now assured, there is no reason for me to act on a principle.

I long to see my grandson, Heinrich.

I will await your reply. But I implore you to do this. My apartments are large enough to keep my grandson comfortably even overnight. Do not deprive my grandson of acquaintance with me, and – through me – his other ancestors. Do not condemn me to exile and loneliness. Do not be heartless. Be a son to me.

Your father,
Oberstleutnant Wilhelm-Werner Mertz von Haydenreich

-

September 20, 1922
Neustrelitz am Schliersee
Bavarian Alps

Oberstleutnant Wilhelm-Werner Mertz von Haydenreich
Munich, Bavaria

Dear Father,

Thank you for clarifying the mystery of how you came to give Karl a saxophone. He has attacked it with enthusiasm and already produces a quality tone. There is no question that he has a talent.

Let me address your proposal for visits with Karl. I think you are in the right on this. Karl spends too much time as it is in this house of ghosts, with his ailing, dying father. This is why he visits his Grandma (this is what he calls Johanna Breslau) from time to time. He should visit his grandfather, too. Also, you are correct that you are his most direct connection to the Haydenreich family line. God knows I have my disagreements with our traditions. But he should know his own family. He should understand where he came from and whence he might go.

But my consent to these visits is based on your acceptance of two conditions.

First, you are not to arrange for any lessons in love for Karl of the type you provided for Willy when he was roughly the same age. I suspect Willy's distaste for the female sex likely began in his mother's womb. Even so, those dismal encounters with whoever your mistress was at the time (I forget the name) did nothing except confirm him in his disinclination. For the rest of his life, he could not speak of them without shuddering. So, please, allow Karl to discover the joys of manhood in his own way and in his own time.

The second is this matter of 'good Jews', as you said in your letter. When you write in this way of Rosamunde and Johanna, it is fully evident to me that you view them as exceptions to the general villainy you attribute to Jewish people. Knowing you as I do, I imagine you are also a confirmed believer in 'the Stab in the Back' by Jews, Bolsheviks, and others, as an explanation of the defeat of the Army. As you might guess, I do not share these views. I do not seek to alter your opinions on these subjects. They don't matter to me. But Karl does matter. I do not want him to be subjected to these views of yours, which his mother, his stepmother, and I myself reject in their entirety. There will be time enough for him to come to his own opinions later in his life. There is no need to introduce him to your ideas at this time.

If you will give me your word on these two matters, then we can proceed to specific arrangements. I will obtain the holiday and feast schedule, and send it to you in the next post. Do not expect that he will spend all these days with you, as he enjoys visiting Frau Breslau as well.

I notice you make no request for a meeting with me, or a visit to Neustrelitz. I am of the same mind. We do better apart. There is no need to write more. As for the rest, your stipend will be continued on the same terms and amounts. However, with the decline in value of the mark, I have arranged with the bank that it be paid in Swiss francs. You should find that more convenient.

Your son,
Heinrich

1923

-

Excerpt from: A History of Germany in the Twentieth Century
Josef Behrens
Alfred A Knopf (1964)

Adolf Hitler did not come at once to ascendancy in the Nazi Party. It was his success as a 'drawing card', in speeches made in the beer halls and gathering places of Munich, beginning in 1921, that brought him to prominence. He had what might be called these days 'star power'. Muncheners came to hear him for the entertainment value, as well as the political rallying point. His ability to draw crowds gave the Nazi Party, no different in philosophy or program than countless other ultra-nationalist parties, an advantage over all of them.

-

-

May 3, 1923
Neustrelitz am Schliersee
Bavarian Alps

From the Journals of Karl von Haydenreich (published 1986):

I am just returned from a visit to my grandfather in Munich, and the two most exciting days of my life. I have seen the new Germany and I have discovered a man of destiny. I sing the glorious name of ADOLF HITLER!!! The True Wild Wolf in the Woods!!!!!

I will record everything while it is still green in memory, while my soul still glows white hot, while my heart still bursts with exaltation! I took the train to Munich on April 30 as planned. Grandma met me and I spent the night in her house. The next day we had lunch and saw a film with the American comedian Chaplin, *The Kid*. It was very amusing. Then she walked with me over to Grandfather's apartment on Falkenberg Strasse, and I bade her farewell.

There was unusual commotion on the Stachus and Marienplatz. Knots of men in groups of two or three, a few larger, were everywhere to be seen, discussing something of importance. There were Brown Shirts and the swastika everywhere, more than I had ever seen. I heard fierce arguments and shouting all over. I wondered what had occurred. But Grandfather told me what had happened.

May 1 is the day on which the Bolsheviks and Jews celebrate the Devil's work they have done in Russia and hope to do in Germany. But Hitler and the NSDAP hoped to interrupt these brazen ceremonies that make a mockery of all the good people in the nation. He had his Brown Shirts armed and organized to disrupt this disgusting affair. But the pig, von Lossow, the head of the Reichswehr, had ordered the Brown Shirts to stand down – but he let the Communists and Socialists have their demonstration! Hitler was furious, but he obeyed the order. Grandfather said there would be a day when he would give the orders, but that was not this day. I asked if von Lossow was a Jew, but Grandfather said no, simply a traitorous German, of whom there are many. (Someday he will pay for his crimes!)

But the men who wear Brown Shirts are real men, not cowardly Jews. They put on their shirts! They went to the street! There were fights and brawls as they gave the Bolsheviks and Socialists what they deserve! That is what I had seen on the Stachus and elsewhere. That's what I call men!

Grandfather had told me a great deal about the Stab in the Back and the treachery of the Bolshevik Jews who betrayed my uncle, my father, and so many other noble Germans. He is certain that Hitler is the man who will one day put all this right. Then Grandfather asked me all at once if I wished to hear Hitler speak that very evening. Of course I did! There had been so much talk of him, from Grandfather and others, of the clear vision with which he sees Germany's enemies and the vigor with which he denounces them! I had longed to see and hear this man for myself, but it had not been possible on the other visits. But this time I was finally to see and hear Hitler speak, which excited me very much.

Then we went back to Grandfather's apartments, with Frau Brehmer, and I read more of the *Protocols of the Elders of Zion*. I could scarcely believe any race of men capable of such cunning and deceit, but Grandfather says that it is all true and Jews are not like other men. He says Mummi and Grandma are good people who do not know what villainy goes on, and are probably deceived themselves by the Elders.

Once more, he made me swear on my honor not to tell Papa. Does he think I am a baby? I am a man of honor, I need only swear once. It is true I don't like keeping this secret, but Grandfather says it is necessary. One day it will be all right, when Papa sees the truth!

Then, in the evening, we went to hear the speech. It was in the Circus Krone, where Grandma has taken me to see the circus. I was surprised an important political meeting would take place there. But Grandfather said the Party rented it because it was the largest hall in Munich and a great many people wanted to hear Hitler.

They were right to get a large hall, because it was filled to overflowing. People were milling about, drinking beer, the sound rising like the rush of a small stream after a storm. I felt my pulse pound, my breath grow short. Some of the men still had their weapons from the morning, in case of disruption. Grandfather introduced me to some of his friends, and his old military comrades. He was proud of me, I could tell, and I was proud to be with him. They made kind jokes about my youth. Then one suggested I enroll in the Party lists. Grandfather and I thought that was a capital idea, and so it was done.

So now I am a member of the National Socialist Party! I think I am the youngest member!

Then, all at once, there was Hitler! He was not there, and then he was, like a mighty wizard! I heard someone say 'Hitler', then another, then a chorus – then everyone had spied him, the whole assembly rose as one, and there was a gigantic roar, a deafening thunder! It went on and on, with shouts and whistles, foot stamping, and wild, wild applause. An electric current buzzed through the hall – we were seeing the hope and future of Germany, in the form of a lone, solitary man!

Then he began to speak, softly at first, so that the deafening roar in a nonce became the deepest of hushes. Everyone strained to hear. But soon enough his voice rose – then rose again. Words poured out, in a torrent of force and crystal logic that swept us all along – I was just one more small chip on the stream! He spoke of the events of the day – he said that May Day had always symbolized in nature a renewal of body and spirit, that this meaning also applied to nations – but that this nation was too feeble and decayed for renewal. The German people had become senile with internationalism, thanks to the Jews. He wondered if there was any creative vigor left in Germany. I felt his despair as he spoke, I suffered with him, I felt my German soul lacerated and torn.

But then, with fire in his voice, with his eyes blazing, he promised renewal – renewal that will be born of the devotion of our party, of us National Socialists, of love, faith, and hope – how we love our country with fanatical love, we have faith in our rights as a nation, and from this we derive hope of a rebirth of our beloved Germany. We will be equally fanatical in our hatred of

110

its enemies and never give up our dream of a Reich in which there is no Soviet state, no Jewish star of David, but only the Swastika, the one true symbol of German labor. Then we will have a true rebirth and be worthy of a May celebration. Everyone stood and cheered again and again – for the truth of this was self-evident, we all felt its truth to the marrow of our bones!

He spoke then of inflation. I don't understand it, but I know what it is. It costs more marks to buy a chocolate bar than there are marks in the whole universe. It frightens me. It frightens everyone. What will become of us all? My own family is safe, for Grandfather had the foresight to invest a large part of our wealth in Swiss marks and other foreign currencies. But what of my friends?? What about Mummi's family and Grandma?

Hitler said it was the Socialist government who were the thieves, for continuing to print these worthless scraps of paper that make everything else worthless and ruin us all. These were the loudest cheers yet – for here is a man who is not afraid to tell the truth – who denounces the Jew Socialists and November traitors outright – who will not be silenced! I knew then I was listening to a man of destiny, the man brought forth to lead our Germany back to the heights on which it stood in the old days!

I felt a fever had broken out in me. I could not sleep. I tossed and turned in my bed, remembering the roar, throwing the pillow up and down, trying to commit to memory all Hitler had said. The next day, I came home. I left my armband with Grandfather. He will obtain a brown shirt for me, too, which he will also keep at his apartment, since Papa must not know. My conscience bothers me, keeping these secrets from him, but someday he will see things as they are, and I will tell him the truth.

All hail Adolf Hitler!! All hail the future!

-

Excerpt from: A History of Germany in the Twentieth Century
Josef Behrens
Alfred A Knopf (1964)

The National Socialists had obtained enough mass and momentum by the end of 1923 to attempt the seizure of power by force – a revolution. The fiasco known to history as the Beer Hall Putsch, led by Hitler, occurred on November 9 and 10, 1923 . . .

-

From the Journals of Karl von Haydenreich (published 1986):

With all my strength, I recall my promise to myself to tell the truth always – and so I will do. But it will not be an easy task to recount the two most shameful, horrible days of my life, or describe the wretched, silly fool I have made of myself. But I will do my best. Like my father, I will always keep my promises.

On November 8, in the morning, I took the train to Munich for a planned visit with my Grandma and Grandfather. Grandma's servant met me at the station and took me to her apartments. Grandma and I had a nice visit, then she took me to lunch at the Hofbrauhaus. Then we shopped at Herties' for jazz records. I found three new records by the American negress Bessie Smith, which pleased me very much. Grandma Johanna then bade me farewell, and I made my way to Grandfather's apartments. It was perhaps 5:00 in the evening.

He was extremely excited. Then I became excited too, because I could tell that something was up. After a while, he took me aside. He could not speak in front of Frau Brehmer, who disapproves – she thinks he is too old for these things.

'*Tonight is the night,*' he whispered to me. '*Tonight witnesses the birth of the renewed Germany.*' Then I felt myself quiver and nearly explode, for I knew what he meant. Hitler and our Nazis intended to seize power that very evening! He told me everything. The government officials had called a meeting at the Burgerbraukeller. There the arch-traitor, Commissioner General Gustav Kahr, would announce his plans for the government. All of the officials of the Bavarian State would be there, before a big, public crowd. But what these traitors did not know was that Adolf Hitler had decided to use the opportunity to seize the power of the State and begin the redemption of Germany. All over the city, the Brown Shirts were leaving their jobs, putting on their uniforms, and preparing to storm the meeting.

I wanted so much to witness this and be a part of it. But Grandfather said it would go on too late for a boy my age and might be dangerous, so he would not take me. I was crushed, but he promised me there would be much to see in the morning, and he would take me then. We dined about 7:00. Then he put on his own Brown Shirt and went to the Burgerbraukeller. He left me in the company of Frau Brehmer.

I could not keep still. I paced and went to the window, so as to hear the sound of shots or the commotion of a crowd. But the night was cold and still. Frau Brehmer insisted we play cards. We sat on the sofa and played bezique. All at once she said she was hot, and went to her room. When she came back, she was in her chemise. When she sat down on the sofa, I could smell her perfume. When she leaned down to gather her cards, I could see her breasts. This made me feel very strange. I did not know what to think or do. I forgot all about Hitler and the new Germany. I tried to avert my gaze, but I could not take my eyes away from her breasts, large and round. Finally, I apologized for myself, for I knew she knew where my eyes went. But she laughed and said she did not mind being admired by such a handsome young man. This confused me more. Then she said it was enough for this night to look. She put away the cards, and went to bed. I could not sleep. My mind was besieged with thoughts, men in their Brown Shirts, snatches of speeches, all this mixed up and confused with Frau Brehmer and her negligee. I wanted Grandfather to come home and settle my mind. But finally, the hour grew late, and he had not returned. Despite myself, I fell asleep on the couch.

Grandfather shook me awake the next morning. Only then did I find out what had happened the night before. The hall filled completely with burghers and others, and NSDAP men, who were dressed like the others and gave no sign of what was to come. Hitler was not there. Kahr was in the midst of a long, boring speech, when Hitler did arrive, in a red Mercedes. The Brown Shirts arrived at the same time in trucks and prepared for the revolution. When they were ready, Hitler stormed into the hall, with the others following. At first, nothing happened, but then he climbed on a chair and fired a shot through the ceiling. He shouted aloud that the hall was surrounded and that the revolution had begun. Then he and his men pushed their way through the hall, to the podium, and took Kahr, the chief of police, and the head of the Reichswehr, prisoner. He herded all three of them into a back room to discuss how things would be reorganized in the future. Meanwhile, Hermann Goering set up a machine gun, so everyone knew they meant business. What a sight it must have been!

But Kahr and the others would not concede. Hitler brought them back to the podium and made a speech to the crowd, a wonderful speech, demanding that they give way. The crowd caught his spirit, and the clamor and shouting became an uproar. But still they would not acquiesce. General Ludendorff himself was sent for, and he himself came to the hall. Then they could see for themselves what they were up against, and agreed to Hitler's terms. The hall exploded in a riot of cheering, for the revolution, the renewal, was at hand. Or so they thought.

Hitler left then, to oversee the revolution elsewhere. General Ludendorff was supposed to keep the officials in custody, but he grew bored and accepted their word of honor that they would abide by their agreement. I was surprised and alarmed to hear that the General was so trusting, but Grandfather said they were German officers and their honor was sacred. Then everyone went home. It was about midnight, and I was asleep. So Grandfather had waited until morning to tell me all this.

'*Come,*' he said then, '*this will be a day you will remember all your life!*' We had sausages for breakfast, I got on my brown shirt, armband, and coat, and then we set out on foot for the Burgerbraukeller. It was about 1.5 kilometers away, on the other side of the river. Most of the S.A. was there, but some had spread out over the city, jubilant with success. We started out. I was more excited than I have ever been, more than Christmas or my birthday. The day was cold and cloudy, but I had to stop myself from running and singing.

But then we came to the corner of Neuhauser and Frausen Strassen. I saw that the windows of Rosenbaum's Bakery had been broken, and all the bread and schnitzel were gone – stolen. Brown Shirts were loitering about, eating the bread, and smiling and happy, as if they were not thieves, but had done a great and wonderful deed. But I know Herr Rosenbaum. He is not a banker, but a nice man who had always been kind to me

'*Grandfather,*' I said, '*I don't understand. Herr Rosenbaum is a good man. Why is this?*'

'*Even good Jews need a lesson now and then,*' he answered. These words shocked me, as if I had been struck. I felt sick to my stomach, I wanted to vomit. All my excitement vanished. I wanted to go home, or back to Grandma. But we were walking briskly and there was no opportunity to say this.

We reached the Burgerbraukeller at about ten o'clock. There was a huge number of Brown Shirts milling about. They had been there all night, most of them drinking and eating. But some had done brutal things, like breaking the glass at the bakery. They frightened me as they had not previously. All of them were very happy with Hitler's success the night before, but now they did not know what came next or what to do. They milled about aimlessly, like sheep. I did not say it aloud, but I was reminded of school, when we are in

114

the schoolyard for games, and the schoolmaster has not come and we don't know what to do. Grandfather pointed out Ludendorff to me, who stood as tall and erect as a steeple. But he seemed as confused as everyone else. Hitler was nowhere to be seen.

Then we heard rumors that the revolution had failed after all. Honor or not, Kahr and the others had broken their promise to Ludendorff the moment they were free of custody. Now the army and police were opposed to Hitler and us. Grandfather said this could not be true, and went off to find out what was happening. I was to wait for him. A fat, bald man named Streicher was giving a speech, but he was not nearly as good as Hitler and no one was listening. A brass band played the same march, over and over. They were awful. It was cold and a little snow fell, and I was bored.

Grandfather was gone for a long while. The men around me didn't seem nearly as nice and jaunty as they had when I first came to the Beer Hall. They made crude jokes. Some seemed to be jeering at my brown shirt and youth. Others looked at me in a way that made me nervous. Finally, one came over, a handsome fellow, and apologized for the others. He complimented me on my uniform. I was about to thank him, when Grandfather returned. He asked the man if he was a friend of Rohm. The man said he was, and Grandfather told him to go away and not to bother me again. I did not understand any of this, which made me feel worse. I didn't see any history being made. I wanted even more to go home.

At last Hitler appeared. He seemed pale and tired. I heard someone say he had not slept at all. He was dressed in a very odd way, wearing a trench coat over a cutaway suit coat, like the suit Clemenceau wears in photographs. Grandfather said he had dressed so, in the event he became head of government that very night. Even so, he seemed ridiculous to me, like Chaplin or a circus clown. This day he was not anything like the man who gave the speeches.

He went over to confer with Ludendorff. Grandfather stepped away to hear what they were saying. When he came back, he was very excited. It was true that the police and army were now ordered to oppose us. But Ludendorff had decided to march all the way to Berlin, and Hitler had agreed. The march would be a call to arms for all good Germans. They would join us in revolution and renewal, our numbers swelling as the streams joined the river, and the new Germany would be born! Grandfather and I would not march the entire distance, of course, but we would march with them through Munich and a little way beyond, to witness this wonder begin.

115

That was what had been decided. I was excited again. I thought that I was really going to see something! But then there was more aimless milling about, and crude jokes, and boredom. By the time everything was organized, it was about noon. The day was not a good one, very cold and even with snow flurries. I wondered whether anything was ever going to happen.

But finally, the procession did begin. As we marched away from the Burgerbraukeller, my spirits began to rise. It was as Hitler had predicted, people began to open their windows and cheer. Customers came out of the shops and waved and saluted. A girl, my age and very pretty, standing by her father, even waved at me. But I was too shy to wave back.

Hitler and Ludendorff led the way, but Grandfather and I were very close to the front, only five rows behind. Right in the center were the flag bearers, carrying the German Imperial Flag, the Swastika, and the flag of the Bund Oberland. They were strong men, they held the staffs up high, and the flags flew bravely. We were among the Sixth S.A. Company, the most ferocious of all the fighters.

We set forth down the way Grandfather and I had come, up Frauen Street, towards Neuhasser and Marienplatz. The band had gone home, which I did not miss, because they were terrible. We made our own music, singing out as we stepped. Grandfather's tenor could be heard above the rest, pure, clear, and strong. Many heads turned to admire him. I felt proud to be beside him. People began to come out of their houses and shops. Many fell in beside us. It was as though the whole city was waking to the new revolution, becoming alive again in a new day. I thought all the boredom might be worth it.

But then we approached the river and Ludwig's Bridge. There we saw a line of policemen astraddle the bridge, blocking our way. This frightened me enormously – they had real guns, and they were pointed at us, real guns! But Grandfather was so calm he made me calm (or less nervous, anyway). He said it was all a bluff, for show – they were mostly old soldiers, and would never shoot at their former comrades. I hoped he was right, for Hitler and Ludendorff continued to march. I wondered what I would do if they did fire.

We were almost upon them, when some of the bigger men charged forward straight into the line of policemen! I was sure they would shoot, but Grandfather was right. They did not shoot, but gave way at once, letting us pass. We went through the line and crossed the bridge, I saw some of them laughing. One waved his hat in salute. I thought they would join us if they could.

116

I felt my breath returning and realized I had been holding it for a long time. I was more scared than I knew. But I thought nothing could stop us now. As we crossed the bridge onto the road, we joined arms like comrades and sang all the louder. Now, more and more of the city folk joined the column, despite the cold and the snow. Hitler and Ludendorff marched proudly, in even steps, at the head of our column. On either side of the street, men from the Ministry were putting up posters proclaiming that the Revolution was treason. But as quickly as they did, our men left the ranks and tore them down. There were scuffles and fights. But it seemed more funny than real. Now I was very glad I had come, for I was certain this was a Great Event – it was all really happening! And I was there – I thought how my schoolmates would envy me the tale!

That's what I thought right then.

We marched up the Tal. There was another cordon of police, but they scattered as the first had. But then we reached the Marienplatz. A huge swastika flag had been hung from one of the balconies. There were street clowns and food vendors, and a mass of people. Our column lost its shape, with marchers spilling out to buy food and celebrate. Others were singing patriotic songs as loudly as they could. The streetcar could barely move for the mass of people. It was like a carnival or street festival. For a moment, I thought the march had ended, at least for now, and the celebration had begun.

But then we began to march again. We left the Marienplatz and made our way into the Odeonsplatz. The plan was to march up Theatiner Strasse, but now there were more police. They blocked the way. They seemed much more determined than the first ones.

I thought I had been frightened the first time, but now I was truly frightened. This was not the same mood. These policemen seemed grim and determined. The others in our column felt this change in intent, for everyone became silent. Grandfather tried to reassure me, but I could tell he was uncertain himself. But then a few pushed toward the police as before, but this time, this time – they did not yield. But they did not fire their guns either. They pushed back, with batons and yells, and serious fights, men with broken bones and blood streaming everywhere. Grandfather said it would be all right and I tried to believe him. But the men shoved and cursed ever more fiercely, there was more blood, and we were pushed slowly back.

Then it happened. One of our men pushed hard at a policeman, and got a huge whack across his face from a police stick. He was only a few feet away

117

from me. Then, before anyone could stop him, he pulled out a pistol and fired at a police sergeant. I cried out to stop, but it was no good. The shot rang out.

Then . . . then . . . everyone began shooting. It must be what war is like. I stood petrified, too frightened to move. *'Get down!'* Grandfather shouted, and pulled me down. Bullets whizzed around everywhere. I saw men fall and blood spurt out of their wounds. Some lay still as statues, and I knew I saw dead men, for the first time in my life. It was a horrible, horrible sight. Right next to me was a man shot in the chest. The spreading blood stained his tunic, and I could see air bubbles popping over the wound. I wish, how I wish I could forget all that. But I can't.

Finally, the shooting ended. I tried to rise, I don't know why, mostly to run, or help, or do something. But as I rose, someone running by me knocked me down, right on top of the wounded man, who shouted out in agony. I looked behind me and saw that the man who had knocked me down was . . . Adolf Hitler himself, running right by all the dead and wounded men . . . running to a car . . . running away! The door opened and he put his hand on the top to enter. As he did, my eyes met his, for a long, long moment. I could see fear in them, shame in them. For that moment, in that instant, he might even have thought of changing his mind and staying with his fallen comrades. But then he entered the car. The door closed and the car sped away. Hitler, the coward, had abandoned us.

Then I tried to rise again. When I put my hand down to push, the man underneath shrieked with pain. I wanted to help him, I felt I had to help him, but I had no idea what to do. There were screams and shouts everywhere, and men running in all directions. Suddenly I felt Grandfather's hand on my arm. *'Run, Karl,'* he said. *'We must leave here!'*

We ran, back down the street toward the Odeonsplatz. Grandfather led, moving more quickly than I had ever seen him. We were running, I thought, running from the police, like ordinary criminals! We would be arrested if they caught us, and taken to jail! I knew this was true, but could not believe it. Everything had changed so quickly! I felt wetness on my tunic, in my hair, and realized I was covered in the blood of the wounded man. Then I could smell the blood and feel its stickiness – it made me sick to my stomach. I felt hot and dizzy. I felt as if I might vomit or faint. All around the buildings began to shimmy and blur. I tried to catch my breath, I gulped for air as we ran, but I could not do it. All the oxygen in the world seemed to have vanished.

118

We rounded a corner and ran straight into someone, almost knocking them over. Idiotically, I thought it might be Hitler, returning to us. But it was not. It was my grandmother, going in the other direction. '*Excuse me, sirs,*' she began – but then she looked more closely.

'*Karl?*' she gasped, '*Karl? Is that you?*' She looked at me more closely. '*What is this? You have – is this blood? Are you hurt? What is this!?!*'

'*Karl is fine,*' my grandfather said. '*Please, madam, we must be going. Good day to you.*'

She did not appear to hear him. '*And this grime on your shirt? Is that gunpowder? What is this uniform?*' Then she spied my armband and her hand went to her mouth. '*Oh, my God!! This is blood!*'

'*Madam –*' my grandfather began again.

'*Herr Oberstleutnant,*' Grandma said, '*did you take Karl down to that march? Where there were guns? And all that shooting?! Is that where you have been!?*'

'*There was not supposed to be shooting,*' Grandfather replied. '*It was supposed –*'

'*You did! You did do that! A twelve-year-old boy! Among all those vile men!*'

'*It is not your affair, madam,*' Grandfather answered. '*It is none of your business.*'

'*It most certainly is my business, where Rosamunde's son –*' She paused, then straightened herself. Grandma is a small woman, but she seemed very tall at that moment. '*Come, Karl, you are coming home with me.*'

'*Karl is my grandson,*' Grandfather began.

'*He is my grandson too, Herr Oberstleutnant*' Grandma interrupted, '*he was my daughter's whole world. And I am going to take him home and away from this.*'

'*You can't do this!*' Grandfather shouted, glaring at her. '*He is in my custody, my care!*'

'*Your CARE!?*' She almost spat the words, glaring right back at him. '*Well, no longer. You have done quite enough for one day. Does his father know of this care? He can't – No. I am certain his father hasn't an inkling of this. Karl is coming with me, and away from all this. Come, Karl,*' she said, turning to me.

'*Madam –*' my grandfather hissed. He was purple with rage. He took a step toward her.

'*You would strike me, Herr Oberstleutnant? Here? In the street? So strike me if you dare. Karl is still coming with me!*'

I had never seen Grandfather in such a state. I could not believe my eyes. I was afraid he actually would hit her. '*Grandfather,*' I said, '*please.*'

He seemed to remember himself then. He stepped back, still furious. But he did nothing.

'*So,*' he said at last, '*in the end, a Jew. Always a Jew.*' Then he turned to me. '*Good day, my grandson.*' Then he left, walking quickly away and not looking back. Grandma took a moment to recover herself.

'*This way, Karl,*' she said in a different tone. '*You are covered in filth. You need a bath.*'

We started up the street, more slowly now. But now I felt so dizzy I might faint. The street was as unsteady under my feet as a rowboat on the lake. The blood on my hair and shirt had become dry and sticky, and the smell! The smell!! I thought I might vomit.

'*Grandma,*' I said, '*I feel sick.*'

'*You will feel much better after a bath. Come, Karl. It is not far. You know the way.*'

I had not even recognized the street. It wasn't far. When we reached her home, she showed me in and directed her maid to run a bath. She asked me if I wanted something to eat, but I was not at all hungry. Then she regarded me for a moment and an expression I had never seen came over her.

'*This tunic! This armband! And you among such terrible, awful men! I am glad today your Mummi is with God. For to see you, who was her whole life, in this company would surely have broken her heart.*' I felt tears flood my eyes. She saw this.

'*Karl, I did not mean –*' All at once, her face became twisted. She tried to catch herself, but she began to cry. I had never seen Grandma cry. I could not imagine she could cry. Of all the awful things I saw that day, that was the worst.

I had promised my journal I would be faithful to the truth. This is a promise I must keep, even now. For I too began to weep, as openly as a girl, even more openly than my grandma.

'*I am so sorry, Grandma,*' I choked out. '*I never meant – I did not know – Mummi – I would never –*' I was crying like an infant, too hard to finish a sentence. Once again, I was all atremble. She saw my state. Her own tears ceased. She took me in her arms.

120

'*Now, now, my boy, my wonderful Karl. You are a boy, just a boy. This is hardly your fault. I should not be such an old fool in front of you.*' She cradled me and kissed me, and I took hold of myself.

'*Grandma,*' I said, '*now there is blood on your dress.*'

'*It will wash out,*' she answered, '*as it will wash off you. I think your bath is ready.*'

The bath was quite hot and felt wonderful. I soaked in it a long, long time. I washed my hair again and again, but could not rid myself of the blood smell. Finally, I had done my best and emerged. My nightshirt had been laid out.

'*Grandma,*' I said, '*it is only four in the afternoon.*'

'*But already dark,*' she answered, '*and you need a nap. You have had much, too much, excitement for one day. It would not surprise me if you slept through the night.*'

She was correct. I fell asleep the moment my head touched the pillow. I must have slept for hours. But then came dreams, nightmares in fact. I dreamt of the wounded man rising and pursuing, but somehow he had become Hitler, now with demon eyes. He was about to lay hands on me when I awoke. I was scared, but I felt a familiar presence in the dark room, and my fear left.

'*Mummi?*' I said in my sleep.

'*No,*' came the answer, '*though I am sure she is with you now and always. Just your grandma. Go back to sleep, my darling boy. It is only eleven o'clock. I wired your father this afternoon. He will be here in the morning.*' She gave my forehead the lightest touch with her fingertips, and I fell back asleep almost at once.

I did not wake until it was light. Everything that had happened the day before seemed a bad dream. I lay in bed for a long, long time, waiting for the house to stir. Finally, there was a light rapping on the door. '*Your father is here,*' my Grandma said. He had left the moment he received her wire, arrived late, and spent the night in a hotel.

I dressed and came down to breakfast, which was in the kitchen. Papa had a bowl of porridge before him. He likes a light breakfast. I filled my own bowl and Grandma sat down beside us. I could not meet either of their eyes. No one said anything. Finally, my father looked at me and spoke.

'*I am not at all angry with you, Karl,*' he said. '*But we will speak of this later.*'

'*Yes, Papa.*' I said, with my eyes down. His speech did not make me feel less anxious or guilty. Just then a knock sounded at the front door. My grandmother's maidservant announced that my grandfather had come.

'*I must have a word with him,*' said Papa, '*which might lead to an unpleasant scene. Johanna, can you find something to occupy Karl?*'

'*He bought some jazz records two days ago,*' Grandma said. '*We can listen to the Edison.*'

We went to the parlor and put on the records. I paid little attention to Bessie Smith. I could hear voices from the other room, my grandfather loud and angry, my father's voice calm and steady. After a quarter-hour, I was called into the parlor room. I could see my grandfather remained angry.

'*Come, Karl,*' my father said. '*We will be going home. I am afraid this experiment is over.*'

'*You are his father and you will decide,*' my grandfather said stiffly. '*I only meant the boy to see history as it happens – and understand the condition of his nation!*'

'*In beer halls, where speakers bring pistols? And in marches that end in gunfire?*'

'*I did not take him to the beer hall,*' my grandfather said.

'*But then –*' Papa turned to me, '*how did you spend the evening before?*'

'*I was with Frau Brehmer,*' I answered. '*We played cards.*'

Papa turned again and eyed Grandfather for a long while. '*Even in the other thing?*' he said softly at last. '*Does your word mean anything?*'

'*If his father will not teach him the ways of men, then his grandfather must,*' my grandfather answered. But it seemed to me he could not meet my father's eye.

'*There is truly nothing more to say,*' Papa said. '*Karl, say your farewells to Grandfather. It will be a while before you see him again.*' I stood and Grandfather embraced me. I could feel his arms trembling, but he did not give way to his feelings. '*I did my best,*' he whispered in my ear. '*Remember.*'

Then he left, without a word to Grandma or Papa. We gathered up my things and said farewell. But we did not take my brown shirt and armband. Grandma asked what she should do with them, and Papa told her she could burn them, that I would not be wearing them again. She smiled a big smile at this.

Then we went to the train. Papa said very little as we walked. As we passed Rosenbaum's Bakery, he asked if I wanted some strudel. I could hardly decline, but it was the last place I wanted to go. Herr Rosenbaum was already busy making repairs. He greeted me kindly, as he always has. I felt another rush of unmanly feelings then, and again tears came like a child, trickling down my face. Herr Rosenbaum pretended not to notice. Papa paid for the strudel and we left.

He did not speak for a long time, not until we were on the train. Then he sat back in his seat, with his coat over him, but with the sleeves empty, the way he likes to wear it. '*I think you had better tell me what has been going on, Karl, these last few months,*' he said.

I told him everything. I did not think I could have lied to him, and I did not want to. For a long time, he sat silent, as the train rolled along. I wondered how angry he would be. But when at last he spoke, he wasn't angry at all.

'*Your grandfather is not a bad man, Karl,*' Papa said. '*But he is an old man, narrow, old-fashioned, and, frankly, ignorant of much that goes on in the world. Have you ever wondered how such an unnatural arrangement could come to be, that the son lives on the estate and provides his father with a stipend?*' I straightened up. I had not expected this subject from him (which I had never considered) nor that he would speak to me in this manner. I did not feel so much a child as I had. '*It has to do with his inability to deal with any sort of worldly complexity. Years ago, our family nearly failed and our creditors insisted that I become manager. We only survived because of the generosity of Mummi's father. A Jew. But this fact makes no difference to him. He does not benefit from life experience. He remains a naif.*'

A thought struck me. '*Was it then you met Mummi?*'

'*Yes,*' he said, and his face changed – I could see him return to thoughts of long ago. '*It was then. I met both your mother and Mummi then. Mummi's father introduced me. I think he meant me as a choice for Mummi, but her best friend, your mother Charlotte, was there, and I was so smitten I paid no attention to her.*' He smiled to himself. '*Two beauties, one blonde, one dark. I was a fortunate young man.*'

For the first time in my life, my father addressed me as a man. I wondered if I had grown up the day before. Does facing bullets do that, I wondered? He was silent for a long moment, then took a deep breath.

'*There is no Jewish conspiracy, Karl. This book your grandfather had you read, The Protocols of the Elders of Zion, is complete fiction, based on a novel. About 20 years ago, the Russian Czar's secret police used the novel to create the Protocols, to embarrass his political opponents. But it is all a fantasy.*'

'*But why —*' I began.

'*Because people believe what they wish to believe, my son. Anyone can find this out for himself, but people who want to believe don't bother. When the book became popular in some circles, I made my own investigations. I even obtained a copy of the novel, for my own amusement. I had no idea your grandfather was aware of it, though it is the sort of thing he fancies. But now I am afraid I must insist you read this book, which is hard luck for you, as it is a very bad novel.*' Papa smiled at his joke, and I smiled, too, relieved that he was not angry and that he treated me so much like a grown-up. Another question arose in my mind.

'*Did my mother hate the Jews?*' I asked.

'*Charlotte?*' His surprise was evident. '*No, God no. She had no patience with anti-Semites. She admired the Breslau family without reservation, and Rosamunde was her best friend on earth. She was already long out of patience with your grandfather and uncle, before God called her, though the occasion had never arisen to express her attitudes.*' Suddenly he smiled to himself. '*My goodness, what a row she would have made had she seen that spectacle yesterday! She would have slapped your grandfather in the face.*'

'*And Mummi?*'

'*Would have acted much in the manner of your grandmother, spirited you away, and then put herself through agonies of doubt that she was somehow responsible. Both your mother and Mummi were strong women, but in different ways. Mummi was not nearly so bold.*' He smiled again. '*I see both of them in you. Two angels always with you, a blonde one and a dark one.*' I remembered that Grandma had said something similar. '*So perhaps you, too, are a lucky young man.*'

He became quiet again, fatigued, from his lungs. I felt much, much better. The train rolled on for a time, while I thought of what he said, and all that had passed. Somehow the confusion had lifted. But there was much I did not understand.

'*Hitler seemed so right, so certain,*' I said.

'*Hitler,*' he said softly. '*Did Grandfather ever tell you that he served in my regiment? No? Well, he did. In fact, I rescued him from the gas attack at the end of the War. He earned his medals fairly enough, but he did not serve in the trenches. He was a dispatch runner at headquarters. And he was no more a man of iron than anyone else. He was not blinded by the gas, as I have heard he claims. It was a disease of the mind, a nervous disorder – a breakdown. The other wounded men found his hysteria somewhat amusing. They laughed at him behind his back. I can believe he played the coward yesterday. He does not have strong nerves.*'

I thought of the fear I had seen in his eyes when he fled in the car. '*What was he like, Papa?*' I asked.

'*A queer sort. An odd duck. He had no family, no sweetheart, no close friends. His only home seemed to be the War. I did not think much about him at the time, but looking back now, it seems to me there was a terrible vacancy in him, a void. I have known a few others like that. They know they are not like other men, that some essential quality is missing. They have no ability to love, and therefore an infinite capacity for hate. Hitler's hatred does not begin with the Jews, but it ends with them. It begins with himself.*'

He became truly quiet then, as he does when he is exhausted. '*I am becoming quite fatigued, Karl. I am going to have to nap a little. The main thing about Adolf Hitler is that he was completely unimportant. It annoys me that I must talk about him, particularly with you. He does not matter. But you do. What lessons you should draw from all this, and how you should live your life – these are ultimately decisions that you yourself must make. I can only tell you what I think.*'

'*Yes, Papa,*' I said. I had much more to consider.

He settled back in his seat, and closed his eyes. His breathing became soft and regular. But then, all at once, he woke for a moment.

'*One last thing,*' my father said, '*very important.*'

'*I have decided you should continue your education in England.*'

A View of the Lake

1924

-

Oberst Heinrich-Werner Mertz von Haydenreich
Neustrelitz am Schliersee

Herr Oberst,

... [T]herefore, I must candidly inform you that my business matters
are such that I do not have the leisure to escort the boy to Rutland.

But I would not be fair to either one of us if I left the matter there. I
must in additional candor inform you that I feel neither kinship nor friendship
with you or any member of the Haydenreich family. In my considered
judgment, you exploited my sister's goodness of heart and willingness to please
to obtain a nursemaid for your two motherless children. In so doing, you caused
her to give up the urban society of Munich, in which she had delighted, and any
number of young men far more eligible than yourself, and estrange herself from
her devoted family. Now she lies buried in your churchyard, far from
everything she truly loved.

I wish I could find it in my heart to forgive you these trespasses, but I
cannot. Please do not trouble me with any more requests of this nature.

Sincerely,
Frederic Breslau

-

Herr Frederick Breslau
Breslau and Breslau
Munich, Germany

Dear Fritz,

A mutual acquaintance of ours, having overheard something you said, has brought to my attention your appallingly rude and discourteous response to a request made by Oberst von Haydenreich.

Whether you acknowledge the fact or not, Heinrich von Haydenreich was the great love of your sister's life. He loved her in turn, and would have justified all, had time served their cause better. She lies in the grave she would have chosen herself. She was as devoted to Karl – 'the boy' – as if he had been her own flesh and blood. In disdaining him, you disdain her.

I cannot threaten you with any more than a mother's gravest displeasure if you persist in this attitude. But you will have incurred that, and I will do my best to make my feelings known to all.

I implore you to behave honorably in this matter . . .

Your very disappointed,

Mama

-

January 20, 1924
Uppingham School
Rutland, England

From the Journals of Karl von Haydenreich (published 1986):

Today is Sunday and marks three weeks since I have been at Uppingham School.

I did not protest when Papa told me of his plans for my further education. I thought it might be a great adventure. I have read and heard so much about England! Papa told me about Uppingham School right before New Year. It sounded exciting, so much more exciting than a gymnasium.

But everything has turned out so much different than I expected. For one thing, Papa was too ill to take me to the school. I had to go with Mummi's brother Fritz, who I would call 'uncle', except he will not let me do so. He dislikes me intensely, though no one, not even Grandma, will tell me why. He would not even have done this, but Grandma made him do so. He took me, but as rapidly as possible. He would not let me use my French or English, or stop to see any sights. On top of everything, I got seasick on the Channel crossing.

We were only in London for a few hours, then on to Rutland, where the Uppingham School is located. There was a car waiting for us at the station at Leicester. After a brief ride, we were at the school. It was as picturesque as the pictures I had seen, and my spirits rose for a moment. But already I was homesick. It is all so different than Neustrelitz.

I met with Headmaster Owens, who seems a kind man. He explained the rules and traditions of Uppingham to me. As he recited them, these seemed not much different than those in my school, but, O! How strange they sounded on foreign soil. I wanted very much to go home right then. I even wished for Uncle Fritz to stay on, but he left as soon as he had left me with the Headmaster, without even a farewell. Then I was all alone.

The classes are not so difficult. My English is more than good enough, because of Mummi – and Papa asked the Headmaster to have me study French instead of Latin – so the French she taught me is also very useful. I even like the classes in which I know little, such as history and geography. They are interesting.

But between classes I keep to myself. No one likes me or wants to be friends. The English winter is as bleak and cold as Bavaria. The only kind face is the German teacher, Herr Frauenthal, who has made a hobby of Yiddish and knows and likes Sholom Aleichem, Mummi's favorite. He invited me to his office and we talked of this, in Yiddish, which was great fun. The only place I find any peace are in the music practice rooms, where I play my saxophone and clarinet, and pretend I am Sidney Bechet. Uppingham has a great reputation for its music, which is why I think Papa chose it. But I can't stay in the practice rooms all the time. Sooner or later, I must go back to the house, and then I am all alone.

I miss all my friends. Everything I knew and loved is so far, far away. I wish I were dead.

-

Excerpt from: A Twentieth Century Life
Albert Sommerville
Houghton, Mifflin (1959)

At the beginning of Spring term in 1924, a buzz went around the school that a new boy had joined the school. Not only was he reputed to be German, but he was from a family of Bavarian nobility. As we were all little barbarians, we were prepared to do our best to continue the Great War in the halls of Uppingham – and would have done so, had not the strictest instructions, accompanied by the direst of threats, come down from on high, to leave the new arrival in peace.

As it happened, the new boy, Karl von Haydenreich by name, was very quiet and kept strictly to himself. I had no inkling that he was destined to become my best friend in life – in fact, at first, his familiarity with the German instructor, a Herr Frauenthal, a German and a Yid, put me off. In any case, like generations of Sommervilles before me, I was at Uppingham to obtain my place at the University before launching myself off to add to the glory of the British Empire. Friendships with German strangers did not fit into that plan.

However, Fate, that sly rearranger of destinies, had its own plans. About two weeks into term, I ventured into one of the practice rooms, to undertake my usual heroic assault against the Baldwin piano. I was hammering away, when, pausing for breath, I heard someone in one of the adjoining rooms producing sublime tones from a woodwind. I ceased beleaguering my poor instrument and crept stealthily toward the room from whence the sound was coming. After opening the door as quietly as I could, I beheld Karl, playing on a tenor saxophone, and as well as anyone I had ever heard. Best of all, he was practicing a song by the American Irving Berlin, *Alexander's Ragtime Band*, a jazz number.

As I watched silently, he put the saxophone back in the case and took out a clarinet from another one. He was as good, if not better, on that. I listened, rapt, until suddenly, he sensed my presence and wheeled around. I was the one who should have been discomfited, but he seemed even more profoundly embarrassed than I was. I could only express my unreserved admiration for the quality of his play, and for his choice of music. He began to relax a little, and then – very shyly – suggested we might practice together. Well! I knew already he was way beyond my level, but I could hardly say no to such an invitation.

We went back to my practice room and, for the first time in my life, I was making music with another human being. Not that this was in any way due to me. I was the same relentless hacker as always. But Karl was already so good that my own deficiencies seemed to disappear. We played the Berlin tune, and then a song, *Swanee,* by another American, Gershwin, that sounded even better. By then, I knew we had to invite him to join the band, and I could hardly wait to tell Jenkins and Fitzmorris.

For I must pause here to confess to another one of my innumerable youthful indiscretions. At the beginning of Michaelmas term, I had joined a band that had been formed by a classmate, Roger Jenkins. I was already a jazz fiend, having become addicted during my excursions to the West End. Jenkins, who had somehow obtained a bass fiddle from somewhere, had persuaded his friend, John Fitzmorris, who dabbled on the trumpet, to join him in the band. I was, of course, the pianist. It was a good try, and we enjoyed our attempts to make music. But the candid truth is that we were terrible.

This was in the back of my mind as Karl and I began what was to be a lifelong friendship. I soon discovered that he wasn't standoffish at all, just shy and lonely, and in truth miserable, though he put up a manly front about it. These revelations made me feel a bit small, for I had misjudged him in the same manner as all the others.

I invited him to come to the next band practice, which we had scheduled for that very evening. He did come. It was obvious to all after only a few moments that Karl was miles beyond any of us. We played our usual cacophonous rendition of *Alexander's Ragtime Band.* Then Karl suggested a simplification of the piano bass line that enabled Jenkins to match my rhythm with a technique within his ability, and altered Fitz's line to one more manageable for him. Then we played the number again, Karl harmonized his clarinet with Fitz – and by God! we were a band! Not a very good band, I hasten to add, but, to the wonderment of all of us, we were making music for the first time – truly making music! This was one of the most thrilling moments of my life.

Thus we became a band. At the same moment that happened, we all knew we had a leader, and who it was. Jenkins' nose was a bit out of joint, but he had to accept the reality. Then Karl surprised us all. He announced he knew a lad who played a splendid set of drums – Joshua Goldberg, another fifth former. This startled us a bit – Goldberg was, after all, a Yid, so we had never considered him. But Karl insisted he sit in, and he proved to be a capital drummer. As I became better acquainted with him, it was also apparent he was a regular chap.

(My views and that of my party are so often misunderstood on this point. I would never deny that exceptional specimens of splendid manhood occur in all races, even among Africans and Indians. It is the general run of the race that constitutes the menace.)

The Uppingham Five had been born. But we did not immediately seek out any public forum. Karl insisted that we rehearse to a point of high proficiency and broaden our repertoire. We did just that throughout that spring term, at every reasonably free hour, becoming more excited and confident with each passing day.

By term's end, Karl had become the best friend I had ever made in my life. With my parents' consent, I invited him to spend the holidays with my family at the family estate.

-

May 17, 1924
Neustrelitz am Schliersee

Lady Lucinda Sommerville
Windermere Castle
Windermere, Westmoreland

Dear Lady Sommerville,

Karl had already forewarned me of the invitation you were so kind to extend to him, and had sought my consent. I am touched by your solicitude on his and my behalf. But the fact is that my family estate is a cold and desolate place for a boy of his age. He will be much better served by spending the holiday with your family and the school friends he has made. My consent is freely and gladly given.

I will expect him for a visit of a fortnight at the end of the holiday, and will make appropriate arrangements. As for spending money, I will provide you a draft, to be given to him at regular intervals, depending on his good behavior in your home.

It would be my pleasure to extend my own hospitality and the hospitality of this estate to the Sommerville family, next summer or the summer after, as it suits your convenience.

My thanks again for your kindness, to me, and to Karl.

Yours very truly,

Heinrich von Haydenreich

-

Excerpt from: A Twentieth Century Life
Albert Sommerville
Houghton, Mifflin (1959)

The summer of 1924 was the happiest time of my life. Karl and I were inseparable. We practiced every day, expanding our horizons and skills (my skills, I should say, my friend's were already truly expansive). Jenkins, Fitzmorris, and Goldberg visited several times, to broaden the repertoire of the band. My father and brother were somewhat taken aback by the invitation to Goldberg, until I assured them of his exceptional personal and musical qualities, which they were soon enough to observe for themselves. We were also able to swot up on some reading that lay ahead both at Uppingham and University, this while availing ourselves of all the pleasures of youth and country.

It was a marvelous time!

Karl made himself instantly popular with both household and servants, and particularly my mother. Of course, his manners were impeccable – but he was also so naturally appreciative of even the smallest gestures of kindness and courtesy that he won the hearts of all. I had been concerned that his German nationality would cause problems with those who had suffered a loss in the War, which nearly everyone had. But his English was so good and his manner so open, that no unpleasantness ever arose.

When term recommenced in the fall, the Uppingham Five were ready to audition before Mr. Pendleton, the music master. Though he was certainly no jazz aficionado, he was sufficiently impressed by our competence to permit us to perform at one of the school assemblies. Our reception was riotous, our classmates erupting with applause. We were quite a change from the staid chorales to which they had been accustomed.

In addition to a meteoric rise in our status with our classmates, our triumph led to a series of engagements at churches, social functions, and school dances – what the jazz musicians of this day call 'gigs'. School rules did not permit us to accept all the invitations that were offered, but we appeared often enough to obtain a very modest (and very brief) celebrity.

It was a very heady experience for a boy like me, who to that point in my life had been shy to the point of welcoming anonymity. I began to conduct myself with a confidence and firmness of purpose, that had previously been conspicuous in their absence. The alteration in my manner was the subject of comment by Reverend Owens to my parents. Theretofore my family had regarded me as a prototypically frivolous younger son, destined for mediocrity or disgrace. For the first time, I received letters from my father in which he took me into his confidence, sharing his thoughts and political plans in full. I knew I had Karl to thank for this marvelous, even miraculous, transformation into what I recognize now as the first stage of mature manhood.

Our friendship had become like no other in my life, for he had done for me what no one else ever did – and which, once done, was never to be undone.

1925

-

January 8, 1925
Neustrelitz am Schliersee

Major Dwight D. Eisenhower
Panama Canal Zone
Panama City, Panama

Dear Ike,

From Neustrelitz across the world, once again I extend my hand to my American friend.

. . . I must acquaint you with some unpleasant family news. In February, my father initiated a lawsuit against the Neustrelitz development. This was clearly a response to the November incident, although of course not stated as such. My counselors assured me the suit was utterly without merit. However, after a time I decided to settle the matter, as the money sum (though significant to my father) was quite affordable to the resort. But the counselors had the final word, for my father passed away only a few weeks after the settlement was paid – a windfall for his mistress and whatever charities he had chosen to support.

In truth, I felt more relief in my father's passing than grief, and then a profound sadness and regret – sadness and regret that after all the years we had come to such a sorry end. All I could do was make the firm resolution that matters would go better with Karl and myself, to the extent I could manage it. And so I shall.

As it happened, my father's death and funeral coincided with Karl's visit at the end of the term holiday. He was more moved by his grandfather's death than I was – and yet I could see Karl had not yet forgiven him for his bringing about my son's infatuation with the man Hitler (who is in prison now, by the way, and very much a spent force). His visit was the highlight of my summer, and all who dwell here. For a few brief days, the house was vibrant and youthful again, as when his sister and Rosamunde were alive. Yet I could see Karl could hardly wait to tear himself away and be back in England. He detests this place, and not without reason. He is gone now, and the vitality with him, and we are as we were. I miss him acutely. My son does not know this.

Which brings me to the last. I am all but certain I shall not be sending you another Christmas greeting next year. The cloak of pen and ink conceals how short of breath and life I have become, in this ancient house with its dying master. I have redone my will. I have created a trust for Karl, to be managed formally by my former brother-in-law Frederick Breslau. Despite his enmity to me, he is a man of the strictest rectitude in financial matters. I trust his integrity with respect to the funds, but not his charity with respect to Karl.

But your kindness of heart I do trust, Ike. I remember the note to Bechet when Karl was just another boy at the table. I would therefore like to appoint you as co-trustee, with the final responsibility of disbursements to Karl. I have enclosed the appropriate forms in both German and English. This would not require any return to Europe. The duties can be discharged by correspondence. Also, I do not expect such a service to be performed gratis. The trust document provides for a small, but appropriate fee and expenses, which I believe you will find sufficient. If not, please advise me at once, as I would not wish to impose on your generosity.

Please do me this one last favor. Be good to my son, and to yourself. The best of everything to you and yours.

Your friend, always,

Heinz

-

Excerpt from: My Name is Ike - Reflections on Fifty Years of Service as Soldier and Statesman
Senator Dwight D. Eisenhower
Random House (1986)

. . .[O]f course I accepted. I would probably have done it gratis.

What Heinz thought of as a 'small fee' proved to make a huge difference to a family living on a major's salary in the United States Army. I was grateful to Heinz, but it was not the reason I became trustee for Karl. The reason was friendship.

Of course, as matters worked out, the payments led to endless comment, speculation, and conspiracy paranoia. I guess the whole affair comes under the heading that no good deed goes unpunished . . .

-

Excerpt from: A Twentieth Century Life
Albert Sommerville
Houghton, Mifflin (1959)

. . . Karl also blossomed that fall. He grew to his full height, a bit over six foot tall. With fine blonde hair and his blue eyes, he looked like a Nordic god. Years later, when I chanced to view the portrait of his mother in the Haydenreich family estate, I realized Karl resembled his mother a bit more than his father. Also, his mother had been quite statuesque, nearly as tall as his father. He inherited her height.

When he played his woodwinds, sax or clarinet, eyes closed, lost in a musical ecstasy, the impression he made was unforgettable. But also, in that strange, mysterious tribal manner in which women communicate, they all seemed to have become aware that he was (a) Bavarian nobility and (b) the sole heir to a considerable fortune. The natural outcome was that our engagements were crowded with girls and women, the majority clustering around Karl, losing themselves in blissful adoration of our band leader. But there were also more than a few who noticed Fitz, Jenkins, Goldberg, and the modest writer of these lines.

All this was heady stuff, and marvelous nourishment for the ego – but, I hasten to add, the ego only. There is a French saying, *si jeunesse savait, si vieillesse pouvait* – if youth but knew, if age but could. We were all as innocent as lambs, Karl in particular. Thus, none of this female appreciation made any impression. Only much, much later, when all was decades behind, did any of us realize what might have been possible. I am sure my readers understand without the need for further explanation.

But I doubt if Karl even then would have been wont to indulge in a series of casual dalliances. Mind you, he had a fine sense of humor and a wonderful ear for jokes. But from the first I knew him, there was always a core seriousness of purpose in him that at times was way, way beyond his years. It was the reason he was so much better a musician than the rest of us. He already considered that music might be his calling, and applied himself accordingly. (He was so accomplished in fact that, with school permission, he sat in with professionals at the village from time to time – at age 15!)

He tried his hand at composition, too. But his product was surprisingly bland, compared to the inventiveness and energy he displayed when performing on the woodwinds. He was much keener about his songs than performance. I know we all shared the same low opinion of his work – but, uncharacteristically diplomatic for boys that age, we kept our thoughts to ourselves. Karl was too good a friend, and too tolerant of our inadequacies on our various instruments, to be subject to any scathing adolescent criticism. Instead, we simply insisted our audiences demanded popular tunes, which was true enough.

As the summer term neared, my expectation was that my family would accept the invitation so kindly reciprocated by Karl's father, and that we would visit Bavaria. I was keen to go. But Father became a candidate in a by-election against a particularly odious Laborite, and my older brother Bernard had to swot up on some tutorials to continue at Oxford. We were forced to delay the adventure for a year.

I was disappointed, but not horribly so. I anticipated another summer as good as the one the year before had been.

Alas, it was not to be.

June 11, 1925
Uppingham School
Rutland, England

Oberst Heinrich-Werner Mertz von Haydenreich
Neustrelitz am Schliersee

Concerning: Karl von Haydenreich:

My dear Oberst,

I thought it appropriate to append a note to Karl's term report to provide you with a more personal evaluation of his progress here at Uppingham. In a word, his showing has been splendid. As you can see from his marks, he excels at languages, and his mathematical skills are also more than adequate. His showing in other subjects is also excellent. Karl is certainly bright enough to read for Oxford, if that is his and your ambition, with matriculation a virtual certainty.

. . . I would close simply by saying that Karl to date has been a more than worthy addition to our student body, and has in fact enriched life at Uppingham considerably. You have every reason to be proud of your outstanding son.

Sincerely,

The mst Reverend Reginald Herbert Owen
Headmaster, Uppingham School

June 28, 1925
Neustrelitz am Schliersee

The mst Reverend Reginald Herbert Owens
Headmaster, Uppingham School
Rutland, England

My dear Headmaster,

My apologies both for the brevity of this letter and the strange hand. I am too indisposed to maintain myself long at my desk, so have dictated it to my obliging housekeeper.

Many thanks for the extended report about my son. Karl is old enough to make his own decisions on career and University. He is aware that my preference is that he return to Germany, but he will make up his own mind. My thanks again.

Sincerely,

Colonel Heinrich-Mertz von Haydenreich
(by his housekeeper's hand)

P.S. I trust your discretion to keep the degree of my present infirmity a matter of strictest confidence, particularly with respect to Karl.

-

August 2, 1925
Neustrelitz am Schliersee

Master Karl von Haydenreich
Windermere Castle
Windermere, Westmorland

YOUR FATHER GRAVELY ILL STOP RECOVERY NOT EXPECTED STOP ASKING FOR YOU STOP COME QUICKLY STOP FRAU HILDEGARDE SCHALLERT

-

Excerpt from: A Twentieth Century Life
Albert Sommerville
Houghton, Mifflin (1959)

Karl was on his way to the train within 30 minutes of the receipt of the telegram. My father's staff had made travel arrangements for him before he reached London.

But he was too late. He was not in time to bid farewell to his father.

-

Undated letter, received August 14, 1925
Neustrelitz am Schliersee
One of three letters from Heinrich-Werner von Haydenreich to Karl-Wilhelm von Haydenreich, delivered post-mortem

My beloved son Karl,

I have left you a reminiscence about my lost, lovely little girl, your sister Magdalena, and another about your marvelous mother Charlotte. I hope

139

you will treasure them always. This third letter is about your stepmother, Rosamunde, your Mummi.

I do not wish to be misunderstood. I loved your mother. It is a huge frustration to me that you never felt her touch, heard her voice – for she was extraordinary. You will hear the idle tongues of fools' whisper about the man who married two women, best friends, in succession. There is nothing to it. I was honorable with both women, in the time I had with them. I would not choose between them.

But it is my belief that it befalls to every man to meet one woman who haunts his life, who both comforts and afflicts him. In my life, that was Rosamunde Breslau, my Rosamunde, your Mummi. She sacrificed much to become my wife, yours and Lena's stepmother. She left a big city, rich with diversions, to live in a small, rural village. In her own mind, she could never escape your mother's shadow. She came as a stranger in a strange land, Jewish in a small village where Jews were objects of suspicion and hatred. She made herself beloved among the same people who were prepared to despise her. But she lived in constant clouds of self-doubt, perpetually anxious that her good deeds were insufficient, unworthy, or misunderstood.

I meant to make all this good. I had made plans for us, the same ones you have witnessed become reality since the war. I meant for us to have a rich life together, the life she deserved. What fools we mortals are! The Sarajevo incident occurred only a few months after I was finished with service to the Prince, the absurd and hellish war began and I was called back into service. Soon all was done, and nothing had been made good. Rosamunde never had the child of her own she deserved. She lived the last years of her life mostly apart from me and the others she loved. Then she was gone.

You will make your way in the world of men, succeed there. Of that I am certain. You will learn that honor among men is always conditioned by the weight of the world – what is possible, what is not. But it is the promises made to women that are sacred. With these, phrases such as 'I meant well' or 'Fate intervened' signify nothing. There is only the deed, done or undone. My story with Mummi is of undone deeds, and the bitterness of time lost.

It is that thought I leave you, and with it, the fervent prayer that you find a woman worthy of the promises of the sort I once made, and do for her what I did not do for your Mummi. Make all good for her. Make what should happen, happen. In that way, perhaps some good may still come of all this.

As for the rest, it was for the best that you go to England. But be aware that I missed you acutely these last years. Your presence always brightened this house, your voice was always the one I most wished to hear. You should know these things.

And last, know I have been proud of you every day of your life, and always will be. If I have not said this enough in my lifetime, I say it now. May you hear it in perpetuity hereafter.

Your father,

Heinrich-Werner von Haydenreich

P.S. See to it that the portraits of Mummi and your mother are exchanged monthly, as I have done these last years. One or more of the staff may have a favorite. But this must not be.

Your Father.

-

Excerpt from: *A Twentieth Century Life*
Albert Sommerville
Houghton, Mifflin (1959)

I did not see him again until September. He did not seem changed all that much, perhaps a bit more subdued. At first, he did not speak of his father. I did not feel it was my place to press him. He only spoke up when we had our first rehearsal. We were all a bit uncomfortable, but a bit shy to address the matter directly, or even offer condolences. I had come to like and respect Goldberg, but he could on occasion exhibit the pushiness of his race. He put the question boldly to Karl.

'*Are you holding steady, old bean?*' he asked.

I have never forgotten Karl's reply, for it spoke both to some of the mysteries of his life and his essential gravity.

'*Just fine, chums,*' he said, '*but I will tell you something. If I were you, I'd find out a bit more about your paters while the time is at hand – for you may discover there's more to the blokes than you could possibly realize. I had thought I'd known my father. But I found out I barely knew him at all.*'

Before this could descend to an embarrassing sentimentality, Karl blew the first bars of Chopin's *Funeral March* and we all laughed. Then we began the set and the rehearsal, and the moment passed into history. But the conversation has stayed with me.

-

Mister Karl von Haydenreich
Uppingham School
Rutland, England

Dear Karl,

I just received news from Frederick Breslau of your father's passing. He was a man like few I have known. I will miss him more than I can say. I am sorry for your grief, but I feel my own great sorrow as well.

I don't know if you remember me, but I was the American soldier who tried to keep up with you in Paris a few years ago. From now on, however, we will have a closer relationship. Your dad advised me in his last Christmas letter to me that he had nominated me to be the discretionary trustee of your estate until you come of age. But he did not tell me I'm guardian as well.

It's a bit more than I bargained for, but I will discharge the responsibility. I don't know what advice I can give you, but it's yours if you need it. As for the funds, short of heading to Monte Carlo and putting everything on red, you tell me what you need and you will have it. I think you're old enough to know what you want.

My condolences again. Let me know if I can help you in any way.

Sincerely,
Major Dwight D. Eisenhower
United States Army

-

September 25, 1925
Uppingham School
Rutland, England

Major Dwight D. Eisenhower
Command and General Staff College
Fort Leavenworth, Kansas

Dear Major Eisenhower,

Of course, I remember you. My father spoke of you from time to time, and always in the highest terms. My thanks and appreciation for your condolences, and your warm offer of help.

For now, though, there is little I need. I am in the upper form at Uppingham, on course to graduate the year after next. My headmaster is pleased with my progress, and urges me to read for Oxford or Cambridge or a good German university. Perhaps in the end I will do that.

But music is my passion. I intend to apply to either the Stern Conservatory or the Berliner Hochschule for Musik, to study composition. I am also going to arrange for study with someone in the woodwind section of the Berliner Philharmonic, to make some progress with the clarinet and saxophone. Perhaps in time I will audition for the orchestra. It is not out of the question.

So I think I am getting on with my life. Of course, I am still grieving for my father, who I realize I hardly knew. I deeply appreciate your letter and your good wishes.

I will write you at Christmas.

Sincerely,

Karl

P.S. I would never stake the entire family fortune on red. I am not a Communist. I would put it on black.

K.

1926

-

-

Excerpt from: Service to the State - in War and Peace
Major General Werner von Blomberg
Reichswehr Press (1949)

.... I vacationed at Neustrelitz in 1926, 1928, and 1929, but I never met Karl von Haydenreich, who was still a boy. We had no relationship before he joined the Reichswehr. Speculation to the contrary is nonsense.

-

Excerpt from: A Twentieth Century Life
Albert Sommerville
Houghton, Mifflin (1959)

It was not until the summer of 1926 that the Sommerville family made the first of our many, many visits to Neustrelitz – in my case, first as son, later as husband, finally as father. The first occasion set the pattern. Then, and later, and always, the appropriate fee is proffered. Then, and later, and always, it is declined. These days it is his widow Elizabeth, acting as trustee for their children who declines, but in her own way. In lieu of payment, she requests a donation to some cause I despise – Home Rule for India or Ireland, some Yid charity, the welfare fund of a labor union, that sort of thing. Always I comply, without a murmur of protest. It is something of an ongoing joke between us.

I realized the moment I exited the station on that first visit that I was in one of the most beautiful places on earth – the lake with its deep placid blue, the sky above with light fleecy clouds, and everywhere the smell of pine scent. The resort itself is laid out in exquisite taste, with concentric circles, centered around a small but perfect hotel. (These days there is a second hotel with circles, a twin of the first.) Looking down over all is the mansion, a castle really, with a magnificent medieval grandeur, where Karl was born and where the family lived.

Father was involved that summer with the preliminaries that led to the formation of the British Imperial Party, and Bernard once again was in an academic scrape. Neither could remain more than a fortnight. But Mother and I stayed several weeks, and had wonderful fun. I had matured enough in the preceding year that she allowed me a degree of freedom – or, to be more accurate, I had matured enough due to Karl's influence that she trusted *him* to keep us out of situations. We cavorted with considerable liberty that summer, our second to last.

I was too youthful to understand the implications of some of my friend's behavior. Although the mansion had been modernized and large enough for him to share with the resident manager (who had even prepared quarters for him), he preferred to stay in a small cabin nearby. I learned later that was the cabin in which his stepmother had dwelt during her initial stay there. Also, although there were diversions in abundance at the resort, and we did avail ourselves of many of them, Karl constantly suggested excursions to Munich and elsewhere. This frustrated me a bit, as I wished to explore the activities nearer at hand in a bit more depth.

It was left to my mother, with a mother's insight, to dispel my bafflement. '*Albert,*' she said, '*he detests this place – and he has good reason. He only remains here because of us.*' Then I understood.

We went by train to Munich on several occasions. This was the first major European city with which I became familiar, even before London. On two occasions, Karl's grandmother, Frau Johanna, gave us lunch. She was a marvelous woman, a model of grace, delicacy, and surprising wit, the sort that does credit to any race. (If only the other Yids would follow her example!) She clearly doted on Karl, and he on her, despite the absence of a direct blood connection.

The first time we visited the Krone Circus, Karl told me the story of his youthful infatuation with the National Socialist Party, the event that had led to his enrollment at Uppingham. He made the story hugely amusing, and I laughed as if it were a big, colossally humorous joke. But I understood how acutely embarrassing he still found the incident. I don't recall if he mentioned Hitler by name. If so, it would not have registered with me, as the name meant nothing at that time.

I could not tell him that the principles of National Socialism were virtually identical with the program for the British Imperial Party that my father and brother were then in the process of organizing. I knew by then that there were some matters of essential political principle on which I and my best friend would never agree.

It was better to say nothing.

-

145

Major Dwight D. Eisenhower
Command and General Staff College
Fort Leavenworth, Kansas

Dear Ike,

I have some good news. Last week, I auditioned before Herrn Richard Mufeld and Ernst Kornberger of the Dresden Philharmonic, which was in London on tour. I performed on both clarinet and saxophone. They both congratulated me afterward and I learned I would be recommended without qualification to the Berlin Hochschule of Arts. I will be able to study composition, as well as my instruments.

I have discussed this decision with Headmaster Owens, who has great wisdom in these matters. He agrees with me, that this is the right time for me to seek my heart's desire and find out what future music might hold for me. There will be time enough to try other things if that does not work out.

Herr Breslau informs me I must have your consent to authorize payment. I have enclosed the forms and directions for the tuition payment. Please authorize it as soon as it is convenient for you.

This is the course I want to pursue now, Ike. Thank you for your help.

I am very, very excited. I can hardly wait to find out what the future holds.

Sincerely,

Karl

-

Excerpt from: *A Twentieth Century Life*
Albert Sommerville
Houghton, Mifflin (1959)

The band ceased to exist in our last year of school. Jenkins and Fitzmorris had departed. Goldberg and I were beginning to view other, larger horizons. Karl decided to try his chances with a musical career. He arranged for an audition for himself with a pair of senior musicians from a touring German orchestra, and gained admission to the prestigious Berlin Hochschule. We all celebrated.

Karl joined many of my own tutorials. He had no interest, of course, in a career in Britain or the Empire, but he did wish to keep the possibility of

146

Oxford alive. I became more and more uncomfortably aware of how much our views on essential matters diverged. For example, we both attended a history lecture on the subject of the exploits of the great 18th-Century imperialists, Clive in India, Wolfe at the Battle of Quebec, and so on. After it was over, I asked Karl jokingly what he, a German, had thought of it. He answered quite seriously that he didn't care too much for empires, and the British Empire was no different.

I was so shocked I was speechless. There would have been considerable ill feeling, or we might even have come to blows, if Karl hadn't been such a capital fellow.

For in the last analysis, he *was* a capital fellow, a prince among men, with a God-given nobility that I respected and admired. Our friendship transcended any disagreement.

1927

-

January 18, 1927
Karlsfeld
Near Munich, in the district of Dachau

Master Karl von Haydenreich
Uppingham School
Rutland, England
[By special messenger]

Dear Karl,

It is with regret I inform you of the passing of my mother, Frau Johanna Breslau, on the 10th of this month. She left certain specific items to you, phonograph records that I will be shipping to you by regular post. But it is not of this I write.

When her will was read, a matter arose with which I cannot deal as trustee of your estate, that requires your personal attention. In her will, my mother expressed a specific intention to be interred beside my sister Rosamunde, in Neustrelitz. I can only assign this whimsy to advancing old age, since the Breslau family owns its own considerable plot in Munich. It is there, beside my father, that she should be buried. My sister insisted on her own wishes in this matter, as she always did. You are probably too young to remember the arguments about this in 1919, but in the end, she got her way.

My mother is a different matter. She belongs with her own family. It would be a great convenience, both as a matter of law and of courtesy in a time of grief, if you could, on behalf of the von Haydenreich family, politely decline permission for this burial. No one would gainsay you. You have every right to deny space in your family's estate to a comparative stranger. In so doing, you will have the gratitude of the entire Breslau family in that event.

Please provide your consent by wire, as funeral arrangements are delayed pending resolution of this matter.

With thanks in advance,
Herr Frederick Breslau
Breslau and Breslau

-

January 26, 1927
Uppingham School
Rutland, England

COMING AT ONCE STOP HOPE TO ATTEND SERVICES STOP DO
NOT KNOW WHAT TO DO ABOUT GRANDMA'S WILL STOP KARL

February 20, 1927
Uppingham School
Rutland, England

From the Journals of Karl von Haydenreich (published 1986):

I am back in school after three weeks in Munich and Neustrelitz, with
so much to relate that I must record it now. As always, my journal, I consecrate
myself to truth above all, particularly when the truth is unpleasant and painful
to recall.

With Reverend Owens' permission, I left school as soon as I could
after receiving Uncle Frederick's letter. Albert was kind enough to phone his
father, and once again his staff made the detailed arrangements before I was on
the train – they have had too much experience with this. My masters gave me
assignments, and I took my books. I tried to busy myself with my studies, but I
was too torn between grief and anger to give attention to them.

How could my uncle be so nonchalant with this awful news . . . as if I
had no more relation to Grandma than a peasant in China?! Then grief would
replace anger when I thought of Grandma, and her love and cheerfulness, how
she took care of me when Mummi died, and later – and my eyes would flood. I
will never see her again! More than once I nearly gave way to unmanly tears.
But I am 16 years of age, too old for childish displays.

Uncle Fritz met me at the station when I reached Munich. He was all
smiles and good cheer, and full of apologies for the late notice. He seemed
sincere, but I had not forgotten how cold he was to me when he escorted me to
Uppingham. He told me there have been Masses said and other ceremonies, but
he had postponed the funeral until the matter of the place of burial could be
resolved. However, there was to be a major remembrance at Grandma's
apartments the next morning. He had had it delayed four days for me. He
suggested that afterward we meet at his offices to discuss the request in her
will.

The next day I attended the remembrance. Her friends and family
came and went, and shared memories of her. I had memories of my own, but I
could not share them, as I was too choked with tears and sorrow to speak. I did
not wish to play the child or the fool. So I said
little, and may have been misunderstood.

149

Several persons did approach me. Evidently, Grandma's request had become generally known, and it was also known that the decision rested with me. Everyone had an opinion. Some sided with the request, others were strongly opposed. My great-aunt Gertrude, my grandmother's sister, thought her sister should be buried with the Breslau family. But she is a meek person, and I was not sure she was speaking for herself. Frau Schallert had come from Neustrelitz to attend. She had respected and admired Frau Breslau, and hoped she would lie in rest with Mummi. She said she had prepared her staff for any decision.

After all was done, I went over to my uncle's offices. I was not looking forward to the interview. Uncle Fritz sat me down, then launched into a long, long speech. He spoke to me of the family heritage of the Breslau's, of how many relations were in repose in their family crypt, that his father lay there, of how long his mother and father had been married and loyal to each other, and much more. He said honoring my Grandma's request would be a major humiliation to his family. He urged me to deny the request and uphold the honor of both our families.

He moved me deeply, and my first thought was to do as he wished. But then I thought I should at least read the will, and learn from her own words why Grandma wished to be buried at Neustrelitz. I asked to see the document. It was apparent this did not please my uncle at all, but he summoned his secretary.

While we were waiting, I looked about his office. There, on one wall, was a picture of Adolf Hitler and, underneath, a Nazi insignia. I could scarcely believe my eyes. My uncle noticed the direction of my eyes.

'*Are you a member of the Nazi Party?*' I asked. I could not keep the astonishment out of my voice.

'*Of course,*' he answered. '*Hitler and his followers are the best chance for Germany to escape the slavery of Versailles – to reclaim its rightful glory.*' He noticed my bewilderment. '*You would know better if you had lived through Eisner and the Red days. The Bolsheviks are the great menace. Hitler understands this better than any man in Germany.*'

Only then did he become perplexed. '*But surely you share these beliefs. Your grandfather was one of Hitler's earliest and most fervent supporters.*'

His secretary interrupted us then, with the will. But before I looked at it, I had to understand.

'But surely you know what Hitler says about Jews?' I asked.

'I am not a Jew,' he answered – he seemed almost affronted. *'The Breslau family are not Jewish. We have been Christian for two generations.'* He glanced up and saw my reaction. *'I can understand your confusion – my sister Rosamunde always had a fond, foolish sympathy for the old culture.'* He smiled. *'Yiddish, for example. My goodness. But the more sensible members of the family prefer modernity. We are German Catholics, not Jews.'*

I nodded understanding, which he mistook for assent. *'Hitler uses this Jewish theme to secure the loyalty of the masses,'* he continued, as I bent over the will. *'It means nothing.'* He became silent as I read.

My grandma's wish was expressed in a handwritten addition to the main document. I felt tears come to my eyes as I recognized the handwriting, from the birthday and holiday greetings she had always sent me. I committed the essential passage to memory. It read:

With the consent of the von Haydenreich family, I should like to be buried beside my beloved daughter Rosamunde and her husband, at the place where she found true love and her greatest happiness. I should like to lie beside her and share the same view of the lake as God has granted my daughter and my son-in-law.

Tears then did overcome me. My uncle had the good sense not to say anything. But when I had dried my eyes, he did remark that the time had come for a decision. In this he was right. But I felt a sudden need to leave the offices, to stroll about Munich, and think. Uncle Frederick was not pleased by this, but had no choice but to agree.

It was a cold, bright day. I needed my coat. I walked through the central city, trying to organize my thoughts, but distracted by the sheer beauty of the city in bright light. I don't know how, but I found myself at the spot near the Odeonsplatz, where the shots had been fired on the day my grandfather and I marched with Hitler. Suddenly I was flooded by memories . . . my grandfather's tenor, Ludendorff marching proud and erect through the bullets, the smell of blood and cement.

All at once I noticed flowers and candles at the spot where I fell atop the wounded man and Hitler fled. I did not understand at first. Then I realized these remembrances had been placed there by persons who regarded the events of that day as heroic. The thought struck me that these memorials were the same in kind as the flowers on Mummi's grave. But the ones there were truth, and these were a complete fraud. This thought made me angry, very angry.

151

Other memories surged forward. The broken window at Herr Rosenbaum's bakery – and my grandmother – my Grandma! Her boldness confronting Grandfather – the way she took me home, and cared for me – but most of all – most of all – the look on her face when she saw me in the brown shirt. Then I wondered what she would think if she could see Hitler's photograph in her son's office. Perhaps she had seen it.

I knew my decision then. I stopped at the telegraph office to send a wire to Frau Schallert. Then I went back to Frederick Breslau's office.

He threw away any semblance of good will. He did not even try to pretend. He denounced me and my father and my entire family. He said my father had deliberately alienated Mummi from her family. . . that he had marooned her far away from the City she loved and the life she savored . . . that he had deliberately thrust myself and Lena at his soft-hearted, soft-headed sister in order to obtain a nursemaid and governess. . . that he had deliberately done as much as possible to sow discord in the Breslau family. . . and now this. He saw now I was my father's son, the same monster of ego and ingratitude that my father had been. He then cursed my entire family as a rat pack of fools and spendthrifts, and a blight on Bavaria.

I fought off tears again as I listened. I have been raised to show respect to my elders, and so I did not leave. Finally, he stopped, and asked if I had reconsidered the matter. I told him my resolution was firm. He then forbade me to call him 'uncle' or consider any member of the Breslau family as kindred. He told me that he would no longer serve as trustee, but would find another banker to serve. Then he sat down and, without looking at me, ordered me out of the office. I began to leave, when he looked up and spoke.

'*I cannot stop you from doing what you will do,*' he said, '*but, rest assured, I will not forget this insult. This is one indignity too many. Now go – out of my sight.*'

The funeral at Neustrelitz was two days later. It was another bright day. I witnessed the interment – my Grandma will have the view of the lake she wanted. There were many fewer persons present than had been at the remembrance, but I believe those who were there were the ones who truly cared for her. Then I came home.

I don't know even now whether my decision was the correct one. I am going to write to Ike and ask for his opinion. I hope he approves me.

-

February 28, 1927
Command and General Staff College
Fort Leavenworth, Kansas

Mister Karl von Haydenreich
Uppingham School
Rutland, England

Dear Karl,

Thanks for your letter. It explains a somewhat mystifying communication I received from Frederick Breslau. He has resigned his share of the trustee responsibility for you to someone named Hjalmar Schacht, of the Danat Bank. This should not make any practical difference to your plans.

As to the rest, I believe you handled this awkward situation very well. I can say with confidence your father would be extremely proud of you . . .

Sincerely,

Ike

-

Excerpt from: A Twentieth Century Life
Albert Sommerville
Houghton, Mifflin (1959)

The only time I dined with Karl at the manse was on the very last day of our stay in 1927. Generally, he avoided his family home if he possibly could, but that day was the exception. It was just he and I that mid-afternoon. We were in a valedictory mood. Though we had been graduates for only a few weeks, Uppingham seemed a lifetime distant. In a day or two, we would be separating, he on his way to Berlin and the Hochschule, and myself going up to Oxford. I felt the pang of the imminent separation acutely.

'Come,' he said, a little shyly, *'there is something I would like to show you.'* We walked through the intimate quarters of the house toward the garden at the back. A magnificent portrait of a truly beautiful German princess hung on one wall. I hardly needed to ask, but I did anyway, out of courtesy. *'My mother,'* Karl said, *'the one I never met. Mummi's portrait will be there next month – my father insisted.'* Then we were through the house and in the open air out back.

The scene shone magnificently in the late August sunlight, with the lake never broader or more blue. But then I realized we had come to a modest family plot, a gravesite. It was canopied by oak trees (a change from the ubiquitous pine) that framed the splendid vista below.

153

'*This is where they all reside now,*' he said quietly. One by one, he pointed out the resting places of the persons he had mentioned so infrequently, but always with great feeling when he did. There before us were the gravesites of his sister, his father, his mother, his stepmother, his uncle Willy – all the persons he had known, loved, and lost. Even in my callow youth, I understood that this was a moment of the most solemn intimacy. I felt privileged.

Flowers adorned two of the graves. I asked about that. '*Mummi,*' he said, '*and her mother. The townspeople have kept Mummi's grave fresh with flowers ever since she was buried there. They honor my grandmother to honor her – it would not be right otherwise.*' Then he gestured. '*My father lies beside Mummi, and my mother Charlotte beside him.*' He smiled suddenly. '*My father requested Father Kugler, under the Confessional seal, orient his body in the casket, then close it – so no one will ever know which of the women he loved is on the left, which on the right. My father thought of things like that.*' He pointed towards his grandmother's memorial. '*Grandma shares the same view of the lake as Mummi,*' he said. '*I saw to that.*'

He spoke for a while, remembering them all, particularly his sister Lena. '*She would have been just the girl for you, old chap, lively and very, very pretty. You would, of course, have had no chance at all.*' Neither of us wanted the moment to become lugubrious, so we joked for a while about how I would have fared with his sister, even indulging in some of the adolescent cant with which boys of our age concealed our ignorance of the opposite sex. Then, at once, he was silent and as serious as he ever was.

'*I cannot escape the thought,*' he said, '*that their only existence is in my memory. When I am gone, they will all be gone with me.*'

This made me uncomfortable. '*But your Mummi is remembered,*' I said. '*The flowers on her grave. The portrait.*'

He shook his head. '*It is only a picture. They loved her, but I am the only one left who truly knew her. I am the only one who knew my sister. My father?*' He smiled suddenly. '*Well, I didn't know him, but neither did anyone else. And my mother Charlotte lives only in me – there are no other relatives.*' Then he was silent again, and as serious as I had ever known him – which for Karl was awfully serious indeed.

'*I feel I must justify this in my own life somehow,*' he said. '*There must be a reason why I alone am left out of all of them.*'

This made me exceedingly uncomfortable. '*You can't consecrate your life to the dead, old bean,*' I said. '*I doubt they would want you to do that.*'

154

'*Oh, nothing that drastic,*' he answered. '*Just to do something that makes sense of all this.*'

'*You can't let your heart lead your head,*' I said.

'*The heart must always lead,*' he answered. '*It has the greater wisdom.*'

Now, I knew this to be nonsense. In the world of affairs, in matters of empire and power, in insisting on the natural orders of men, the head must always rule. Without the light of reason, we would all be as savage as Africans. But I said nothing. I had been honored by an invitation to the most sacred place in his life, and I respected the profundity of his feeling even as I questioned it.

'*Old bean,*' he said suddenly, as if he understood my thoughts, '*Albert, has it ever occurred to you that you may be a better man than either your father and brother? Precisely because your heart is sounder?*'

I realized then how high an opinion he had of me, far higher than anyone else. I was touched, but too young to be anything but disconcerted, to the point of reddening embarrassment. Then we both became self-conscious, as boys will, changed the subject to other, trivial matters, and went back inside. The next day, I bade farewell, both to Karl and the happiest time of my life. My mother and I departed for home, and Oxford. A few days later, Karl went on his way. We never met at Neustrelitz again.

The Cold Light of Day

***Excerpt from: My Name is Ike - Reflections on Fifty Years of Service as
Soldier and Statesman
Senator Dwight D. Eisenhower
Random House (1986)***

Historians who write looking back at events long after the fact too
often forget how accidental and personal human life really is. Karl didn't
abandon music and join the Reichswehr with any fixed plan to do anything.
Sure, there was a large element of patriotism in his change of direction. He saw
what was happening in Germany, and he didn't like it.

But the basic motivation was purely personal – a reaction to the
biggest disappointment of his life.

***Excerpt from: A History of Germany in the Twentieth Century
Josef Behrens
Alfred A Knopf (1964)***

Ironically, the cities of Berlin and Munich changed personalities
during the brief life of the Weimar Republic. The former, which had been a
dour provincial city during the reign of the Kaisers, became the most open,
liberated city in the world, the cutting edge of avant garde art, music, and
literature, and daring experiments in sex and lifestyles. The latter, before the
war the most cosmopolitan city in Europe, never recovered from the traumas of
1919. It became a cesspool of rightwing and reactionary politics.

***November 19, 1927
Hochschule fur Musik
Berlin, Germanr***

Mister Albert Sommerville
Jesus College, Oxford University
Oxford, England

Dear Old Bean,

. . . [C]lasses are not that difficult, in elementary counterpoint and harmony. Of course, there are performance classes as well. But I also play at three different night clubs (or cabarets, as they call them) sometimes as many as four nights a week. This is more educational than anything in the academic curriculum.

I don't just mean simply musical education, old chum. My eyes popped at some of the sights I saw. Yours would, too. . . men dressed as women, men with men, women with women, men with two women, many dressed (or undressed) in ways that the good masters at Uppingham could scarcely imagine. One night, a woman sat in the front row of tables, dressed in severe men's clothing, with a monkey on a leash, dressed in a tuxedo! It is like that! Berlin after dark is another world, an Arabian Nights' tale come to life.

My one disappointment is that my compositions have not yet been deemed worthy enough to be programmed on any of the school recitals. But my day will come . . .

Your old German chum,

Karl

-

December 19, 1927
Hochschule fur Musik
Berlin, Germany

Mister Albert Sommerville
Jesus College, Oxford University
Oxford, England

Dear Old Bean,
. . . I have made a new friend, a young composer named Kurt Weill, who writes his own extraordinary blend of old and new – jazz, but like nothing you've ever heard before! Jazz, yes, but with his own peculiarly European twist. He likes the way I play my saxophone, and we became friends. I am enclosing some sheet music – take a look at it. Perhaps we'll have a go at it this summer.

Another Jew, poor Albert – another one you'd like in spite of yourself. You'll just have to get used to that . . .

From far-off Berlin,

Karl

1928

-

March 6, 1928
Berlin, Germany

From the Journals of Karl von Haydenreich (published 1986):

    . . . [P]assed a small stand walking from class, from which three Brown Shirts – Nazis – were distributing leaflets and literature. I was disconcerted – I had thought the Hitler phenomenon was a matter of historical interest only.

    I found myself more bothered by this encounter than I would have thought . . .

-

April 11, 1928
Berlin, Germany

From the Journals of Karl von Haydenreich (Published 1986):

    . . . [T]he reception of my song at the Katakombe was not what I had hoped. Perhaps it was the absence of lyrics . . .

-

April 18, 1928
Hochschule fur Musik
Berlin, Germany

Mister Albert Sommerville
Jesus College, Oxford University
Oxford, England

    Dear Old Bean,
    Your frustration that I do not write more of romantic exploits breathes through your lines, old chum. But I must disappoint you. True, I have crossed the equator and live on the other side of the world. Berlin is a different universe in that way. But the sad reality is that girls prove to be as mysterious, elusive, and frustrating, when they are attainable, as when they are not. You will find this out for yourself soon enough.
    In my circumstances, they fall into two classes – a precious few with an innocence and vulnerability with which one feels he must not trifle, and the larger number, with a hardness and cynicism that in turn dismays me. They remind me of my grandfather's fancy woman, to whom he entrusted my

160

education one fine night a few years ago. (I never told you of this – it is not a memory of which I am fond). These are not desirable attachments.

Thus, old bean, I find myself condemned, if not entirely to celibacy, at least to seriousness, and must send you elsewhere for fodder for your lurid imaginings.

Wishing you your own good luck in these matters,

Karl

-

May 2, 1928
Berlin, Germany

From the Journals of Karl von Haydenreich (Published 1986):

... [A] party at Weill's place, in celebration of May Day. Brecht was there, as much of a pig as Kurt is a prince. He had too much to drink, and started in on me – my noble blood, the property at Neustrelitz, all of it – a complete hypocrite – he fancies himself a Communist, but denies himself nothing. Somehow he had heard of the reception of my song at the Katakombe. He railed on and on about the lack of talent in the upper classes, their uselessness, and how their red blood (meaning my red blood) will one day pour down the gutters. He was clever in this and others laughed and joined in. No one wants to take him on. Everyone knows the success of Three Penny Opera is due to Kurt's music and not Brecht's dreadful prose. But no one says that out loud.

Kurt said that a man who played the saxophone with the energy I do, must be a man of the people, which made the crowd laugh. I was thankful and pleased. But then I realized that if Brecht had heard my song, so had Kurt . . . and he said nothing at all about that . . .

-

May 3, 1928
Berlin, Germany

From the Journals of Karl von Haydenreich (Published 1986):

... [P]assed the Nazi stand again. Some copies of *Mein Kampf,* Hitler's autobiography, were for sale. On impulse, I bought one.

I began to read at home, but the book is not worth reading – endless, turgid rantings of schoolboy views of humanity and the world, with savage condemnations of Jews and other 'inferiors'. I thought to dismiss it, but I found myself becoming angry, then furious – not at the opinions, but the effrontery. I

161

know this man. My father knew him. I remember the fear in his eyes at Marienplatz, and how he ran. A man of his sort has no right to opine about anyone . . .

-

May 10, 1928
Berlin, Germany

From the Journals of Karl von Haydenreich (Published 1986):

. . . [M]y quintet was not selected for the annual student program in June. I could not believe my eyes when I saw the list. I worked for months on that piece. I know the composition has merit, I am certain of it!

I at once sought out Professor Hindemith, who was still in his offices. He is always a gentleman, and kind, though in this instant his kindness devastated me. He informed me that my quintet was in good form, intelligent, and studious – but lacked something of the essence – lacked a soul (my words). He noticed how crestfallen I was, and tried to reassure me. I was a superb performer; my musicianship was of the highest caliber; there are many other places and routes in music besides composition. I thanked him for this thought, and left, with my whole being in an uproar.

NO!!! Forever no!!! I cannot accept this as my fate. I cannot believe that I can get near enough to Olympus to see the mountain top, yet am permanently consigned to a place in upper Hades! *'My musicianship is of the highest caliber, but lacks something of the essence.'* Let me put that in plain language, my dear Professor. What you mean in plain words is that I am a studious mediocrity, long on diligence, short on talent.

I spit on this judgment! I defy this courteous condemnation! Curse Hindemith and all his kindness! During the next year, I will devote all my energy, all my talents, to proving Brecht, and Professor Hindemith, and all of them, completely in the wrong – and I will hear them say so out loud.

-

October 21, 1928
Berlin, Germany

From the Journals of Karl von Haydenreich (Published 1986):

. . . [T]here are perceptibly more Brown Shirts on the streets these days. The Nationalist Socialist Party is apparently gaining strength. I find this phenomenon perplexing, and annoying.

162

1929

-

Excerpt from: A History of Germany in the Twentieth Century
Josef Behrens
Alfred A Knopf (1964)

The prosperity of the Weimar Republic, even in the golden period of the mid-twenties, was always something of an economic illusion, resting as it did on the base of easy American credit. In 1929, when that credit became gradually unavailable, the Republic began to wobble. The fragility became apparent as early as the first quarter of the year, long before the stock market crash in October. Economic indicators became negative, and unemployment rolls began to swell . . .

-

January 17, 1929
Berlin, Germany

From the Journals of Karl von Haydenreich (Published 1986):

. . . [P]erformed two new songs at the Katakombe. They did not go well. I must do better.

After the performance, I went to a late night gathering at Weill's quarters. Some of Brecht's Bolshevik friends were there, clothing in disarray, crowing about a fight with the Nazis they had just left. They are too full of themselves to realize that such puerile means will not bring their revolutionary end any closer. But it is the fights they like, not the cause. Everyone knows that.

Weill was there, and noticed my mood. I weakened and told him of my disappointment. Kurt is a good fellow, and showed sympathy. He asked to look at my songs. We went into a room away from the others, and I showed him one of them. He said it was not too bad, all it needed was a little work. Then he picked up a pen, and made some modifications. He altered the time signature of the chorus, reworked three of the first sixteen bars, and made some other alterations. The effect of all was to transform the key to E minor, and the tempo into a brisk ⁷⁄₈.

The effect was miraculous. My dead, leaden song was alive and marvelous! Kurt is a genius! I was profoundly grateful at the time, and thanked him genuinely.

163

But now? As I think of it? Why could I not see the changes he saw so easily? I would have done this effortlessly, naturally, when playing my woodwinds. Why does it all become so difficult when I have pen in hand?

What is wrong with me?

-

April 2, 1929
Berlin, Germany

From the Journals of Karl von Haydenreich (Published 1986):
    . . .[C]ompleted my submission and presented it to Professor Hindemith – a song cycle, 12 in all, written in modern jazz idiom.

This is good work, possibly even masterwork. I await the Professor's verdict with confidence and large hope . . .

-

May 3, 1929
Berlin, Germany

From the Journals of Karl von Haydenreich (Published 1986):

Rejected again – and junior works from students who just joined the Hochschule in the fall, accepted, placed on the program! This time I did not have to seek Professor Hindemith out – he sent his assistant with a note, requesting I meet him in his offices.

He was as gentle as he always is. But he stated, without emphasis or malice but in words as plain as these, that my work as a composer in these songs, and elsewhere, lacked the touch of originality that might make them notable. He complimented me again on my skill on the woodwind instruments and my musicianship. He reminded me of the careers and opportunities in music apart from composing. He mentioned performing. He mentioned conducting. To this I could only reply that I regarded those sorts of lives as dilettantes' lives, and I did not propose to live mine as a dilettante. I had always intended to make my mark in music in my study and recording studios. Anything less will not do.

Professor Hindemith was silent for a moment, then switched subjects. Suddenly he was speaking of the larger world outside of music. I understood what he implied. His words were nails in my ears. He said that he had noted my composure and maturity, which he considered remarkable for a youth not yet 21. I informed him that, so far from being 21, I was not yet 19, which caused him to raise his eyebrows and remark that in that case I was truly remarkable. I

164

was not flattered by his praise. I knew he had only made it to soften the judgment of death he was pronouncing on everything I ever wanted.

I could not accept this with saintly meekness. Instead, I offered a suggestion that I had already been pondering. I said I might rent the Katakombe for a session, possibly after hours, during which my song cycle, and some others that had been unfairly rejected by the faculty, might be performed. Professor Hindemith thought this an excellent idea, and assured me that obtaining the necessary permissions would not be a problem. I asked him if he would do me the favor of selecting the other student works for the program, as I do not wish to make enemies.

Professor Hindemith answered that he would be delighted to do so, provided I made one commitment in turn to him – that I would not myself join in the performance of my own work, but take my place in the audience. This was a sensible condition, and I accepted at once.

So. We shall see what happens, in the tasting of the pudding. I cannot deny the fact that Professor Hindemith's kindness and his allusion to other types of life made a deep, unsettling impression. He did not enjoy what he was saying. His praise of my other capabilities seemed sincere.

I am completely confused. I don't know what to think.

-

May 9, 1929
Berlin, Germany

From the Journals of Karl von Haydenreich (Published 1986):

. . . I have made the arrangements for my concert at the Katakombe, after hours, on June 13th. There will be wine, beer, and a party as well. Now we shall see!

-

June 14, 1929
Berlin, Germany

From the Journals of Karl von Haydenreich (Published 1986):

7:00 a.m.

This, above all, to thine own self be true. The motto of my journal always. This morning, as I write in the cold light of day, this motto has never been more important.

The Katakombe cleared the regular customers about 11:00. Some of my party were already waiting outside. There was beer in abundance, and sausages and buns. I wanted the feeling of a festival, for everyone to have a

165

good time. My friends drank, and ate, and laughed, for a good thirty minutes or so, before taking their seats. Kurt was there, and Brecht and his whole crowd.

I was far more nervous than I ever am when playing myself. (Klaus Junge took the saxophone part.) Lotte, Kurt's girlfriend, had agreed to sing my work. She sings his songs magnificently, and I did not even try to conceal the considerable influence his work has had on mine. He had even rehearsed with her when I was occupied with the organization. So now there were twelve songs to hear, and I could only pray they would go well.

A soft drum beat, a tap on the snare, and Lotte began. I was transfixed at once. This was the first time I had ever heard my music played when I was not involved in its performance. I could not believe my ears. After a few bars, I looked around. Everyone was attentive, patient, paying attention. Kurt was focused on Lotte alone, mouthing the lyrics, still coaching her. He's a good friend. Brecht was involved with his Bolshevik friends.

Lotte finished the first song in the cycle. There was light applause, and she began the second. I remained transfixed, as if hearing everything I had ever written for the first time. The second was no different than the first. Perhaps the applause at the end was a bit warmer. I couldn't tell. Lotte finished the third song, and began the fourth. I knew by that time it would be the same for all. It didn't matter to me any longer whether the rest were sung. But Lotte would of course complete the program.

She was midway through the fourth when there was a commotion at the entrance to the club. A half-dozen or so Nazis, with their brown shirts and swastikas, were demanding entrance. Perhaps they had smelled the food. Harold informed them that a private party was in progress, but they raised their voices and pushed forward. An argument began. Then Brecht and his group arose, and confronted them. The voices became even louder.

The musicians put down their instruments. Lotte stopped singing. Everyone rose then. I was still in my trance, too lost in my own thoughts to realize what was occurring. Then, suddenly, there was push, a push back, a shove, and then a shove back. Then all was pandemonium, with fists and shouting, and beer flying everywhere. Nazis were swinging roundhouse, American punches, Reds were raising chairs and shouting.

All this snapped me out of my spell. I saw a Nazi point at Kurt (who wears his ancestry on his face) – '*Jew!*' – and start for him. I moved to stop him, but Lotte darted forward first and smashed a beer mug into the Nazi's

166

mouth. (Lotte is a tough girl. The rumor is Kurt met her when she was walking the streets. I have never asked.) The man staggered back.

Then I saw Chloe, a young, slight, pretty waitress in the grasp of another Nazi hooligan. She was a girl with whom I felt a bond, since she and I were together for a while when I first came to Berlin. I pulled the man away from her, then shoved him back toward the larger battle. He might have come after me, but a Communist or student or someone confronted him, and he had no opportunity.

'*Quickly!*' I said to Kurt, Lotte, and Chloe, and we made our way out the back entrance, the same escape the musicians had made – and Brecht as well, who deserted his comrades at the first show of force. I always suspected he was a coward. Kurt and Lotte were laughing at this huge adventure, and bade me good night. Chloe was more shaken. I offered to see her to the trolley, as she lives way across the city. But she was too upset to go home unescorted. I offered her the couch at my own apartment, which she accepted gratefully. (She is with someone else now.)

She took the couch when we arrived, and I went to bed. But I could not sleep. My mind was churning with what I had heard in the audience. Suddenly Chloe slipped into the bed beside me. She had taken off all her clothing. '*It is not natural to sleep apart*', she whispered, and, indeed, it was not. On a different night, I might have reminded myself of the others in her life and declined. But on this night, I accepted the consolation she offered, with gratitude. Finally, I slept.

But now she is gone, mercifully without recriminations or second thoughts.

Now, in the cold light of day, I must consider what I heard last night.

I must consider how I am going to live my life.

11:00 am.

I am no composer. My songs are worthless – bland, flavorless, student exercises. They are not even bad enough to be interesting. They are simply flat and lifeless. Everyone knew it but me – not just Professor Hindemith, but Albert, Jenkins, Fitz and Goldberg back at Uppingham. They all knew. They were all too kind to tell me. The one talent I wish most desperately to possess is one which God has denied me.

For an hour or two I sat at my table in the most profound despair. But then it was as if the sun had broken through the clouds. There are other ways to live. There are infinite choices. I recalled the advice Professor Hindemith had urged on me. Now I understood him. I don't have to build my life around music. With this thought came the most exhilarating sense of freedom, as a convict breaking out of a cell! I did not have to beat my head ceaselessly against a locked door! Perhaps somewhere in my inner self I had known as surely as the others that music was not my destiny! And knowing that, embracing that . . . I am free!!!

So.

What now?

-

July 14, 1929
Berlin, Germany

From the Journals of Karl von Haydenreich (Published 1986):

The school halls seemed surprisingly empty today. I learned later a great number of students had gone to hear Hitler address the Student Union. I hope this was only to satisfy curiosity . . .

-

July 31, 1929
Hochschule fur Musik
Berlin, Germany

The mst Reverend Reginald Herbert Owens
Headmaster, Uppingham School
Rutland, England

Dear Reverend Owen,

I am considering entering University either in Berlin or Heidelberg, and possibly reading history, economics, or law. This alteration of plan must come as a surprise to you, but I have come to realize that the paths in music I wished to follow are barred to me, and no hope for it.

If you could recommend a suitable tutor or counselor in Berlin, I would be eternally grateful . . .

Sincerely,

Karl von Haydenreich

-

August 18, 1929
Hochschule fur Musik
Berlin, Germany

Major Dwight D. Eisenhower
Department of War
Washington, D.C.

Dear Ike,

. . . [S]o as not to surprise you, I am going to be requesting consent to the application of funds for tuition, books, and other expenses related to enrollment in the University. My plan is to read history and economics. I have been forced to realize there were limitations to what I could accomplish as a musician. This was a very bitter pill for me to swallow, as you Americans would say. But I think I have digested it.

But now I will surprise you more. I am also giving serious thought to following your path and joining the Reichswehr, the Army. There is a storm coming in Germany. Everyone can feel it. There are too many discontented people and too much new affection for violent men and causes. We Germans are not so lucky as you Americans or my British friends. There is neither loyalty nor trust in this Weimar government, which shakes in the wind like the last, forlorn leaf on a barren tree. When the storm comes, the only institution which will stand firm is the Army, in which the public does have confidence. I have begun to wonder if that is where my duty lies.

In the meantime, though, I will begin at University, if you would be pleased to approve the expenditures . . .

Your friend,

Karl

-

Excerpt from: My Name is Ike - Reflections on Fifty Years of Service as Soldier and Statesman
Senator Dwight D. Eisenhower
Random House (1986)

. . . [I] kept the letter Karl sent me in which he first mentioned the possibility he might become a military officer – not because I thought it was in any way prophetic. It was the first time I heard the echoes of his father's voice in his letters.

-

Excerpt from: A History of Germany in the Twentieth Century
Josef Behrens
Alfred A Knopf (1964)

By the end of the summer of 1929, the stability of the Weimar Republic hung on two slender threads. One was the personality of Gustav Stresemann, the extraordinarily capable Foreign Minister, whose force of personality was felt throughout the government. The other was the continued

169

availability of easy credit from the United States, even though that had diminished substantially during the year. But on October 3rd, Stresemann died suddenly of a stroke. On October 24th, the American stock market collapsed. In a month, the Republic lost both its credibility and its economic stability.

The times, which had been uncertain, became frighteningly bad.

1930

-

From the Journals of Karl von Haydenreich (Published 1986):

. . . [F]orgot my scarf, so I purchased one from a street peddler. We chatted. He had been forced to sell his bakery in 1926 at too low a price, to meet creditors' demands. He blamed Jews for this. (I did not argue.) Now he ekes out a living with his cart. He has just joined the National Socialists. He has no hope of any change from the present government – *at least the Nazis promise action!*

There must be hundreds of thousands of bitter men like this all over Germany. Seeing no hope, they become Communists or Nazis. Meanwhile the Republic does nothing, the breadlines get longer, and the bitterness becomes more intense, each passing day.

My new course of study seems far off and distant compared to what I see happening all around me . . .

-

February 18, 1930
Berlin, Germany

From the Journals of Karl von Haydenreich (Published 1986):

. . . [P]apers full of reports of another massive street brawl between Nazis and Bolsheviks. At Kurt's house, Brecht is full of glee at the imminent Revolution and subsequent blood bath. The hunger on the streets does not stop him from gorging himself on Kurt's food. Swine . . .

-

Excerpt from: Eyewitness!
The True Story of the Fiasco on the Rhine and the Siege of the Reich Chancellery
Oberfeldwebel (formerly) Victor H. Becker
Houghton, Mifflin (1950)

I had a good little chauffeur's business in Berlin in the 20s, three cars and drivers and looking for a fourth. Then came the Crash, and kerblam!! Everything went to hell.

So . . . back to the Army, which I thought I'd left for good in 1919. Fortunately, the Reichswehr needed drivers and car mechanics.

March 21, 1930
Berlin, Germany

Mister Albert Sommerville
Jesus College, Oxford University
Oxford, England

Dear Fledgling Barrister,

. . .[H]ate to wax all serious with you, old bean, but the state of
Germany is a good deal more parlous than jolly old England. There you wonder
if the Prime Minister can weather the economic storm. But here we wonder if
the entire ship of State will capsize – for we Germans do not have the
confidence in our ship with which you British are blessed.

A man of integrity must decide where he stands in this chaos. I am
questioning whether I have the right to the tidy life of a student just now . . .

-

April 11, 1930
Berlin, Germany

From the Journals of Karl von Haydenreich (Published 1986):

.. . . [R]eceived the quarterly accounting from Herr Schacht.
Neustrelitz had its best winter in history. The rich are not touched by any of this
calamity. They never are.

I reside on an island of prosperity in a sea of misery and hunger. This
does not sit well with me . . .

-

April 21, 1930
Berlin, Germany

Mister Albert Sommerville
Jesus College, Oxford University
Oxford, England

Dear Most Junior of Clerks,

. . . [H]old on to your hat, old bean, for I have come to a momentous
life decision.

When I am done with examinations in a fortnight, I am going to join
the Army.

A Wedding at Grossenbrode

May 1, 1930
Jesus College,
Oxford University

Herr Karl von Haydenreich
Hochschule fur Musik

      Dear idiot,

      . . .[F]or God's sake, come to your senses, old bean, before it's too late

. . .

      NO ONE joins the army these days. Certainly no one of our set . . .

                  Your appalled friend,

                     Albert

Excerpt from: Service to the State - in War and Peace
Major General Werner von Blomberg
Reichswehr Press (1949)

      I was not involved in the recruitment of Karl von Haydenreich into the
Reichswehr. This is another instance in which rumors have usurped the place of
reality.

Excerpt from: A General Speaks - the Autobiography of Kurt von
Hammerstein Equord
Major General Kurt von Hammerstein Equord
Reichswehr Press (1986)

      . . . [I] first learned of the application of Karl von Haydenreich to the
Reichswehr from William Groner, at that time the Minister of Defense. This
was in the spring of 1930.

      Because the times had become so bad, a huge number of young men
attempted to join the Army. These were normally rejected routinely, because of
the Versailles limitations. But to be contacted by someone bearing the name of
one of the most distinguished noble families in Bavaria was unusual. To receive

an application from a young man in possession of a substantial private income, a student living in Berlin, prepared to surrender all the pleasure of that vibrant city for the primitive brutality of a military barracks, was extraordinary. The circumstances were so unique that Groner felt compelled to investigate further.

His meeting with von Haydenreich sufficiently impressed him with the young man's earnestness, sincerity, and personal qualities, that he referred the matter to me. I knew the family as well as anyone still in service. The father was an outstanding officer, though very much of his own stripe; the uncle was dashing and quite capable; the grandfather? The less said of him, the better. The question was which, if any of these, Karl von Haydenreich resembled. Therefore, I invited him to lunch, and an interview thereafter.

I could see he was very much his father's son. But that did not end the matter. Although it is not widely known among non-Germans, and these days not even to most German youth, the road to an officer's commission in the Reichswehr is one of the rockiest roads of any army on Earth. An officer candidate spends the first eighteen months in ranks and barracks with ordinary soldiers, subject to the same drills, training, and privations. While performing his regular duties, he also receives basic officer training in the afternoons. After eighteen months, he then becomes an ensign, equivalent to corporal's rank. Finally, in the third year, he is promoted to sergeant's rank, and sent to a specialized school for formal education as an officer. His training may continue for years thereafter. All this is dependent on passing examinations of considerable difficulty at every point. A soldier's life is a hard, arduous life, that not that many adopt by choice, and even fewer among the indulged youth of the Weimar Republic.

But Karl surprised me. He had fully informed himself about officer's training. He impressed me also with his seriousness and a remarkable maturity for a young man of his age (he was not yet twenty). This led inevitably to the next inquiry. What had motivated him to make such an unusual decision?

He answered forthrightly that he believed that a crisis had overtaken Germany, such that the Republic as presently constituted was certain to fail. He believed the Army was the only institution capable of maintaining order and stability until some more permanent and popular order of government was established. These were views that had been widely, if privately, expressed among many military and civilian leaders of my acquaintance (and which I shared). But it was remarkable to hear them voiced by one so young.

I reminded him that the Reichswehr was resolutely apolitical, a fundamental policy established and enforced by von Seekt, and a good one. He answered that he had no special politics, simply an aversion to violence and crude, brutal solutions to complex problems. His mother had raised him, he said, to believe in the benevolence and nobility of all men, without being any less German. (The mother he mentioned was in fact his stepmother, but I did not know that at the time.)

I left our meeting mightily impressed. The diminished ranks needed men of the versatility and flexibility of mind that Heinrich von Haydenreich had possessed, and that his son had clearly inherited.

To my surprise, von Blomberg also seconded the application, simply on the strength of the von Haydenreich family's military tradition. His statement in his memoirs that he was not involved in the recruitment does not match my recollection.

-

May 23, 1930
Berlin, Germany

Major General Werner von Blomberg
Headquarters, Reichswehr
Berlin, Germany

My esteemed General,

It has come to the attention of the National Socialist Party that Karl von Haydenreich has applied to join the Reichswehr for officer training.

Be advised that Herr von Haydenreich is a long-time member of the National Socialist Party, at one time being its youngest member. His family estates have long supported the Party financially. His sympathies are unquestionable.

The Party would therefore endorse his application with enthusiasm.

Sincerely,

/s/Heinrich Himmler
Reichsfuhrer, S.S.

-

Excerpt from: A General Speaks - the Autobiography of Kurt von Hammerstein Equord
Major General Kurt von Hammerstein Equord
Reichswehr (1986)

. . . [T]he recruitment of a conservatory-trained musician, an expert performer on clarinet and saxophone, became known instantly throughout the entire Army.

From the beginning, von Haydenreich was extremely popular with officers of all ranks and assignments.

August 25, 1930
Regimental barracks
Munich, Germany

The Honorable Albert Sommerville
Oxford, England

Dear Unworthy Civilian,

My apologies for such a belated letter. But, truth be told, I have been so harried, so fatigued, so constantly breathless, that I lacked the time either to gather my thoughts or the words to express them. Everything in my life has been so utterly changed. I had foreknowledge of what to expect, and these expectations were correct. But nothing prepared me for the actual experience.

On the first full day of my enlistment, I was rudely shaken awake, thrust into ranks, and marched from pillar to post. On day two, icy water was poured over my head, and a rude voice denounced me as less worthy than the 'shit in a latrine' – these were the words actually used! I knew then I had been plunged into a world so primitive I would scarce believe it existed – wooden barracks shared with two dozen other men; simple pallets for beds; clean, but rough bedding; a single uniform of dull, coarse grey-green wool.

Thus it goes, every day. Up at dawn, formation into rank, endless drills and marches, basic courses on personal hygiene and maintenance of barracks, uniform, weapons, and so forth. We are responsible as a unit for the cleanliness of latrines and barracks, as well as food preparation – tasks that are assigned in rotation or as minor discipline. We all learn the work our servants do in the life outside the Army. This is a soldier's life!

The first fortnight was so difficult I could only recall your warnings and consider the horrid possibility I might be forced to confess you were right. I had thought I was in decent physical condition. I learned within two days I was not. Every muscle ached to the bone. I was bleary eyed with lack of sleep, completely exhausted from the regimen of march and drill. The tasks we must learn by rote are so simple they are difficult. Failure (at first) is the norm, and

177

the cause of caustic, obscene ridicule. Our training officers are not gentle persons.

There was only one other officer-candidate in our unit, a Prussian boy three years my junior, a general's son. The conduct and performance of we two candidates were the subject of the strictest scrutiny and harshest comment, since we are, in theory, future officers and our performance superior to others. In theory only – of course, at the beginning we are no better than anyone else. The other candidate did not last a week, but withdrew and left for home. I alone am left as officer-candidate.

But, old chum, I must tell you, even at the start, there was something bracing about this primitive new life. It was as if I had stepped out of a stuffy room into a crisp, fresh breeze. The muscles that were sore and groaning are now hard, toned, and a bit more pronounced. I have come to love the early light of dawn. I take pride in mastering the simple soldiering skills that seemed impossibly elusive in the first weeks. With this mastery comes the discovery that my sergeant taskmasters are not quite the ogrish tyrants they pretend to be. There is a personal reality in all this that was missing at the Hochschule. I feel as if I had not been grounded before, and now I am.

Besides, the rationale that drew me to this calling seems more concrete than ever. Conditions in Germany have worsened – millions unemployed, real hunger in some places, the Republic ruling by emergency decree for nearly two years now, without anyone's confidence, and no end in sight. If Germany is to avoid a Bolshevik revolution, or a descent into its own odious version of Mussolini's Fascism, it will only be because of the stability of the Army. Sorry to wax serious, old bean, but this is rather serious stuff.

Music? This is perhaps the best news of all. Three times already I have been called away for musicales, and two more beckon. The Germans are a musical people, and the military no different. My modest reputation preceded me into service. Everyone seems to know of it. So the summonses arrive, I make my way to the appointed place, meet my fellows, discuss our repertoire, pick up my saxophone, and then . . .

The miracle occurs. With my saxophone in my hands, the sheer joy of making music, the untrammeled bliss that used to be mine . . . all that I thought was lost to me forever . . . returns! Free from the burden of expectations with which I tortured myself, the rapturous ecstasy I used to know is mine again. All that is missing is . . . *you*, old friend, and the Uppingham Five. I look about, hoping to see you hard at work at the keyboard, and all the others. But all there are about me are strangers in Reichswehr uniforms. Still, it is a small burden. We must get together again, Albert, and make music again. We must!

Then the dance or musicale is over, and it is a dash back to the barracks, and a resumption of the strict Spartan regime I described. It's a strange life I have chosen, different than anything I imagined. Yet it suits me, and the renewed gift of music is the proof.

The one major frustration is the one we endured at Uppingham, returned now in full, furious force. At night and off time, my comrades and I talk of one subject only – women. I am no different now than the others. Berlin and the clubs, with all the available girls, seem a distant dream, a Paradise Lost. On some feverish nights, I recall all the opportunities that were so recently, so easily at hand. I wonder how I could ever have been so mad as to resist them.

You might recall how I wrote you once I had given myself 'if not to celibacy, at least to seriousness'? Old bean, this was the most incredibly foolish nonsense any man ever wrote. Make hay while the sun shines, is the motto I would now suggest to you. Take this to heart, from someone living in a sunless clime with no hay in sight anywhere. It is the best advice you will ever get.

Your comrade, whether in arms or not,

Karl

-

Excerpt from: Destiny Betrayed - A Chronicle of Treason
Harald Quandt
Franz Eher Nachfolger Gmbh (1952)

. . .[v]on Haydenreich used his genuine, but limited musical skills, and his morbid interest in American jazz, to insinuate himself into the hierarchy of command . . .

-

Excerpt from: A History of Germany in the Twentieth Century
Josef Behrens
Alfred A Knopf (1964)

. . . [B]etween 1930 and 1932, every economy in the Western world collapsed. The effects were particularly acute in Germany. Its phantasmal prosperity vanished. The Weimar Republic had never been accepted by the public at large. The one opinion shared by all, conservatives, radicals, moderates, was that the government would not be able to resolve the crisis. Three different prime ministers tried to form governments between 1930 and 1932. None succeeded in forming a coalition – the various political parties were

179

unable to agree. The government thus ruled by emergency decree rather than consensus.

As the public lost confidence in the government, the radical parties gained ground. Both the Communists and various Conservative parties made substantial gains in the election polls. In particular, Hitler's National Socialist Party went from a minor fringe party in 1929 to the second largest party in the Reichstag by mid-1931. . .

1931

-

March 25, 1931
Adlon Hotel
Berlin, Germany

(*From the Journals of Karl von Haydenreich (Published 1986):*

. . . [D]ay four of leave, first day back in Berlin. The city seems so much the same, so much different. The Nazis everywhere and much bolder. They solicit without restraint, heckle those who pass by without responding. Two of them taunted an older Jewish woman on the corner, directly obstructing her path. I would have intervened, but two passersby came to her aid before me. There were words, but nothing else – a policeman nearby doubtless the reason, though he did not prevent the taunting. What is it all coming to?

Then lunch with Kurt. He was kind enough to invite me back to the Hochschule, where he played for me some sketches for a song ballet based on the seven sins of Christian theology – extraordinary stuff. I borrowed a clarinet, and together we made music based on his music for an hour or so. I was in good form; he was appreciative, and wondered aloud if I could realize my spontaneous inspirations during performance, in a formal composition. But I know I am no composer.

In the evening, a party at Brecht's. Mostly old friends, including Kurt, and welcoming enough. They did not know what to make of me. I was not in uniform, but they sensed the   transformation. And my own reactions to them? Their conversation, which I once thought sophisticated and substantial, seemed to me trivial and empty. Brecht prated on and on and on about revolution, as if bloodshed were only a word one reads in a book. Of course, he has no interest in the plight of that poor Jewish woman this morning. He never does. None of them do.

A week before, my platoon had assumed the point role in an exercise to capture a bridge. We succeeded. I earned a commendation. I thought the satisfaction was not much different than a triumph in a boy's game at Uppingham, and smiled at myself for taking so much pleasure in the modest achievement. But last night this puerile feat seemed more of the moment than anything Brecht had to say. I even felt a nostalgia for the rude simplicity of the barracks I left. Of course – I smile as I write this – when I am back in Dresden,

I will miss the soft sheets and maid service at the Adlon. There is no fully pleasing the inner man.

Some of the girls were intrigued by the presence of a creature as exotic as an officer-candidate in their midst. One of them, Theresa, whom I had known only slightly before, came home with me. A pleasant night, and she left only a while ago, on good terms. But the encounter left me hollow and restless. When one is in the grip of barracks fever, it is easy to forget how much more one wants and needs from a woman than simply the physical satisfaction . . .

-

September 3, 1931
Office of the Assistant Secretary of War
Washington D.C.

Officer-candidate Kari von Haydenreich
c/o Reichswehr Headquarters
Berlin, Germany

Dear Karl,

Congratulations on attaining your 21st birthday! Welcome to manhood, as I have already welcomed you to the brotherhood of arms . . .

. . . [Y]ou might not have known that the trust created by your father's will gives me the power to continue the trust until your 30th birthday, if I conclude you are still too young to assume full responsibility for your own affairs. I wrote to Dr. Schacht, the financial trustee, on this issue. We are both in agreement that such an extension would be nonsense. You will always have the benefit of my friendship and advice, but this day forward, you will be fully responsible for your own affairs.

I do think it would be a good idea for you to meet with the Neustrelitz managers as soon as practicable . . .

Your friend,

Ike

-

November 23, 1931
Regimental barracks
Dresden, Germany

From the Journals of Karl von Haydenreich (Published 1986):

. . . [A] nice note today from Claus, one of my second cousins in Munich. He asks me to join him and six others in an ensemble at a wedding ceremony, to take place on the first day of the new year. The groom is from another Munich musical family, with the name 'Heydrich'.

I am happy to accept . . .

Excerpt from: *A Twentieth Century Life*
Albert Sommerville
Houghton, Mifflin (1959)

. . . [B]etween my studies and Karl's military obligations, I did not visit with Karl until late November of 1931, when I accompanied my father as his secretary to a conference in Munich. (My older brother was already too far gone in the dipsomania that ravaged his life to be of any use.) At the same time, Karl took leave to come down and meet with the managerial staff of the Neustrelitz resort, the ones who in fact conducted its day-to-day business.

The conference I attended was with like-minded, eminent personages from Germany and Great Britain, all concerned with stemming the rising tide of Bolshevism and firmly maintaining the Teutonic-Anglo-Saxon tradition. The topic was the meteoric rise of the National Socialist Party and Adolf Hitler, and what uses might be made of that phenomenon. No one present had any real regard for Hitler. He was viewed by all as a crude, simplistic man, totally unfit for any actual responsibility. Yet there was no question he had been able to galvanize a mass movement that had the potential to become both a bulwark against Yiddish Bolshevism and a force for racial purity. The topic of the conference was methods to exploit the movement itself, while maintaining control of its leader. Any number of useful, constructive proposals were broached and debated.

I described all this forthrightly to Karl later when we met. I knew he did not agree with the politics, but I was surprised that he viewed Hitler in a totally different light than the conference. '*He is too egotistical to be anyone's catspaw,*' he said, '*and far more cunning than you and your friends realize. You underestimate the danger.*'

History, of course, is the judge of which of us was correct. But then I asked a question that had perplexed me during the conference. Considering what I knew Karl believed, why was the Neustrelitz resort one of the major financial supporters of the Nazi Party? (Dr. Schacht had mentioned this in passing.) His look of incredulous horror was so spontaneous and natural it was unintentionally comic. I burst out laughing.

'You mean my money is paying for the shithead's motorcar and aeroplane?' he sputtered. *'Surely you are joking.'*

'I'm afraid I'm quite serious,' I laughed.

His first impulse was to cancel the monthly donations at once. But in that spirit in which friendship triumphs over any petty matter, I suggested he was far wiser to continue the donations without change, keeping his own private views as private as possible. He began to object, then became thoughtful. At the end, this was the course of action he decided to adopt.

This was natural enough advice – yet I have come to regret the giving of it as much as anything I have done in my life. The road that cost me the companionship of my dearest friend was a long one, with many twisting turns. Yet I believe the first step was taken that day, with that throwaway remark.

I had with me a companion whose name I will not divulge, as she has gone on to a quiet life and a stately marriage. I planned to continue on to Neustrelitz after the conference, for some winter sports, courtesy of Karl's generosity. I knew Karl would not be with me. He went there as infrequently as he possibly could. But I was surprised that Karl had not brought anyone with him. It made for an awkward threesome on occasion. He told me in confidence that he had become weary of sexual escapades for their own sake, and was in search of something that was more than mere adventure.

This was less than six weeks before he met Elizabeth. I do not believe that was a coincidence. I believe Fate speaks in that way.

-

December 14, 1931
Regimental barracks
Dresden, Germany

From the Journals of Karl von Haydenreich (Published 1986):

. . . Christ! Damnation! I am well and truly shat upon! I learn today that the wedding is not in Munich, but in Grossenbrode, far up on the Baltic Coast! Claus did not mention that little fact – deliberately, I would bet!

So now I must look forward to a ten-hour train ride on New Year's Eve . . .

1932

-

January 2, 1932
Regimental barracks
Dresden, Germany

From the Journals of Karl von Haydenreich (Published 1986):

As the poet said, 'so fair and foul a day I have not seen'. It is yesterday to which I refer.

The foul? I attended the worst wedding in the world.

The fair? Elizabeth! All the foulness dazzled away in an instant!

I left Munich at noon, and arrived at Grossenbrode at 10:00 that evening. The next day is when the foul began, at the church. Swastikas and Brown Shirts everywhere! Good God, what had I gotten myself into?! It seems the bridegroom Reinhard is a ranking member of the Nazi elite, and his bride is an even more fervent supporter of that cause. His groomsmen could not even assemble in the church, for they are all wanted men. But the police could not easily intervene in the cemetery. So it was there these S.A. and S.S. Nazis formed up an honor guard, dressed in white shirts and black trousers.

The bride and groom proceeded into the church between these two abysmal caricatures of military lines, parading as if they were being saluted by a royal brigade. Then the pastor (another Nazi) preached a Nazi sermon. Once the vows were exchanged, the bride and groom left the church to the strains of . . . not Mendelssohn (no Jewish music here!), but the Horst Wessel song! Outside the church, the police closed in. Several of the groomsmen were arrested, as their own anthem played. It was an absolute farce, straight out of comic opera! I only wish Kurt could have seen it.

Of course, they'd brought along their banners and flags. They could not display them at the church. But there they were throughout the banquet hall, a sea of crimson red and swastikas. Then Reinhard Heydrich re-appeared in his new S.S. uniform, a mess of shiny black and silver colors. When he presented himself, his superior, one Heinrich Himmler, announced his promotion to some new rank in the S.S., and all cheered. Every mention of the name '*Hitler*' drew louder cheers.

Worse. Who should be seated among the most honored guests, but my old uncle and trustee Frederic Breslau, not caring a fig that his hosts and the Nazi pastor describe his friends and family as germs, vermin, and worse. (As

185

for the Nazis, I suppose if you lend them money enough, they don't care who your grandfather was.) I took this as an omen. The gods were directing me to take my leave as soon as possible. I cased my instruments, bade my farewells, and I would have left . . . but then . . .

I caught sight of the most enchanting girl I had ever seen. She was seated with an older couple, likely her parents, the three alone at a small table, stiff and uncomfortable, speaking to no one. Her hair was bobbed, short, and blonde, with lively blue eyes, and a pert nose. Even seated, in a trim, formal grey dress, the grace of her slim figure was apparent. She looked about the room, with an alert, disapproving intelligence.

I could not tear my eyes away. She declined all offers to dance or celebrate. Even so, I had to take my chance. I put down my case and approached her table.

She at first declined my invitation. But I made it clear I was not of the same company as the wedding party. Perhaps, too, she noticed the abject, beseeching look in my eye. In any case, she looked to her father for consent, who granted it with a curt nod. Her voice was pure music, as enchanting as everything else about her. I led her to a waltz, that I conducted with appropriate formality, and was able to say a bit more. To hold her in my arms was heaven. She seemed to warm to me a bit, or perhaps this was my fervid imagination. Then I felt an imperious tap on my shoulder.

It was Heydrich, in his uniform. He had taken it upon himself to remind me that I was a hired musician and not one of the guests. I should have known he was that type. Paying a Roland for an Oliver, I informed him that I was an officer-candidate on leave, that I had joined the performance as a favor to family, and stated my name and title. Rarely do I do this, but it gave me great pleasure to embarrass him in front of his guests.

'*I do not believe you,*' he said, with incredible rudeness. I felt my ears go red, for the insult was intolerable, particularly before the girl. Fortunately, others in the throng who had recognized me corrected him on the spot. Even my uncle, with no little reluctance, vouched for me. Heydrich knew then that he was in the wrong, and an apology was due.

'*I regret my remark,*' he said, in a tone that was not regretful at all, glared at me, turned on his heel, and rejoined the wedding table. Rage inflamed me. I took two steps after him – I am myself no longer a soft man. Then I remembered the greater thing.

186

Disaster! The girl and her family were gone, embarrassed, or had seen enough. I felt that all light had fled the world. My devastation was so complete and obvious, that an older woman seated next to the abandoned table summoned me over with a gesture. *'Would I like to know the name of the girl and her family?'* she asked with a smile. She did not know me, but enjoyed assisting young love. This angel of mercy was not a friend of the family, but they had introduced themselves to her.

Thus I learned her name – Elizabeth Golsing, and that she is – Glory be to God! – a Munchener! They live in the Harlaching district. Her father is a respected jurist. My new friend did not know more than this, but it is enough. I have already written my agents in Munich to find out her residential address. I must see her again!

Then I bid my musician companions farewell and left. Heydrich fixed me with another look as I packed my clarinet. I met his glare with one of my own. I would that I was charitable enough to wish bride and groom happiness. But in truth I am not. May they both go to the Devil, with Hitler and all their Nazi friends!

So that was the fair and foul day, and the fair part worth an infinity of foulness. I must see Elizabeth again! What will I do if she rejects me? Ah, I cannot endure the thought!

-

January 28, 1932
Harlaching District,
Munich, Germany

Herr Karl von Haydenreich
Company Headquarters
Dresden, Germany

Dear Officer Haydenreich,

I have received your letter of January 15th. Of course, I remember the dance we briefly shared at the wedding of Lina van Oten. Thank you for the many fine compliments.

However, I would never permit a member of a family notorious for its support of the Nazi Party, and its contemptible anti-Semitism, to call upon me. Please find another young woman on whom to bestow your attention.

Sincerely,

Fraulein Elizabeth Golsing

-

February 2nd, 1932
Regimental barracks
Dresden, Germany

Fraulein Elizabeth Golsing
Grunwalder Strasse 16
Munich, Germany

Dear Fraulein Golsing,

I implore you with all my strength to allow me to call on you, on your whole family, to give my explanations on the subject of Nazis and other matters. Were the matter not so serious, were my heart not so torn, I could even find humor in this turn of events. In the interest of brevity, I will simply state that I am not one with my family on the matter of either the Nazi Party or our valuable Jewish fellow citizens – nor were my father, mother, or stepmother. I regard Adolf Hitler as a despicable person.

I beg you to permit me to make my explanations, not simply to you, but to your parents, to your entire family. If you do not grant me such a privilege, I will go my way in the manner of a gentleman, but treasuring always the memory of our one, brief dance. Whatever befalls, I will store those precious moments in the sacred keep of my heart.

Very truly yours,
Your true friend,
Karl von Haydenreich

-

February 11, 1932
Regimental barracks
Dresden, Germany

From the Journals of Karl von Haydenreich (Published 1986):

An odd day.

It began in the field, with small force maneuvers. My company was assigned the task of storming and securing an entrenched field battery position. Despite the cold, it was an interesting exercise to which my men responded with enthusiasm. We had made all preparations for the assault, when a messenger arrived, summoning me to field headquarters.

At first, I thought this was an element of the exercise. But I was greeted by a member of von Blomberg's staff, a Major Kurt Spielbauer, and a man in plain clothes named Muller. I was invited to take a seat. Thereafter, for a good thirty minutes, perhaps longer, I was subjected to intense questioning about my political attitudes. What did I think of the present state of affairs in Germany? The Communists? The Social Democrats? The Steel Helmets? The Nazis? Whom did I support for Chancellor?

I realized then I was being subjected to a political vetting of some sort. As the questioning went on, it became clearer still that this was being done on behalf of the Nazi Party. The interview was thus completely illegal. However, if von Blomberg was behind it, there was nothing to be gained by protest. Under these circumstances, I felt no obligation to be truthful. I remembered Albert's advice about the donations. I emphasized my loyalty to the Army and my belief in the importance of its political neutrality. I did not say anything outrageously false. But I did – deliberately – give the impression of sympathy. The man in the plain clothes surprised me by asking about my presence at the Beer Hall Putsch nine years before, and my membership in the Nazi Party. This astonished me. I would not have thought anyone remembered. But not so.

Then the interview was over, the two men thanked me for my time, and apologized for interrupting my training.

What does this mean? I am completely baffled.

–

February 13, 1932
Harlaching District,
Munich, Germany

Herr Karl von Haydenreich
Company Headquarters
Dresden, Germany

Dear Officer von Haydenreich,

Your letter did intrigue me. There is one member of my family who believes we should hear your explanations. If Sunday, March 6, three weeks from the posting of this letter, is convenient for you, we will expect you at about 1:00, after luncheon.

I look forward to meeting you again, and hearing whatever it is you have to say.

Sincerely,
Fraulein Elizabeth Golsing

–

February 13, 1932
Berlin, Germany

189

SD File No. 112384
Subject: Haydenreich, Karl von
Report on interview conducted February 11, 1932

On February 11, I conducted an interview with Officer-Candidate Karl von Haydenreich at the field headquarters of his company outside Dresden. Present also was Major Kurt Spielbauer of the staff of Brigadier General Werner von Blomberg.

Von Haydenreich gave guarded, but entirely satisfactory answers to all questions. In particular, he emphasized the profundity of the impression that his presence at the Munich Putsch had made upon him. He also volunteered the fact that his father had been the commanding officer of the Fuhrer in the Great War, and had commented on the enduring memory his father had of the Fuhrer's singularity and resolve.

The subject seems politically reliable in all respects. Major Spielbauer concurs. He seems well fit for the assignment Herr Major General von Blomberg has in mind.

Respectfully,

Agent Heinrich Muller, S. D.

(Handwritten note appended)

Keep a watchful eye on this one. I don't trust him. R. Heydrich

-

March 7, 1932
Regimental barracks
Dresden, Germany

From the Journals of Karl von Haydenreich (Published 1986):

. . .[I] arrived at the Golsing home precisely at 1:00, not wishing to be early and not knowing how the family regarded fashionable tardiness. A maid showed me to the front parlor, where the family sat seated – father, mother, older brother, and Elizabeth. She was not as beautiful as I remembered her, but even more interesting and alert. We introduced ourselves formally, father, Paul, mother, Margaret, older brother, Martin, and Elizabeth. I accepted a cup of tea.

I had decided there was no other course for me but the full truth. I am a terrible liar in any case. I told the four of them forthrightly of my life – of my father, of my mother Charlotte, of Mummi, my sister Lena, of the terrible days in 1919, my grandfather, my presence at the Putsch, my education in England, the Hochschule, my decision to become an officer, and the reasons for it. I told them that there were many people, who (like me) despised Hitler, but very few

190

who knew him to be a coward and a fraud as I did. I told them my family's support of the Nazi Party was done by my family, mostly by my grandfather and my trustees, without my knowledge or consent.

I paused, about to continue, when Margaret spoke.

'*Karl, you should know I was the one who suggested to Elizabeth we should hear you out. I knew your mother, and father, and Rosamunde Breslau, quite well. I was part of their set when Heinz was in Munich in 1905, though not one of the main ones. They made quite a trio – Heinz and Lottie and Rosa, as we called her – the blonde princess and the dark princess. We all knew your father was wooing Charlotte. Rosamunde seemed quite content to play the part of friend and chaperone. None of us realized how keenly she felt her own disappointment until years later. But you know the story better than anyone.*'

I was overwhelmed. I have met so few persons outside the Neustrelitz household who knew my mother and Mummi. I was trying to collect my thoughts when she spoke again. '*Der tayvl iz nit azoy shvarts vi men molt im*' [The Devil is not as black as you paint him], she said, looking toward Elizabeth, and then laughed lightly at my surprise. '*We all learned a little Yiddish from Rosa.*'

I was amazed, but I could not just stand there, gaping like a dummy. I had to say something. '*I am – I mean – I don't - you have taken me completely by surprise, Frau Golsing. Der mentsh trakht un got lakht*' [Man plans and God laughs]. The whole family smiled. '*Mummi,*' I said, '*that's what I called her. Yiddish was our favorite.*'

Then Martin spoke, for the first time. '*Mit eyn tokhes ken men nit tantsn af tsvey khasenes*' [You can't dance at two weddings with one rump]. Margaret laughed, but the Judge pursed his lips. '*Really, Martin!*' Elizabeth said.

Somehow, finally, I was able to remind myself that I was a Reichswehr officer-candidate, and not a schoolboy. I recovered my composure. I thanked Margaret profusely, then added that I should like to call on her in any case, for in my adult life I have never met anyone who knew my mother Charlotte well. Mummi and Father told me stories of her, of course, but I was too young then.

Margaret smiled at me. '*I am quite certain that I am not the one on whom you wish to call, Karl.*' She turned to her husband. '*I could not believe that three such persons as Charlotte Eisen, Heinrich Haydenreich, and Rosamunde Breslau could produce a devotee of Adolf Hitler. It simply was not*

191

possible. Charlotte despised anti-Semites. Rosamunde was her best friend. Heinrich made his embarrassment at his family's attitude known to all. Your explanations' – she turned back to me – *'as well as your Yiddish – are close to what I expected. I am completely satisfied with them. Do you agree, Judge?'*

The father Werner looked directly at me. *'My wife does not always speak for both of us,'* he said, *'but in this case, she does. I knew your father, not as well socially as Margaret, but well enough to know that he was a man of honor and sense. I was perplexed by your apparent association with these . . . swine. I'm glad you have clarified the matter. I have no objection at all if you call on my daughter. Of course, the ultimate voice on the matter is that of Elizabeth herself.'*

Then he turned to his wife. *'Come, Mother. We have heard enough for today. It's time to leave the young people to themselves.'*

He rose on that word, and gave his arm to his wife. She smiled at me, and allowed her husband to escort her out of the room. Martin, Elizabeth, and I were left. Elizabeth met my eyes with a cool, implacable look.

'You may have persuaded Mother and Papa, Herr von Haydenreich,' she said evenly. *'I still have my doubts.'*

Then Martin leapt to his feet. *'Oh, do be truthful, Elli!'* he exclaimed. *'So strong, so handsome, so dignified!'* he continued, in a falsetto voice. *'O why, God, why does he have to be a Nazi?!'*

'Martin!' Elizabeth cried, turning beet red. But he did not hear her. He continued in the same falsetto voice, one joke and absurdity following another with the rapidity of a machine gun. He was no longer impersonating his sister, I realized, but some German girl created on the spur of the moment from his own imagination. He was overwhelmingly funny. I tried not to laugh, for fear of offending Elizabeth – but I could not help myself. Then I was relieved to see Elizabeth overcome with laughter herself.

Then abruptly he stopped and extended his hand. *'I'm Martin Golsing,'* he said in his natural voice, *'Elli's big brother. I had to let you know Elli is not quite as stern as she wishes to appear. Because I rather like you myself.'*

I shook his hand, still laughing. *'Come,'* I said, *'let me give you both dinner.'*

-

March 9, 1932
Harlaching District,
Munich, Germany

Herr Karl von Haydenreich
Company Headquarters
Munich, Germany

Dear Officer Haydenreich,

Thank you for the courteous visit you paid to me and my family on Sunday, and for the dinner you provided for my brother and myself. I will look forward to your next visit, if such should occur.

I must confide in you and trust your honor. While I am in no way betrothed, I have come to a certain understanding with a young man of my acquaintance. The understanding is not such that I cannot receive your visits. My family is not aware of this situation, so I must trust your discretion. But I would not be honorable myself if I did not inform you of this circumstance.

With fondest wishes,

Fraulein Elizabeth Golsing

-

March 11, 1932
Regimental barracks
Munich, Germany

From the Journals of Karl von Haydenreich (Published 1986):

Ah, girls . . . they use uncertainty like a dueling sword! Elizabeth writes that I may have a rival, or perhaps I do not – for what sort of understanding can this be, that permits her to receive other callers? And of which her family is unaware? A rather informal one, I would think.

Enough. No more. I silence the doubts of the inner voice with another letter to Elizabeth.

The days pass like centuries until I can see her again. Saturday awaits!

-

Excerpt from: A History of Germany in the Twentieth Century
Josef Behrens
Alfred A Knopf (1964)

. . . [D]uring 1932, repetitive elections plagued Germany. On March 13th, in the Presidential election, Hindenburg came ahead of all other candidates, with Hitler next. But he did not win a majority of the votes. A run-off election was scheduled on April 10th . . .

April 14, 1932
Regimental barracks
Munich, Germany

From the Journals of Karl von Haydenreich (Published 1986):

. . . [I] have never known anyone like Martin Golsing. He has an infinite wit, a genius for spontaneity, and not a serious bone in his body. Today we walked past the National Socialist Party headquarters on our way to the cinema. There were a few Brown Shirts outside. Hitler had finished second to Hindenburg, God be praised. They were disappointed men. Suddenly Martin put his two fingers to his upper lip, caricaturing Hitler's moustache, turned in their direction, and began an impassioned, improvised, utterly ludicrous speech in the unmistakably thick Austrian accent of Hitler, in which he blamed everything and everybody else for his defeat in the election.

Martin was incredibly funny, but Elizabeth and I could not laugh. The Nazis became infuriated, for Martin's jokes were deadly accurate. It was a lucky thing I was in uniform, or it might have come to a fight. As it was, they shook their fists and shouted their own curses – utterly humorless pigs.

Afterwards, Elizabeth was furious with him. *'These are dangerous men,'* she said, *'and brutes. You must not mock them.'* I added my own cautions, for in this Elizabeth was right. He should not take such risks. But Martin is completely fearless. *'Why should they complain?'* was his rejoinder. *'I mock the Communists as well.'* And so he does.

I have become inordinately fond of him. If I did not already have a best friend, Martin would be that person. He is always brimming with fun and high spirits. Elizabeth adores him, as does his mother. With one exception, everyone he meets delights in him.

The one exception is his father, the Judge. The Judge is a good man, even something of a Social Democrat, but ponderous. Everyone, including wife and friends, call him 'Judge'. He cannot accept that his daughter, three years the younger, is his serious child, and his son's gift is for lightness and mirth. Elizabeth has the loftiest plans for an eminent career in law and beyond, while . . . Martin? I doubt he has any plans beyond next week. There is also the fact that he is one of those who has little or no interest in girls. I believe this troubles the Judge so much he does not admit the fact to himself. But I met enough of that sort in Berlin to know and not to care.

194

A good thing, that I like him as much as I do, for it is the strict rule of the family that Martin must accompany Elizabeth whenever I am with her. She apparently has no disagreement with this. Do I have a rival or not? On the one hand, she is warm and supple in my arms when I dance with her, and takes my hand without hesitation. She seems always free to meet me. On the other hand, she seems perfectly satisfied to share my company with her brother. We have no more than the chance moment or two alone, with which she seems to be content. I most certainly am not.

But I have lost my heart to Elizabeth, and that is that. I have never met anyone in the least like her, with her own brand of high spirits, her fierce ambition, and her own special, unique intelligence. I will not give up my passion for her.

And I will succeed.

April 16, 1932
Regimental barracks
Dresden, Germany

From the Journals of Karl von Haydenreich (Published 1986):

. . . [H]eard some gossip today about Heydrich, my 'friend' from the wedding at Grossenbrode. Evidently a capable enough naval officer, but lacking any moral sense. He behaved so dishonorably to a young woman to whom he was betrothed that he was court martialed. Having no prospects anywhere else, he became a Nazi, and the worst kind, high in the ranks of the S.S. He is already infamous among those brutes for his coldness.

A real piece of pig shit, in short. It is odd how one can sometimes sense such qualities, at slightest acquaintance . . .

April 28, 1932
Regimental barracks
Dresden, Germany

From the Journals of Karl von Haydenreich (Published 1986):

. . . [W]hen we returned to her home, Martin unexpectedly made his farewells as quickly as he could and vanished with a last joke. He had never done that before. For the first time, I was alone with Elizabeth.

I seized the opportunity he'd given me. I took her hand and pulled her to me. She gasped, but came into my arms. '*You are so bold,*' she whispered, but then I kissed her fully, once and then again. All at once, she was kissing

195

me, passionately, my mouth, neck, face, repeatedly, as if she could not help herself. This was wonderful – but even as I felt her eagerness, I sensed that these were strange sensations for her, passions that confused her as much as pleased her. I just held her, trembling in my arms, for a moment.

'*Please understand, I do not know what came over me,*' she said. '*This is not typical of me.*' Then she looked up at me, still in my embrace, and I could see real fear in her eyes.

'*Please tell me,*' she said, '*that you are not trifling with me. That I am not just another girl.*'

'*You are not just another girl,*' I answered. '*You are the only girl. Upon my soul.*'

'*Then for my part, I will tell you that I informed my other friend this week that we no longer have an understanding. I do not mean by this*' – she could see the delight in my eyes – '*that I have made a choice of any sort. Only that I should like to be free to make one, without any inhibition, if a time comes when I am presented with one.*'

At that, her father could be heard, summoning her into the depths of the house. There was only time for a farewell, a squeeze of the hand, and a parting kiss. Then I was out the door.

As I moved down the sidewalk, Martin stood up from the bench where he had been waiting. '*I thought tonight for once I would not be the perfect chaperone,*' he said. '*I hope you made good use of the opportunity.*'

'*Thank you,*' I answered. '*We did.*'

'*But I must warn you,*' he continued, '*if you hurt my little sister – worse, if you should break Elli's heart – I will give you a thrashing you will never in your life forget.*' Martin is at least two inches shorter than I, far more slender, nor has he had the benefit of any military training. But he was not joking in this matter, as deadly serious as only a jester can be when he becomes serious. For a moment, I did not know what to say.

Then I clapped him on the shoulder. '*A fine way to speak to your future brother-in-law,*' I said, giving him his own sort of answer. Then I grinned at him, and walked on to the station.

This was a wonderful day.

-

Excerpt from: *A General Speaks - the Autobiography of Kurt von Hammerstein Equord*

Major General Kurt von Hammerstein Equord
Reichswehr Press (1986)

... [T]he possibility of assigning von Haydenreich to the Abwehr was first mentioned by von Blomberg, in a private conversation with me during a break in a staff conference in the spring of 1932.

The domination of foreign intelligence by Naval officers had been a concern of the Reichswehr for some time. Karl von Haydenreich's linguistic skills and his education abroad made him ideal for the Abwehr. But I was quite sure von Blomberg had other motives beside the benefits to the Reichswehr. He did not hide the sympathy he felt for Adolf Hitler and the Nazi Party. I was certain that the suggestion had been prompted by the Party.

But I did not oppose the proposal. I had my own opinion of Karl von Haydenreich. Von Blomberg may have had his plans. I had plans of my own. The worsening climate of German politics, and particularly the increasing public acceptance of Hitler, had become a grave concern of mine. In reaction, I had begun to assemble a cadre of officers of impeccable honor and loyalty to the larger German State. I did not foresee rebellion or revolution, let alone the events of 1936. I simply wished to create a core of officers who could be trusted not to be corrupted by the Nazis. My view of Karl von Haydenreich was that a young man of his intelligence and capability would be a valuable addition to my group.

So I had my reasons and von Blomberg had his.

June 16, 1932
Regimental barracks
Dresden, Germany

From the Journals of Karl von Haydenreich (Published 1986):

... [I]'m in a daze ...

I escorted Elizabeth and Martin to the last of the lectures before her examinations. The subject, on the alteration of some aspects of German family law by the Reformation, was interesting. But it was more enlightening to see the seriousness with which Elizabeth addressed her questions to the lecturer, and the respect that they received. Clearly, she was regarded as a scholar to be reckoned with. She has set lofty goals for herself, this love of mine, and not without reason.

Then to dinner, and dancing at a jazz club of my acquaintance. It was hard to reconcile the bright, laughing girl in my arms with the dedicated student

197

of two hours before, but they were one and the same. Martin danced with several girls, never the same one twice, and amused almost everyone with his constant stream of wit. Almost everyone – there were the inevitable glowers from the Nazis in our midst. Martin didn't care.

Then I brought her home. Martin vanished, as has become his custom, and Elizabeth was in my arms even before the door had closed – as has become our custom. We were as passionate as usual, then suddenly, with no special indication . . . more so. Her breath came in shorter gasps, her hands clutched at my back and neck. I realized then that she had surrendered, or was prepared to.

'So,' she breathed, '*tonight you are to be Napoleon? And I am to surrender?*'

Thus, the question was upon me – not an easy one – what were we to be to each other? What consequence? I have felt the powerful pull of my own flesh from the start. The yearning to possess her as a man has bedeviled my nights and haunted my days. Now, on this night, she was of the same mind, and mine to take.

Yet, in loving her I have come to know her well. On this night, she might surrender her honor to me with free, wild passion. On the morrow, she would be consumed with doubt and bitter self-recrimination. She is more curious about my student life in Berlin than I would like. She still wonders if I am nothing but a clever Lothario, and she my next intended conquest. These doubts would become an agony of second thought if I proceeded as Napoleon.

Yet I could not pretend that we had not reached a point where a decision of some kind was required. In that moment, I knew what it had to be.

I drew back a bit, which surprised her. '*I want you,*' I said, '*more than anything. But not as your lover. As my wife.*'

Elizabeth released herself from my embrace and pulled back on the couch. Her wonderful face shone pale in the darkness. She searched for breath. '*Karl,*' she gulped, '*do I understand you? You are proposing marriage to me?*'

'*Yes,*' I said, going forward in the only way it was possible to go forward. '*I love you. There is no one else for me but you. There will never be anyone else. Will you marry me?*'

'*Karl,*' she whispered, '*please get me a glass of water. I feel very faint.*' I rose and got the water, and some for myself – I felt faint as well. (What had I done?) After she had drunk and recovered herself, she spoke.

'*You must know the direction of my heart,*' she said. '*But I cannot give you an answer until you have spoken to my father.*'

'*Of course,*' I said. '*But please – do not request this of me if it is to be an exercise in futility. Give me reason to hope.*'

At this, she bestowed on me the smile that is the food of the gods. '*I thought you knew the direction of my heart well enough that I did not have to say,*' she said gently. '*Of course, speak to my father. You have every reason to hope.*'

With that, I took her hand, and our minds and hearts were one in that moment. An odd thing, then – the enormity of the undertaking we had just made dawned on both of us, and drove all passion into the void. The chastity that had been a scourge and torment a moment before was now the natural order of the world. I told Elizabeth I would speak to her father on the next leave, as there was no time left on this one. She nodded, kissed me lightly, then took her leave, and went upstairs, as overwhelmed as me. I wrote a short note to the Judge, to the effect that I wished to speak to him the next time I called. (He will surely deduce what it is I mean to discuss.)

I left the note on the front table, then found my coat and saw myself to the door. As I made to leave, Elizabeth suddenly reappeared at the stairs, half dressed, and raced across the room. She flung herself into my arms, and kissed me with a passion and violence that I had not dreamed existed in the world.

'*Why?*' I said, confused.

'*Because you deserve a much better kiss than the last one,*' she breathed. '*I love you.*' Then she turned and ran upstairs as rapidly as she had run down.

So. I am secretly – for the moment – betrothed – and not a little dazed. Is it really so simple? Is the future decided as easily as this? In an evening, on a kiss? It seems unnaturally straightforward. Should I be anxious about the easiness of all this? Or am I one of those luckless louts, destined always to doubt and second-guess his good fortune? Ah, me . . .

--

June 22, 1932
Neustrelitz, Bavaria

Mister Albert Sommerville
Sommersby and Smith
London, England

Dear Forlorn Bachelor,

. . . [B]ig news and little. I shall start with the little.

This past week, I have completed the two years of ordinary military training. As of Tuesday, I will be a sergeant, an officer of the non-commissioned type. Next is the fabled war college, for both general and specialized officer's training. Signals and communications is the branch for which I feel most apt, and the Reichswehr apparently agrees. Normally this is undertaken in the course of assignment to a battalion. We shall see where fate takes me – not too far from Munich, I hope!

So much for the little news.

The Big News I indicated in the salutation. But details must wait until I have a meeting with someone's father. You can guess . . .

Your friend,

Karl

-

Excerpt from: *A History of Germany in the Twentieth Century*
Josef Behrens
Alfred A Knopf (1964)

. . . [I]f the United States had managed to restore its own economy, and with it the flow of credit to the German Republic, the situation might have stabilized. But the New World was caught in a crisis of its own – perhaps not one as grave as the German, because of the stability of its institutions, but a grave one nonetheless. Unemployment skyrocketed. Business investments sank to catastrophic lows. Breadlines stretched out over city blocks in many major cities.

In many urban areas, the dispossessed and impoverished gathered together in shanty towns, which were derisively named 'Hoovervilles'. Perhaps the saddest of these was in Washington D.C. itself, where some 43,000 men, veterans of the Great War, came directly to the nation's capital to demand early payment of a bonus the Congress had promised for joining the Army. They called themselves the Bonus Army. A large and embarrassing Hooverville came to exist in the same environment as the federal government.

The House of Representatives passed the measure, but it failed the Senate. The Bonus Army refused to leave. Ultimately, the group had to be dispersed by force, by the same army of which they had been part only 15 years earlier . . .

-

Excerpt from: *My Name is Ike - Reflections on Fifty Years of Service as Soldier and Statesman*

200

. . . I faced the gravest crisis to that point in my career in the summer of 1932. A number of good men, some of whom I am sure I had once commanded, down on their luck and desperate, formed what they called a Bonus Army, and camped out in Washington until a bonus they'd been promised for wartime service was paid. It wasn't due for a few years, but it was then, in 1932, that they needed the money. The House of Representatives saw the rightness of that, and passed a bill. But the stuffed shirts in the Senate wouldn't go along. The poor ex-doughboys got nothing.

Then things got sad and ugly. The Bonus Army refused to leave. The government sent the police out, to make the men disperse, but there weren't nearly enough of them to do the job. The Attorney General had the bright idea of them being dispersed by the Army. Douglas MacArthur, the highest-ranking officer in the Army, took personal charge of the affair. Up to that point, he and I had been friends. In fact, I was one of his protégés.

But not then. I told him straight out that he was making a horrible mistake in taking on the assignment. I also told him there was no way I was going to participate in what I knew would be a fiasco, or worse. MacArthur fixed me with one of those looks he had, and found someone else to do the job. A major named George Patton took the command.

When the troops first appeared, the men in the Bonus Army cheered. They thought their old comrades were coming to support them. But then the martinet Patton ordered a cavalry charge. He had the infantry fix bayonets and go after these men, who were nothing more than American soldiers who needed a break. He used tear gas and other weapons of war to get them moving. He succeeded, but he disgraced himself at the same time. The streets were lined with spectators who saw all this, mostly government workers come out of their offices to watch. You could hear them all yelling '*Shame! Shame!*' – and they were right.

General MacArthur had a lot of fine qualities, but respecting someone for standing up to him on principle was not one of them. That was particularly the case when he was being roasted in the newspapers – nor did it help that I'd warned him, and I'd been right. I found myself summoned to his office for a royal dressing down. I was also told that if I had any sense I'd look for a career for myself out of the Army – because I had no future in any army that he commanded – and he intended to be commander for a long, long time.

I left the office, shaken to my roots. I was a soldier. I had no wish to be anything but a soldier. I talked it over with Mamie that night, and we both agreed that simply leaving the Army would be foolish and even cowardly. I'd been in the right, not Doug MacArthur. We were going to stay. But it did mean I had to find some assignment that would keep me out of MacArthur's path to the extent possible.

It was that path that led me to my destiny in Germany.

-

June 29, 1932
Regimental barracks
Munich, German

From the Journals of Karl von Haydenreich (Published 1986)

. . . [T]he Judge opened the door and invited me into his study. Elizabeth, Martin, and Margaret waited in the large room outside.

'*So you wish to marry my daughter?*' He said. '*And she, you?*'

'*Yes, sir,*' I said.

'*You are both youthful,*' he continued, '*but old enough to know your own minds. I am aware of your financial circumstances. I do not need reassurance about your ability to support a family. And I have made my own assessment of your character. I have no doubts on that point, either.*'

I almost sighed my relief. But then he continued. '*Before I give my consent,*' he said, '*I do have two questions for you.*' I became alert again. '*The first is what you intend to do with your life. I understand that the present crisis drew you into the Reichswehr. But do you intend to make a career of it? What happens when the crisis is over?*'

'*I don't plan a life in the Army,*' I answered. '*When – or if – Germany returns to a normal state of affairs, I will resign my commission as soon as it is honorable to do so. What comes next I don't know. My father was a diplomat in service to Prince Rupprecht – perhaps public service of that type. What is certain is that I won't return to musical studies, or content myself with managing the resort. How Elizabeth is faring in her legal career will make a great deal of difference.*'

He nodded in agreement. '*An honest answer,*' he said, '*and that is quite sufficient.*'

'*The second question,*' he said, '*is more pointed. You explained how your estate's support of the Nazis was begun without your consent or*

202

knowledge. But I am curious whether you have cut off that support since you discovered the truth.'

'No, sir,' I said, '*I have not. The reason –*'

He held up his hand to stay me. '*I can guess the reason. You see no reason to turn all your cards face up at this time. You feel you may do better service to the nation if your true opinions remain a personal matter. Is that accurate?*'

'*Yes, sir,*' I answered. '*I hope that does not cause a problem.*'

'*Not at all,*' he replied. '*This is exactly what I would do in your situation. You are under neither legal nor moral obligation to disclose such matters to these creatures. But it does mean I will require an undertaking from you. There is going to be a parliamentary election in another month, and I believe Hitler and his friends are going to do very well. Are you familiar with the poet Dante?*'

'*As a historical figure? Yes, sir.*' I was a bit confused. '*But I am not familiar with his work.*'

'*At one point in the Inferno, he compares the city of Florence, with its constant political shifts, to a sick man twisting on a pallet. What is true for men is true for nations. A sick man or nation in great distress can mistake a deadly poison for a healing medicine. I believe that is happening. I think Hitler and the Nazis are going to come to power, and their rule will be far more poisonous than any of us can imagine.*'

'*I hope you are wrong,*' I answered.

'*I hope so, too,*' he said, '*but if I am right, you may find yourself playing a very dangerous game, among brutal, vicious men — men who possess no honor or integrity, or respect for those who do. My daughter is a very courageous and committed young woman. I could only wish my son shared those qualities.*' I would have liked to tell him how wrong he was, but this was not the time.

'*The same honor that compels a man to oppose these brutes also compels him to keep his loved ones as far from harm as possible. Do you share that view?*'

'*Yes, sir,*' I answered. I knew where he was going

'*Elizabeth is a bright and courageous girl. She would in all likelihood insist on sharing these dangers with you,*' he continued, '*if she knew of them. What you must promise me is that you will not allow that to happen – under any circumstance – no matter how she insists, or what you may say to her – you will not share any of these risks with her.'*

'*That is an easy undertaking to give,*' I answered. '*Of course.*'

'*I mean,*' he emphasized, '*even if that means lying to Elizabeth directly to her face. No matter what promises you make to her, the one made to me is the one I require you to honor.*'

'*I understood you,*' I said. '*You have my word.*'

The Judge then arose from his chair, and came around his desk. '*Then,*' he said, '*you have my consent. It is up to Elizabeth to make her decision.*'

We left his study, and went into the next room. I did indulge myself in a bit of theater then. I did not say a single word to the anxious faces, but simply took Elizabeth by the hand and led her into the parlor. Before she could reproach me, I sank to one knee.

'*Elizabeth Golsing, will you marry me? Will you do me the honor to become my wife?*'

She was caught between tears and laughter. '*Karl – I – do you love me, Karl? As I do you?*'

'*Till the end of time,*' I answered. '*And beyond.*'

'*Then yes!*' she said, '*yes!*' and pulled me to my feet. '*A thousand times, yes!*'

Then the house became a festival of joy and celebration. I had brought with me a ring, which delighted Elizabeth – and which naturally didn't fit. We shall take care of it on the next leave.

-

Excerpt from: A History of Germany in the Twentieth Century
Josef Behrens
Alfred A Knopf (1964)

. . . [T]he Presidential election and run-off were followed only three months later by Parliamentary elections. Hitler scoured the country, by car and – a novelty – aeroplane. The National Socialist program was as always vague to the point of indecipherable, but it promised action and renewal.

On July 31st, German voters gave the Nazi Party its largest plurality yet. It became the largest Party in the Reichstag, though not yet a majority.

-

Excerpt from: A Twentieth Century Life
Albert Sommerville
Houghton, Mifflin (1959)

. . . [K]arl requested that I act as best man at his wedding, which task I accepted immediately. At the same time, he invited me to Munich in mid-August, to meet his bride and prospective in-laws. He took rooms for the two of us for the duration.

This was my first meeting with the woman who would one day become the formidable Elizabeth Whittingham, simultaneously my archenemy and my best friend, Karl's wife and widow, and the mother of his children. Whatever differences in ideology have divided us, we have always been united in grief and an aching sense of loss. Nothing in our first meeting foretold any of this. I encountered a charming young woman, with sparkling good looks and a lively wit, that did not entirely conceal a keen intelligence and seriousness of purpose. I could appreciate her fine qualities and congratulate Karl on his bride-to-be, without being in the least bit jealous. I have always preferred my female companions to be a bit more frivolous and not so heavily endowed with brains as Elizabeth.

I also met Martin, her brother. We became fast friends instantly. That was the usual outcome on meeting Martin. He was a constant bubbling fountain of jokes and hilarity, in perpetual motion – an utterly delightful person. We three young men dubbed ourselves the Three Musketeers for the fortnight, and engaged in all sorts of fun. Truth be told, the third musketeer was as often Elizabeth as it was Karl. He had to spend considerable time preparing for examinations that might save him a full year at the War College. We spent a few days at Neustrelitz, but he did not accompany us there. In any case, it was a wonderful fortnight.

Karl had asked me to lay my political convictions to one side when we were with Elizabeth's family. Indeed, I did have to bite my tongue on occasion, what with the continual praise of all things universal, and German Jewry in particular. But this was not quite the exercise in self-discipline that it otherwise might have been. The difference in perception of Hitler and the National Socialist movement that split the British Imperial Party was beginning to become apparent.

From the start, I had looked askance at the degree of thuggery and sheer brutality in the Nazi Party. It is one thing to insist on the importance of Empire and the continued dominance of the European peoples over the less worthy races of the world. It is quite another to countenance street brawls, window breaking, and the harassment of girls and old women on street corners. That summer, von Papen, the Chancellor, had ended a prohibition on demonstrations by Hitler's Brown Shirts, the Sturmabteilung, or S.A. The result had been continual clashes with the Bolsheviks, and any number of utterly disgraceful incidents of hooliganism and petty cruelty. These were all reported in the press, with the usual scandalmongering, certainly, but founded on too much truth to be easily dismissed.

I saw at once these crudities were a grave threat to our cause. But I was unable at that time to make my father and brother bestir themselves. They were too enamored of Hitler and the progress he had made with the German public to recognize the problems his savagery was likely to produce in the longer term. This looming dispute was very much on my mind during the fortnight at Neustrelitz. Thus, I was ill-disposed to express any disagreement with the consternation over the Nazis expressed by all the members of the Golsing family. Whatever our disagreements over the larger principles, I shared their low opinion of flesh-and-blood Nazis.

I was more put off by his father's occasional disparagement of Martin. The Golsings were basically a happy family, perhaps a bit too open-minded, but with a sound base of conservative German family values. But the Judge (as the father was called by everyone) could not avoid remarking all too frequently on what he regarded as Martin's frivolousness and lack of direction. The qualities that everyone else admired – his son's cleverness, his constant high spirits, his irreverence – annoyed him. I might have taken Martin's part in this, since I had endured my own share of this theme in my own life. But I had made promises to Karl, and I respected them.

The Golsings repaid Karl's hospitality with a splendid dinner two days before my departure from Munich. It became a feast of reminiscence, with Frau Golsing recalling the days of her youth spent with Charlotte and Rosamunde Breslau. Her recollections were high spirited and hilarious. But though Karl joined in the general laughter, I could see him falling into the triste that so often afflicted him when those memories arose. He added nothing of his own. He spent the next day on a long letter of apology and explanation to Frau Golsing.

-

September 1, 1932
Munich, Bavaria

206

Mister Albert Sommerville
Sommersby and Smith
London, England

Dear Best of All Men,

. . . [A] slight change of calendar date, which I fervently hope does not discommode you. When the wedding date was disclosed to family, Elizabeth's grandmother Gertrude (her father's mother) made violent objections. She herself was married in mid-January. This led to rumors that the marriage was performed in haste, because of the delicacy of her condition. This would be insult enough to her honor if the rumors were false. But unfortunately, they were true.

The older Frau therefore insists to the Judge that her granddaughter be married in mid-January, in the interest of the non-existent family tradition that was the supposed reason for the date of her wedding. Otherwise, all the old gossip will resume. Her son, the Judge, perforce agrees, and the rest of her family has no choice.

Thus, the wedding date is now the horrifically wintry day of January 29, 1933. This means our wedding trip must be delayed until the summer. But at least Elizabeth and I will not have a conventional anniversary. PLEASE do plan to attend . . .

Your eager, but beleaguered, friend,

Karl

-

September 25, 1932
Berlin, Germany

SD File No. 112384
Subject: Haydenreich, Karl von
Information as of 25/9/32

. . . [O]fficer-candidate Haydenreich passed examinations in language, history, and so on, sufficient to excuse a full year's study at the War College. He is regarded by his superiors as a young officer of outstanding promise.

Summary: Officer-candidate von Haydenreich is considered a reliable Party member. His future career in the Reichswehr may provide promising opportunities for the Party.

-

207

Excerpt from: A History of Germany in the Twentieth Century
Josef Behrens
Alfred A Knopf (1964)

. . . [T]he fifth and last election in the election-tormented year of 1932 took place on November 6, 1932. The National Socialist Party lost some ground, but remained the largest party in the Reichstag.

It was apparent that Hitler could not be kept out of the government. Quietly, the Nazis began to make plans for their accession to power . . .

-

November 8, 1932
Munich, Bavaria

Mister Albert Sommerville
Sommersby and Smith
London, England

Dear Fellow Sufferer,

I had quite forgotten, during the years away from Bavaria, that I am a member of a Bavarian noble family and heir to a title. This fact, however, has not escaped the attention of either my bride or her mother.

I am enclosing a list of the formal occasions, starting four days before the actual wedding. You will take special note of the procession to the cathedral by horse-drawn carriage . . .

Your forlorn friend.

Karl

-

Excerpt from: A General Speaks - the Autobiography of Kurt von
Hammerstein Equord
Major General Kurt von Hammerstein Equord
Reichswehr Press (1951 and1986)

. . . [v]on Blomberg once again brought up the subject of young Haydenreich. His evaluations were superb. He had passed examinations in foreign languages, history, and so on that advanced him nearly a full year in the War College. Von Blomberg recommended that he be assigned to the Abwehr as soon as practicable, and attached to the appropriate battalion in Berlin to complete his education in the War College.

I concurred with this plan . . .

-

December 14, 1932
Munich, Germany

From the Journals of Karl von Haydenreich (Published 1986):

The eternal (and infernal) brouhaha of wedding preparations interrupted today, by extraordinary orders today, from the Reichswehr. I am assigned to the Abwehr! The War College to be completed in rank in Berlin! At first, I was too stunned to react. Then, I sought out Elizabeth, as soon as it was convenient. She had assumed we would remain in Munich or be posted to one of the provinces. I did not know how she would react to a posting to Berlin.

But after her initial shock had passed, she was delighted. She gave voice to some thoughts she had not shared with me earlier. Her father casts a huge shadow in legal circles in Munich. Making her own mark had been a concern to her. The legal and judicial colleges in Berlin are excellent. There will be no problems with enrollment, given her high academic prestige here. The assignment also means billeting in Berlin, not a garrison in some dull provincial town. As we considered the prospect, it seemed more and more attractive. Berlin! With all its culture and excitement!

I bid farewell to my beloved in high spirits. It is only now, back in my quarters, that doubts begin to trouble me.

Why the Abwehr?? Why such an unusual posting?

How much is this to do with the Nazi Party?

1933

-

January 30, 1933
Hof Bayerischer
Munich, Germany

From the Journals of Karl von Haydenreich (Published 1986):

So. It has happened.

We were awakened in mid-morning by the commotion outside, loud enough to penetrate to the recesses of our suite. I arose and opened the curtains. There, far below in the square, were dozens, possibly hundreds, of Brown Shirts, shouting and celebrating. Some were already staggering drunk, though the hour was only 10 o'clock in the morning. Without taking time to dress, Elizabeth was beside me. We watched in silence. We both knew what had happened. The news of the meetings in Berlin, the negotiations, penetrated even the crush of the hysteria of a wedding.

'*So this is how we begin,*' she murmured, and took my hand. Then the staggering realization struck me again with force. Elizabeth Golsing, now Elizabeth Golsing-von Haydenreich, has become my wife – and nothing can alter that fact. And Hitler has become the ruler of Germany, and nothing can alter that fact either. An abyss separates this day from yesterday.

Yesterday? Yesterday was my wedding day. I wish I could remember more of it. But it passed in a daze of confusion and euphoria. There was the huge cathedral, with more flowers than I believed could be gathered in wintertime; a blaze of candles; Elizabeth in a gown more radiant than sunshine; and then a horse-drawn carriage, closed because of the season, driving us away from the church. Truth be told, I don't remember the vows or ring, but there it is on her finger, so it must have happened. The banquet followed, at which Albert demonstrated a distressingly complete recollection of every personal embarrassment I have experienced, and an English gift for discrete humor. This I wish I could forget.

But throughout the afternoon there was the constant overhang of the events in Berlin. Amidst the congratulations and gaiety, the hall buzzed with political talk. Most of the guests knew the Judge only as a German conservative nationalist, and were not aware of his actual attitudes. Others believed me to be a Nazi sympathizer. We received a series of subtle congratulations, that we did nothing to correct.

Then, at last, we were alone, in the hotel suite. After a long while, Elizabeth appeared, in her nightgown, apprehensive but expectant. Then, finally, after so many months and so much longing, I did take her into my arms for the first time as her husband. And here my account must interrupt itself, for my custom of candor with my journal will not be observed in this instance. But after a while, Elizabeth lay in my arms, head on my shoulder, as close to me as one human being can be to another. She joked that she now knew why the foolish virgins were foolish, so I was relieved to know it had gone well.

But even then, I could not escape the whispers of the afternoon. Suddenly the memory of my father's last letter flashed into my mind. I stirred then, enough so that Elizabeth asked me what I was thinking. I told her then, in far greater detail than I had ever spoken, of my father and Mummi, and what he had written in that letter – the importance of Mummi's happiness to him, and his frustration that he had not been able to secure it. I had expected Elizabeth would find these notions protective and reassuring. But I felt at once her restlessness on my shoulder. Suddenly she sat up in bed, with all the gravitas of her father. In an instant, she had transformed herself from paramour to the judge she will one day be.

'*Karl,*' she said, '*it is not the same. Rosamunde Breslau – your Mummi – was alone in the world, abandoned by her family in your village of strangers. Back then, a woman in her place could not make her own way alone. She needed your father's protection. But times are different. I have no such need. We are the modern couple; we look out for each other. You do not have to take care of me. You must not believe you do.*'

I nodded, but she was not satisfied. '*You frighten me, Karl, talking this way. You must not endanger yourself. I love you too much, you are too important to me. You must promise me to forget all about this letter and this so-called obligation. I am certain your father did not mean to be understood so – not in these times, in these circumstances. You must promise me to be sensible.*'

She met my eyes directly, and I made the promise she demanded – the promise which her father had foreseen and made me vow to dishonor. If the crisis should ever come, I know which oath is of greater solemnity. My mind wandered to Berlin. What was happening there was bad, I knew. I could only hope it was not the worst. These brutish men simply could not be ignored, if she and I, or any of us, were to live happily. But then she stirred, and I became aware of her beauty, in all its natural splendor. In a moment, all the larger world was forgotten. We became passionate again, and were so engaged until late into the night. This was the reason we were late to breakfast.

I did not need to hear the news the next day. I knew the moment I walked into the dining room. Our hosts were reacting as if we all had attended a funeral the day before, and not a wedding. The Judge stared into space; Frau Golsing wrung her handkerchief in anxious worry; Martin for once seemed lost for wit and life. Outside, I could hear the jubilant Stormtroopers. I knew what the headlines shouted before I even saw them.

HINDENBERG SUMMONS HITLER! HITLER TO BECOME CHANCELLOR! NSDAP FORMS NEW GOVERNMENT!

We took our place at the table, surrounded by tables full of anxious, fearful German people. The only exception was a group of Nazis at a corner table, getting rowdily and noisily drunk on one bottle of champagne after another – this at 11:15 a.m. I would have given long odds that they did not expect to pay a bill, that none would even be presented to them. Pigs.

We did our best to make small talk, of the joyous type for which one would hope after a large wedding has gone off well (which it had). But no one's heart was really in it. I felt Elizabeth slip a note into my hand. I read it discreetly:

Please let us make our excuses, then take me back to bed.

Yes. Our own garden. A private fortress.

At least on this day.

212

The Judge and the Jester

Excerpt from: A Twentieth Century Life
Albert Sommerville
Houghton, Mifflin (1959)

. . . [I] left Karl in possession of his beautiful bride, and proceeded to Berlin by train. I was to meet Father and my brother Bernard for conferences with various officials in the German government. When I left Munich, the Nazis were not yet in power. By the scheduled time of our appointments the next day, that had changed. The difference in bearing and attitude was at once apparent. I felt some apprehension, but I must say that Herr Goering could not have been more courteous and gracious.

That night I was witness to one of the most magnificent spectacles of the century. Hitler stood at the window of the Chancery, while thousands and thousands of Nazis paraded underneath, each with his torch. The parade went on for hour after hour – a symbolic purging and renewal, the refiner's fire leading to a new and renewed Germany. There was a primitive, magnificent barbarism to the pageant, one that had to move even the dullest of dullards. At that time, I could certainly believe staid old England could have done with a healthy measure of this primal energy. Our ancient, prim institutions seemed so dull and listless in comparison.

February 1, 1933
34 Kantstrasse, Schoneberg District
Berlin, Germany

From the Journals of Karl von Haydenreich (Published 1986):

. . . [W]e did not bid farewell to the wedding party until well after 3:00, barely in time to board the 4:30 train for Berlin. The dreadful political news of the day could only dampen, not defeat, our high spirits.

Once on the train, Elizabeth at first continued to reassure me that the lodgings she and her mother had chosen and furnished for us in Berlin would meet my every expectation. (She proved to be entirely right.) I tried to comprehend the overwhelming fact that this marvelous girl was now my wife, for now and always. But by and by we subsided into the mundane. Elizabeth picked up the newspapers of the day. Suddenly she straightened up and paled. I asked her what was the matter.

'*God in heaven, Karl, that imbecile von Papen not only made Hitler Chancellor,*' she said, '*He gave the Nazis control of the police in Prussia and Germany.*'

I understood her point at once. How can the Nazis be policed, when they themselves are the police?

-

February 8th, 1933
Washington, D.C.

General George V. Mosley,
Assistant Secretary of War
Washington, D.C.

Dear General Mosley,

. . . [I] am hoping to find an appointment, commensurate with my seniority and command training. I know you are familiar with the circumstances under which I was assigned to Fort Leavenworth, and the political and personal differences between myself and General MacArthur that lay behind it. I know you are familiar with my capabilities as a military officer.

Very truly yours,
Major Dwight D. Eisenhower

-

Excerpt from: A History of Germany in the Twentieth Century
Josef Behrens
Alfred A Knopf (1964)

. . . [F]ollowing the accession of Hitler to power, the National Socialist Party succeeded in 'Nazifying' the nation with astonishing speed. Social clubs, sporting clubs, youth organizations – even hobbyists, such as associations of stamp and coin collectors – were reformed to reflect a commitment to National Socialist ideals and principles. To some extent, this was consensual, to some extent, it reflected political forces. With the Nazis in control of the civic institutions, resistance to the pressure – legal or illegal – was impossible.

The only institutions that remained independent were the churches, and the Reichswehr.

215

March 1, 1933
34 Kantstrasse, Schoneberg District
Berlin, Germany

From the Journals of Karl von Haydenreich (Published 1986):

We were blasted out of sleep at 10:30 p.m. by a chorus of howling sirens. I jumped to the window and pulled the drapes aside. Fire fighters and trucks raced by our window as we watched. More sirens joined the commotion. From a distance, we could see a huge red glow, and even a pillar of fire. Neighbors all around us came out of their apartments and homes to see what was occurring. The whispers seemed to come from everywhere . . . *'It's the Reichstag . . . the Reichstag is on fire . . . the Reichstag is burning . . .'*

We watched for the better part of the hour, as the trucks and noise tore the night apart. Then, since we could do nothing but watch, we returned to bed. Elizabeth had a lecture, I had my duties, and there was nothing to do, and nothing more to see. I was drifting off to sleep, when Elizabeth startled me awake. She sat bolt up in bed.

'They did it themselves,' she said. *'The Nazis. They did it so they can accuse the Communists.'*

Excerpt from: A General Speaks - the Autobiography of Kurt von Hammerstein Equord
Major General Kurt von Hammerstein Equord
Reichswehr Press (1986)

. . . [T]he inroads that Adolf Hitler and his Party had made into German society were a grave concern to me. With relentless cynicism, the Nazis exploited the 'crisis' to eliminate every element of legitimate opposition to their rule. Overnight, Germany became a one-party State. None of the statesmen who had so improvidently granted Hitler power had reckoned on the sheer amorality and ruthlessness of the man.

These developments made it all the more imperative that the Reichswehr maintain its strict neutrality with respect to civic politics. Unfortunately, some officers with Nazi sympathies, most notably von Blomberg, were quick to find occasions to undermine Seekt's policy of non-involvement in the political process. I am convinced that his relationship with von Haydenreich began out of that motive . . .

216

March 4, 1933
34 Kantstrasse, Schoneberg District
Berlin, Germany

From the Journals of Karl von Haydenreich (Published 1986):

. . . [T]he most extraordinary summons today. At about 10:00 in the morning, I was ordered to report at once to the headquarters of Major General Werner von Blomberg, the Minister of Defense himself. I wondered if the order had something to do with some failing of mine at either the Abwehr or the War College, although I believe I am discharging both responsibilities satisfactorily.

When I arrived at the General's offices, I was surprised to find myself ushered into his presence immediately. I realized I was to have an unwitnessed colloquy with the General. There were no others in the room. Apparently, this was by design.

General von Blomberg took a long time to get to the point. But gradually he gave me to understand that he expects me to report to him personally every fortnight or so on activities at the Abwehr. The Reichswehr has long been concerned that the agency is dominated by the Navy; that its intelligence analysis is colored by naval concerns; that it does not reflect a balanced approach to military matters. He also said that many persons in the ministry were worried that certain persons in the Abwehr were '*irrational*' – his word – in their opposition to the new regime, to the degree that they might subvert the activity of the Agency. He directs me also to report to him on these personalities. (By 'certain persons', he meant von Bredow, the Abwehr chief, whose hostility to Hitler is well known). The reports will be oral, and for his ears only.

I listened to these comments with as an expressionless a demeanor as I could manage. But what sort of fool did he take me for? No secretary, no witnesses, no written reports. What von Blomberg was ordering me to do was spy for the Nazi Party, on whatever opposition there may be to it in the intelligence agency. He knows full well this violates the most solemn undertakings of Reichswehr officers. Suddenly I understood what the political vetting of last spring had been about. Suddenly I understood the purpose of this unusual assignment to the Abwehr.

I heard the General out. When he was done, I simply acknowledged my understanding of the order, stood up, and saluted (the Nazi salute, as I wished him to have no doubt of my enthusiasm for his project) and left. But behind the soldier's mask of duty I was in turmoil. I completed my duties at the

217

Abwehr, and later a tactics class at school, in a daze. What should I do about this strange, new order? How could I comply with von Blomberg's demands without betraying any of my colleagues? How much of this should I disclose to Elizabeth? Should I discuss this with her? What of my promise to the Judge?

But when I arrived at our apartment, I was immediately engulfed. I had never seen Elizabeth in such a state. She was sputtering with anger. She had been on the second floor at the law library, when there was a commotion at the door. Someone shouted – in the quiet of the library – that the S.A. were in the building, that they were forcing all the Jews out of the courts and the library. Some of Elizabeth's classmates, some she liked, immediately rose and began to pack up their books. Then the Brown Shirts did enter. Without even the pretense of courtesy, their leader ordered all the non-Aryans out. Those who did not leave at once were the subject of a rude inspection of features. A big lout of a Nazi had the effrontery to appraise my wife's looks and assess her Aryan status. (I felt my own blood begin to rush as she told me of this insult.)

The thug was satisfied easily enough with her racial purity, but then had the temerity to question her right as a woman to pursue legal studies. '*Shouldn't she be at home? Or doing woman's work?*' Elizabeth blistered his ears with her response, but all the brute did was laugh at her dismissively. '*A typical gymnasium bully,*' she said, '*no more fit for university than a seal in a circus act. Yet his kind ruled the day!*'

Recounting the events rekindled her anger. All at once she was sputtering, and this time giving way to tears of fury and frustration. I took her in my arms to soothe her, and also to quiet myself, for I was inwardly enraged that my wife should be insulted so, with me elsewhere and not able to protect her. These strong emotions led to strong passion. Soon we were comforting each other in the most ancient manner.

Afterwards, she lay in my arms. '*This should be our delight,*' she said, '*not our refuge.*' I did not answer, lost in my own thoughts. Elizabeth turned her head at this. '*What are you thinking, Karl?*' she asked.

'*Only of you,*' I answered, but this was not true. I was thinking of the meeting with von Blomberg and the promise I had made to the Judge. I decided in that instant not to say anything to my wife about that. '*It's a dangerous game,*' the Judge had said. Maybe – but I don't know if the game has even begun. It holds little danger at present. I am certainly not going to betray any of the fellows at the Abwehr. I like most of them, but even the ones I dislike I would not give over to the Nazis. But the prosaic fact is, that there is nothing to

218

report – nothing of what the General fears, anyway. The only reports the General is going to hear are of the usual tittle-tattle and petty disputes. That is all there is.

Even so, I shall keep my silence with my wife. The further away Elizabeth is from this, the better, I think.

-

Excerpt from: Service to the State - in War and Peace
Major General Werner von Blomberg
Reichswehr Press (1949)

. . . [C]ontrary to the insinuations made by my political opponents, I never had any relationship with Karl von Haydenreich, other than as the interest of the Reichswehr would require. He was on an appropriate, but unusual assignment and training path. Naturally, I took pains to satisfy myself that his military education was proceeding satisfactorily. But that was all.

-

March 7, 1933
Washington, D.C.

The Honorable Patrick J. Hurley
Secretary of War
Washington, D.C.

Dear Mr. Secretary.

. . . [I] believe you are familiar with my qualifications and capability, due to my service with General Mosley. I of course will serve to the best of my ability where ordered, but I believe my present post is the result of personal and professional differences with General MacArthur, over the dispersal of the Bonus Army. My service record speaks for itself.

I am therefore presenting my case to you, in the hope that you are aware of some position in the Army or the Department of War more commensurate with my career to date than the present post . . .

Very truly yours,
Major Dwight D. Eisenhower

-

March 9, 1933
34 Kantstrasse, Schoneberg District
Berlin, Germany

From the Journals of Karl von Haydenreich (Published 1986):

Martin has been arrested!

This thunderbolt struck yesterday, in a telegram from Frau Golsing. We were able to place a phone call last night. My mother-in-law was agitated to near hysteria. The Judge was contacting friends, foes, anyone he knows, to find out the whereabouts of his son and secure his release. Elizabeth kept her calm throughout, and assisted her father in what seemed to me good, practical ways.

Of course, Martin has committed no crime. This is some political revenge, from one of the Nazis he ridiculed – completely absurd, even on those terms, because Martin has no politics.

But I fear for him. He is not the sort to do well in a prison.

My wife is *en route* to Munich as we speak. How she covers her lectures, I don't know – but she will. Her poise last night was remarkable. She talked only of problems and solutions.

But I see through the mask. She is petrified with fear for her brother.

-

March 11, 1933
34 Kantstrasse, Schoneberg District
Berlin, Germany

From the Journals of Karl von Haydenreich (Published 1986):

Elizabeth called. Martin is in a temporary prison situated at the Dachau suburb. The Nazis have converted an old munitions factory into a facility for political prisoners – Communists, socialists, anyone they consider a foe, including harmless jesters like Martin. I said that sounded better than an ordinary prison, but Elizabeth is of the opposite opinion. None of the legal protections for regular prisoners are likely to be in place, or respected. Dachau will be run the way the Nazi brutes want it to be run. (Her voice broke then. I longed to take her in my arms and comfort her.)

The Judge is using all his energies to secure Martin's release. Frau Golsing has been making calls on those of her friends with husbands who might have influence, so far without result. We can only wait. I heard all this, frustrated by my own inability to help. Then I bade a good night to Elizabeth over the phone. I am astonished how much I miss her. After only a few weeks of life together. I am one-half of a whole.

Not a quarter-hour later came a soft knock on the door. I wondered who this could be, expecting a caller who had some relation to Martin's arrest. But there stood Kurt and Lotte, suitcases in hand. Kurt apologized for not calling on us sooner – he had meant to, but there were professional obligations. But today he was warned that his name is on a list – and how could it not be? A

220

Jew and an avant-garde composer. Doubtless only his fame has saved him so far. Now he knows his string has run out. They are leaving at once. By morning's light, they will be gone. He called to say farewell, which touched me.

'Has it truly come to this?' I asked. He sighed, and gave me the news. The master of ceremonies at the Katakombe has disappeared. A well-known actor, Jewish, homosexual, and Communist, threw himself out a fourth-story window. There are many others. Kurt has already stayed longer than was truly safe. Only the good chance of a well-placed admirer has saved him.

And Brecht? I had to ask. But of course he left weeks ago, at the first whiff of danger. Typical – that sheep in wolf's clothing – with all his chatter of revolution and bloody streets, he would hide under the bed in a pool of his own urine at the sound of gunfire. But who knows how much his absurd prattle contributed to this disaster?? And now he is fled and my harmless brother-in-law is at Dachau.

On that note, Kurt and Lotte took their leave, and I was alone. I tried to sleep but a restless anguish held me in its grip. When will I see Kurt again? Or Martin? I expected the rise of Hitler to bring dark times, but nothing like the waking nightmare of the last days. Suddenly the isolation was unbearable. I rose from bed, found my saxophone, cut a reed, and played for a while, American 'blues' jazz. It had been a long time since I played music I liked, just because I liked it. It helped lift the melancholy, but only a little. I wished this life was anything but what it has become. I wished that I was in an orchestra, or I was an impresario, or even greeting my guests at Neustrelitz.

Anything but this.

—

March 27, 1933
Offices of Charles Curtis
Washington, D.C.

Major Dwight D. Eisenhower
Washington, D.C.

Dear Major Eisenhower,

. . . [I] think you know how limited are the powers of a Vice-President, and particularly one leaving office . . .

However, I did happen to encounter George Dern, who, as you know, is shortly to be appointed Secretary of War, and mentioned your situation to him. Dern was infuriated by the way our Administration handled the Bonus Army, and is thus sympathetic to your plight. He noted that the present military

221

attaché in Berlin has indicated his reluctance to serve beyond the new year, and requested a transfer. Dern noted that your background, skills, and lineage would make you an excellent candidate for that position.

I recognize that the post of attaché is not generally considered by military officers to be as desirable as a command assignment. But the assignment would have the advantage of placing you outside the influence of General MacArthur, and on another continent.

I think Secretary Dern can ensure that the Secretaries of State and Army will consider your request positively. I would urge you to give this opportunity your utmost consideration.

Sincerely,

Charles Curtis

(formerly) Vice-President, United States

-

March 30, 1933
34 Kantstrasse, Schoneberg District
Berlin, Germany

From the Journals of Karl von Haydenreich (Published 1986):

At last, the welcome news that Martin is released, at 5 p.m. yesterday, and returned home. Better yet, I am due for a three-day pass.

So, off tonight to Munich, and a celebration for Martin. After three weeks, I can once again kiss my bride . . .

-

April 4, 1933
Munich, Germany

From the Journals of Karl von Haydenreich (Published 1986):

March 31

How little I know of human nature.

I had expected I would find unbounded joy in the Golsing household. But Elizabeth greeted me at the door with an uncertain smile; Frau Golsing could barely meet my eye; and Martin? He was nowhere to be seen. The women informed me that he disappeared into his room the instant he arrived home. Since then he has only emerged briefly for meals. He exchanges words only upon necessity, and then as few as possible. I asked them if it would do for me to visit him in his room. Elizabeth and her mother both enthusiastically supported the suggestion, hoping that my company could bring him back to himself.

222

When I tapped on Martin's door, he allowed me to enter in a cordial enough voice. As I pushed open the door, I espied him, lying on his back, turned away from me, staring at the wall. There was no sign of any book or other diversion. I asked him to face me and did my best to engage him in one of our old dialogues. He answered me politely enough, once even smiling slightly, but in monosyllables or head shakes. When at last I boldly inquired as to what had happened in Dachau, he said nothing, but simply half-closed his eyes.

I knew then why my wife and her mother were worried, for now I shared their worries. This person was not the Martin I had known – had not merely known, had loved. All the jauntiness was gone. All the high spirits were fled. Something fundamental, something at the core, had been broken – and I had no conception of when, if ever, it would be mended.

There was no celebration that evening. There was not even a shared meal. The Judge returned home from his courtroom. He was as anxious as his wife, but his anxiety took the form of a vexed exasperation, an impatience, which all three of us hoped he would master. No one was truly hungry, so it was decided to eat informally. Elizabeth went up to see Martin, and returned a moment later to inform us that her brother wished to eat in his room. Her father scowled at the notion, but it seemed better to accommodate Martin than confront him. Over her father's disapproving gaze, she prepared a tray for her brother and took it up to him.

The four of us ate our own dinner a short while later, but barely spoke, over the table or afterward. Elizabeth and I at last retired to our room. When I closed the door behind us, I found her striding the floor, arms folded, with quick, impatient steps, as she does when she is angry or upset.

'*You know what they did to him, my husband,*' she said. '*We both do. Rape. Forcible pederasty.*' She looked up and saw my expression. '*Oh, for heaven's sake, Karl, do you think I am a fool? Or a porcelain doll? You think I don't know of these things? I study law. I mean to be a judge. Forcible pederasty. Fucked in the butt. That is what happened.*'

'*I know you are not a fool or a doll, Elizabeth,*' I said. '*Your language surprised me is all. I thought it better not to speak so candidly of such stuff. It does not salve the wound. It pours salt on it.*'

'*But how can we obtain redress or cure if we cannot even*' – she began – '*or perhaps you are right. My mother could never – nor my father – perhaps it is only a matter of time healing –*' then she put her hands to her face and began to sob. '*I have lost Martin, I have lost my brother.*' I took her into my arms and onto my shoulder. Her body began to soften.

'*I'm sorry, my husband,*' she said, '*I should not have spoken so.*' She clutched at me. This is the essence of the woman I married. One moment she is her father's daughter, with all his stern ambition, the next her mother's, wishing only to be the same sort of pliant, dutiful German Frau as Margaret – all the more difficult because Elizabeth and I both know Elizabeth is the brighter of the two of us.

'*You said nothing untoward,*' I said, '*and perhaps things that had to be said. But I think we must go to sleep now. Everything looks better in the morning.*'

Then we did go to bed, and slept, but nervously and fitfully.

Nothing looked better in the morning.

April 1

The household arose late as no one had slept well. The Judge had already departed to his chambers. We breakfasted lightly and informally, then were surprised and delighted when Martin made an appearance. He had hardly recovered his old self, but he did make a brave try, smiling wanly and even attempting a joke or two. Elizabeth and Frau Golsing decided on the moment to have a celebratory dinner that evening. Martin gamely agreed, but declined to participate in any way except sitting down to the dinner. It fell to myself and Elizabeth to conduct the marketing and procure the foodstuffs for the cook.

I set out on foot, and decided to make my first stop at Rosenbaum's Bakery. But when I rounded the corner, I espied a crowd of milling, confused shoppers. A strong young Nazi in a brown shirt and armband was standing in front of the entrance. The preceding Sunday, Goebbels had announced a symbolic boycott of all Jewish shops and businesses. It was to last only a day, as an expression of national resolve. This Saturday, April 1, was that day – the day of the Boycott.

The crowd was mostly older women. I would imagine some had been coming to Rosenbaum's for decades, buying fresh bread and pastry for their Saturday dinner. But now the stony-faced young Stormtrooper stood at the doorway, preventing their entry. His friends had scrawled a crude obscenity in large, yellow letters across the bakery window. The shoppers milled about, not knowing exactly what to do. Inside I could see Rosenbaum, hardly changed from the kindly baker I remembered as a child, as confused and helpless as his sometimes customers – but frightened, too, as who would not be? Some of his

224

customers looked back at him with the same yearning look. They could have been Paramus and Thisbe, young lovers separated by a wall. I could have laughed out loud, if I did not want to shout with rage.

I found myself becoming furious. For a moment, I was tempted to push boldly by the S.A. man and into the store, and damn the consequences! But then I remembered Martin and his broken spirit, the cloud under which he remained. So was it with all the rest, I imagine. We all have hostages. I turned away, embarrassed and ashamed. We were all embarrassed and ashamed. Only the Nazis strutted. God bless Mummi and Grandma in their peaceful graves, and spared the sight of this!

I purchased the bread and strudel from a different bakery, not nearly as good as Rosenbaum's, and returned home. We managed to maintain conversation and appearances during the afternoon. The women helped the cook with the food, a pleasant chore. The Judge returned from his offices, in a foul mood – supposedly over the state of the nation, but we all knew better. Martin did not appear.

But he did come down for dinner, when at last it was served. Crispy duck with mushroom stuffing, a favorite of Martin's. But it did not work. A pall hung over the table. Our attempts at gaiety were forced and artificial. Then Frau Golsing made an innocuous remark, about the number of Nazi troopers in the street – and, of a sudden, Martin's eyes flooded with tears. He did not weep. He kept control of himself to that degree. But he could not help the tears.

The Judge lost all control. Without any restraint, he upbraided Martin for his weakness, calling into question his courage and manhood. I knew that at once this was wrong, as wrong as it was possible to be. We all did. I even believe the Judge, too, knew it was wrong. But he could not help himself or stop himself. He went on and on, while the rest of us did our utmost to quiet him without challenging his authority. To no avail.

Martin did not respond to anything his father said. His eyes in fact dried. Suddenly, abruptly, he stood up, composed himself, turned to his mother, and begged formally to be excused. He said not a word to his father or any of us. The Judge was too taken aback by this deliberate affront to say anything. Frau Golsing made some fluttery gesture – then Martin turned and left the table, without even acknowledging his father's presence. He had not eaten anything. The Judge became silent as well. We sat in silence for a while, all appetite having vanished. Then Elizabeth begged everyone's indulgence, and she and I departed the table as well. I do not believe anyone had so much as a morsel.

This time it was she who closed the door behind us. I felt the imminence of something enormously significant. *'I had hoped for a better time, my husband,'* she began, *'but there is not going to be a good time. I am pregnant, Karl. I am going to bear your son.'* (This last was a joke, for Elizabeth knows full well I would prefer a daughter, in the memory of my poor forgotten Lena.)

I took her hand. *'My God, Elizabeth,'* I said, *'this is wonderful. When?'*

'November,' she answered. *'Karl, I am afraid to tell my parents. I think my father will find this another reason to disparage Martin, comparing him to me. Am I right?'*

I thought for a long while. *'I think you are,'* I answered, *'but it is a secret we must not keep for too long.'*

'There surely will be a better time,' Elizabeth said. *'We will be back in Berlin tomorrow. I will phone my mother and give her the news. She can find the right moment.'*

-

Excerpt from: A General Speaks - the Autobiography of Kurt von Hammerstein Equord
Major General Kurt von Hammerstein Equord
Reichswehr Press (1986)

. . . [M]y opposition to Nazi influence in the Reichswehr was initially based on the importance of military neutrality and the importance of abstention from civil affairs.

But as time went on, I became more and more disturbed by the lengths to which the corporal and his cronies would go to eliminate any opposition to their regime, including opposition which was loyal without question to the German Reich itself. Accounts of barbarities in the concentration camps began to circulate, with convincing credibility.

But in the early days, I was reluctant to act. Most of my opposition circle was similarly disposed. We all hoped for better.

-

April 8, 1933
34 Kantstrasse, Schoneberg District
Berlin, Germany

226

From the Journals of Karl von Haydenreich (Published 1986):

... [M]ade my first report to von Blomberg today, recounting some personal friction among the Abwehr staff, and a difference of opinion about the direction of Rumanian politics. (If he takes the trouble to check, he will find that the difference is already reflected in the intelligence assessment.)

The report was evidently sufficient ...

-

April 12, 1933
34 Kantstrasse, Schoneberg District
Berlin, Germany

Mister Albert Sommerville
Sommersby and Smith
London, England

Greetings, Albert,

I am proud to inform you that I will receive my commission on May 20, subject to the completion of a field exercise in artillery in July and August of this summer. Your classmate will thus be a fully commissioned officer in the Reichswehr!

I would like to share my celebrations with some of my classmates from Uppingham. I am sure there are some who are doing business in Germany. If you would be so kind as to advise me of anyone in or near Berlin, I would be deeply appreciative.

Meanwhile, the Third Reich continues to grow in power and in the hearts of all loyal Germans!

Heil Hitler!
Officer-candidate Karl von Haydenreich

-

Excerpt from: A Twentieth Century Life
Albert Sommerville
Houghton, Mifflin (1959)

... [O]ne hardly needed the acumen of Sherlock Holmes to understand the background of the strange letter I received from my friend in April of 1933. The Emergency Decrees enacted after the Reichstag Fire had permitted the Gestapo (as it had come to be called) to inspect mail and tap telephone conversations at random. Karl could not be certain his letter would not be read. None of our old chums at Uppingham would have the remotest interest in celebrating his commission, as he knew perfectly well. What he was

227

really requesting was a messenger who could be trusted to deliver safely our private communications.

As it happened, there was someone, a perfect someone. Jenkins, our old bassist, was employed in the Berlin office of Lloyd's (which was the Neustrelitz insurer). He could be trusted absolutely to pass on communications with complete discretion . . .

-

May 2, 1933
34 Kantstrasse, Schoneberg District
Berlin, Germany
(By hand delivery)

Mister Albert Sommerville
Sommersby and Smith
London, England

Dear Old Bean,

The news, as the Bard would say, is too fair and foul for our usual joking.

The fair is that Elizabeth is pregnant. I will be a father sometime in early November, if the doctors are correct.

But before you congratulate me, the foul news is so foul that it all but blights the fair. My brother-in-law Martin – lively, mischievous, brilliant Martin, the epitome of wit – was arrested by the S.A. in early March. They kept him three weeks, then released him without charge. But he has not been the same since. Elizabeth suspects he was forcibly buggered (the candor with which she expressed the thought would have shocked you), and I think she is right. In any case, he was subject to some extreme treatment, which he will not discuss. He is not the same man.

But there is worse. The Judge is unable to mask his disapproval. He scolds Martin incessantly for not showing more manly attitudes towards this wretched injustice. Elizabeth, her mother, and I all see this attitude of his as the worst possible. Yet he seems unable to control himself. The result is that Martin becomes more and more withdrawn, Frau Golsing is in agonies of pain, and the house completely divided.

The strife was so great, that Elizabeth decided to withhold her good news during our stay there. She did phone her mother a day later, but the Judge still does not know, nor will, until we can be sure it will not loose another artillery barrage in his war against his son. That this is a consideration will tell you how truly frightful things are.

Elizabeth had intended to go to Munich after her examinations to attempt to interpose some sanity. (Her not appearing for examination would be the proverbial last straw for the Judge.) But the news about the commission I included in the joke letter was truthful. I suggested it might be more prudent to invite Martin to our quarters in Berlin, than for Elizabeth to travel. There will be room enough while I am here, and room in abundance when I am gone on maneuvers in July. Elizabeth at once agreed this was the better idea, and so it shall be.

Wish us all luck, old bean, and include us in whatever prayers you do say, for these are trying times indeed, and we are in great need of prayer.

Your old, true friend,

Karl

-

May 20, 1933
34 Kantstrasse, Schoneberg District
Berlin, Germany

From the Journals of Karl von Haydenreich (Published 1986):

. . . To my great surprise, when I presented myself for the ceremony, all the major staff had assembled. Even von Hammerstein, the Chief of Staff himself, was present!

Champagne and hot hors d'oeuvres were in place. We were to do no more work that afternoon. The commission was duly bestowed, there was a bit of applause, then the champagne was opened, and we became informal. Something extraordinary happened then. Von Hammerstein came over to me and offered his congratulations. Then he lowered his voice and spoke to me confidentially.

'*I had the good fortune to know both your father and your grandfather,*' he said. '*They were two very different men. Tell me, then – are you your father's son? Or your grandfather's?*'

I understood fully what he meant. I answered that, in every respect, I was my father's son.

'*Ah,*' he replied. '*As I thought.*'

Then he surprised me by inquiring after Elizabeth and the Golsing family. It happened we had more mutual friends and acquaintances than I knew. He was aware of the arrest. I told him that Elizabeth was quite well, and the family recovering – a polite, but necessary, fiction in such surroundings. Von Hammerstein shook his head.

'*Disgraceful*,' he muttered. In what way, or how, I am not sure, for he said nothing more and moved on to someone else. But the single word stayed with me.

Then the reception was over, and we all bid each other *auf wiedersehen*. Von Hammerstein said nothing more to me. But I did have interesting news to share with Elizabeth. There is more afoot in the Reichswehr than I had any idea.

-

June 16, 1933
34 Kantstrasse, Schoneberg District
Berlin, Germany

From the Journals of Karl von Haydenreich (Published 1986):

Martin is dead.

Martin is dead.

Martin is dead. My brother-in-law, my friend, with his special gifts of life and wit . . . dead. I write these words, but I can scarcely believe what I write. Yet they are true. Martin is dead!

The maid found him hanging from the top of the window sill this morning. He had made a noose out of bed sheets. It was the day after Elizabeth had completed her examinations. He must have thought of that. Then he did a deed he had been surely contemplating for some time.

Elizabeth has already left, gone on the first train leaving. I informed the Abwehr, and received emergency medical leave at once. The earliest train to Munich is tonight at 6.

But Martin will still be dead.

-

June 17, 1933
Munich, Germany

From the Journals of Karl von Haydenreich (Published 1986):

This is sorrow beyond sorrow, worse than anything I have known since Lena and Mummi.

The house is desolate. Both the Judge and Frau Golsing are secluded in separate bedrooms. Both have been given prescriptions by their physicians. The Judge is more heavily sedated than his wife. The maid who found Martin gave notice and left at once. Elizabeth is in charge, trying to hold the household

230

together and make the necessary arrangements. But she herself has not come to terms with this. I offered to take charge of the funeral, to which she agreed at once.

What happened is this. Elizabeth finished her examinations on the afternoon of the 15th. As usual, she achieved splendid results. She reported this to her family by telephone. In Munich, the family gathered to celebrate. For the first time in weeks, Martin appeared lively and in good humor. He even humorously thanked his father for his sound advice of the last few weeks before. The Judge for his part made a partial apology of his own, admitting that he had been much too harsh. All seemed to be well.

Now it is so painfully apparent that the reason for my brother-in-law's high spirits was that the time had arrived to act on a decision he had made some time before, now that his beloved little sister would not be thrown off course. And so he acted.

The maid did not find a note, but Elizabeth and I were certain there was one. We found it, concealed in the pages of a collection of librettos by the British humorist Gilbert, of whose operettas Martin was extremely fond. It was sad and touching, and blamed no one. We showed it to the parents. Frau Golsing took some comfort from it, but the Judge took none at all.

Tomorrow, the priest, and the issue of consecrated soil. For tonight, I do my best to give comfort to father, mother, and sister, even though the heart of this mere brother-in-law is breaking right along with theirs.

-

Undated
Munich, Bavaria
Note found in personal effects of Martin Golsing

Dear Mama, Papa, Elli – you too, Karl,

Please, please, no one should feel blame or distress or guilt about what I have done. It is no one's fault.

What I learned in my weeks at Dachau is that there is no place in this world for someone like me. Nor is it a world that I want to live in. Since the feeling seems to be mutual, and the vote unanimous, it only makes sense to perform the Happy Dispatch (as Gilbert put it).

I love you all. (You too, Karl.) Don't feel bad, Papa, you only said aloud what was my inmost thought. There is no place for me here, and so I am leaving.

231

Love to all,

Martin

-

From the Journals of Karl von Haydenreich (Published 1986):

I went on foot to the Church to see Father von Ritter, as he is named. It still seems a bad dream. With every step, I imagined Martin would leap out of a corner and celebrate the wonderful joke he had played. But Martin is dead, and it is not a dream. Part of the route lay along the path I had walked with my grandfather in 1923. It was littered with Nazis paying homage to the spot where the Putsch ended, which they regard as a sacred site. Well, it is not sacred at all, but a wretched, cursed spot, and may all their souls be damned to Hell. As I was not in uniform, they were less than respectful.

You never know who you will get these days. Nazis are everywhere. Perhaps this priest would prove to be another fool like the one at Heydrich's wedding. But on meeting him, I could sense the good father had his own similar doubts about me, sounding me out in the same way as I was him. Finally, we felt confident enough of each other to discuss the matter candidly. '*Murdered,*' he said, the moment I mentioned the S.A. and Dachau. '*We shall proceed on that basis.*' I went back to the Golsings with that small particle of good news.

The funeral was today, in the same cathedral in which Elizabeth and I were wed five months ago. It was not well-attended. I had hoped that more of his friends and classmates would attend. But the political taint is already known and feared. There were men in suits loitering about the cathedral entrance – plainclothes Party men? One cannot be sure. One is not sure of anything now. We all live on our own little islands.

Father von Ritter did an admirable job. He had only our notes and recollections, yet somehow he managed to speak personally about Martin, as if he had known him in life. Elizabeth and her mother wept without cease. Lost in their own grief, they paid little attention to the Judge. Yet he is beginning to concern me.

He has said very little since my arrival. He has expressed no grief about his son. A stranger hearing of this might consider this an attitude of noble stoicism in the wake of such an unbearable tragedy. But this is not that. I believe the anguish he suffers is at the core of his being, and too acute and

232

tormenting even to express to his own family. On my own, I attempted to engage him on these matters. In a private moment, I reminded him that the responsibility for Martin's fate rested solely in the hands of the swine who arrested him and mistreated him while in custody. I risked a rebuke in this, as he is the head of this family, not I, and his grief a matter of his own concern.

But he did not rebuke me. He simply acknowledged, with the most perfunctory nod, that I had spoken, and indicated he had nothing more to say on the subject. He offered nothing of his own thoughts. He might as easily have been a bad stage actor. While Elizabeth and her mother have shed tears without number, he has yet to exhibit even moist eyes. This is not the father-in-law I know. Something is wrong, something is very wrong. Yet I alone seem to have noticed this.

Elizabeth is still too lost in mourning for her brother even to raise the subject of her father, let alone discuss it. Tomorrow we shall return to Berlin. Maybe then.

-

Excerpt from: Destiny Betrayed - A Chronicle of Treason
Harald Quandt
Franz Eher Nachfolger Gmbh (1952)

. . . [T]he suicide of his brother-in-law Martin Golsing is suggested as the motive or even an excuse for von Haydenreich's treason by his defenders. But Golsing was an ephemeral type of person, a man of no importance. Had he lived, he would almost certainly have worn the pink badge. One does not overthrow governments on behalf of this sort . . .

-

Excerpt from: A Twentieth Century Life
Albert Sommerville
Houghton, Mifflin (1959)

. . . [T]he death of Martin Golsing, a brilliant, harmless fellow, and someone I know I would have liked enormously on more acquaintance, shook me to my core. By what possible rationale could such an atrocious act of indifferent malice be justified?

The incident solidified my growing distaste for the Nazis. The creation of bulwarks and defenses against the Yid and Bolshevik was of paramount importance. But how was it possible to build broad public support for those principles, when the most significant State that had adopted them, perpetrated such barbarities in their name?

July 5, 1933
34 Kantstrasse, Schoneberg District
Berlin, Germany

From the Journals of Karl von Haydenreich (Published 1986):

. . . [W]hat troubled me during Martin's funeral is now evident to all. The Judge is not himself. There was first a letter from Frau Golsing, and then a long, long call last night.

He has been late to his court sessions, which he has never been in his entire career. His judicial opinions are short, almost perfunctory, with none of the refined scholarship for which he is renowned. Elizabeth suspects they were the drafts he had on hand before Martin's death. When he is home, he does no reading, but sleeps or naps. His appetite has vanished. Margaret believes he may have lost as much as two kilos in three weeks.

We can all see the cause easily enough. He is consumed by inner torment. An alienist or psychiatrist is what is required. We all know that. But Elizabeth and her mother are convinced that the Judge will not hear of it. They are likely right.

Besides, there is another consideration, one of which I was not aware. During the time when Martin was at Dachau, the Judge received a formal letter from the Ministry of Interior, which contained a questionnaire. It required the Judge declare in detail the political parties to which he belonged, the clubs, the social organizations, all his affiliations, and, of course, his racial descent as far back as he knew it. The answers were required by what was called the Act for the Reestablishment of the Civil Service, which everyone knew was a device to Nazify the whole of the government bureaucracy – not even thinly disguised.

Elizabeth had been outraged by the implication. '*What is the point of studying law*,' she asked her father, '*when law itself is disappearing?*'

But at the time her father, preoccupied with Martin's release and certain of his stature, had shrugged his shoulders. '*Because better times will come*,' he answered. '*This, too, shall pass.*'

But the questionnaire had never been returned, and now he was infirm of mind. If the Golsing family did anything so public as consult an alienist on his behalf, he would certainly be removed from office. Both mother and daughter believed the better choice was to hope the Judge would somehow find the inner strength to cure himself. We all knew this to be a forlorn hope, but I could not disagree with it.

Then Elizabeth began to pack her bags. It is apparent to both of us that her parents are in desperate need of her presence. The paper she is preparing can be finished in Munich easily enough – in any case, I am bound for field maneuvers for the next two months. But the separation weighed on both of us.

'*You know this means our son –*'

'*Daughter*,' I interrupted, to make her smile, and she did smile –

'*Son*,' she went on, '*will be born in Munich?*' For a woman in her condition cannot be journeying incessantly between Berlin and Munich.

She will be gone from me tomorrow. Another long, miserable separation . . .

July 28, 1933
On Summer Maneuvers
Pomerania, Germany

From the Journals of Karl von Haydenreich (Published 1986):

In the field.

Morning – Entrusted with a complicated field maneuver. The storming of a fortified point of vantage (an old farmhouse playing that part). The exercise seemed simple enough – a flanking movement followed by a straightforward assault – basic textbook. But I saw the position also had an ambuscade potential. I revised the plans accordingly . . . and . . . yes! The ambush had not been foreseen in the defense preparation – which defenders were extremely surprised and quickly surrounded. The farmhouse/fortress fell easily.

For a moment, for a moment only, the fog of gloom that has pervaded this bleak summer was lifted. It embarrasses, even frightens me, how keenly I relish these petty triumphs. It is this aspect of soldiery I like best. Best of all, the defenders were led by two of the more committed and stupid Nazis.

Afternoon – A letter from Elizabeth brings me down to the ground of my life. The Judge is not improving. His condition is becoming worse. Elizabeth recounts one incident. He was reading a popular journal, and suddenly smiled – a rare occurrence these days. He muttered to himself, '*he would have made good jokes out of that.*' Then he rose without saying more, and took to his bed, as he does most days. He has books with him, but the women think he is reading the same chapters over and over and over. He continues to lose weight.

He is obviously in no condition to conduct judicial matters. Frau Golsing has shown resources in the crisis that I never suspected she possessed. She persuaded Doctor Rosenthal, a longtime family friend, to direct a letter to the Ministry of Interior to the effect that the Judge has a condition of the heart that requires an extended convalescence, and little work. Of course, the Nazis are delighted to substitute one of their own for the best and most intelligent judge in Bavaria.

But this tactic will only succeed for a short while. At some time, we must confront the disease of the spirit that inflicts my father-in-law. How and when that is to be done, and what remedies there may be, are completely beyond me.

If only it were as simple as storming a farmhouse!

-

August 27, 1933
Washington, D.C.

Leutnant Karl van Haydenreich
% Reichswehr Headquarters
Berlin, Germany

Dear Karl,

I have to share some news with you. I've been appointed the military attaché for the United States government to its embassy in Berlin, starting the first of January. It's not much of an honor, to be truthful with you. It's the result of a little disagreement I had with a fellow further up the command chain. I'll tell you all about it when we meet, if you don't find it too boring.

But at least it gets me back to Europe and the chance to meet up with you. There are some interesting things happening in Germany, somewhat exciting and somewhat perplexing. I am excited to be posted to Berlin.

If you drop me a line at the Berlin embassy, they'll hold it for me. I don't know where you're stationed or if you're still in Munich, but a military attaché is on a long leash, so I can work it out. I really want to see you.

Your friend,

Ike

-

October 9, 1933
34 Kantstrasse, Schoneberg District
Berlin, Germany

From the Journals of Karl von Haydenreich (Published 1986):

. . . [H]e almost never leaves his bedroom now. They tell me he looks skeletal. Perhaps the Judge does not want to live, and is deliberately starving himself. It is a natural speculation. Not even Elizabeth's swelling belly and the promise of hope it implies, brings him any consolation.

The Judge must see a psychiatrist. It has become a necessity. I wish we had Doctor Rosenthal available. But he is gone, fled to Canada three weeks ago. No one in Munich can be trusted.

Now it falls to me – to find someone in Berlin who can be trusted. But how? I know no physicians here.

October 10, 1933
34 Kantstrasse, Schoneberg District
Berlin, Germany

From the Journals of Karl von Haydenreich (Published 1986):

. . . [C]alled on Professor Hindemith at the Hochschule. He seemed delighted to see me. He even invited me to take a chair in the woodwind section at a concert on Saturday. I was forced to decline, then came directly to the matter at hand. The tendency of musicians and other artists to suffer from temperamental and emotional distress is well known. Professor Hindemith had surely had experience with such situations. I had come to him, to inquire if he had any knowledge of a doctor who specializes in such complaints – someone whose discretion can be trusted absolutely.

The professor provided a reference instantly – a physician by the name of Erik Landauer. He hesitated for a moment, then added that Landauer is Jewish, as are most doctors practicing in that area of medicine. Many of them have already fled Germany. Hindemith said he would have recommended this man even if all the others were still in practice. But he thought I should know of his race, in case I had some objection. Hindemith is in an uncertain position. His wife is half-Jewish.

I was moved by his trust (I was in full uniform), as he might easily have provided me with no name. I told him that if he believed I would have any objection, the professor had mistaken me for someone else. Then I thanked him, with the truest sincerity possible, for his necessary candor four years before. His relief at hearing this was obvious. I told him, too, of my rediscovery of the joy of music once free of the burdens of ambition. We parted on this note, both our eyes somewhat moist.

237

Then off to Landauer's offices, for there was no time to lose. A Brown Shirt standing outside glared at me as I entered, but I ignored him. I found the doctor in and unoccupied, since his patient list has declined dramatically since the boycott in April. The outline of the 'Juden' on his door is still there. It could not be completely eradicated.

I knew within a few moments we had found our man. Doctor Landauer was gentle, sympathetic, and knowledgeable – and he is unoccupied. He agreed to a consultation in Munich this very weekend. Our only disagreement was the amount of the fee he quoted, which I knew was far too low. Perhaps the Nazis have made him shy. I insisted on paying him the fair fee, about twice what he asked. It is sometimes helpful to have money in this world.

I also told him I could arrange lodgings of his choice at Neustrelitz, should he choose to vacation there. But Dr. Landauer declined this addition to the fee.

'*By next summer*,' he said, in a soft voice, '*I do not think that German Jews will be allowed to visit to such places.* '\

-

October 13, 1933
34 Kantstrasse, Schoneberg District
Berlin, Germany

From the Journals of Karl von Haydenreich (Published 1986):

Elizabeth and Dr. Landauer phoned tonight from Munich. First, the doctor spoke. He repeated what he had told Elizabeth and her mother. The Judge is afflicted with a severe depression, that has reached a pathological state. He needs intensive medical treatment, and in an institution or dedicated private home.

He then became practical. In the present political climate, he does not trust any institution in Germany to provide decent care. The Nazis have infected this aspect of German life as they have infected all the others. The mentally ill, the feeble-minded, the senile, and the like are termed 'useless eaters'. Persons who used to be the objects of pity and compassion are now condemned in the same way as criminals, Jews, and Bolsheviks – racial traitors, all affronts to the ideal of the master race. Sympathy for them is a sign of racial weakness. A strong, healthy people cast them out without remorse. So Hitler believes. Fortunately, there is still too much human decency left in this nation

238

for this barbarism to be enforced rigorously. But in general, the institutions can no longer be trusted.

Doctor Landauer therefore suggested that the Judge either resign his office, or take an extended leave of absence, and seek treatment in Switzerland, particularly Zurich. He is familiar with good, civilized clinics there, and can make all the necessary arrangements. He cannot assure me that there will be a cure. But in all probability, we will avoid the worst, suicide or even death by malnourishment. Call it what it is – self-starvation.

I would have thought that such a drastic recommendation would be resisted by Elizabeth and Frau Golsing. But not so. It happened that Margaret had already given thought to the possibility of leaving Germany. It solves the problem of discretion with the Nazi authorities. Also, she had made her own inquiries about the state of German asylums. Switzerland was an obvious destination. Thus, she accepted the doctor's suggestion instantly, and with gratitude. Landauer had been directed to begin making arrangements immediately. Given the state to which the Judge had descended, the matter was urgent.

Elizabeth took the line. She spoke crisply, and in her lawyer's voice. Her mother and she had already compiled a list of tasks for the plan. But she emphasized this was a plan only, until the Judge consented – for as a matter of law, all of the Golsing properties were under his control. Nothing could be done without his permission. Since a legal proceeding to declare him incompetent is out of the question, he must give his consent. Both women were concerned that a request for consent might lift him out of his torpor, and that he would not necessarily be rational at that time. They had decided on a family meeting on November 1, at which time all the necessary documents would be presented to the Judge. My wife requested I be there if I possibly could, to assist with the burden of persuasion, if it should come to that.

Of course, I will be present. The day is too sad and important for there to be any question of that.

-

October 14, 1933
34 Kantstrasse, Schoneberg District
Berlin, Germany

From the Journals of Karl von Haydenreich (Published 1986):

. . . [S]ixth report to Blomberg. Now his office is festooned with two small Nazi flags – he does not even bother to conceal his allegiance. I provided the usual gossip and chitchat, and the usual report of nothing amiss.

Blomberg greeted this report of no activity with relief. This puzzled me, but then suddenly, I understood the reason for these reports. They were not to provide evidence of plots, but the opposite, to provide reassurance of <u>no</u> plots, no resentment bubbling beneath the surface, no conspiracies brewing.

So this is it. Blomberg and above him, Hitler, are still afraid of the Army. I had not seen that so clearly before.

-

October 20, 1933
34 Kantstrasse, Schoneberg District
Berlin, Germany

From the Journals of Karl von Haydenreich (Published 1986):

. . . [A] letter from Elizabeth . . .

. . . [T]hey had expected to entrust the Golsing home to the hands of an agent for lease. But a willing renter approached almost at once. This is a Gert Schafer, an assistant Gauleiter and an important Party official. But when Schafer met with Frau Golsing, he suggested a rental less than half of what had been proposed, or what the house would have brought just a year ago. Schafer pointed out that a great number of homes of good quality were on the market, because of the emigration of all 'the rich Jews' and other undesirables. Rental rates are depressed in consequence. He was quite smug on this.

Frau Golsing answered politely that she would herself burn her house to the ground, before she would accept a lease payment so low. She also told Schafer that she would make her own inquiries. If he had anything to do with Dachau or the Brown Shirts, she would not lease to him at any price. (In this crisis, she has displayed a resilience and an indomitability of spirit that were invisible when her husband was head of the house.) Schafer left, much less smug than when he arrived.

But he returned a few hours later, with a letter from the Gauleiter himself, verifying that Schafer was an ordinary city official and Party member, and not connected with the S.A. or police. He had been an ordinary clerk in the Munich city government, until the Nazis elevated him. He also had a letter from a local bank, guaranteeing for a five-year period, lease payments in the amount Frau Golsing demanded. The letter was signed by Frederick Breslau, my old reluctant uncle, and the best friend of the Nazi Party in Munich.

Thus, the die is cast, as the Roman said, subject only to the Judge's consent. The lease will be signed on November 1, and the property available by November 15.

Events move apace . . .

-

November 1, 1933
Munich, Germany
From the Journals of Karl von Haydenreich (Published 1986):
. . . [S]o, the family meeting . . .

Margaret, Elizabeth, Dr. Landauer, and the family solicitor, a kindly man named Helmut Treskow, were present. The Judge remained upstairs until his presence was required. The home looked entirely different from when I first presented myself. Much of the furniture, and the books in the library, had already been removed to the warehouse. The oil paintings and other items of value were draped with drop cloths, preparatory for moving. The entire house was a shroud over ruined lives.

Documents were stacked on the desk of the front room. The lease was among them – so were resignations from various professional societies, social clubs, a letter to the Ministry of Interior, and so on. Elizabeth and Treskow did a brief, final review for accuracy. Then the time had come to summon the Judge. We all prepared ourselves for a last argument.

But it did not happen. I had arrived too late the night before to visit with the Judge. I had not seen him in four months. With all the warnings about the change in his appearance, I was nonetheless shocked. He was dressed in a bathrobe, not bothering to change. He must have lost at least 20 – maybe 25 – kilos. His beard was gray, stubbly, and irregular – I wondered if Frau Golsing had been shaving him. He moved in hesitant steps, with automatic gestures. I understood instantly how urgent his case had become. I myself came close to weeping.

There was no argument. In a gentle voice, Frau Golsing told him they would be moving to Zurich, and it would be necessary for him to sign some papers. He shrugged, nodded, and picked up the pen. She could have told him he was to be buried alive that afternoon and I doubt it would have made a difference. He signed everything in a matter of minutes, without bothering to read a word – this, the man who had not long before been the preeminent jurist in Munich! Then he looked up.

241

'*Is that all?*' he said. '*May I be excused?*' This was in the manner of a polite child.

'*Of course, Judge,*' Frau Golsing replied. The Judge arose on that word, shambled out of the room, and up the stairs. Only after he left did Margaret allow herself the relief of tears. '*That it would come to this,*' she sobbed. Then she turned to Elizabeth.

'*And I will not be able to care for my grandchild,*' she went on.

I put my hand on Elizabeth's shoulder. I guaranteed my mother-in-law that we would be in Zurich for Christmas, or as soon as Elizabeth and the baby could travel. With that, she dried her eyes and returned to the matters at hand. Elizabeth and Treskow reviewed all the documents and letters, Margaret sealed them and prepared them for mailing. Then we awaited Schafer and his solicitor, due after lunch.

When they arrived, there were four in number – Schafer, his own solicitor, and two other Party members. These proved to be his grown sons. All of them had swastika armbands. Margaret could not conceal her surprise at the solicitor.

'*Albert,*' she said. '*You, a Nazi?*'

'*Since March, Frau Golsing,*' he answered. '*A practical decision.*' The older Nazis refer to these latecomers to National Socialism as 'March Flowers' and have nothing but contempt for them. This may be the only opinion I share with them.

The four had obviously been celebrating at lunch. Their cheeks were flushed, their breath alcoholic, their manner boisterous. Schafer and his sons could not conceal their glee at acquiring the right to live in the house that the Golsing family had occupied for three centuries. They behaved as if this colossal change in their fortune was the rightful reward for some heroic act of great merit. Frau Golsing reminded them sharply that it was still her house, and belonged to a judge. Schafer then recovered enough sobriety to remember that the contract was not signed, and had the good sense to quiet down and in fact order his sons out of the house.

We got down to business then. Having discovered Dr. Landauer was Jewish, Schafer and the solicitor (Albert Weber by name) ostentatiously ignored him, not even extending the courtesy of a greeting. Weber reviewed the lease, far too quickly to be meaningful. Elizabeth rolled her eyes. Then he pronounced it in good order, and Schafer signed. He would take occupancy on December 1st, or two weeks after Elizabeth gave birth, whichever was later.

Then it was over. Schafer and the others left the house, off for more celebration. We could hear their voices rise again outside. We had a quiet luncheon, then bid goodbye to Dr. Landauer, with the most profound gratitude. Frau Golsing went up to be with the Judge. I took Elizabeth to her room and lay down beside her. She was huge with child.

'I would have thought you would feel more sadness,' I remarked.

'I would have last year,' she answered. *'But not now. Not since Martin. Not since my father. Now I know how you feel about Neustrelitz.'*

That evening, I encountered Dr. Landauer on the train platform, also bound for Berlin. I informed him I planned to send him an additional honorarium, as I felt the fee we had discussed was not adequate to the services he had rendered. He acquiesced without demurrer. As he is not the sort of man to accept unearned moneys, I knew I had done right.

I asked him then if he intended to leave Germany. He smiled the weary philosophical smile I had come to know well. *'No,'* he said, *'I have responsibilities here, people, patients. I can't desert them. Not every family has the resources yours does.'*

'Besides,' he added, *'how long can it last? How bad can it get?'*

-

November 6, 1933
34 Kantstrasse, Schoneberg District
Berlin, Germany

From the Journals of Karl von Haydenreich (Published 1986):

For unto us a child is born! Elizabeth has her way, as always – unto us, a son is given!! Martin Heinrich-Werner von Haydenreich has come into the world!!

I had intended to be in Munich for the birth. But late last night, I received word that labor had begun that afternoon, ten days before schedule. It was already too late for timely travel. Extremely frustrating!

I could not speak to Elizabeth until this morning, after she had slept. Our son is fine and doing well, despite his slightly early entrance into the world. Even through the phone, her happiness radiated across the universe. Like me, she can scarcely believe the event – we are parents, we are the creators of a new human being. My impatience to see, to touch, to hold my son overwhelms me! But, alas, not for another unendurable fortnight, until the scheduled leave. The nursery is furnished, the nanny will be with Elizabeth and

Martin by week's end. But there is still much to do in Munich – also, best not to travel until mother and son have gathered some strength.

But I am a father! My wife has presented me with a son! Sing hallelujah to the highest heaven!

-

November 9, 1933
34 Kantstrasse, Schoneberg District
Berlin, Germany

From the Journals of Karl von Haydenreich (Published 1986):

. . .{W]e had all hoped that the birth of our child would bring the Judge out of his state. But not so.

He heard the news with the same listlessness he shows to everything. Not even the revelation that there is a new Martin in the world made any difference to him.

The preparations proceed without break, the Golsing family will leave Munich, leave the house where it has resided for three hundred years, on November 29th. One private car will take Judge Golsing and his wife to Zurich. The next day, another will take my son and his parents to our home in Berlin

And all will start anew.

-

November 29, 1933
Municb, Germany

From the Journals of Karl von Haydenreich (Published 1986):

Saw the Judge and Frau Golsing off today, by private car. Elizabeth put up a brave front, but I knew the thoughts behind the mask. When will she see her parents again? Margaret hugged little Martin and kissed him again and again. When will she again have the pleasure of holding her grandchild in her own home?

The day was further marred by the review of the exit papers. Everything was in order – and yet the officious oaf could not resist a pompous lecture about the Fatherland, the Fuhrer (as some have begun to call Hitler), our duty of loyalty, our obligation to stand firm – as if seeking treatment for an elderly, grief-stricken man was a moral failing, a betrayal of Germany. I managed to draw him out a bit, feigning politeness. As I thought, he had no medical background, not even any higher education. He was another Nazi party loyalist elevated way, way above his station and ability. It is the order of the day.

But these crude, implicit insults had to be endured, for the little tin asshole had the power to make major difficulties. Finally, we saw the last of him. The car was ready. Essential furnishings had been sent ahead. The Judge came down the stairs, in a suit. It was as if a scarecrow made of sticks had appeared. Margaret bid an extended, teary farewell to her daughter, little Martin, and me. Elizabeth, too, was lost in tears.

Then they were off, down the road, to a new and strange land.

Elizabeth, Martin, and I will spend the last night of the three hundred years in this ancient, deserted family home. Tomorrow, we are off to Berlin.

-

December 28, 1933
Shutzstauffel headquarters
Berlin, Germany

SD File No. 112384
Subject: Haydenreich, Karl von

Concerning: Letter addressed to von Haydenreich, from an American military officer, Dwight D. Eisenhower, date 27/8/33. Opened, examined, and resealed 29/8/33. Reviewed, 28/12/33

. . . [E]isenhower appears to be an old family friend. However, he is the new American military attaché in Berlin, effective 1/1/34, and von Haydenreich is attached to the Abwehr. Eisenhower also describes the New Order as 'exciting and perplexing'.

Surveillance is indicated.

Luncheons at the Adlon Hotel

1934

-

Excerpt from: My Name is Ike - Reflections on Fifty Years of Service as Soldier and Statesman
Dwight D. Eisenhower
Random House (1986)

I came to Berlin in 1934 to get as far away as I possibly could from MacArthur and the shambles my military career had become. I had no other ambition. I didn't know that the years in Germany would become the most important of my life, that they would catapult me to heights of which I had never dreamt, or that they would change the direction of history decisively. I'll leave it to others to decide whether my elevation was deserved or justified. But most people do think the change in history was a good one. Generally, I agree with that.

'Generally'? I know much, too much, about the personal cost to be sure of anything. Not a day goes by when I don't revisit those years. Some days I think I'd do what I did all over again. On other days, I'd change everything. It's an easy thing to blather about the 'greater good' or the 'best interest of humanity' when the axe is falling elsewhere. It's a different matter when you personally know where, and on whom, it did fall, and what an enormous price was paid.

Then you never stop your second-guessing. You live with doubts and 'what-ifs' forever after.

But all that lay in front of me at the beginning of 1934. I arrived in Berlin in the first week of January, as grass green as any other American. I was on my own, ahead of Mamie by about a month. The idea was I'd set us up, then she'd come over, and then our sons, when the school term was done. I would have looked up Karl first thing, but he was off in Zurich with his wife and their new baby, on what I thought then was a vacation.

I didn't know what to expect. There had been a lot of publicity in the US in 1933, about Dachau, the concentration camps, the wave of political arrests and the police abuses, the campaign against the Jews, and all the rest. Most Americans were appalled by that, though there were a few who admired the brisk pace Hitler had set for the new Germany. I was more or less in the 'appalled' camp, but I really didn't know what to expect.

What I did find, I never would have guessed in a hundred years. Berlin turned out to be an ordinary city, with all the ordinary, routine patterns of life in any other big city. People worked, played, socialized, and so on in the same way as everywhere else. There was nothing exceptional. Oh, there were Nazi posters and Nazi newspapers, all right, the same as there are political posters and newspapers everywhere. But mostly, it was all so ordinary.

It was only when you scratched just a bit beneath the surface that you realized how deep the Nazi inroads were. Karl described the process, in words I still remember. *'It's a subtle thing, Ike,'* he said. *'An S.A. man stands outside a psychiatrist's office, to make callers uncomfortable. A boycott of the Jewish businesses for just one day, to single them out. The brutalities take place well out of sight, to persons the people don't like. Day by day everything is apparently the same, and no one notices how much life changes.'* That's the reason it took me a while to catch on.

There was also much more political tension than I would have guessed. The first inkling I had of that was from Reichswehr command itself, beginning at the top – with General von Hammerstein himself.

-

Excerpt from: A General Speaks - the Autobiography of Kurt von Hammerstein Equord
Major General Kurt von Hammerstein Equord
Reichswehr Press (1986)

I first met the future Senator Eisenhower in early January 1934 at a reception for military attachés. He was an open, engaging personality, an easy man to like. He had the earnestness and naiveté typical of an American approaching German politics for the first time. While it was not my role as Chief of Staff to educate him in these complexities, I was sufficiently impressed with him to suggest others, both in and out of the military, who might provide him with more insight.

-

Excerpt from: My Name is Ike - Reflections on Fifty Years of Service as Soldier and Statesman
Dwight D. Eisenhower
Random House (1986)

What I learned in those first few weeks was that Hitler was not wholly the master of his own house – at least, not yet. He had eliminated most of the formal political opposition, but there were still some powerful opponents left in the government and, more important, in the Reichswehr. But by far his biggest problem was in his own party, in the form of Ernst Rohm and the Brown Shirts, the S.A. They had become a million strong, Hitler's private army, which he'd used to do the work too dirty even for the Gestapo – in their private prisons, in Dachau, and on street corners throughout Germany. But now all that work was done. Rohm was pressuring Hitler and the rest of the Nazi leadership for what Rohm thought was their just reward.

Did I say private army? I should have said 'private mob'. They'd been recruited throughout the 20s from the dregs of German society – criminals, hooligans, bullies, and thugs, too lazy, incompetent, or disorderly to find real jobs. They were the ones who bullied and harassed foes of the Nazis, intimidating Jewish businesses, starting street fights with Communists, breaking heads, and sometimes even kidnapping their enemies. It was as if an American politician had used a lynch mob to help obliterate the organized opposition to his election – and now that mob was demanding its tribute.

But providing the reward was impossible. Hitler was personally popular with the German people, but that was as far as Nazi popularity went. The public hated and feared the S.A. If Hitler allowed Rohm any degree of political or social power, he'd alienate all of the more traditional and nationalist conservatives, whose support he needed. He'd also alienate the Reichswehr leadership, which had the most negative view possible of the Brown Shirts.

So, with all his success, Hitler still had major, looming problems.

-

January 21, 1934
34 Kantstrasse, Schoneberg District
Berlin, Germany

From the Journals of Karl von Haydenreich (Published 1986):

. . . [T]wo letters. The first from Zurich. The Judge is as listless and indifferent as ever. We had hoped the Christmas visit and a meeting with his new grandson would cause some change. But not so. We can only hope that something will change.

The second, a note from my old trustee, Major Eisenhower, now the American military attaché. Can we meet for lunch? We certainly can. I cannot think of anyone I am more eager to meet . . .

Excerpt from: My Name is Ike - Reflections on Fifty Years of Service as Soldier and Statesman
Dwight D. Eisenhower
Random House (1986)

Most people who know me would tell you that I have my fair share, and then some, of cold blood. But I must admit it warmed a bit as I waited in the lobby for Karl. It had been fifteen years since I had seen him. From afar, I had been a second father to him. From afar, I had administered his estate, seen to his education, and shared his frustrations and triumphs. The fees that Heinz had regarded as nominal had made a major difference to me and my family. Outside of my own folks, there was no one to whom I was closer. But for whatever reason, we had never exchanged photographs. I hadn't seen him in a decade and a half. The world had changed unimaginably in that time.

But suddenly there he was, unmistakably Karl, in the lobby of the Adlon hotel, smiling, striding towards me. Cold-blooded Ike had to turn away to regain a measure of composure.

He stood a tad over six feet tall – he had inherited his mother's and uncle's height. He had his father's aspect and alertness, but not much more in the way of direct resemblance. (People who knew them said he took after his mother more than his dad.) Blond and blue-eyed, in his Reichswehr uniform, he seemed the epitome of the Aryan demigods portrayed in the crude Nazi propaganda circulating in Berlin. I felt the silliest, most irrational pride in who he was and what he had become. He was not my son, I knew that – and yet . . . godson . . . I felt I finally understood the meaning of that relationship.

He shook my hand and then we embraced, the most natural gesture in the world. I brought him up to date on the events that had brought me to Berlin and he shared his news. His young son was two months old. What with all the travel and dislocation, news of that event had reached me only after I arrived in Berlin. I gave him my and Mamie's warmest congratulations, and made a date to visit his family as soon as convenient after she arrived. After we had finished exchanging the basic news, however, by slow degrees we descended from intimate talk to chit-chat and meaningless cordiality. The warmth with which we had begun seemed to have cooled. Karl was then smiling and talking, but saying nothing. I wondered if I'd said or done something wrong.

All at once, he suggested a walk. I was baffled at this, but agreed. We paid our bill and walked outside into a bright winter's early afternoon. Karl led

251

the way to the Tiergarten, still smiling, still saying next to nothing. Then he spoke.

'*We were being watched at the restaurant,*' he said quietly. '*It was impossible to speak freely there.*' I found that hard to believe. '*You are only a junior officer,*' I said.

'*I am in a unique position,*' he answered. '*My assignment at the Abwehr is quite unusual. Von Blomberg used his influence to place me there, believing I could be a useful spy for the Nazis. He is a Nazi sympathizer, and believes I am as well.*'

'*You, a Nazi, Karl?*' I answered. '*That's incredible.*'

'*I am no Nazi, Ike,*' he smiled. '*Quite the contrary. But, come, I have time this afternoon. Let me tell you everything.*'

Then he told me of the full catastrophe that had overtaken the Golsing family the year before, of the false arrest of his harmless, witty brother-in-law, of the breakdown of his father-in-law, and his in-laws' self-exile in Zurich. Only then did I realize he had not been away on a simple family vacation. I learned then, too, of his grandfather's involvement with the Nazi Party, Karl's own infatuation when he was 13, his enrollment in the Party as likely its youngest member at the time, his presence at the Beer Hall Putsch (now sacred history in Nazi lore). There, he witnessed Adolf Hitler run away from his comrades in panicky fear for his life. I found out, too, for the first time that my friend Heinrich had been Hitler's commanding officer in the Great War – that came as a thunderbolt of a surprise. All this detailed personal biography came as news to me. Heinrich had never bothered to mention it. It hadn't been important before the Nazis came to power.

It was then and there I first realized that Karl, in addition to becoming a close friend, might also be a very, very valuable resource.

-

February 10, 1934
Berlin, Germany

SD File No. 112384
Subject: Haydenreich, Karl von
Summary of Surveillance Reports, 14/1/34-8/2/34: Subject and Major Dwight D. Eisenhower

The subject von Haydenreich met Major Eisenhower on three separate occasions between the dates noted, in the Adlon Hotel.

What dialog between the two men that could be overheard is summarized in the detailed report. It is of a banal nature – family, jazz music, athletics, and so on.

Background checks indicate that Eisenhower is a longtime family friend of the von Haydenreich family. The relationship is thus of long standing, and not formed as a result of Eisenhower's assignment as military attaché.

The Eisenhower family emigrated from Germany in the 18th century to Pennsylvania, and then Kansas. There is no evidence of tainted Jewish blood.

Surveillance will continue, but there is no evidence of anti-Nazi or anti-Reich activity.

February 9, 1934
/s/Unterscharger Gustav Dorf

(*Handwritten note appended*)
I know von Haydenreich personally. I do not trust him.
Surveillance to be not only continued, but enhanced. R. Heydrich, 15-2-34]

-

Excerpt from: Service to the State - in War and Peace
Major General Werner von Blomberg
Reichswehr Press (1949)

. . . [I]n the first few months of 1934, Rohm began to demand that his entire irregular army be joined with the regular Reichswehr, with all their self-designated ranks and orders (including officers) left the same. The ruffians would thus gain all the privileges of military status, without, however, submitting to any of the discipline or training, or exhibiting any of the devotion to duty, that is the pride of the German Army.

This was out of the question, and I told Hitler so. People who believe I was an unthinking puppet of the Third Reich forget such matters . . .

-

Excerpt from: My Name is Ike - Reflections on Fifty Years of Service as
Soldier and Statesman
Dwight D. Eisenhower
Random House (1986)

The end for Mamie came within two weeks of her arrival, almost before there was a beginning. By coincidence, it occurred the night we met Karl's family. He waited until Mamie arrived to invite us over to meet his wife and their new son Martin. Martin was already adorable at age three months. It was a memorable night, as it happened – my first meeting with the woman who

253

was to become my lifelong friend and political ally, Elizabeth Whittingham, as the world has known her these last forty years. But of course, that night we met her as Elizabeth Golsing von Haydenreich. She turned out to be not only beautiful and charming, but also one of those frighteningly brilliant women you meet every now and then, that many men go out of their way to avoid.

But not Karl, and the three of them – the youthful husband and wife, and their baby – won our hearts instantly. Elizabeth was making her way through her legal studies, at the top of her class despite the pregnancy and birth, and despite constant petty insult and harassment from the Nazis in the class. (The Nazis thought all women should confine themselves to kitchen, church, and children – another of their primitive bigotries.) We didn't talk much politics, but enough for me to know she detested Hitler and the Nazis even more than Karl.

Becoming friends with a nice, welcoming family seemed to clinch the deal for Mamie. But as we were walking back to our quarters at the Embassy hotel, we came upon a big crowd and a street band, with music. Then we saw a column of S.A., the Brown Shirts, and between two big ones, at the very head of the column, a figure that looked like a clown. We moved up, thinking it was some kind of celebration. But as the column got closer, we saw it wasn't a clown at all. It was a girl, a young woman, a pitiful sight, as terrified as an adult could be. There was a sign draped around her neck, which you didn't need German to understand – '*I have given myself to a Jew.*' That was her crime and the only reason for all the commotion.

And the onlookers? None of them helped or even booed the tormentors. Instead, they were jeering and catcalling at the poor woman, along with the Brown Shirts. I will tell you, it made me sick to my stomach. But that was tame compared to Mamie's reaction. When we reached our place, she literally *was* sick. I told her everyone, including Hitler, knew he had to do something about the Brown Shirts. I said I'd bet the bystanders were all Nazis themselves.

But she answered me back that it didn't make any difference. '*I think it is already too late for Germany,*' she said. '*I don't want to be around those people. I don't want my children around these people. I only hope it changes for Karl and Elizabeth before that wonderful baby grows up.*' And that was that. I loved and needed Mamie, I wanted her with me desperately. If I hadn't painted myself into a corner with the Army, I'd have gone straight home with her. But that was not possible.

We arranged passage back home as quickly as we could – and a week later she was gone.

So I spent the next three years without my wife and family. I'm not the sort to find consolation elsewhere, if you know what I mean. The upshot is that Karl and Elizabeth became my other family during my stay. I already thought of him as godson. It was a rare fortnight when I didn't dine with them at least once.

‑

February 18, 1934
34 Kantstrasse, Schoneberg District
Berlin, Germany

From the Journals of Karl von Haydenreich (Published 1986):

Afternoon

. . . [E]lizabeth having come home last night with one account too many of muttered corridor insults and passing uncouth remarks, I found my patience outworn. The time for a response was long overdue. I spent some time deciding exactly what that would be.

Today, shortly after the midday break for lunch, I left the Abwehr and appeared at Elizabeth's carrel at the University a few minutes before the lecture was to begin. She was startled. '*Karl,*' she exclaimed, '*why are you here?*'

'*I decided to escort you to the lecture today,*' I replied.

This surprised her even more, then she understood. She gathered her notes and took my elbow. '*I shall never,*' she whispered, '*forgive you for this!*' I had expected that reaction. But I had already made up my mind.

As we proceeded towards the lecture hall, I met the eyes of every student who passed. More than a few wore Brown Shirts. I said nothing, but kept my eyes cold and focused, my expression calm and formal. Sometimes it is useful to wear a Reichswehr uniform, to stand well off the ground, and to be known to have had military training with weapons and personal combat. I knew from my own school days that any open expression of the protective anger I felt on behalf of my wife would be met with jeering and ridicule – that is always the way with that type – and they would resume their harassment the very next day.

But if I said nothing, but implied all, made each wonder for a moment about unknown consequences, and perhaps feel the deep shame of his own cowardice . . . no juvenile response was possible. As each one met my gaze in succession, then turned away in haste, I thought the tactic might succeed. The

255

worst of the lot (Elizabeth had once pointed him out) was a corpulent Brown Shirt named Braun. He held my gaze for a long moment. I cocked my head, as if to ask, *do you truly want to challenge me?* Then he, too, broke off the look and found something else to take up his attention.

I escorted Elizabeth to her seat, then bade farewell, ignoring the steely glare she bestowed on me – a far fiercer glare than any I had bestowed on her classmates. I had known I would have to deal with that consequence, but later. Then I turned and went back to my duties at the Abwehr.

Evening

Elizabeth returned home, took Martin into her arms from the nurse, and played with him for a while, conspicuously not saying anything to me. She waited for that until we were alone in our bedroom. Then it was if a cannonade had begun on the Western front. How could I do such a thing? Did I not trust her to deal with such rabble? Did I really think she needed the protection of her husband? And so on – and on – and on – in this vein, until she announced she would be sleeping in the nursery for the foreseeable future, until she had quite recovered from her fury.

She did just that, leaving me alone in the larger room. I know her well enough to have expected such – and yet I remain pleased with myself. Whatever her personal stature, it was necessary for me to make my own presence felt. I will brook no insult to my wife.

—

February 23, 1934
34 Kantstrasse, Schoneberg District
Berlin, Germany

From the Journals of Karl von Haydenreich (Published 1986):

. . . [I] had resigned myself to another night alone in the big bedroom, when the door opened and Elizabeth slid into the bed and into my arms. She was wearing her bridal nightgown.

'*I am still very angry with you, my husband,*' she said. '*But you should know why.*'

'*Why is that, my wife?*' I asked.

'*Because I like it too much when you play the hero for me,*' she said. '*They are the feelings of a schoolgirl. I cannot be a dreamy schoolgirl if I am to make an impression in the law. I cannot be the maiden waiting for the prince on horseback to save her.*'

'*Did our promenade at least discourage some of these fools?*' I asked.

256

'Oh, yes,' she said, *'they have been noticeably more silent. And – Karl – though you should not have behaved as you did – you were <u>wonderful</u>! I suppose I must forgive you . . . just this once.'*

With that, she turned out the light . . .

-

Excerpt from: *A Twentieth Century Life*
Albert Sommerville
Houghton, Mifflin (1959)

. . . [A]t the beginning of March, Father returned from Berlin with the news that our German friends were losing patience with Hitler. As appreciative as they were of his firm stance against the Bolsheviks, his determination to re-establish the privileges of the Teutonic race, and the new energy in Germany, they were unnerved by the brutalities and general rowdiness of the S.A. More than that, Ernst Rohm apparently took the 'Socialist' element of the Nazi program seriously. He had no more affection for the traditional German elite than did the Bolsheviks. He was stridently insisting on a 'Second Revolution', a massive redistribution of wealth and power. This, of course, made the elite nervous, extremely wary, and inclined to rethink its support of Hitler.

As welcome as the news was that Father had begun to waver in his bland acceptance of Nazi tactics, it was a bit exasperating that the same points that he disregarded when I made them, took on weight and significance when raised by others. This state of affairs went on until 1939, when events forced me to assume leadership of the Party.

-

Excerpt from: *My Name is Ike - Reflections on Fifty Years of Service as Soldier and Statesman*
Dwight D. Eisenhower
Random House (1986)

. . . [I]t was on one of our strolls in early May, that Karl informed me that he and Elizabeth were expecting another child. I congratulated him, and he smiled mysteriously. *'It is the consequence of playing the hero,'* he said. This baffled me, but I knew he was enjoying some private joke and left it alone.

He then told me that Elizabeth had decided to go to Neustrelitz after her examinations were complete, to show little Martin his ancestral home for the first time. Since one doesn't question the whims of a pregnant woman, Karl had acquiesced. He would be joining her at the end of June, when he was due extended leave. He knew I had leave coming myself. The suggestion that I visit

257

to provide some companionship to Elizabeth in the time before he could join her was natural and inevitable.

I accepted at once. I was as curious about Neustrelitz as I had been about Karl. I would have visited months before, if Mamie hadn't gone home.

-

Excerpt from: A History of Germany in the Twentieth Century
Josef Behrens
Alfred A Knopf (1964)

. . . Rohm conducted himself with increasing boldness. He met openly with Kurt Schleicher, the general who had preceded Hitler as Chancellor, with other members of the military, and even with foreign emissaries from Britain and France. His dissatisfaction with the reluctance of Hitler to act on what he regarded as the just and fair demands of the Sturmabteilung became more and more evident.

Other opponents were beginning to raise their voices. Students at the University of Frankfurt conspicuously arose and walked out of a speech given by a ranking Nazi. German conservatives, and even reactionaries, made no secret of their alarm at the demons they had unloosed. Franz von Papen, the Vice-Chancellor, continued to seek a political solution that would involve the restoration of the monarchy.

All this culminated on June 17th. On that day, at the University of Marburg, von Papen delivered a blistering speech, denouncing the excesses of the Nazis. The speech was received with rapturous applause by the assembled students. Goebbels did his best to suppress its publication, but it obtained wide circulation anyway. At a horse race meeting a few days later, von Papen was greeted with spontaneous cheers of '*Marburg! Marburg!*' by bystanders . . .

-

Excerpt from: My Name is Ike - Reflections on Fifty Years of Service as
Soldier and Statesman
Dwight D. Eisenhower
Random House (1986)

I'd formed a view in my mind's eye from what Heinz had said, but in no way did it prepare me for the reality. As God is my witness, Neustrelitz is the most beautiful place on earth. A crystal blue lake meets a cloudless blue sky, framed by the most picturesque mountains and pine forests imaginable.

So this was where my old friend Heinz had been born, lived, and died. I discovered an entire world who had known and loved him long before a chance meeting in Paris. Johanna Schallert was closing in on her 80th year, but she was still the efficient, no-nonsense housekeeper. She'd been Heinz's nursemaid in her youth, and his children's in her middle age. She missed Karl acutely. She was full of reminiscence about him, a small, lively boy who made the old, stone walls resound, first with his scamperings about the halls, later with his saxophone and the American songs he played incessantly on his gramophone. There were other servants who went back almost as far. Now the family retinue had been reduced to caretaking, and providing service to the occasional family wealthy and privileged enough to rent the large manse in its entirety for their stay. Our visit was thus a cause for huge celebration, since visits from Karl had been a rare event his entire adult life.

Elizabeth and I let Frau Schallert do her best to spoil little Martin, while we explored the castle and grounds. I viewed the splendid portraits of both Charlotte and Rosamunde, Rosamunde's being the prominent one that month. We visited the old town, the towers, the outbuildings, and, of course, the gravesite by the lake, with its profound tranquility. Soldier or not, I choked up at the site of those headstones, a response which Elizabeth was tactful enough to ignore. We both noticed the fresh flowers on the graves of the Breslau women, placed there daily. I understand this practice continues to this very day.

Karl did not arrive until the last week of June. My stay and his overlapped by only a few days.

-

Excerpt from: Destiny Betrayed - A Chronicle of Treason
Harald Quandt
Franz Eher Nachfolger Gmbh (1952)

. . . [I]t was the custom of Ernst Rohm to grant furlough to the S.A. for the two summer months beginning around June 1st. He himself and the other members of the senior leadership took a summer holiday in the Bavarian Alps, at which they could indulge in excesses of alcohol and their disgusting perversions to their hearts' delight. In 1934, the occasion was set for the beginning of July at the Tiergensee resort.

So it was that the Fuhrer seized the opportunity to eliminate the cancer with the swiftness and precision of a surgeon.

The Reichswehr command designated a junior officer to serve as observer and report. As it happened, Karl von Haydenreich was on leave at his own family's resort in Neustrelitz, only a few kilometers distant from the one rented by Rohm. Thus, this duty fell to him. It is impossible to believe this was a 'mere' coincidence . . .

June 28, 1934
Neustrelitz am Schliersee
Bavaria

From the Journals of Karl von Haydenreich (Published 1986):

. . . [H]ell and damnation! Here four days on a leave I have awaited for six months, and special orders arrive by telegram.

. . . [S]omething extraordinary must be afoot . . .

July 3, 1934
Neustrelitz am Schliersee

From the Journals of Karl von Haydenreich (Published 1986):

. . . [I] made my way to the Munich Aerodrome as ordered. Three black trucks and a throng of men, mustered in rough military order, were in front of the control tower. As we drew closer, I could make out that they were all military troops – no S.S. or S.A.

I reported to the Aerodrome offices, where I was met by General Wilhelm Adam, the commander of the Munich military district, and his chief of staff, Lieutenant Ludwig Kubler. Adam was courteous enough, Kubler quite brusque and abrupt. Kubler had additional orders for me that the Reichswehr had not wished to send by ordinary telegraph.

These were somewhat mysterious. Addressed to me by rank and station rather than name, I was ordered to accompany the persons who would arrive shortly by aeroplane, observe their activity, and report in detail to the Abwehr and General Blomberg. Under no circumstances was I to participate in any activity or operation, but limit my activity to observing and reporting. This left me as much in the dark as before, though I now had some suspicions. The 'persons' I was to accompany were not referred to by any military designation. There were not that many personages in Germany whose protection was important enough to justify mustering an entire local battalion on short notice.

Shortly after 4:00 a.m., we heard the distant buzzing of a plane approaching the field. Then a Junker became visible as it neared the runway. It circled once, then landed, between the red and blue lights along the runway. As it pulled up, I could see black shirted S.S. men moving about the cabin. A

260

mechanic in the interior opened the door. Out of the plane stepped Der Fuhrer himself, Adolf Hitler. I heard the troops around me gasp, almost in unison.

Close behind him followed Goebbels, then Adolf Wagner, the Minister of Interior for Bavaria. Hitler strode forward quickly, not even pausing to salute. Wagner kept pace; Goebbels limped behind them, trying to catch up. Hitler stopped abruptly before us, saluted sloppily, and moved on toward the phones. He did not pay me any attention, let alone recognize me, for which I was profoundly grateful.

We stood there, in that crisp cool of a dawn that betokens a hot day. Inside the tower, the phone rang continuously – calls from Berlin, mostly for Hitler, mostly from Himmler. Once or twice, Goebbels took the line. With the Reichswehr mustered to provide protection for Hitler, and grim looking S.S. troops in numbers, one did not need a fortune teller to know what was in the air. Some action against the S.A. was about to occur. But with all the phone calls, it was also apparent that there was much improvisation in the plan.

Suddenly I myself was summoned to the phone. I stepped by Wagner and Goebbels as casually as I could. Hitler himself handed me the receiver, shot me a quick glance, then turned and resumed his conference with Wagner and Goebbels. On the other end of the line was von Blomberg. He amplified my orders. The Reichswehr wanted an observer of the events that were to come. I had been chosen because of my proximity while on leave, my assignment with the Abwehr, and (I assumed) my relationship with von Blomberg. I was to report in person to von Blomberg, the balance of my leave deferred until after the report was made. I signaled my understanding, clicked my heels, and replaced the receiver. The phone rang immediately, Goebbels picked it up, listened, and handed it to Hitler.

But soon the calls were finished. The time had come to depart. I was beckoned to the back seat of the Mercedes, with Hitler himself and Goebbels. I was concerned I might breach some point of Nazi etiquette of which I was unaware, but fortunately I might as well have been invisible. The two were engaged in rapid conversation in low voices, too quick and freighted with their own prior discussions to pay any attention to me. After a few minutes, we were at the outskirts of Munich.

Dawn was breaking. We passed small groups of Brown Shirts on street corners, most of whom had clearly caroused the night away. Some supported comrades staggering with drink. Others were engaged in loud argument or singing as they wended homeward. Only then did the obvious occur to me, that the S.A. was on its summer furlough, and all of them were celebrating midsummer in some form or other. The timing of this action was not an accident.

None of them noticed Hitler as the black Mercedes sped by. He had fallen silent, lost in thought. But then we were at the Brown House, formerly Party headquarters, but now serving as the central offices of the Ministry of the Interior of Bavaria. Since the night before, it had been full of Brown Shirts, carousing and singing. Some of them were sleeping on benches outside. Apparently, none of those awake had noticed S.S. men taking up positions outside. Perhaps they assumed they were sentries. But more black uniformed S.S. troops were arriving, cars pulling up with screeching brakes, a commotion beginning. Some of the sleepers stirred. Hitler leaped out of the car, and raced up the steps and into the building. I followed, trying to keep up.

The corridors were dark and unlit. The commotion inside and out brought the building slowly to life. Men began to stir inside the offices. A few doors cracked open. Hitler strode briskly up the stairs to the third floor, and then to the reception desk before Wagner's office. A fat S.A. officer in a stained brown shirt was seated there. He lifted his head – and his face froze, almost disbelieving, at the apparition before him, the Fuhrer himself. He half rose, and began a Nazi salute, but Hitler went straight to him, his hands open. The S.A. officer drew back reflexively.

'*Lock him up!*' Hitler shouted. '*He is a traitor! They are all traitors!*' He stepped up to the man and tore the insignia off his tunic. He was so envenomed with fury his features were distorted by a facial tic. Spittle dripped off a corner of his mouth. I could only wish the German people could see him in this state. Two S.S. men grabbed the flabbergasted Schneidhuber (as he turned out to be named) and dragged him away. Meanwhile, Goebbels and Wagner had entered the office, taken seats at the desk, pulled out files, and begun compiling lists of men to be arrested. They made no secret of this. Hitler paced up and down as they worked, still in a rage.

They telephoned the local S.A. leader, a man named Schmidt, and ordered him to report to Wagner's office. He was there in minutes, and pushed his way through the crowd – there must have been 30 men in the office by then. Hitler stepped up to him. Once again, he ripped the gold braid off his shoulders – I had thought such gestures were only done at the cinema or on stage. '*You are under arrest! You will be shot! Traitor!*' he screamed. Schmidt, like

Schneidhuber, was stupefied, struck so dumb with surprise he said nothing. Then he too, was dragged away.

I learned later that such scenes were taking place all over Munich – S.A. men suddenly arrested, accused of treason, and marched to prison. The black-shirted S.S. men were posted at the railway to arrest any of the brown-shirted S.A. force who tried to leave or arrive. No one in the Brown Building was permitted to leave.

The lists of arrestees were completed. Hitler conferred with Wagner for a few moments, then made to depart with Goebbels. It was a little before 6. As my orders were to accompany them, I stayed with those two. We left the building, going towards a convoy of waiting cars. Hitler's movements were convulsive and jerky, still ablaze with anger. Then we were off. The destination given the driver was Tiergensee, the resort at which Rohm was vacationing.

Our car was in the lead. I was in the back seat with Goebbels and Hitler. I felt the breathlessness and urgency that had gripped the morning slacken its hold. Without turning my head, I stole a glance at Hitler, seated in the center of the back seat. I had last seen him at close range eleven years before, when he fled from the Odeonsplatz as the Beer Hall Putsch collapsed. He had been thinner then, with more color. Now he was flabbier, pastier, in the manner of a middle-aged civil servant who does not exercise sufficiently. Off the stage, away from the podium and the radio microphone, he was any ordinary German you might meet.

He talked incessantly, almost raving, speaking wildly of traitors, treason, personal betrayal. I could see he was deliberately working himself up, driving himself into a fit. Goebbels seconded everything he said. The two of them, the hysteric and the toady, could not have made a more contemptible impression. I straightened my head and attempted to be inconspicuous. Neither man took any notice of me at first.

Then, without warning, Hitler turned to me. '*What is your opinion of all this?*' he demanded. Any expression of opinion was dangerous, that was obvious. I remarked that politics was not the province of a Reichswehr officer, that my assignment was merely to observe and report. This answer seemed satisfactory.

Then, all at once, he peered at me more intensely.

'*What is your name?*' he demanded again. '*Have we met?*'

Well, of course we had met, eleven years before, when his eyes found mine, just before he fled his comrades at the Odeonsplatz. But it would be madness even to hint at that. I recited my name with formal politeness, and disclaimed any prior meeting.

'*Von Haydenreich?*' Hitler said. '*That was the name of my commanding officer in the Great War. Did he ever speak of me?*'

'*He was my father,*' I answered. '*He was badly gassed at the end of the war, and in bad health for most of my life. He once remarked, after the Party became significant, that you were a good soldier. But otherwise he said very little of his service.*' A complete falsehood, but I did not owe Hitler truth.

'*Yes,*' Hitler nodded, '*like many another fine warrior. Your father was a man I admired without reservation. Stabbed in the back like the rest.*' Then he realized he had lost the edge of his rage. He said something about Rohm's disloyalty; Goebbels goaded him again; and gradually he worked himself into another full storm of fury. The car raced on.

Then we were approaching the Hotel Hanselbauer at Tergensee, where Rohm and the senior officers of the Brown Shirts were vacationing. Just ahead of us were two truckloads of S.S. men, dispatched before us. Goebbels shouted out a greeting to the commander, Sepp Dietrich. I had not met him, but I knew the name. He was the commander of the Liebstandarte Adolf Hitler, Hitler's S.S. bodyguard, fanatically loyal to him personally.

The S.S. men leapt out of the trucks even before they had stopped moving and raced toward the building. The soft grass surrounding the entrance muffled their footsteps as they encircled the entire structure. There was no human noise, either inside the hotel or out. The only sound was the twittering of the summer birds. Hitler took his position before the front door, flanked by two S.S. men with drawn weapons.

Then it began. One of the S.S. men kicked open the door, and the others surged in. I could hear exclamations, guttural, sleepy cries. I entered and saw the S.S. troops stride through the corridors, thrusting the maids aside, flinging doors open without warning. Then the S.A. men, many half asleep or hung over, nearly all in undergarments or sleepwear, were driven through the corridors, with shouts and blows. They were pushed toward Hitler, who himself began the arrests, shouting at them, screaming in fury that they were traitors, vile, despicable. As in Munich, the typical reaction was amazement, bewilderment. No one had any idea what Hitler was talking about. Some tried reflexively to salute.

Then Hitler and his comrades moved to Rohm's room. Hitler himself began to pound on the door, shouting his name, and demanding that Rohm open the door. At last, Rohm flung it open. Hitler pushed his way in, screaming insults and denouncing Rohm as a traitor. Like the others, Rohm was too stupefied to reply at first, then began to protest his innocence. Hitler interrupted him with more shouts, accusing him again of arrogance and treason. Then, to my amazement, the fearsome Ernst Rohm, with his hideous scar and his arrogant swagger, collapsed into meekness. He became silent. Hitler regarded him contemptuously for a moment, then declared he was under arrest. Two S.S. men moved to either side of the door. Then Hitler turned on his heel and rushed off down the corridor, to make more arrests and denunciations.

Rohm was herded down the corridor and into the cellar with the others. I followed them and peered into the cellar. There they were, the elite of the formidable Brown Shirts, in their undershirts, numb and silent. The only sounds were the weeping of one or two adolescent boys, who had been found in bed with older officers and were now to share their fate. To my shock, I saw Braun, Elizabeth's principal tormentor, among them. He was only half-dressed. He had likely been in bed with one of the S.A. officers. Now his pudgy face was lined with tension and fear.

I felt sorry for him. I felt sorry for all of them. I could not help myself. I knew in one sense it was an unworthy emotion. These were the men who had bullied and terrorized all Germany, choosing their victims with sadistic whimsy. They had tortured Martin to the point of suicide, they had murdered him as surely as if they had pointed a pistol at his temple and pulled the trigger. There had been many, many other victims. Now they were about to suffer consequences that they earned many times over – and yet I felt sympathy for them, in their confusion and fear.

Beyond sympathy, I found myself unnerved and angered by this tawdry spectacle – yes, strangely angered. For a time, I did not understand myself. Then, suddenly, I understood the reason. I had witnessed such a grotesque perversion of truth this morning that I had become involuntarily angry. These men were not traitors to Adolf Hitler. The truth was that they were fanatically devoted to him, always had been, and remained devoted even now. They had exhibited that devotion throughout the morning, making grim, comic fools of themselves – pledging their loyalty to, or attempting to salute, a man shouting maniacal denunciations in their faces — even as they were being thrown into cellars. Murderers, sadists, pederasts, human vermin – all true. But traitors? Perhaps this was the only accusation of the lot that was not true. The truth was *he* was the traitor to *them*.

Hitler continued to rage, refusing to be calmed. The word 'rabid' sprang to mind. At times, he had actually foamed at the mouth. He *knew* that the accusations he was shouting were absolute lies. I knew he knew and then, all at once, I fully understood the mechanism. He used the sheer magnitude of the lie to his benefit. He transformed the energy he had to exert to force himself to believe this preposterous hypocrisy into a manic, hysterical rage that swept aside all opposition, including his own awareness of the truth. The objects of his fury were too cowed and intimidated by its intensity to give him the lie. As I watched, he drove himself to even stormier heights.

Somehow Dietrich had procured a tour bus, to transport the prisoners to Munich. As Rohm and the others were herded towards it, I heard another engine. Approaching down the same road was another open truck, this time crammed with Brown Shirts. I surmised this was Rohm's personal guard, the Stabswache, come to rescue their leader from his plight. The truck roared in, and the Brown Shirts jumped off with weapons. For a long moment, they confronted the black-shirted S.S. men, both parties grim but uncertain. At that moment, the outcome once again had become uncertain.

But for a moment only. Then Hitler strode up to them. Since it was necessary for him now to be calm, he had calmed himself. Peremptorily he announced that he was their Fuhrer, that they were sworn to obey him – and then he ordered them back into the truck and back to Munich. They hesitated, but he stood firm. Then, after a long moment of sullen silence, the S.A. men saluted Hitler in unison (he did not return it), remounted the truck, and drove away. The scene became completely calm. Then the Fuhrer began anew the process of enraging himself.

A few minutes later, Goebbels summoned me to the telephone. It was von Blomberg, who asked me directly if the scene was orderly. I informed him truthfully that it was, and that the entire morning had been orderly. No one arrested had offered resistance. He then told me then that my mission of observation was ended. He reinstated my leave (welcome news!). As events had unfolded, he saw no need for an immediate report. He did direct me to report to him personally, as soon as I returned to Berlin. Hitler and the others were already gone in the Mercedes, back to Munich. So was the bus with the prisoners. I was left to make my own way home, which was not difficult, as the Handlebauer is much closer to Neustrelitz than Munich.

July 5

It has been five days. Enough time to pause and reflect.

266

I told everything to Elizabeth as soon after my return, as I had recovered breath. She saw at once what had escaped me. '*There were no police?*' she said. '*No warrants or process of the court? Then this was murder. But it is the Reichstag fire again. The people will approve because they feared and detested the S.A.*'

She was also sure that the circle of violence would extend well beyond the S.A. '*It will not be just here, in Bavaria. He will not lose the opportunity. He will include his other enemies, and claim they were conspirators with Rohm.*' I wondered about that, when first she spoke. But she was right again. The days have passed and we learned what else had happened that night. There were operations in Berlin and elsewhere, all timed to occur at the same time as the Munich arrests.

Rank and position had meant nothing. Two Reichswehr generals had been murdered, von Bredow, whom I had liked, and Schleicher, whom I had detested . . . but Reichswehr generals! Von Papen – the vice Chancellor! – had only barely escaped arrest. Goebbels insisted that all those who suffered were involved with the S.A. But he provided no more explanations, confident that none would be required.

The same cynical excuse masked plain, simple, primitive revenge. Jung, the writer of the Marburg speech, had been murdered. So, too, in Munich was the retired mayor, von Kahr, hacked to death in a ditch. Von Kahr was 73, long retired from politics, and with no connection to the S.A. He did not pose the slightest risk to anyone. But he had been one of the officials present on the night of the Beer Hall Putsch, the one my grandfather would not take me to. He had embarrassed Hitler that long ago night and morning. The Fuhrer never forgot an insult.

I asked Elizabeth if she had ever met von Kahr. Indeed she had. He and his wife had even been to the Golsing home, for rather stuffy, formal dinners. She hadn't liked him – he was rather stuffy and formal himself.

'*Did he ever mention Hitler?*' I asked.

'*Only after he became prominent,*' she answered. '*He regretted very much the leniency Hitler received in 1923. He regretted that he had not been exiled or executed, according to the law.*'

'*I am sure he regretted it much more in that ditch,*' I said.

Then I told her that Braun had been among those arrested with Rohm. To my surprise, her eyes filled with tears. My wife is not a woman who cries often. Only for her brother did I ever see her weep without inhibition. Perhaps her condition had something to do with it.

'*Tears for Braun?*' I said. '*But he was a contemptible pig.*'

'*I weep because he was a contemptible pig,*' she said. '*Was that reason enough to shoot him?*'

Excerpt from: A General Speaks - the Autobiography of Kurt von Hammerstein Equord
Major General Kurt von Hammerstein Equord
Reichswehr Press (1986)

. . . [T]he Night of the Long Knives was the most profound shock of my life. The corporal had had the audacity to include two Reichswehr generals in the ambit of his vengeance. Von Schleicher was murdered in his own front parlor, along with his wife. He was a compulsive intriguer who doubtless had met and plotted with Rohm. Von Bredow was tied to a chair in his basement and shot five times. He was von Schleicher's confederate. But they were Reichswehr generals – and whatever they might have planned for Hitler, they were not remotely traitors to the German nation.

Even if these men had been in league with the S.A. leadership, were their acts so menacing that they must perforce be executed without arrest or trial? And what of Schleicher's wife? Whose only act of treason had been to answer the door when the S.S. knocked? What of her? To me, the question answered itself.

There had been other barbaric acts committed that day, more in keeping with the practice of an American gangster or an Oriental despot than the leader of the German Republic. They deserved the greatest condemnation and criminal punishment. But to my amazement, there was nothing – no reaction from the public or Reichswehr command. I attended Schleicher's funeral – I, and I alone. I was astounded. I realized then that there was not going to be a trial or proceeding, or consequence of any kind. Von Blomberg and Reichenau had evidently been far more successful at compromising the Army than I had been aware.

Hitler made a speech. He passed all his brutalities off as a necessary reaction to an emergency – and, incredibly, that was that. At first, I could not believe that would be all. Yet it was – from the public, from the Army. Their relief that Hitler had put the S.A. in its place was so great that they accepted his inadequate explanations without more.

The time had come for deep reflection. Neither the Kaiser, nor any of the crowned heads of Europe, nor any of their ministers, nor even the Czar, had used murder and random violence in this manner. The corporal was not a politician like any other, and the Nazi Party not like any other. They presented a peril to the German nation that was unparalleled – and growing in danger. I had never in my career questioned the principle of political neutrality for a serving officer in the Army. But now, for the first time in my professional life, I began to wonder where my duty as German citizen and German general might lie.

But what to do? I pondered these matters to the point of obsession over the next few weeks.

Excerpt from: My Name is Ike - Reflections on Fifty Years of Service as Soldier and Statesman
Dwight D. Eisenhower
Random House (1986)

Karl returned to Berlin a few days later, temporarily alone. Elizabeth decided to stay on at Neustrelitz for a few more days. We met for lunch as usual.

I asked Karl for his thoughts on the recent events. It was only then I learned that he had been the officer designated by the Reichswehr to observe that morning. He gave me an account of Hitler's behavior that was worse than anything I had imagined.

'*I wish I could report on this,*' I told him.

'*But I expect you to report, Ike,*' Karl answered. '*I want you to. It's important that powerful people know what Hitler is really like.*'

'*Karl,*' I said patiently, '*you are identified as the Reichswehr observer. If I write a report, everyone will know you are the source.*'

'*I know it is a dangerous game we are about to play,*' he said, '*and I am duty-bound to protect Elizabeth and Martin and my unborn child. But people must know this. You are a clever man, and you have met many people in Germany. Surely you can conceal how you know what you know.*'

'*Yes,*' I answered slowly, '*I can do that.*' I thought about it all for a moment – what I could do, what I should do, what Karl wanted, how dangerous a game it really was . . . and I decided to go forward. In truth, it was not a terribly significant decision. Gathering intelligence of that type was exactly what the United States Army expected me to do. My hesitation was based solely on concern for Karl. For me, there wasn't much to think about.

But what I did not know is that personalities and decisions being made elsewhere in Berlin would give my decision a momentousness that I could not possibly have imagined . . . in fact, never did imagine, until it all blew up in my face a few years later.

And if you've wondered when all that doubt and second-guessing I mentioned earlier begins . . . it begins right there.

-

Excerpt from: A General Speaks - the Autobiography of Kurt von Hammerstein Equord
Major General Kurt von Hammerstein Equord
Reichswehr Press (1986)

. . . [B]y August I had come to my decision. The corporal, an émigré Austrian vagabond with no special attainments or accomplishments, attempted to seal off all opposition in the Army by requiring all personnel to swear an oath of loyalty to him personally. The form of vow was well beyond what any Kaiser, caliph, king, or tsar had ever required. It was taken in mass formation in late July. I did not regard myself bound in the slightest by this preposterous farce, nor did any officer I respected.

But it was, in the words of the proverb, the last straw. The Nazi regime was intolerable. I had already formed a loose circle of opponents of the Nazis within the Army command – without, however, any particular objective. Events had now gone too far for talk. I decided to cull from that circle a core group who shared my sense of alarm, and were prepared to seek the overthrow of the Nazi regime, when and if circumstances permitted. I am aware in writing this, that I am providing fodder for Quandt and other apologetic historians of his ilk. But the implication that a revolutionary cabal was formed then is one I do deny. Nothing was planned, beyond a principled opposition ready to oppose, and, possibly, depose Hitler, if the occasion arose. All we were prepared to do at that time was stand ready.

I should clarify. That was all *we* were prepared to do as a group. But I had already chosen a bolder strategy for myself alone, one that was only possible for an officer as above suspicion as the ranking officer in the Reichswehr (or Wehrmacht, as newly christened by the corporal. The strategy had been chosen. But I was still in search of the tactic, the method.

270

Then I learned that von Blomberg had received a report about the June 28th event from a young Reichswehr officer, who was none other than Karl von Haydenreich. I obtained a copy of the report, which was bland and non-controversial. I was sure he had much more to say on the subject. Therefore, I summoned him to my offices, for an interview – this despite the rumors that he was a committed Nazi sympathizer, spying on the Abwehr for von Blomberg.

He was noncommittal at first, as was I. Neither of us was sure of the other. But I reminded him of the interview we had had when he applied to the Reichswehr. I also recalled the question I had put to him at his commission – was he truly his father's son? At that, the mask of duty slipped a bit. I was encouraged enough by this to take the huge risk of laying my own convictions (though not my plans) in front of him. With those confidences lingering in the air, I asked him if he had anything to add to the report. Von Haydenreich hesitated for only a moment – and then he, too, spoke as freely as I had. He provided details of Hitler's conduct and bloodlust that fully confirmed the worst of my opinions about the man.

Then he surprised me by asking if I knew how well-acquainted he was with Adolf Hitler. I invited him to continue. I was astounded to learn how much coincidental involvement the Haydenreich family had had with the man. Young Haydenreich himself had actually been a witness to the corporal's behavior at the time of the Munich Putsch.

'*What, then, do you think of him?*' I asked at the end.

'*That he is a worthless coward, a fraud, and a criminal,*' von Haydenreich said promptly.

'*And the outcome?*' I asked. '*The dissolution of the S.A.?*'

'*Dissolution?*' he said. '*He replaced it with the S.S. – much more efficient and dangerous. He also eliminated all the opposition in government – most of whom despised the S.A. as much as he did. You must have noticed this.*'

'*Yes,*' I said, '*and I am in agreement with you.*' But I had one final question for him before I took him fully into my confidence. '*If these are your true opinions, why do you spy for von Blomberg?*'

Young Haydenreich almost jumped out of his skin at this, but then he composed himself. '*Von Blomberg believes I spy for him,*' he said. '*But I tell him only enough to dull his curiosity. The General believes what he wants to believe about my sympathies.*'

'*I see,*' I said. With that, I came to a critical decision – to take Karl von Haydenreich fully into my confidence. I became completely open about my own thinking and some of the preliminary plans I had made. At the end, I asked him if he would be willing to repeat his reports to other officers sympathetic to my aims. *'With pleasure,'* he replied. He hesitated a bit, and I inquired of his thoughts.

'I have already circulated a report,' he said, *'through my friend Major Eisenhower, the American. It was my hope that publicizing the Fuhrer's conduct will bring about a crisis.'*

'I see,' I said, *'and I am in complete sympathy.'* This last disclosure confirmed the judgment I had tentatively made of young von Haydenreich. I had found my man.

'I'm having a small gathering at my home this Saturday,' I said. *'I'm sure your saxophone would be a valuable addition to the music. Your wife is invited, too. Perhaps during the evening, I can introduce you to other officers whose views might interest you.'*

'I would be delighted to attend, sir,' he answered. *'My wife Elizabeth is in the last months of a difficult pregnancy. Her health may preclude her presence.'*

'Of course,' I answered. Then I had a final thought.

'That American friend of yours,' I said, *'Major Eisenhower. I've met him. Is he completely trustworthy?'*

-

Excerpt from: My Name is Ike - Reflections on Fifty Years of Service as Soldier and Statesman
Dwight D. Eisenhower
Random House (1986)

I was on furlough during August and September of 1934 – two months at home with Mamie and my sons. It was a tonic that I desperately needed. I didn't want to go back to Germany. What had looked ordinary to me in 1933 no longer did. I did not want to return to that world of weird, funhouse mirrors that the Nazis had created.

But I had no choice. There was no place else to go. So back I went.

I resumed with Karl and Elizabeth within a week, though I did not see nearly as much of them as before. Her pregnancy was advanced, the baby due in December. Just how she kept up with her studies in that condition, enduring the muttered insults and whispered indignities, amazes me. But Elizabeth is that kind of amazing woman. However, she simply wasn't up to much socializing in what little free time she had. Karl was even more musically active than usual.

His talents had been discovered (or, more accurately, rediscovered) by some prominent members of the Wehrmacht General Staff. Our meetings were reduced to the lunches that Karl and I shared from time to time.

It was at the second of these that Karl invited me for another of our walks in the Tiergarten. It was a crisp, early autumn afternoon in October. We were talking of everything and nothing, when he turned to me.

'*I have a matter of extreme sensitivity and importance to discuss with you,*' he said.

An Arrow Loosed Into The Air

Excerpt from: A History of Germany in the Twentieth Century
Josef Behrens
Alfred A Knopf (1964)

Beginning in the autumn of 1934 and lasting through March 1936 (the date 'the Order' was received), the policies and priorities of the British and French governments were first affected, then decisively influenced by an extraordinary intelligence resource the British developed inside the German government.

His own statements establish that Senator Dwight D. Eisenhower, then the military attaché for the United States, was the individual primarily responsible for the actual delivery of the material to the British officials. Karl von Haydenreich has long been suspected of being the primary agent inside German government, though his participation is a matter of hot debate and conjecture. Who else may have been involved is unknown . . .

Excerpt from: My Name is Ike - Reflections on Fifty Years of Service as
Soldier and Statesman
Dwight D. Eisenhower
Random House (1986)

That conversation was the first of the great turning points of my life that occurred during those years in Berlin. Karl, a bit shyly, but without undue embarrassment, asked me directly if I would be willing to furnish information obtained from a highly-placed Wehrmacht source, to representatives of the British and French governments.

I was not expecting that request. But I can't say I was surprised, either, not after the report about the Night of the Long Knives that Karl had given me earlier that summer. It was no surprise to me that there was organized resistance to Hitler in the Wehrmacht. It was certainly no surprise that Karl was a part of it. Thus, it did not come as any surprise to me that I might be asked to play an active role in that resistance.

But I also knew instantly that a watershed moment had arrived. Every prudential consideration indicated that I should emphatically refuse. It was one thing to write a report to my own government about information I'd received from a German officer. That was my job. It was quite another to deliver information stolen from the host government to one of its adversaries. That is an act of espionage. A person who does such things is a spy. There is no way spying or espionage in any form can be confused with the proper role of a military attaché. (I was forcibly and repeatedly reminded of that fact during the Senate hearings of 1937, but I knew it already.) Just what my status would be if the Nazis ever discovered me, I had no idea.

Not just the Nazis . . . there'd be hell to pay if my own people found out. The Ivy League stuffed shirts who ran the State Department were determined to play nice with Hitler. There were more than a few committed anti-Semites in the ranks who secretly approved of his anti-Jew policies. Ambassador Dodd, who was a great guy, was trying to set them straight, but getting nowhere. I had already burned my military prospects back in Washington with MacArthur. Now Karl was asking me to put the shattered remnants of whatever was left of my career on the line.

So there was every practical reason to turn him down.

'*Sure,*' I said, without a pause for breath. '*Tell me how I can help.*'

I'd already seen and heard enough of the Third Reich to know where my real duty lay. The hell with practicality.

November 13, 1934
Cavendish Square
London, England

Mr. A. A. Milne
Cotchford Farm
Hartfield, East Sussex

My dear Milne,

. . . [T]he war mongers never rest. You would think Churchill and his like would have learned better in the Great War, but not so. What do we English care how Hitler cleans his own house, or how he may have blathered in the dawn of his career? Haven't we all blathered? Who other than a few troglodytes like Churchill believe in the villainy of this man?

By all accounts, Herr Hitler means us no harm. He has only the best interests of the German people at heart. They suffered more in the Great War than we did. That will not inhibit the Prime Minister and the others from undermining and demonizing Hitler in the interest of perpetuating French and English hegemony on the continent. We must not permit this . . .

Yours,

Sir Robert Cecil

-

Excerpt from: My Name is Ike - Reflections on Fifty Years of Service as Soldier and Statesman
Dwight D. Eisenhower
Random House (1986)

Karl did not inform me who or what the source of the information was, and I didn't ask. We both understood that the less I knew the better. We did discuss the mechanism. The means were rather simple. The source and I used the same book, the same standard edition of the German Lutheran Bible – easy to obtain, and beyond suspicion. The notes and the verifying information was a basic book cipher – simple, but virtually undetectable in a civilian context. Even in war time, it's a tough code for professional cryptographers to break.

I never asked directly, but it was an easy guess that Karl obtained the report during the musical events he attended. Live music was a staple of German military hospitality, and Karl's virtuosity was such that he was in demand everywhere. When his source had something to provide, the encoded notes were interleaved into Karl's music scores. Karl left the musicales with the documents in his scores. These he in turn inserted into another musical score that he browsed over at one of the half-dozen music stores he frequented. These would be retrieved by me.

The mechanics were simple enough, and virtually foolproof. It was the human factor that bothered me. The Germans had spies of their own in both the British and French governments. I trusted Karl, but maybe he himself was being manipulated and tested by someone wondering about his in-laws. On my side, I had a fairly low opinion of the British military liaison officer to whom I would most likely deliver the material. Major William Keller was a blustering type of military man who liked his whiskey neat, and often, big on blather, and very low on intelligence. The need to trust his discretion to any degree bothered me quite a bit.

I was also bothered by Karl's insistence that the entire undertaking be kept secret from Elizabeth. Mind you, the good sense of that was obvious enough. But I liked Elizabeth, did not like keeping information from her, and

278

the practical fact was that she was too damn smart not to figure out that something was up. Karl scrupulously avoided any mention of our arrangement in his journal or any other writing. But she was too keen not to wonder what was going on.

Nonetheless, whatever our misgivings, we began our perilous journey that fall. Only two weeks had passed before Karl mentioned casually that there was a music score that might interest me at one of his favorite shops.

-

Excerpt from: Destiny Betrayed - A Chronicle of Treason
Harald Quandt
Franz Eher Nachfolger Gmbh (1952)

. . . [O]nly the naive require direct proof of treason. Even the densest villains and traitors have enough animal cunning to cover their tracks.

. . . [V]on Hammerstein made the acquaintance of von Haydenreich and invited him to numerous musical soirées. Von Haydenreich was a longtime friend of the American military attaché Eisenhower. Eisenhower had accepted large sums of money from von Haydenreich in the past. Eisenhower admits he was the person who delivered the stolen documents to the British and French. His conspiracy of silence with whomever the traitor was, is a meaningless comedy to anyone with discerning intelligence.

The pattern is obvious to anyone – except for those Jewish thinkers determined to confuse and obscure . . .

-

Excerpt from: My Name is Ike - Reflections on Fifty Years of Service as
Soldier and Statesman
Dwight D. Eisenhower
Random House (1986)

. . . [T]he exact name of the first music I purchased fled my memory a long time ago – some piano music by Chopin, I think. Karl made a casual mention of it in one of our meetings. Two days later, I was at the right shop, found the piece in the used section, and bought it. Since I don't play myself, I told the clerk I was picking it up for a friend. (There really *was* a friend, who did play, and was my one American ally in the venture, since (s)he spoke German as well. (S)he despised Hitler even more than I did. I will not identify my friend here. By the time these memoirs appear, that person will either have made his or her role known, or will have departed into history on that person's own terms. In either case, it's not a choice for me to make, so I will respect that confidentiality here.)

The Third Reich back then was hardly the police state the Soviet Union became. A walk of a mile or so with a piece of music under my arm, with an insert presented in an obscure, semi-musical form, was not much of an adventure. But I walked that walk in as full a state of adrenaline alert as I had ever been in combat. You can fool your intellect, but never your instincts. What I was doing was dangerous, very dangerous, never mind the low probability of discovery, and my guts knew it.

But nothing did happen, then or later. (In fact, until this very day, with the publication of my memoirs and von Hammerstein's, no one ever discovered our method. As all the world knows, when the catastrophe did arrive, it was from an entirely different direction.) I went to my friend's office, closed the door, and we began to decode the enclosure. Of course, we were novices to cryptography that first day, so it took quite a while. But finally, we were done, my friend did a hasty translation, and we evaluated what was before us. The first page was simply a list of unannounced officer promotions, intended to prove the *bona fides* of the informant. But the second and third pages . . .

'*My goodness*,' I said weakly. My friend was silent for a long, long time.

'*Whatever you need, Ike*,' (s)he said at last. '*I'll support you any way I can.*'

–

Excerpt from: *A General Speaks - the Autobiography of Kurt von Hammerstein Equord*
Major General Kurt von Hammerstein Equord
Reichswehr Press (1986)

. . . [C]ircumstances and a mutual detestation of Hitler had brought von Haydenreich and myself together. But I was pleased to discover human qualities in him that I appreciated and respected – a profound nobility of spirit rare in any young man, and a true graciousness and gentleness of soul. These latter traits may not seem to be of the essence of a sound military character, but you may trust me that they are. In no little time, a profound friendship developed between us.

I also had some initial concern that some explanations about the presence of von Haydenreich as a musician might be required. But, unexpectedly, he proved to be superbly talented. Not only was he accepted by the others, he soon assumed a leadership position in most of the ensembles in which he participated. My musicians accepted him as a peer without a murmur.

The pleasure he derived from the simple act of music-making was apparent and touching. Once, in one of our rare informal moments, he confided in me that these satisfactions were almost reward enough for the risks he was undertaking . . .

Excerpt from: My Name is Ike - Reflections on Fifty Years of Service as Soldier and Statesman
Dwight D. Eisenhower
Random House (1986)

The next day I sought out Major Keller at his offices. '*Here,*' I said, '*I have something that might interest you.*' I slid the envelope over to him.

'*What is this?*' he asked upon opening it, a bit warily. I couldn't blame him. On a stranger's desktop, it looked like nothing so much as a schoolboy's bad essay, nothing that could ever be important to anyone.

'*Only the best intelligence you'll ever get on the intentions of the Nazi government.*' I didn't like Keller or respect his judgment. The puffery was essential to make him understand that his own career might be jeopardized if he did not respond appropriately. I could see in his eyes he got the point.

'*Who's your contact?*' he asked.

'*I'm not going to tell you that,*' I answered. '*You'll find the document authenticates itself. And to answer your next question, no, my government does not know what I'm doing. This is wholly my own affair. So keep your mouth shut about me, too. If my own embassy finds out, I'm going to be on the next ship back to the States, probably lashed to the foremast. Your Prime Minister wouldn't be happy if that happened. He's going to want as much of this stuff as we can provide.*' I wasn't so sure of the truth of that last, but it was another point that had to be made. I needed Keller intimidated into speechlessness.

I became even less certain about the British in the three weeks that followed. Nothing happened. I wondered if Keller had followed through, or if the British government was so lackadaisical that it didn't matter. The silence angered me. We had loosed an arrow of considerable significance into the air, at considerable risk, and it didn't seem to make any difference to anyone.

Then, in late October, during a military exercise we both were observing, Keller sidled up to me. '*Whitehall wants as much of that stuff as you can provide it,*' he said stiffly, as if I'd offended him. I knew at once what had

281

occurred. The Wehrmacht promotion list had come out and thus verified the report – and that made the dynamite that was in it suddenly of the highest importance. Keller had likely received a dressing down for handling it casually. I couldn't say I was surprised or displeased. It was further confirmation that we were being taken seriously. I was a little disappointed that London hadn't taken it a little further and replaced him. He was too loose a cannon for my taste. I would have preferred someone, anyone, with a bit more seriousness and discretion.

But the loosed arrow had found its target after all. It was my pleasure to inform Karl of that fact when next we met. As it happened, he had another document ready for delivery to me.

-

Excerpt from: Ma Vie Publique, 1929 -1940
Albert Sarraut
Editions du Cerf (1955)

. . . [B]eginning in late 1934, the British government began receiving extraordinarily detailed intelligence of the actual intentions of the Chancellor of Germany, the self-styled Fuhrer, Adolf Hitler, as expressed in statements he made in meetings with the General Staff of the Wehrmacht. The British Prime Minister MacDonald was sufficiently concerned to share the product with the French government.

I did not see the actual documents until I myself became premier. But even after the fact, they were enough to cause the gravest possible concern . . .

-

November 18, 1934
34 Kantstrasse, Schoneberg District
Berlin, Germany

From the Journals of Karl von Haydenreich (Published 1986):
. . . I was encasing my clarinet, on my way to an event at the General's, when Elizabeth addressed me. The invitation had of course been addressed to both of us, but she had declined, as she is now quite large with child and indisposed. But then, of a sudden she was questioning me deeply about this event and then all the others. We had been in Berlin for nearly two years. Everyone knew I could play. Why all at once was my saxophone so popular with von Hammerstein's circle of friends? What took place at these events besides music?

.

282

Why this sudden curiosity, I wondered. Was she jealous? Our baby is now only a month away. But she insisted that was not so. *'It is my intuition. There is something odd about all this, Karl,'* she said. *'What is going on?'*

I reassured her that it was coincidence. Despite my reputation, General von Hammerstein probably hadn't known I played the saxophone. He had learned of this recently, and now he and his friends desired my presence. That was all.

'But you said the General had been present at other performances of yours, when you were in training. How could your gift be a new discovery?'

'I really don't know.' Then for good measure, I took her in my arms. Large belly or small, she has no rival and never will. There is only one for me, and always will be. She knows that, but perhaps it was wise to say it aloud.

She let the matter drop. Perhaps, despite her protestations, she was troubled by the thought of another woman.

-

Excerpt from: My Life in Office
Stanley Baldwin
Houghton, Mifflin (1947)

In late October of 1934, I received a summons to the Prime Minister's offices. I can't be sure of the precise date the because I was not a member of the Government. All I can state with certainty is that I was contacted by the Prime Minister's Office and advised that the Government was in receipt of material that it felt must be shared with the shadow cabinet. I was advised to make an appointment with the appropriate secretary to review the documents. I could take all the time I wished, but the material could not be copied or removed from the office. This was all quite mysterious, but there was no more said than that. Naturally, I was intrigued and made the requested appointment within a day or two.

At the appointed hour, I was ushered into a small alcove, accompanied by the same secretary. On a small table in the center of the room, with a single chair, were three binders. I was invited to sit and examine the material for as long as I liked, but also informed that no notes would be permitted. At first, these seemed like strict protocols for what were, after all, intelligence reports.

But I understood the necessity for the strictness almost as soon as I began my examination. By that time, the government had received three separate reports from the German intelligence source. Each one consisted of only a few pages in the original German, then an English translation by the same source. Each one had its own separate dossier, with dozens and dozens of collateral reports collated beneath. Collectively and individually, they had been subjected to an extraordinarily thorough analysis by several different intelligence agencies, all of which had confirmed their authenticity – in the case of some agencies, with considerable reluctance.

I began with the latest, the one that had brought me to the alcove. I was presented with a detailed summary of a conference that Adolf Hitler had held with the top generals of the Wehrmacht (as Hitler had renamed the Reichswehr) and the Staff command in mid-October. At that time, he had directly discussed his plans for the full rearmament of Germany as quickly as the task could be accomplished. Once the state, the military, and the people were war ready, he fully intended to embroil Germany in a full-scale continental war. The purpose was to secure additional territory for the German race in Eastern Europe. The peoples presently living there would be eliminated or enslaved, as would the other races Hitler deemed unworthy, most notably the Jews. He rationalized all these horrific plans by references to the crude Darwinism of *Mein Kampf.* Persons of Aryan stock, being the master race, were blessed with a moral imperative to confront and destroy lesser races and their nations. This horrific ambition was expressed in cold, unambiguous language that could not be rationalized.

I perused the first two documents as well. They were more of the same. Collectively, they put the lie to the public protestations of the German Chancellor that his ambitions for the new Germany extended no further than redress of the grievances of the Versailles Treaty. Instead, there was talk of a Third Reich and an empire that would last a thousand years. The unknown source had added the comment that by no means had the entire Wehrmacht Staff succumbed to this talk of slaves and empire. But he also noted that even the hesitant ones acquiesced to the vision, due to the immediate benefit of rearmament. He cautioned that success in the diplomatic or limited military exercises would doubtless bring more and more of the doubting Thomases into line with Hitler's vision. He emphasized the fire and conviction with which Hitler discussed his plans for war, and the benefits to Germany.

The dossiers were the product of the truly Herculean efforts our own people had made to ascertain the identity of the provider of this information. The essential *bona fides* of the author had been established in the form of the promotional lists and minor field orders that he furnished in advance of their publication, all of which came to pass as predicted. But who was he? All three reports had been subject to the most searching and painstaking analysis, down to the ink used to write the reports. It had produced nothing. All that could be said definitively is that the source had a high position in the Wehrmacht and was scrupulous about his loyalty to it. There was no military intelligence that was remotely useful in a military context; it was apparent that the writer had taken great pains not to divulge anything that could do damage to the German Army. (I noticed a grudging respect for this in the military analyses.) All that could be deduced with certainty was that he was profoundly anti-Nazi and determined to bring about the fall of Hitler.

The British contact on the scene, a major named Keller, did know the name of the go-between who had furnished the reports. Keller had indicated early on that he was quite willing to disclose the identity, despite having given an undertaking not to do so. But since that person was a representative of a neutral country, pursuing that avenue of inquiry promised little and might endanger the flow of information. Keller had been soundly admonished for his casual willingness to break a solemn promise and was kept on a short tether thereafter. This seemed a prudent course of action to me. But it left us with no real method of ascertaining the source of information. For the time being, we would have to trust in his continued good will and detestation of Hitler.

I left with my mind roiled in thought. By the worst possible bad luck, the German people, or the forces of history, had placed at the head of Germany a criminal psychopath of the most loathsome and despicable type. He was a far greater threat to peace than any king, Kaiser, or czar had ever been, and would remain so until and unless something was done.

But what, exactly? The British public, made rightfully cynical by the rhetorical excesses of the Great War, would never countenance any bold act of opposition, nor would the French. The proverbial problem of the mice with the bell was what the British government faced.

I almost felt sorry for MacDonald. We had our very different views on what ailed England, and what the right remedies might be. But, like myself, the domestic agenda was the one that interested him. The last thing he wanted on his plate was a major problem of foreign policy. But there it was.

I would have felt sorrier still for him, were I not aware that (if the mood of the voting public could be trusted) this problem would soon devolve from him to me.

-

November 19, 1934

34 Kantstrasse, Schoneberg District
Berlin, Germany
From the Journals of Karl von Haydenreich (Published 1986):

. . . [G]reeted by Elizabeth at the door. Her mood, absolute exultation – news from Zurich – positive news – at last! After this long, endless darkness! The latest photographs of Martin in his little sailor suit, have had an effect! They stirred something inside the Judge. For the first time in years, he showed a spark of interest in what lay outside his chamber door. He asked for more pictures, inquired after me, after Martin, after Elizabeth, her studies, her pregnancy. Then he arose, dressed himself as of old, and shaved.

This happened about a week ago. Every day now, he walks outside in his overcoat, reads the newspapers, and takes coffee at a coffee house on the square. Day by day, he shakes off the lethargy. Each passing day, he becomes someone who resembles the man we all knew and respected . . .

-

Excerpt from: Destiny Betrayed - A Chronicle of Treason
Harald Quandt
Franz Eher Nachfolger Gmbh (1952)

. . . [I]t is a base lie, it is the most baseless lie, that Adolf Hitler was ever a warmonger. His *Mein Kampf* was no more than a long philosophical rumination, one completely removed from the practicalities of rule – a simple distinction that he made clearly to all of Europe and the world shortly after he took office . . .

. . . [T]he Fuhrer was a man of peace . . .

-

Excerpt from: A Twentieth Century Life
Albert Sommerville
Houghton, Mifflin (1959)

In November of 1934, I attended the annual rally of the Nazi Party in Nuremberg with my father. We were planning our own international conference in the spring, and were hoping to obtain Hitler's support.

But I would have been glad for the opportunity to attend in any case. These gatherings of the National Socialist Party had been annual events since the mid 20's, but since its ascent to power, the rallies had become increasingly large and spectacular. I found the pageantry at the 1934 rally an extraordinary, thrilling spectacle. The film the woman director Riefenstahl made of the event is remarkable, but even that does not do it justice.

Row after row, rank after rank of German citizens, from all walks of life, arrayed in phalanx after phalanx, dedicating their lives and loyalty to the new Germany and the Fuhrer. It was an overwhelming, magnificent display. The thuggery that had so disturbed me seemed to belong to another time and world. My father and brother had formed the Imperial Party in 1927, when the Nazis were a long running joke in Germany. How far they had come, how pitiful our progress in comparison!

As to the man himself, my father and I shared a luncheon with Hitler and several of his supporters, mostly German, but a few international. The Fuhrer (as he had recently come to be called) made a most favorable impression at the lunch – relaxed and engaging, in his element. He had put paid to the S.A. and won back the allegiance of most of the traditional Conservative nationalists who had wondered about him. Once more, he had become the man of the hour, the man on whom all things depended. His awareness of that fact was a tonic to him. It is easy to be charming when you're being lionized.

I revised my favorable opinion somewhat downward the next day, after a private audience with Hitler and my father. The Fuhrer was obviously intelligent, but with an extremely narrow focus. The themes were all about Germany, and its resurgence, and its rightful place in the world. He swore that he abjured war, that his ambitions were only to restore the natural borders of the German state. But there was a bellicosity to his tone that undercut his sincerity. On this occasion, he was not at all charming. I mentioned my misgivings to my father, but he brushed them aside. He was too pleased with Hitler's promise to send delegates to our conference to be critical.

Then we were off to Italy, and the Fascisti. There was not even time for a visit with Karl. He had not been able to attend Nuremberg due to Elizabeth's condition. I missed him on that occasion.

December 10, 1934
34 Kantstrasse, Schoneberg District
Berlin, German

From the Journals of Karl von Haydenreich (Published 1986):

So today I have become the father of two sons! Wilhelm Karl is born into the world! Elizabeth began feeling pain in the middle of the afternoon yesterday. She somehow finished her lecture (!) before she had herself driven to the hospital, and notified me. Then, somewhat after midnight, Wilhelm made his debut!

287

Elizabeth gave me her marvelous smile. '*So now we have replaced my brother and your uncle, my husband,*' she said. '*Next time, our little Lena. I promise.*'

Now I am home, lost in wonder at the blessings of my two sons, and the divine grace that brought Elizabeth to me in my life and loneliness.

1935

-

Excerpt from: A General Speaks - the Autobiography of Kurt von Hammerstein Equord
Major General Kurt von Hammerstein Equord
Reichswehr Press (1986)

. . . [W]e had been successful in delivering to the British information about the true character and intentions of the corporal. But in these initial months, no opportunity for the type of political embarrassment that might depose him had arisen. Then, in late January of 1935, fortune and Hitler himself seemed to put the best chance directly into our hands.

At a secret meeting with the Wehrmacht, Hitler in all his arrogance as Fuhrer announced plans to repudiate the Versailles Treaty and all the arms limitations in early March. Conscription would be resumed. Of course, this news was greeted outwardly with tremendous applause. I myself chafed at the humiliations in the Treaty. But as I looked about the room, I could also see any number of general officers with reservations. All of us remembered the horrors of the last war; no one wanted to experience them again; and Germany was completely unprepared for war if the Allies showed any determination. The announcement proposed by the corporal was thus one of extreme high risk.

I thought that the opportunity had come. With just a bit of luck, Hitler could be embarrassed before the entire world, and the German public. There was even the possibility that the chains of Versailles might be broken in the process, peacefully and honorably, since they had become quite unpopular throughout Europe.

I prepared encrypted notes on the meeting at once. Karl was at that time abroad, in Zurich with his in-laws. But they were ready for delivery the moment he returned . . .

-

February 6, 1935
Cavendish Square
London, England

Mr. A. A. Milne
Cotchford Farm,
Hartfield, East Sussex

My dear Milne,

. . . [T]he progress of the League of Nations United in six months has been more than we ever hoped for. There are now over 1,000 committees in every city and hamlet in the nation. More than 500,000 canvassers urge the Peace Ballot from door to door.

And still some cry wolf about Hitler! Have they learned nothing! We must see that the appropriate consequences are visited on those who will not change . . .

Yours for peace,

Robert Cecil

-

February 7, 1935
34 Kantstrasse, Schoneberg District
Berlin, Germany

From the Journals of Karl von Haydenreich (Published 1986):

Home tonight, after five good days in Zurich.

The Judge was indeed himself again. Frau Golsing doted on her grandsons. Martin has reached the age where his every movement and utterance are charming. The only sad moment was the moment of leave-taking. Frau Golsing's eyes flooded at the station when she reflected on the time that might pass before she is with her grandchildren again – for she and the Judge had been clear and decisive. They will not be returning to Munich at any time soon – perhaps never. '*Not,*' he said, '*while those monsters remain in power.*'

I had learned this on the second day, when I joined him for his mid-morning walk. I was loathe to raise the subject of his mental affliction, but he brought it up himself.

'*You have at last forgiven yourself,*' I responded.

'*For my son, Martin?*' I nodded. '*Quite the contrary,*' the Judge continued, '*I will never forgive myself. I have accepted the fact of damnation.*'

'*May I suggest this is too harsh a judgment?*' I said. '*The real blame must be placed on the S.A. and the beasts at Dachau.*'

He waved his hand dismissively. '*That was only one cause,*' he said, '*perhaps not even the main cause. No – I have assessed my case and pronounced judgment on myself. I have fully accepted my own responsibility. Now I look forward to the final judgment – other men dread this, but I look forward to it. I only hope it is my son who sits as judge.*' He looked straight at me. '*In the meantime, I must do my best for Frau Golsing, Elizabeth, and the rest of you.*'

290

That is when he told me they would be staying in Zurich indefinitely. He had deeded the family home already to Elizabeth – we can make our home there if we choose, for the Judge and his wife will never dwell there again. Then he regarded me once more.

'*You could leave, too, if you chose,*' he said. '*I know you do not intend to manage the resort actively. Zurich is as German a city as any you will find in the Reich.*'

I answered that this was not what I wanted for my family at this time – that we were, after all, Germans. He nodded, and we walked on. Then, at once, he turned to me.

'*I asked you for an undertaking before I consented to your marriage,*' he said. '*I assume you remember it.*' I assured him I did. '*I expect you to honor it under all circumstances,*' he answered.

I told him I remained aware that I remained duty-bound to do so, but the circumstances had not yet arisen in which my promise had become meaningful. The Judge gave me a long, appraising look, but said nothing more.

Then we turned for home.

. . .

We were on the train. Elizabeth had just finished nursing Wilhelm, when she raised the same subject. '*I like Zurich, my husband,*' she said, somewhat hesitantly. '*I could complete my studies there. There is no reason we must keep on living in the jungle that Germany has become.*'

'*I do not believe it has come to that just yet, my wife,*' I said. '*Exile also has its price.*'

Elizabeth regarded me with the same appraising gaze that her father had given me a few days before. Then she subsided.

'*As you say, my husband,*' she said.

-

Excerpt from: My Name is Ike - Reflections on Fifty Years of Service as Soldier and Statesman
Dwight D. Eisenhower
Random House (1986)

I did not do much in the way of spying that winter. Karl was involved with his new son, and then off to Zurich after his father-in-law finally showed some signs of coming out of his funk. Hitler was closeted with his Party allies and there were no Wehrmacht conferences that meant anything.

But when I finally did get the word from Karl to pick up something, it was a doozy. Hitler had announced to the military his intention to denounce the Versailles Treaty, to renew military conscription, and to rearm Germany. That was sensational news, and the most alarming development yet. Surely the British and French would respond in some way, particularly with the advance warning we were giving them. And if not . . .

I was becoming impatient and frustrated. I was taking a small risk in doing what I did, but Karl was taking a huge one. We had sent almost a half-dozen reports to the British government by that time, every one of them with more than enough information to show Adolf Hitler as the man he really was. But nothing had happened. It had been like shouting into the wind, and hoping to hear an echo.

But surely this defiance of Versailles was too ominous not to provoke *some* reaction . . .

-

March 13, 1935
Berlin, Germany

S.S. File No. 4358, 11088 (formerly SD: 112384)
Subject(s): Leutnant Karl von Haydenreich

Swartz,

. . . [Y]our reports are unsatisfactory.

The trappings of Party loyalty with this man are ornamental and superficial, a ruse and a distraction. I am certain to the marrow of my bones that von Haydenreich is an ardent foe of the Reich.

Continue the surveillance.

Heydrich

-

Excerpt from: My Life in Office
Stanley Baldwin
Houghton, Mifflin (1947)

. . . [B]etween November of 1934 and February of 1935, the government received only one more report from our anonymous German friend. This led some to speculate that he had either given up hope, or lost interest, or (worst) been found out. But cooler heads suggested that the gap was almost certainly seasonal, and reflected reduced opportunities for observations, due to both Hitler's and the source's other social obligations.

Then, in the first week of February, we received another report, a genuine bombshell. In late January, Hitler had announced to the Wehrmacht his intent to repudiate the Versailles Treaty, sometime in March, after a suitable propaganda campaign. This was the first time we had received early warning of a proposed action of the Nazis.

The information could not have come at a worse time for MacDonald. He was clearly losing the confidence of the public. A general election was inevitable and did come in June, only three months later. Cecil's Peace Movement was making gigantic strides with the intellectuals and the Oxbridge crowd. Although most of the British public was not so militantly anti-war as Cecil and the children's author Milne, it was primarily concerned with recovering from the economic catastrophe of 1929. Not only had the electorate lost interest in enforcing the restrictions of the Versailles Treaty, a significant majority plainly found many of the more draconian provisions embarrassing.

Although I often had reason to question the wisdom of MacDonald, my great rival, and frequently his actions, very seldom did I question his good faith. Alas, this occasion is one on which I must. Outwardly, he took all the appropriate actions. He summoned the right people, he shared the right information with the right degree of gravity, he held the right conferences, he burned midnight oil with all the appropriate fuss and formality, his countenance was correctly serious. We all did all the right things. But I believe we all knew from the outset that nothing substantive would happen.

So it proved. Military action was of course out of the question, but we could have done something. The German public was becoming restless with the amount of sacrifice and belt-tightening that the rearmament required. Trade sanctions of some sort would have been effective, but there would have been repercussions, lost wages from MacDonald's perspective, lost profits from mine. Facing a difficult election, he was unwilling to pay any political price. In the musical chair regime that French politics had become, a Conservative administration was in power. France had much more to lose, but was even more reluctant to act.

Thus, in the end, neither government did anything. Both contented themselves with the ineffectual diplomatic protests, of exactly the type that caused Hitler to sneer at the West and jeer at the ineffectuality of our political will. In this case, he was exactly right. At least we warned Phipps, our ambassador in Berlin, of what was intended, so that he could put up a dignified front. But that was all.

'*How will our friend in Berlin react to this?*' one of the more aggressive Cabinet members asked in despair.

'*I regret that,*' MacDonald answered, '*but ultimately German problems require German solutions.*'

As for me, I gave the Government the loyalty and support I thought my duty required. But I resolved privately that if my chance ever came, I would provide a slightly better show than the Laborites had.

-

March 2, 1935
34 Kantstrasse, Schoneberg District
Berlin, Germany

From the Journals of Karl von Haydenreich (Published 1986):

. . . [S]ummoned today to von Blomberg's office, the first time in several months. He congratulated me again on the Long Knives report, in which I had emphasized the Fuhrer's boldness and heroics. Then he inquired as always about the loyalty of the Abwehr. I was able to reassure him again, truthfully, that there is no overt dissidence of any kind. (I am certain there are more than a few, like me, who remember von Bredow with fondness and regard his murder as an appalling crime. But no one speaks aloud.) This, as always, satisfied him. He reminded himself (and me) that von Bredow's scheming had not occurred on the military premises.

Then, just before he excused me, he smiled and said that an event was forthcoming that should confirm everyone's confidence in the Fuhrer's daring and vision. I told him I had no idea to what he was referring, but would await the future with confidence . . .

-

Excerpt from: *A Twentieth Century Life*
Albert Sommerville
Houghton, Mifflin (1959)

. . . [T]he First International Congress of the Imperial Party, held at the family estates in the first part of March of 1935, was a smashing success. Representatives from Germany, Italy, Hungary, Austria, Poland, and other nations all over Europe attended.

. . . [T]he Germans mercifully did not indulge in too much Nazi bluster, but seemed smug for some reason. Later in the month, we found out what it was . . .

-

Excerpt from: Memoirs
The Right Honourable Eric Phipps
Houghton, Mifflin (1946)

. . . [I] found myself summoned to the Reich Chancellery to hear the dual announcement of the renunciation of both the Versailles Treaty and the end of any negotiation to limit the size of the German Navy or U-boat construction.

This did not come as the surprise Hitler hoped. Forewarned by Whitehall, I was prepared both for the announcement and the Fuhrer's inevitable histrionics. Announcements of this sort were invariably accompanied by hysterical bluster about the indignities suffered by Germany, the insults, degradations, etc. In this case, I simply did not allow myself to be ruffled or even express any surprise. This seemed to take him aback somewhat.

-

March 18, 1935
Headline
New York Times:

> **Germany Renounces Versailles Treaty; Conscription to be Reinstated; Armed Forces to Be Reorganized as Wehrmacht; Protests from Great Britain, France, and Italy**

-

Excerpt from: A General Speaks - the Autobiography of Kurt von Hammerstein Equord
Major General Kurt von Hammerstein Equord
Reichswehr Press (1986)

I will confess to falling to the edge of despair. Of course, I was a German officer. The end of the indignities of Versailles was an event in which I had to rejoice. All around me were jubilant Wehrmacht officers and staff, and rightly so. There was an irresistible satisfaction in the end of subordinate status to the other European powers.

But my personal rejoicing was utterly soured by the adulation that poured upon the head of the corporal, now the Fuhrer not only in name, but in too many of the hearts of my fellow officers. He had proved himself a man of destiny! He had seen the hollow shell of Western power as no one else, and shown it up for the mockery it was! Heil Hitler! To watch the strutting little puppet walk through all this hero-worship, acknowledging Nazi salutes with the

295

tiniest gestures, pretending indifference to it, when the reality was he was intoxicated by his own ego . . . it was almost more than flesh and blood could endure. This had come about despite all the risks my friends and I had taken, the blight some would see on our honor, and all the information and insight we had provided the British. It had all been for nothing.

We might have given up the enterprise then, if it were not for Karl. '*I was educated in England, General,*' he said. '*I understand the politics. British politicians both respect and fear the British public. With an election imminent, political courage is not a trait I would expect from even the best of them. The timing could not have been worse. Hitler was helped in incalculable measure by the state of British politics.*'

'*But he is still the man who broke down at the end of the War, and fled from his comrades in the Putsch,*' he went on. '*A better time will come.*'

So we continued . . . and everyone knows what happened.

-

**Excerpt from: *My Name is Ike - Reflections on Fifty Years of Service as Soldier and Statesman*
Dwight D. Eisenhower
Random House (1986)**

I wasn't the political realist then that I am now.

I walked the streets of Berlin, seething. The German public was jubilant to the point of rejoicing. German national honor had been restored! The chains of Versailles were gone! Of course, if they had known what I knew, that Hitler's bombshell was not simply a matter of renewing national pride, but the first step in a plan to engage Germany in a full-fledged world war within half a decade, there would have been no cheering at all. The German people were no more interested in war than any other people. But, as before, Hitler had been able to dress up his murderous intentions in the trappings of restored nationalism – and so the German people cheered him to the rafters.

But thanks to Karl, I knew better. Thanks to Karl and myself, Ramsay MacDonald knew better – and nothing had happened. The significant risks we had taken were for nothing. We had accomplished nothing. I walked the streets, enraged and furious. Why had we endured all that surveillance? Why had I walked the streets of Berlin with spy reports camouflaged in purchased music, and my heart in my mouth? I was as frustrated that day as I have ever been.

But I was also naïve – and I was also dead wrong. I missed the most important thing. We *had* accomplished something, even though I didn't know it.

We had established our credibility where it mattered. Even if the Prime Minister was not yet willing to act, because of the reluctance of the British public, we had caught his attention.

But I didn't see that at the time. At the time, I came close to giving up completely.

-

April 8, 1935
Berlin, Germany
Offices of the Schutzstaffel
Memo to Ranking S.S. Officers

To All Heads of Station:

Certain behaviors of the English Ambassador Phipps during his recent meetings with the Fuhrer have raised concern that the British may be receiving information from inside the government, or even inside the Wehrmacht itself, about the plans and intentions of the Government.

Please increase all surveillance efforts to the utmost. If there is a traitor, he must be found and punished.

Reichsfuhrer Heinrich Himmler

by: Gruppenfuhrer Reinhard Heydrich

-

Excerpt from: My Name is Ike - Reflections on Fifty Years of Service as
Soldier and Statesman
Dwight D. Eisenhower
Random House (1986)

. . . [A]t the end of April 1935, without any warning, a Gestapo officer in the company of an S.S. lieutenant, called on me at my offices at the Embassy. The Ambassador let them in, but was sufficiently concerned to summon a Marine guard.

I must have passed on a half-dozen packages from Karl by that time. My first thought was that the jig was up, that the Nazis were on to us. I am not a fearful man. Doing military service on a battlefield will make a man fatalistic, in a good way. But I did feel some alarm.

As I have mentioned, a military attaché is not supposed to spy, and particularly not for a nation not his own. I was not in Germany to perform espionage. I didn't know if I had any diplomatic immunity. There was danger in that visit, and no denying it. But that realization somehow solidified my poise, like the unnatural calm you feel on the morning of a battle.

The two of them entered my office. The Gestapo man was in an overcoat and hat, the S.S. fellow in that vicious black uniform they wore. Unlike the S.A. types, who generally showed their fondness for beer in their belly, he was well-proportioned and in excellent shape – not that that was in any way reassuring. The violence and sadism of the S.A. had been random and unfocused. But for the S.S. bastards, the cruelty was tight and deliberate. I was determined not to show them anything in the way of fear. But that did take some effort.

Then they began questioning. It turned out they had come to inquire solely about the social aspects of my relationship with Karl. The questions were all about lunches and dinners, and how I had come to know him. I felt a relief I did my best to conceal. I told the officers the truth, that I stood in the relationship of godfather to Karl, that his father had entrusted him to me – and I produced the letters to that effect, that Heinrich had written me in the years before his death. The officers examined the documents for some time, before they were satisfied. The S.S. man asked if he could take the letters with him, to which I responded that he absolutely could not. I did allow them to copy large portions of the text.

Then they left, without further ado. They hadn't come close to the reality. I relaxed for a moment, but for a moment only. Then I came almost panicky about Karl. It was a funny thing. When it was my hide, I'd been a man of ice. But thinking about what this goonishness could mean to Karl and Elizabeth, I nearly went to pieces. My pulse began to race, and I broke out in a cold sweat.

There was no way to warn him. Besides, we'd discussed the fact that a communication in such circumstances would be the worst thing to do, since it could not possibly be done unobserved. No, I could only hope he'd keep his composure, and that it would blow over . . .

-

April 18, 1935
34 Kantstrasse, Schoneberg District
Berlin, Germany

From the Journals of Karl von Haydenreich (Published 1986):

My family and I received an insulting call this evening. My old friend Muller, now with the S.S. and a Gestapo man whose name I did not learn, came to our door. The subject was my relationship with Ike.

I did not conceal my impatience at this insolence. I informed them coldly that Ike stood in the relationship of godfather to me, in accordance with my father's last wishes, and had for many years. I told them that they must know of the dynamics of the relationship, since both Ike and I were aware that we have been under surveillance since he was posted to Berlin. We were not at war with the United States, I reminded them, nor were likely to be. Now I was going to have to apologize to my godfather for this outrageous discourtesy, an embarrassment to our entire nation.

The Gestapo man was suitably cowed and apologetic, but Muller met ice with ice. *'Loyalty must be constantly reviewed,'* he said, particularly someone with a position like mine. He implied I would do well to give up the relationship. I told him I had no intention of doing anything of the sort. Then I could expect other visits like this one, I was told. I rejoined that I welcomed them, but hoped in the future he would have the common decency to call on me at my station, rather than intruding into my domestic life. We bid each other cold, formal farewells, and I closed the door on him.

Elizabeth was not present at the interview, away at the library, for which I am grateful. She would have been equal parts terrified and infuriated . . .

-

May 2, 1935
The Ballot Worker
Editorial

. . . [W]hile as conscientious believers in peace between peoples and nations we must deplore the resumption of conscription in Germany, we must at the same time remind His Majesty's Government that these measures were the natural result of the harsh and even inhumane terms of the Versailles Treaty.

In our view, the new policy announced by Herr Hitler has been undertaken for the sole purpose of restoring Germany's honor among nations. Whitehall would be making a grave mistake to respond to this gesture in any other but the most conciliatory terms . . .

. . . [L]et me remind the Prime Minister that 500,000 British voters stand behind this position, with our numbers swelling every day . . .

-

Excerpt from: My Life in Office
Stanley Baldwin
Houghton, Mifflin (1947)

. . . [D]omestic issues were in the ascendant at the time I regained the Office of Prime Minister. In addition to those of substance, there was the folly being perpetrated by the Prince of Wales in his infatuation with the American divorcee Wallis Simpson.

But the situation in Germany was never far from my thoughts. Fortunately, our intelligence source, however dismayed he might have been by MacDonald's inaction, resumed providing substantial briefs on the plans, actual views, and personal characteristics of Adolf Hitler. The more light thrown on that venomous egoist, the more disturbing the implications.

However, at the same time, we began to hope that no action of our Government would be required to see to his departure from power. The focus on rearmament and military buildup had starved the German economy of basic consumer goods to the point of real scarcity of basic foodstuffs such as meat and cooking oil. Once the cheering over the Versailles Treaty stopped, the level of grumbling and complaint in Germany rose to such a level that it was reasonable to hope that a spontaneous movement would oust him from power without any foreign intervention.

Adolf Hitler, of course, was not the sort of man to accept the shortages of consumer goods as the consequence of his own misguided policy. He blamed a nonexistent Jewish conspiracy. The result was another deplorable round of violence against innocent German Jews. This time, however, the German public was not so easily deceived.

Excerpt from: Destiny Betrayed - A Chronicle of Treason
Harald Quandt
Franz Eher Nachfolger Gmbh (1952)

. . . [T]hus in one masterstroke did the Fuhrer slash the bonds of Versailles that had kept Germany in the shackles of humiliation and inferiority, and demand that the Reich take its rightful place among nations! Had he never accomplished any other feat, he would still be remembered as one of the great figures of German history. Alas, the vermin who traffic in spite and treason were already at work to sabotage all his achievements! But the full measure of their treachery would not become evident for some time.

In the meantime, the cunning conspiracy of International Jewry took a different revenge. Almost as soon as the Fuhrer had made his bold announcements, prices of basic goods in Germany began to rise – fats and meats, particularly. Some commodities even became scarce. Of course, the conspirators made sure that wages remained low. In this way did the sinister, invisible hand of the Jew make itself known.

The German people were not deceived. They knew full well who their enemies were. Their natural anger and indignation took its form in a series of retaliatory incidents against the traitors, the Jews who walked boldly among them in defiant contempt of their wrath. The international press, dominated as it is by Jews and Bolsheviks, made much of this with the usual nonsense. But it was only the healthy reaction of a vigorous folk to the enemies in their midst.

Excerpt from: *A History of Germany in the Twentieth Century*
Josef Behrens
Alfred A Knopf (1964)

. . . [T]he announcement of the Versailles Treaty was followed in short order by the end of negotiations to limit the size of the German Navy, and the re-institution of military conscription. All these measures were greeted with huge approval by the German public, which saw in them a restoration of German national pride.

But in retrospect, it is also apparent that they were necessary to support the regime. The National Socialist Party could never escape the dilemma of guns and butter. The remilitarization of the German state on which it embarked came at the necessary expense of consumer goods and amenities. When the world economy retreated, the German public was forced to accept a level of deprivation that the French or British public would never have accepted. The reasons had to do with the simple, elemental constraints of economics.

But the Nazis responded by blaming the shortages on the retaliation of International Jewry for Hitler's boldness with Versailles. Outrages and incivilities to German Jews, substantially reduced during the previous year, were renewed and increased, in response to this supposed Jewish conspiracy. However, the German public did not accept either these explanations or these practices as readily as it had in 1933.

The National Socialist movement clearly began to lose its momentum and public support that summer.

Excerpt from: My Name is Ike - Reflections on Fifty Years of Service as
Soldier and Statesman
Dwight D. Eisenhower
Random House (1986)

. . . [I]t was a long bad, summer. The Nazi propaganda machine was turned up to full volume. You saw the occasional street scene with Jews harassed in a manner that was sickening to anyone who encountered it. I was glad Mamie wasn't there. I wished I hadn't been there myself.

But I got the impression that the German people weren't buying. All the yakking about international conspiracies in the world won't make up for the absence of meat on the table. When I was observing maneuvers later in the summer, it was apparent that even in the Wehrmacht there was a great deal of dissension. Everyone but the dullest knew that the Jews weren't *that* powerful. Beyond the circle of the true believers, Hitler had his problems.

I had my own problems. I was not sleeping well. The visit in April from the S.S. and Gestapo weighed heavily on me. Afterwards, it seemed to me the surveillance had increased and was even more noticeable. I was in that state of mind where you jump when a door slams, or start up at a car backfiring. But I was not nearly so concerned about my own safety, as that of Karl, Elizabeth, Martin, and now Willy. The young von Haydenreichs had become a second family to me. I worried about them.

The ongoing duplicity also bothered me. I don't mean the spying; I'd seen enough of Nazi Germany to be certain I was on the side of the right. I mean keeping secrets from Elizabeth. She was now next to certain that something was going on. But she did not know enough to be sure. The constant doubt made her perplexed and anxious. I would have liked to tell her all, but Karl had sworn me to secrecy. It was an oath I had to respect.

Other developments were also frazzling Elizabeth's nerves. In addition to the constant harassment she experienced at school, their household had been joined by a nanny, a sweet eighteen-year-old girl named Helga. But Helga, like all of them at that time, had to be vetted by a Nazi organization – and she was the truest of true believers in National Socialism. Her constant innocent reiteration of the Fuhrer's virtues drove Elizabeth quietly up the wall.

Karl remained calm. Once he confided to me that the privilege of joining the polished group of musicians von Hammerstein had recruited over the years went a long way in quieting his nerves. (Years later, von

Hammerstein told me Karl had said pretty much the same thing to him a few weeks after the whole thing began.) '*I really wish things had worked out better at the Hochschule,*' he said. '*I am much more musician than soldier.*'

'*Do you want to give this up?*' I asked.

'*Oh, no,*' he replied, becoming grim. '*I will see this through. To the end.*'

But to what end? By July, I'd delivered just under a dozen packages to my British friends. Nothing seemed to be happening. Hitler had disavowed Versailles, the Nazis had resumed conscription, and nothing had changed. What difference were we making? Any at all? Sometimes I wondered if anyone was even reading the stuff.

It was a long summer.

June 2, 1935
34 Kantstrasse, Schoneberg District
Berlin, Germany

From the Journals of Karl von Haydenreich (Published 1986):

A bad day. Elizabeth and I had the most savage fight of our marriage.

Martin has begun to use the word 'Juden' as his basic word for 'bad', 'annoying', anything that displeases him. We do not know what to do about this. Today on his outing, he used that word when the nanny and he stepped around dog shit. Helga thought this a huge joke, as did a couple of passersby – and Martin, delighted to please, pointed at the dog shit itself and repeated the word. Helga laughed again when she recounted this tale to Elizabeth and myself. Our nanny is 18, a believer in Hitler and a member of the Hitler Youth. This is where she goes for games, recreation, and companionship. The Party sponsors these. She believes. They all believe.

I knew Elizabeth was seething, but she kept her tongue until we were retired and alone. Then she exploded. How long were we going to stand for this? How long, before Martin begins making baby Hitler salutes and everyone laughs? Are we going to enroll him in a Nazi school? Let him listen to Nazi radio? Join the Hitler Youth?

'*Others must endure this, my husband,*' she said. '*We do not. We have money. We have no family or sentiment about the places we grew up in. We do not have to live in this madhouse.*' She could practice law in any country. I was talented, I could make my way anywhere. '*It need not be Zurich, my husband,*' she said. '*Perhaps in London with Albert – or America, where Ike lives. These*

303

murderous thugs killed my brother and ruined my father. I will not give them my sons!'

To this I could only reply that I was not yet ready to flee . . . that we were Germans . . . that we would be fish out of water elsewhere . . . that there was still much reason to hope for an end to all this. Elizabeth opened her mouth to speak, then stopped.

'*My husband*,' she said, in a completely different soft tone, '*what is going on? What are you doing?'*

'*What do you mean?'* I answered.

'*I mean, with you and Ike and these lunches and this music. What are you doing?'*

'*Nothing is going on except lunches and music*,' I answered.

'*You are lying to me, my husband*,' she said. '*I know it. You are a terrible, terrible liar, Karl.*' Then suddenly her eyes were flooded with tears. '*I said sons. I should have also said husband. If anything happened to you . . . you must not endanger yourself, my husband. I do not want to leave Germany, either. I hate these Nazis as much as you, for what they have done to my country – but you must not risk yourself in opposition. We must flee first. You are my love, and my life – the thought of losing you –*' and then she was full out weeping, and clenching her fists in frustration.

'*I am not lying to you, my wife. Your fears are phantoms.*' Then I took her in my arms, and kissed away her tears. She said nothing, but allowed me to do so. '*I will make you this promise, my wife*,' I said. '*If the Nazis are still in power, we will be gone from here no later than the end of next year – 1936. We can begin making plans next summer. Is that sufficient?'*

'*I wish it were now*,' she said, '*tomorrow. But yes, it is sufficient, my husband. And what is it you are doing now? Don't distract me like that.*' But I continued distracting her in the most ancient of ways, and she did not protest again. Later, she lay in my arms.

'*You promise?'* she said. '*The end of 1936?'*

'*I promise*,' I answered, '*the end of 1936. And I am not lying to you.*'

'*Yes, you are*,' Elizabeth said, '*but no more tonight.*' Then she turned and went to sleep.

-

Excerpt from: A General Speaks - the Autobiography of Kurt von Hammerstein Equord

304

Major General Kurt von Hammerstein Equord
Reichswehr Press (1986)

I first met Elizabeth von Haydenreich (now the accomplished Elizabeth Whittingham) in mid-summer of 1935. She had always been included in the invitations I extended. But when my arrangement with Karl began, she was in the later stages of pregnancy and reluctant to appear at formal social occasions. A pattern emerged, and it became von Haydenreich's custom to appear alone and confine himself to the role of performer. But on this occasion, an officers' ball in mid-June, she did accompany her husband. They made a handsome couple. Later, when he was not with the ensemble, they danced with a nonchalant elegance that was charming.

Our formal introduction was unremarkable, but later I found myself standing beside her while Karl was with the band. I did not identify the tune at first, but then was surprised to recognize the *Apprentice's Waltz* from *Meistersinger*, which the band (doubtless at Karl's direction) had arranged in American swing style. It was quite pleasing. I complimented Elizabeth on her husband's musicianship.

'*Yes*,' she said, '*Karl has a musician's gift and a soldier's honor.*' Then she met my eyes. '*It would be a disgrace if anyone imposed on his honor to abuse his musical gift.*' It was a remark and attitude that would have been impertinent from any young woman less forthright and open than Elizabeth von Haydenreich. I knew she was unaware of the full understanding between myself and her husband, for von Haydenreich had demanded this be so. But she clearly had some sense of it. It took a fair degree of self-control to meet her gaze firmly, but I managed to do so. Then I made some irrelevant remark and changed the subject.

In later years, Elizabeth Whittingham, Senator Eisenhower, and I have become friends and allies. The simultaneous publication of my memoirs, and Eisenhower's, and von Haydenreich's journals, are the result of that friendship. But, to her credit, she has never once reminded me of that exchange at the officer's ball.

-

August 16, 1935
34 Kantstrasse, Schoneberg District
Berlin, Germany

Mister Albert Sommerville
Sommersby and Smith
London, England

Dear Albert,

I will be attending the Seventh Party Congress of the NSDAP in Nuremberg between September 10th and 16th. It is my pleasure to invite your attendance, so that a leading member of the British Imperial Party can see for himself the amazing changes that the Nazi Party and the Fuhrer have wrought in the life and spirit of Germany.

Heil Hitler,
Leutnant Karl von Haydenreich

-

Excerpt from: My Name is Ike - Reflections on Fifty Years of Service as Soldier and Statesman
Dwight D. Eisenhower
Random House (1986)

I went to the Nazi rally, the Seventh Party Congress, in Nuremberg that September, with Karl. We were to meet up there with Karl's old school chum, Albert Sommerville. He proved to be almost as charming as Karl. We were mostly a trio, but I had some official duties as attaché, so Karl and Albert had quite a bit of time to themselves.

Everyone knows the Honorable Albert Sommerville these days as a respected member of Parliament and the longtime leader of the British Imperial Party. But back then he was just another personable youngster with a bright future. Much of what his Party stood for was similar to Hitler and the Nazis, so there was much in the rally that he should have approved in theory. But although the spectacle pleased him, the personality cult unnerved him. He agreed with the Nazis in principle, but despised them as men – an interesting point of view. Of course, this wasn't the sort of thing you said aloud during the six days.

I was jumpier during those weeks than I have ever been in my life. The nerviness that had plagued me in the summer was getting worse, not better. Mind you, the pageant was spectacular - parades during the day, bonfires and torchlights at night. But these weren't like our Fourth of July innocence, or the British equivalent. They were fervent, quasi-religious pagan rituals, with Hitler here, Hitler there, Hitler everywhere. Tens of thousands of his loyal followers saluted and roared in unison, swearing their allegiance to him to a degree way,

306

way beyond political loyalty. We were witnessing the creation of a secular religion with Adolf Hitler, a mortal man, at the center, its messianic savior. It scared me. I had to remind myself more than once that this was not the whole of Germany, that just beyond the perimeters of the camp ground lay a German public that was getting increasingly restive with the Nazis, and the sacrifices it was being asked to make for Hitler's vision.

I couldn't get out of my mind what I had been doing with Karl and our unknown friend. I was surrounded by goons and thugs, any one of whom would cheerfully beat me to death if they knew. Intellectually, I knew we were safe. We'd been awfully careful. But what your head knows and what your stomach feels are sometimes two different things. That was my situation then.

Karl, though, was a model of detached composure.

-

Excerpt from: A Twentieth Century Life
Albert Sommerville
Houghton, Mifflin (1959)

. . . I did not truly have need to attend Nuremberg in 1935, but the message in Karl's letter was clear enough. He wanted to meet me there. I found the six days long, exhausting, a bit intimidating, and somewhat numbing. The pageantry I had appreciated in the past had become too familiar. My respect for Hitler, already waning before I arrived, had all but disappeared by the time I left.

Karl was in an odd, ambiguous position. Many of the 'Alte', as they called themselves, the oldest Party members, remembered his grandfather. More than a few remembered him. They all assumed he was as true to the swastika as they were. It was amazing and somewhat unsettling to see him politely and, on occasion, even warmly acknowledging the greetings of the passionate Party members – all the while implacably opposed to all they stood for.

He had his enemies. We chanced across Reinhard Heydrich in his black S.S. uniform, a human serpent. You did not need clairvoyance to know Heydrich hated him. No one would want such a man as a foe, but Karl stood up to him with ice of his own. He told me later the bad blood went back to some minor incident that had occurred at Heydrich's wedding, the very occasion when Karl first met Elizabeth.

But we spent more time with Ike, as Karl called the then Major (now Senator) Dwight D. Eisenhower, than we did with National Socialist Party members. Ike was another one of those persons that seemed to cluster around Karl's life – extraordinary amiable, open, charming. He was relentlessly American, and a naive believer in all the egalitarian nonsense about which Americans are so hopelessly innocent. Yet I liked him – it is impossible to dislike Ike. As is the case with my friendship with Elizabeth, our friendship has withstood the test of time and all manner of disagreements of principle, large and small.

Between the 'Alte', the pageantry, some military business, and Ike, I did not have the opportunity for a meaningful tête-à-tête with Karl until the last day, after the Nuremberg Decrees had been announced. Ike was off somewhere with some Americans. We took the opportunity for a shared libation – and I finally learned why he had wanted me to come to Nuremberg.

'*This has become a very strange nation lately, old chum,*' he said, '*and I may need a favor from you.*'

'*Of course,*' I answered.

'*It may be Elizabeth and I will wish to leave the country on very short notice – and that is not so easy to do anymore. One needs permissions and so on. We Germans have already surrendered more freedoms than you British ever would.*'

'*Why would you have to leave, old chum?*' I was perplexed. '*Are you involved in something?*'

'*No,*' he answered promptly. '*But you know the ambiguity with which I live. Anything can happen. In any case, if I should ever send you a letter with a mention of a desire to see some cricket, would you kindly ignore the mention, but conjure up some appropriate Imperial Party function or other that would be a suitable occasion for a Nazi Wehrmacht officer to attend – something that includes his family? Could you oblige me in that manner? The invitation you extend will be my reason for a sudden departure.*'

'*Of course, old chum,*' I said. '*But I must confess you alarm me. Has Herr Hitler brought it to this?*'

'*Yes and no,*' he replied. '*Ordinary Germany still remains as it was, beneath all the Nazi trappings. But in these times, a man must be prudent.*'

I nodded in agreement, but I must say I was staggered. Karl had invited me to Nuremberg solely to arrange this flight mechanism? Despite his assurance, I was sure matters were much, much worse than he said.

It was in that way that these escape arrangements came into being. I hoped, of course, that the crisis that would call them into being would never arise.

I certainly never dreamt that they would become pertinent within four months.

-

Excerpt from: My Name is Ike - Reflections on Fifty Years of Service as Soldier and Statesman
Dwight D. Eisenhower
Random House (1986)

The Nuremberg Decrees – the Flag Law, the Citizenship Law, the Blood Law, and the barbaric restrictions and humiliations they imposed on German Jews, even those who had long since given up their faith – was the pagan climax of the Rally. (Even Sommerville had been taken aback by the Blood Law. '*It's the boardroom that matters, not the bedroom,*' I recall him muttering.) The Nazis had been demonizing the Jews all summer long for their supposed conspiracy against Germany. This was the capstone. It was disgusting.

But it led unexpectedly to some insights about my own country that I have never forgotten. A few weeks later, I was having a private dinner with Karl and Elizabeth. I mentioned the Decrees, and how uniquely and savagely German they were. I shouldn't have said that. You will not meet a more charming and gracious woman than Elizabeth Whittingham, and particularly as hostess. But there is always a core of pure steel you'd do well to respect. Nicely, but with a distinct hint of ice, she reminded me that the effect of the laws was no different than the Jim Crow laws with which Southerners oppress American Negroes. However unconscionable the Nuremberg Decrees, an American citizen had no moral right to condemn Germany.

Well! – as Jack Benny was saying on the radio at that time– what could I say to that? She was right. For the first time in my life, I had to consider how much my own nation shoots itself in the foot by its abandonment of its own basic principles, with respect to our colored peoples.

For the first time, but hardly the last.

-

November 28, 1935
Minutes of Meeting
Reich Chancellery
Subject: Stapo Report for October 1935 (including Morale Report), Presented

309

by Franz
Weidmann, Adjutant to the Fuhrer
Participants: The Fuhrer, Minister of Propaganda, Minister of the Interior,
Adjutant

The meeting began at 2:30. Adjutant Weidmann presented the Stapo Report. Meats and fats continue to be in short supply. Unemployment continues high. The Gestapo reports an increasing number of public complaints, and several dozen arrests.

Adjutant Weidmann had also received the Morale Report, but was reluctant to present it at that time. The Fuhrer demanded its presentation.

The Gestapo reported serious problems with morale. The lack of faith in the Party that has been noticeable in recent months has extended to the person of the Fuhrer himself. It is said that he is too tolerant of failings in the Party officers, particularly the tendency to indulge in personal extravagance. One can now go for days in Berlin without seeing or hearing the Hitler salute, except among uniformed civil servants and provincials. Comments about the desirability of a military dictatorship or another purge of the Party elite (in the style of the Rohm purge) have also been overheard.

At this point, the Fuhrer interrupted. He did not trouble to hide his anger, but pounded the table and shouted. He declared that the morale of the public was in reality good, not bad, and was made bad by such false reports. He forbade any reports of a similar kind in the future. Then he announced the meeting over and left the room. Frick, the Minister of the Interior, also left.

Goebbels remained. He requested that Weidmann complete the presentation. At its conclusion, he remarked that he agreed with the Fuhrer that, while the mood of the public was overall good, the report made clear that the enemies of the Reich, particularly the Jewish enemies, were increasingly active. They create the problems of wages and shortages, and then exploit them to manufacture popular discontent.

What was needed, he suggested, was something to distract the masses. They had rallied to the Fuhrer when he had dealt with the S.A. and ended the abomination of Versailles. In the excitement of a circus, the empty stomach is forgotten. Perhaps it was time for the New Germany to make its voice heard throughout Europe – and the world. Perhaps it was time for the Party to demonstrate to the people the full extent of what it had achieved.

The Minister of Propaganda said he would speak to the Fuhrer about the matter.

310

-

***Excerpt from: My Name is Ike - Reflections on Fifty Years of Service as
Soldier and Statesman
Dwight D. Eisenhower
Random House (1986)***

With all the talk of saxophone and Hochschule, I only heard Karl play
once. Von Hammerstein held a Christmas reception for all us military attachés,
at which there was music. There he was on the bandstand, performing
Christmas carols arranged in a modern, jazzy style. You could see he was in his
element – eyes half-closed, swaying to the rhythm, an inhabitant of a paradise
that he alone occupied and he alone had created. I felt a paternal pride in
watching him that I had only experienced with my own sons. *This is where he
belongs*, I remember thinking. *This is what he should be doing.*

That's my favorite memory of my godson. Wherever he is now, I hope
he's in the same place he was that day – lost in the pure joy of making music,
not so much performing music as being music itself. That is my favorite
memory of Karl.

The Order

1936

-

Excerpt from: My Life in Office
Stanley Baldwin
Houghton, Mifflin (1947)

. . . [A]t the end of the day, we seized our opportunity. That is all that matters. I like to believe that we would have done so with or without knowledge of the Order.

Perhaps that is only my conceit.

-

Excerpt from: A General Speaks - the Autobiography of Kurt von
Hammerstein Equord
Major General Kurt von Hammerstein Equord
Reichswehr Press (1986)

Adolf Hitler was an adventurer, and not a particularly intelligent man. Sooner or later, one of his adventures was certain to end in disaster. The Rhineland Fiasco was simply the specific case of the general rule. The effect of the Order should not be overestimated.

-

Excerpt from: Destiny Betrayed - A Chronicle of Treason
Harald Quandt
Franz Eher Nachfolger Gmbh (1952)

. . . [A]dolph Hitler, like Caesar and Christ before him, was the victim of betrayal.

The traitor who doomed Adolf Hitler, the Nazi Party, the Third Reich, and condemned Germany to the second rank of European nations for another generation was Karl von Haydenreich, and no other. There is too much coincidence for any but the most perverted, cynical Jew to doubt.

-

Excerpt from: My Name is Ike - Reflections on Fifty Years of Service as
Soldier and Statesman

314

Hitler had to pull another rabbit out of the hat to keep the show going. Because the German people were impatient with him, with good reason, and he really didn't have a program beyond his Looney Tunes notions of *lebensraum.* You didn't have to be Napoleon or Alexander the Great to figure out where he was going to find the rabbit. It had to be on the Rhineland, another subject on which Hitler had done quite a bit of yelping.

All that has gone into the circular file of history now, so let me give you a little refresher. The 'Rhineland' never did have a precise definition. The word referred generally to the western provinces of Germany along the Rhine, including cities such as Cologne and Dusseldorf. But what it meant specifically back then was a 50-kilometer zone extending east back from the Rhine, in which no militarization or fortification of any kind was permitted. The idea was to prevent the sort of military structure that could be used as a staging point for an invasion, such as had happened in 1870 and 1914. The demilitarized zone had first been enforced on Germany in the Treaty of Versailles in 1919, then ratified by the Weimar Republic consensually in the Treaty of Locarno in 1925. It was serious stuff. A violation of the terms gave Britain and France the right to invade and reoccupy the area.

At the time of the Locarno Treaty in 1925, both Britain and France still had troops in the demilitarized zone. Versailles gave both nations the right to occupy the zone until 1935. But matters had gone so well that the British left in 1929, and the French in 1930. The region had been returned to German control by 1936. But the blot on Germany's honor, the 'stain of Versailles', as Hitler liked to say, remained.

Remilitarizing the Rhineland was thus a natural step for a man whose political survival depended on promises to restore Germany to greatness. It was a particularly natural step when ordinary Germans were beginning to see through the charade.

But even so, finding out it was really going to happen was a shock. It was a day in mid-January of 1936 I will never forget. I opened the musical score my friend had delivered, and retrieved a few more pages than usual, with a lot more language. There it was, after translation – the orders, the basic deployment, the decision made, writ large and unequivocal. It was not talk any longer. Hitler was truly going to do it. I wondered how the British and French would react.

I was of two minds. On the one hand, the reoccupation was simply a reorganization of German forces within German borders. Nothing more than a diplomatic response was required. On the other, it was a deliberate violation of two significant international treaties, and a cause for war. That was a disturbing thought. Anyone who fought in the Great War would find it disturbing. The one exception to the rule was Adolf Hitler.

By that time, the silence in reaction to the other information we had delivered had made me cynical. I was sure the West would do nothing. Karl was of a completely different mind. *'This time Hitler has badly overreached himself,'* he said. *'An opportunity will present itself.'* (Years later, I learned that Karl was quoting General von Hammerstein.)

The whole world knows now that Karl and the General were right. But not he, nor anyone, as God is my witness, foresaw the events all the way to the finish.

-

Excerpt from: My Life in Office
Stanley Baldwin
Houghton, Mifflin (1947)

. . . [A]t the beginning of January 1936, the next thunderbolt struck. Our anonymous
German friend provided information to the effect that Hitler had ordered the Wehrmacht to develop plans to reoccupy the Rhineland. In a few months, Adolf Hitler and the Nazi Party planned to execute a military adventure, extending the reach of its armed forces through the agreed-upon demilitarized zone and on to the borders of the German Reich. Not six months before, when MacDonald had chosen passivity, he had assured our ambassador the zone would be respected.

But what to do? What exactly to do? All at once, I found myself more in sympathy with Ramsay MacDonald than I would have liked . . .

-

January 17, 1936
334 Kantstrasse, Schoneberg District
Berlin, Germany

Mister Albert Sommerville
Sommersby and Smith
London, England

Dear Albert,

316

With little Wilhelm now old enough to travel, I find myself keen to revisit the old grounds of Uppingham and take a look once again at a cricket match. (I do miss that sport!) It would be wonderful, too, to present my sons to your mother and father. Your wonderful parents are the closest thing to family that I have left since I lost my father.

A date in late February or early March would suit Elizabeth's academic schedule. Let me know if that is convenient.

My best wishes to you and all of yours,

Heil Hitler!

Karl

-

Excerpt from: *A Twentieth Century Life*
Albert Sommerville
Houghton, Mifflin (1959)

When Karl and I had made our arrangements at the Nuremberg Rally, I had hardly contemplated the thought that I would be called upon to act before four months had passed. But there it was.

Naturally, I responded immediately as we had agreed.

-

January 25, 1936
London, England

Leutnant Karl von Haydenreich
34 Kantstrasse, Schoneberg District
Berlin, Germany

My dear old friend,

With respect to yours of the 17th, I am delighted to invite you (and your wife and sons, of course) to the 1936 Convention of the Imperialist Party.

My father and I will be hosting a series of dinner parties and meetings for prominent, sympathetic individuals between February 15th and March 15th. These persons will be delighted to meet a member of the National Socialist Party with as distinguished a history as your own – a family, moreover, with personal acquaintance with the Fuhrer himself. Please make what arrangements are convenient to you within that interval. My family will be more than eager to reciprocate the hospitality you have shown us over the years. I will notify our German friends accordingly.

317

There should also be ample opportunity to pop over to Uppingham and observe the progress of the cricketers. Let us hope they are not as deplorable as last year's edition!

Let me know of your arrangements as soon as it is convenient for you to make them. My home and hearth are at your disposal.

Heil Hitler

Albert

-

Excerpt from: Destiny Betrayed - A Chronicle of Treason
Harald Quandt
Franz Eher Nachfolger Gmbh (1952)

How can the apologists for Haydenreich possibly account for the fact that he planned the escape of his wife and children at precisely the moment when the Wehrmacht set the date for the reoccupation of the Rhineland?

-

Excerpt from: My Name is Ike - Reflections on Fifty Years of Service as
Soldier and Statesman
Dwight D. Eisenhower
Random House (1986)

Karl told me of his decision to send his wife and sons abroad a week or so after we learned of the Rhineland plans. We were on one of our walks in the Tiergarten. The news surprised me.

'*Don't you think that's a bit excessive?*' I asked.

'*No, Ike, I don't,*' he answered. '*A crisis is coming. Hitler will either fail or succeed. Either way, dangerous times will follow. I want Elizabeth and the boys well away from it.*'

'*More dangerous if he succeeds,*' I joked.

Karl cocked an eyebrow. '*Then we must use all the means at our disposal to ensure that he does not,*' he replied. We walked on.

'*Does Elizabeth know of your thinking on this?*' I asked.

He shrugged uncomfortably. '*You know she does not, Ike,*' he said. '*She must not.*'

-

January 19, 1936
The Ballot Worker
Editorial

. . . [O]ur Government refuses to listen. We recklessly and needlessly endanger the peace of Europe at every turn. Our only response to Herr Hitler

318

and his renewal of Germany? To rearm ourselves! Have we all gone mad? Have we learned nothing?

As much as we all deplore Nazi barbarities, we have all learned, or should have learned, that war is not the answer . . .

Excerpt from: My Life in Office
Stanley Baldwin
Houghton, Mifflin (1947)

In late January1936, our source provided us with the outline of the full operational plan of the Wehrmacht for the reoccupation of the Rhineland. Before that, when the German intent existed only in abstract terms, we could hope for error or change of heart. But now it existed, in a fully realized, concrete form. There was no longer any room for doubt or contrarian speculation. Hitler was going to go forward, engaging in a considered provocation of monumental proportions. He was deliberately challenging the continent to war.

I stared out my window in disbelief. How should we and our French allies respond to this? What practically could we do in reaction? There are issues in public life that perplex and bewilder, but trouble the intellect only. There are others that knot up the stomach, that poison sleep, that sicken the entire frame of nature, and loosen the anchors of the soul. The affair with Hitler was one of the latter. How could we keep the monster from uncaging itself? What, practically, could we do??

Cables began to fly back and forth across the Channel. Albert Sarraut, my counterpart in France, the President of the Council of Ministers, had only been in office six weeks. I pitied him.

February 1, 1930
Berlin, Germany

Major General Werner von Blomberg
Reichswehr Headquarters
Berlin, Germany

My General,

I address you with all due respect, soliciting your aid in a political matter of the utmost gravity and sensitivity. I am invited, along with wife and family, to the conference of the British Imperial Party, to be held in March of this year at the Sommerville family estates. The Sommerville family are personally acquainted with the Fuhrer, and enthusiastic supporters of his policies.

Unfortunately, I will not be able to attend, for reasons known to us both that I will not commit to paper. It is thus even more important that my family make an appearance, to avoid any implication of disapproval or disavowal of the Sommervilles in the weeks to come. Travel permissions have been unaccountably delayed, doubtless owing to the strained relations between Great Britain and the Third Reich. I would like to have these expedited, as time is short.

Your assistance in obtaining these approvals would be greatly appreciated and of inestimable value to the Reich.

With all due respect,

Heil Hitler!

Leutnant Karl von Haydenreich

-

Excerpt from: Ma Vie Publique, 1929 -1940
Albert Sarraut
Editions du Cerf (1955)

For the second time, I stepped into the office of the Presidency of the Council, and this time into a waking nightmare. Within an hour of assuming responsibility I learnt the despicable Hitler had made plans to remilitarize the demilitarized Rhineland zone. The zone had been created precisely to prevent its being used for the military build-up that had preceded such abominations as the invasions in 1870 and 1914. Was France to be stripped of its most important safeguard against German aggression? While the new president – me – searched for the keys to his office?

And with what cunning the Germans had measured the degree of force they intended to use – 14,000 military, lightly armed, without artillery or armor, and 22,000 civilian policemen. It was too small a force to constitute a direct and immediate threat, yet large enough to work a significant and meaningful change in the balance of power. The public would never accept an order of general mobilization in response to so slight a provocation. But if our response, as before, was confined solely to diplomatic channels, it would be perceived by Hitler – correctly – as another sign of the weakness and demoralization of the West.

My one consolation was that Baldwin shared my estimate of the gravity of the situation. He also left me in no doubt of the validity of the information we had received, which had been of the highest quality in the past. He had disagreed completely with the passive reaction of our nations to the Versailles outrage. He emphasized the willingness of the British government to support France in whatever reaction it chose. But naturally, he also insisted that the decision of what means should be utilized, military or otherwise, must be made by my government.

It was there that the true frustration commenced.

-

Excerpt from: Eyewitness!
The True Story of the Fiasco on the Rhine and the Siege of the Reich
Chancellery
Oberfeldwebel (formerly) Victor H. Becker
Houghton, Mifflin (1950)

The plans for the remilitarization of the Rhineland were the darkest of dark secrets to most of the troops. But I was too close to the General not to feel how the wind blew. The news that we were finally going to see action of some sort, even in such a small thing as the occupation of territory that was already German, caused my heart to beat a little harder. Of course, as General von Hammerstein's driver, I was assigned to headquarters, and did not anticipate that I would be participating personally. But, even so . . .

Action at last!

-

February 4, 1936
34 Kantstrasse, Schoneberg District
Berlin, Germany

From the Journals of Karl von Haydenreich (Published 1986):
 . . . [T]ravel permissions and documents finally in hand, doubtless though von Blomberg's intercession. '*The friendship of the Sommerville family is of the greatest importance to the Reich,*' etc. I confirmed the date with Albert by cable. All is in readiness. Departure in only two weeks!

Elizabeth mocks me about the haste and the timing. England in late February? But she is too excited to be seriously cross – her first trip off the Continent! She has made her own contacts with the legal scholars, and hopes to advance her studies and thesis even more rapidly.

I have not yet told her I do not expect to accompany her. There will be argument enough on that day . . .

321

Excerpt from: My Life in Office
Stanley Baldwin
Houghton, Mifflin (1947)

Those were some of the strangest days of my life. I was besieged by a sense of crisis. I rarely left my office, I lost sleep, I had difficulty eating.

What agonies of doubt and indecision! The reoccupation would be the first direct use of military force by Hitler. The line crossed would be fine, but clear. It would have a direct and immediate effect on the balance of power in Europe. But it would take place entirely within the borders of Germany. To risk war on this cause? Send men to their deaths over a provocation this slight? Erect barricades, dig trenches, order artillery barrages? The course of action seemed wildly, horribly disproportionate. Yet the line was clear. To do nothing? The thought was a dead weight in the pit of my stomach.

Outside in London, the world went on in all its ordinary ways, in typically execrable February weather. I might have had the sense that the larger course of history turned on this light pivot, on the action we and the French decided upon in response to Hitler's plans. But beyond my offices, it was humdrum, routine business as usual, including the increasingly aggressive peace movement. The world neither knew nor cared what was imminent in the Rhineland. I strongly suspected that, if it knew, it would still not care. My colleagues and I were all alone.

Everything depended on the decisions of the French government. Sarraut and I were in agreement that some response more forceful than the merely diplomatic was required. But it was here, during the first weeks in February, that our decisions stalled, for the most surprising reasons.

Excerpt from: Ma Vie Publique, 1929 -1940
Albert Sarraut
Editions du Cerf (1955)

. . . [O]ne would have thought that the Minister of War would be the most bellicose of all of us. But not so. General Maurin was an armored wall of resistance to every positive thought. Precious days, ten priceless days, passed, with no agreement to action of any kind. I formed my own private opinion of the reasons for this reluctance. Later, I learned that the other members of the council had come to very much the same conclusion. We all came to believe that a cautiousness welcome in the military after the debacles of the Great War, had in Maurin's case devolved into a disabling fear . . . cowardice, to give it its right name.

Meanwhile, Baldwin awaited our decisions. But there were none forthcoming. Was Adolf Hitler fated to gain a matchless cachet simply because our Minister of War was too craven to act? The prospect horrified me, but as each day passed, it seemed more and more likely.

Then, on February 19th, the miracle occurred.

I will call it by its right name. A miracle.

-

Excerpt from: A General Speaks - the Autobiography of Kurt von Hammerstein Equord
Major General Kurt von Hammerstein Equord
Reichswehr Press (1986)

Let us, as the Americans would say, talk turkey. The reoccupation of the Rhineland was an act of madness. As far as the Reich had advanced in rearmament, its force of arms paled in comparison with Britain and France. The German people were absolutely, and quite sensibly, opposed to war in any form. They wanted no part of the corporal's adolescent views of German destiny.

But it was also an entirely unnecessary adventure, a challenge to the gods that did not have to be issued. Hitler had defied the Allies with his denunciation of Versailles. There was no obstacle to the gradual and systematic development of German military capability to full equality with the other major European nations. The Rhineland could wait. It was not significant in the larger order of things.

These considerations made not the slightest difference to the Fuhrer. Between January and the end of February 1935, there were ceaseless arguments with him at the Wehrmacht and Chancellery. Two things became clear. The first was that his rationale for the operation was political, not military. The National Socialist Party had lost considerable éclat in the year 1935. Ordinary people had begun to realize that their lives had not improved. There was growing resentment of the impositions of the Party and the privileges ranking Party members granted themselves. Above all, there was a growing public abhorrence at the sheer crudeness and brutality of the Nazis.

So the corporal needed a triumph, some sort of coup to justify to the German people the demands he continued to make upon them. This was the real basis for the disastrous decision.

323

The second reality that emerged was that Hitler had begun to believe his own myth. For thirteen years, since the debacle of the Putsch in Munich, he had allowed the Nazi Party members to deify him. He had systematically eliminated any independent thinkers or persons with contrary views. He had surrounded himself with mediocrities and sycophants, men who were accustomed to agree with his every opinion. (I regret to say a fair number of these were senior Wehrmacht officers.) He had thus come to believe in the infallibility of his own judgment, no matter how many uncontroverted facts were arrayed against it. In short, he had become dangerous to his own ambitions, and he did not know it.

The upshot is that the corporal could not be dissuaded from his plans. In vain did the senior members of the General Staff point out the risks, the military pointlessness, the lack of popular support. Hitler was determined to have his coup.

It was from this maelstrom of argument that the Order emerged, significantly later than the general orders. (It was only reduced to final form on February 13th.) That is why it was distributed after the general orders, only to those with a need to know, and given the highest classification of secrecy.

I found myself suddenly in a crisis of conscience. Of course, I knew at once the effect that disclosure of the Order would have on British and French resolution. But I had begun my venture with the intention of exposing Hitler to the world. I had resolved firmly to protect military information, in accordance with my oath. I had gone to the limits of my conscience in disclosing the array of force proposed for the reoccupation. But this was not, strictly speaking, a Wehrmacht determination. Now I had in my hands an actual Wehrmacht order. On the one hand, providing the Order to the Allies might provoke exactly the political crisis I had hoped to achieve. On the other hand . . . it was a Wehrmacht order. To disclose it was to violate my sacred oath as a soldier. I was torn with indecision.

Karl von Haydenreich was the man most instrumental in resolving this chaos of conflicting values and loyalties. In fact, he was probably the person most responsible for the course subsequent events took. He and I happened to meet the day the Order was issued, about the musical program for an event I was hosting. He was, of course, too junior an officer to have knowledge of the Order. But I decided to take him into my confidence. I had come to trust his honor, his discretion, and his judgment.

He was instantly and emphatically of the opinion that the Order must be disclosed. *'Hitler has the madman's advantage,'* he said, *'the criminal's indifference. Other men – the British Prime Minister, the French Premier, even Mussolini – concern themselves with the effect of their actions on their fellow man. They dread war and unnecessary suffering. The Fuhrer does not. For him, the fate of others is meaningless. All that matters to him is his ego and his sense of destiny. Disclosing the Order deprives him of the unfair strategic superiority he enjoys because of the vacancy in his being.'*

He was of a similar mind about the duty we both owed to the Army. This madness, though to be undertaken by the Wehrmacht, was not in truth a Wehrmacht operation. Hitler had ordered it in defiance of all military logic and over the valid objections of the General Staff. To disclose the Order was likely to preserve both the Wehrmacht and its soldiery from disaster, and possibly even destruction, in the longer term.

Of course, these were not new thoughts to me. I did not need the advice of a junior officer decades younger than myself to obtain these perspectives. But to hear them articulated in concrete form with complete confidence by a man whose honor I respected, whatever his youth, clarified my own views on the matter. But then he took our conversation in a different direction, one that changed everything that came after.

'General, what has become of the Order itself?' he asked.

'I still have my copy,' I said. *'It was marked 'destroy after reading', because of the demoralizing effect on the troops if the contents became known. But I have not done so yet.'*

'There could not be more eloquent evidence of the actual attitude of the Fuhrer to the Army,' he remarked. Then his voice took on a heightened urgency. *'General, in this case, if we could provide the Order itself, rather than notes or a paraphrase . . . the actual Order . . . I could get it to Major Eisenhower this evening . . . this might make all the difference.'*

I understood him at once. *'Yes,'* I said, and with that one word my mind became clear and my will firm. *'I will get you the document this afternoon. Expect a summons to my office.'* Then I met his eye. *'There will be danger in this, Leutnant. Much more than in our other dispatches. Take all the sensible precautions.'*

Von Haydenreich knew he was being dismissed. He clicked his heels and saluted. *'I will proceed with the utmost care, sir.'*

I presented him with the Order that afternoon, as I had indicated. I also added some brief notes of my own on a separate sheet.

-

Excerpt from: My Name is Ike - Reflections on Fifty Years of Service as Soldier and Statesman
Dwight D. Eisenhower
Random House (1986)

. . . I received a phone call from Karl that day, inviting me to an impromptu social meeting at his apartments. On the phone, for the benefit of whomever might be listening, he said there was some personal family business to discuss. But I knew something else was up.

Both he and Elizabeth greeted me, but then she excused herself to look after the baby. As soon as she was gone, Karl produced an envelope. '*I believe our opportunity has arrived, Ike. I have something here that I could not leave at the music store. An actual Wehrmacht order.*' He told me briefly about the meeting he had had that day with the source and then about the Order. Then he handed me the envelope, which I put in my coat. Then Elizabeth was back, we bid our farewells, and I walked out into the night.

It was a long walk. I was carrying something that this time could not be explained away if I were to be suddenly apprehended. The envelope seemed to weigh a ton. Every policeman I passed seemed a looming menace. The walk seemed to take forever. But finally, I was back in my own quarters. Then I opened the envelope, all by myself. This was one time I did not want to involve my colleague, as much as I trusted that person.

There it was, with seals, countersignatures, the works, indisputably authentic. I had never seen a Wehrmacht General Order, but I knew enough about military formality to know that what I was looking at was the real deal. I had enough pidgin German to do my own loose translation. I knew immediately I was looking at a monumental, history-changing document.

Destroy After Reading . . . Top Secret . . . for Limited Distribution. In the event of any encounter with organized Allied troops, either French or British, the German forces are ordered to undertake a general retreat, in good order, as quickly as possible, back beyond the border of the unmilitarized zone, as defined by the Locarno Treaty. Contact with the enemy is to be broken off as quickly and efficiently as possible, and to be minimized during the conduct of the retreat. Clashes of arms are completely forbidden during the course of the maneuver, particularly the discharge of firearms . . . Destroy After Reading.

326

There was more, notes from some of the conferences that had led to the issuance of the order. The source had added his own notes, which emphasized one comment of Hitler himself. In the event of a reaction from the Allies, Hitler had said that his troops '*must scurry back to Germany, with their tail between their legs.*' My German was just terrible, then as now, but I knew enough to know that this was an incredibly insulting and dismissive manner of describing a military operation of proud German troops.

The implications were almost too big to grasp immediately. But then I got it. Hitler and the Nazis were bluffing. The whole Rhineland Operation was a bluff. Anyone can call a bluff, if you know the other guy is bluffing. This single document changed everything. I understood instantly why Karl was determined that the British see the original Order. It would be hard to believe, if you didn't see the thing itself.

The British had to have this. I would have been off to the British Embassy that very night, if the hour weren't so late. I scribbled a few notes of my own on how devastating a hasty retreat would be to all of Adolf Hitler's pretensions about a new, glorious Germany, then went to bed, where I hardly slept at all. Bright and early the next morning I was off to the British Embassy with the Order in hand. There was no time to lose.

Keller was his usual oafish self. He always behaved like a horse's behind to me. He'd been dressed down earlier for the casual attitude with which he approached the information we had provided. But he was apparently too well connected to replace. Somehow this time I managed to impress even him that what was in that envelope was critical. It had to be on its way to England in a diplomatic pouch that very day. Afterwards, I learned that that's exactly what happened. Even Keller wasn't that obtuse.

Then I went back to my own post, immeasurably relieved, but now tense in a different way. Surely the British and French would act now. Surely the information we had just provided would reassure even the most timid politician. Surely it would not be a repeat of the Versailles fiasco. But all I could do was wait. All that private cheerleading was just whistling in the dark. I really wasn't sure at all.

As to how it did work out . . . well, I guess the whole world knows that now.

-

Excerpt from: My Life in Office
Stanley Baldwin
Houghton, Mifflin (1947)

I was in conference that morning, attempting to deal with the other major crisis of my administration, the infatuation of the Prince of Wales with Wallis Simpson, when an aide burst in with the notice that a dispatch of extraordinary import had been received from our embassy in Berlin. I was at first annoyed as the conference was not to be interrupted. But when I learned more I understood at once the reason for the interruption, and the excitement. My aides had just seen the Order.

The Germans were going to retreat in the face of the slightest Allied opposition. The withdrawal (if it could even be called that) was to be as rapid as possible, without even maintaining contact with our forces. The entire operation, in short, was revealed to be a bluff. We and the French could put Hitler to the lie without the slightest real risk. The American military attaché who had provided the information (who I now know to be Dwight Eisenhower) had provided the original order. Our Berlin office had done a preliminary assessment of its authenticity. So had our own military intelligence. Both assessments concurred on the veracity of the document. Incredibly, my government was in possession of a genuine copy of a fully authorized Wehrmacht order.

I knew at once this changed everything.

I summoned my cabinet, and certain members of the Opposition, into an emergency conference that afternoon. The meeting lasted the balance of the afternoon, through the dinner hour, and late into the night, finally concluding just before midnight. It was by far the most heated and controversial meeting of my entire political life. This was largely owing to the fact that I made my own views clear at the outset. It was my intention to provide the original of the Order to the French Premier Sarraut, and at the same time indicate my willingness to order a general mobilization if the French did as well. This proposal was met by implacable hostility from the Opposition, and even a sizable fraction of my own Party, who feared the political consequences.

I could understand these considerations. We were all aware of Cecil's burgeoning Peace Ballot movement, which was hugely popular at the Universities and included any number of luminaries. But it soon became apparent that the objections went far, far beyond merely practical political calculations. How could I forget the lessons of the Great War so easily? How could I repeat Asquith's mistakes of 1914 so casually?

It was useless to point out that the Order made it clear that the Nazi move was a bluff, and one that could easily be called. *How could I be so sure? How did I know that the intelligence was not some sort of cunning trap? Or that Hitler might not change his mind and mobilize in turn?* It was even more useless to point out that a German mobilization was out of the question; that German forces were still minuscule compared to the West; that despite the disavowal of Versailles German rearmament had barely begun; that a call to arms would almost certainly result in a popular and/or military uprising on a scale that even Hitler could not risk. *But why take even this small risk to peace?* It was most useless to point out that allowing Herr Hitler to succeed with his bluff was a far greater risk to peace than a mobilization order. They had all had access to our intelligence over the last eighteen months. They all knew that. But my opponents ignored what they knew, as men with fixed views will always ignore inconvenient facts.

Finally, the chimes at midnight were about to sound. I called an end. I told all the participants that the meeting had been called to sound out any rational objections that might exist against my proposal. But having heard none in nearly eight hours, I intended to proceed as I had indicated. I did not take a vote; many of my colleagues had legitimate political concerns, and would not be happy being forced into record. The meeting was then adjourned.

Clement Attlee, the most vocal of my opponents, left, shaking with rage. '*You are a madman, Baldwin,*' he said. '*This is madness. I will make you pay for this. I promise you there will be consequences.*' I replied that I knew that, but they were consequences I must accept. He left without another word.

Meanwhile, our clerks had been busy making copies of the Order, that were so good they were for all practical purposes forgeries. I was determined that the French Premier would have the original. I gave directions to send that copy to Albert Sarraut that very night, midnight or not. I also included a note with assurances that Great Britain was now prepared to stand fully behind France in whatever sensible action it decided to take.

Then I went to bed.

Where I did not sleep well.

-

Excerpt from: Ma Vie Publique, 1929 -1940
Albert Sarraut
Editions du Cerf (1955)

. . . [T]he miracle was in the form of a dispatch from Baldwin, the British Prime Minister. It was hard to believe at first, but both the British and our own evaluations indicated the truth. The German forces in the Rhineland were ordered to retreat at the merest presence of Allied military. We could oppose this dangerous measure by force with full confidence that no widespread war would ensue. A miracle!

I immediately summoned Maurin to share this unprecedented intelligence with him. But to my utter amazement, I found his opinions and advice completely unchanged by this extraordinary knowledge. He was as relentlessly opposed to any demonstration of force as he had been before. He quibbled, he equivocated, he legalized. He even expressed doubts about the intelligence, even though the reliability of the source had been indisputably demonstrated over the past eighteen months.

Enough was enough. Within a few minutes, I had come to a decision unprecedented for a civilian occupying my office. It is one thing to deal with a general who is cautious in the face of an enemy of unknown plans and intent. It is quite another to deal with a general who refuses to act, even when he knows the enemy intends to flee. I informed Maurin that his resignation as Minister of War would be required immediately. Mercifully, I received it on the spot.

It then became necessary to find a replacement. To that end, I called Paul Reynaud, whose vocal advocacy of rearmament had made us political foes. But when I indicated what was afoot and what the stakes were, he accepted the newly vacant position immediately. He was present in the government offices before noon, and even before an official announcement. He absorbed the background with commendable speed.

Even while I was arguing with Maurin, I was thinking about the nature of the military operation France would wish to conduct. The assessment of the neutral (the American attaché Eisenhower, as it happened) was acute and convincing. The object would not be the normal military objective of inflicting maximum damage on the enemy, which would withdraw in any case. Any unnecessary bloodshed would instantly swing international opinion against France. Rather, the object must be to embarrass Hitler and the Nazis, to the maximum extent possible, with the minimum use of force. Hitler had sought a political triumph. We would provide him instead with a political disaster.

Reynaud instantly understood and agreed with these assessments. There then arose the question of what officer, if any, could be trusted to organize a force to accomplish these objectives, and in fact realize them. It was then that the Devil made his presence felt. Reynaud nominated a relatively youthful colonel in the mobile armored division, who had written a book concerning the tactical uses of these vehicles (called 'tanks' these days) with some truly creative ideas. I emphasized to Reynaud that success would require a certain amount of panache, and a gift for the grand gesture.

Then Reynaud smiled and assured me that his nominee possessed those qualities almost to excess. As all the world knows now, his opinion of Colonel Charles De Gaulle on that score proved to be entirely justified.

How was I to know the demon I had unleashed!? How could I possibly have known??

-

Interview with Premier Charles De Gaulle
Le Figaro
June 3, 1952

Before I was summoned to the Presidential palace, I was of the opinion that French politicians were one and all dunderheaded fools, with heads filled with straw and excrement.

I soon learned that that opinion was much, much too generous.

-

February 20, 1936
34 Kantstrasse, Schoneberg District
Berlin, Germany

From the Journals of Karl von Haydenreich (Published 1986):

Two days before departure. Matters came to a head.

Elizabeth left the boys to Helga, and closed the door behind her. '*My husband,*' she said, '*you have not begun your own preparations for our journey.*'

'*Something has come up at the Abwehr,*' I answered. '*I'm unable to leave right now. I'll join you in a few days.*'

'*I don't think you have any intention of joining us,*' she said quietly. '*I don't think you ever did.*'

'*You don't trust my honor in this matter?*' I said.

'*I would trust your honor with my life, my husband,*' Elizabeth answered quietly. '*It is your prudence I question. Please be truthful with me, Karl. There is more to this, I am certain.*'

'*Yes, there is, my wife,*' I said. '*I must beg your forgiveness. I should have been open with you from the start.*' Then I told her of the mad plans being made for the occupation of the Rhineland, the objections of the Wehrmacht, the foolhardiness of Hitler, the real possibility of another general war on the Continent. '*These are the reasons I want you and my sons in England, my darling,*' I finished. '*I should have been truthful from the start.*'

Elizabeth was silent for a long moment. Then she spoke quietly again. '*I believe you, Karl,*' she said, '*but there is still more to it than this. I am certain of it. Ike here so suddenly the other night – these meetings you have – these musical scores you carry, that you don't really need – I am dreadfully afraid.*'

'*There is nothing to be afraid of, my wife,*' I said. '*I am not quite the musician you think I am.*'

'*Yes, you are. Karl, if there is danger, you must tell me,*' she said urgently. '*You must let me share it. You must be truthful with me.*'

I was silent for a while, then took her hand. She shook me off. '*No, my husband, you will not distract me tonight.*' I sighed then. '*Please sit down, then, Elizabeth,*' I said. '*Let us talk.*' She sighed in turn and sat at our bedroom table.

'*You think more clearly than I do,*' I said. '*You must have considered the full consequences of what you ask. I am not lying, but supposing I were? Supposing I permitted you to share these imaginary perils? What would happen to Martin and Willy if we were both arrested? What would become of them? If we both shared your brother's fate?*' Her expression changed. She had thought of this. '*A Nazi orphanage? Some nice Nazi foster parents? There are no perils, my love, other than this Rhineland foolishness. But if there were, to share them is not to halve them. It is to double them.*' Elizabeth said nothing. I took her hand. She did not object.

'*I am not lying to you, my wife. But you must do as I wish in this matter. I have never played the German pater familias before,*' I said, '*and I hope to never again. We are indeed the modern couple. But please honor my wishes now. Believe me, I am in no danger.*'

'*You are lying to me,*' she answered, '*but I will do as you say. Just please, Karl, please, take care of yourself. Be good to yourself. You are my life. You are everything to me.*'

332

The next morning, two limousines called for the three of them at about 8:00 – one for the passengers, one for the luggage. Elizabeth was silent to the last farewell. Then she kissed me with a passion that reminded me of our courtship.

'*Will I ever see you again?*' she said. Her eyes were suddenly moist.

'*Of course, you will*,' I answered. '*Be of good cheer.*' She nodded, then entered the car. The two limousines drove away. I waved from the sidewalk until they were out of sight.

Now I am alone in our apartments. All I can think of is Elizabeth, Martin's clumsy walk, and Wilhelm's first smile. I seem to have returned to all the loneliness of my childhood.

Excerpt from: Ma Vie Publique, 1929-1940
Albert Sarraut
Editions du Cerf (1955)

Seldom have I taken a more instant dislike to anyone than I did to Colonel Charles De Gaulle. Of course, I had no expectation of him of any sympathy for me or my political faction. But what I did not expect was the degree of disdain – from a junior officer, no less – that he took no pains to conceal.

But I must pay the Devil his due. De Gaulle was in my office within two hours of the recommendation of Reynaud. He absorbed the basic elements of the situation with uncanny speed. As soon as he was assured that our intelligence source was unquestionably bona fide, he asked no more questions. And it was he who first sensed the full potential of the political embarrassment these events permitted us to visit on the National Socialist Party and its shoddy Fuhrer.

De Gaulle endorsed the views of the American major Eisenhower (as he is now known to be) completely. He suggested that we treat these Nazi plans as an opportunity rather than a danger. He strongly urged that we allow the reoccupation to proceed, letting Hitler sow the wind and reap the whirlwind. No one in our military had even considered this before he raised the possibility. But the suggestion had so much obvious appeal that the Ministry acceded at once. Given his head, within the next hour, he had laid out the elements of a military response that would yield the maximum political advantage, in terms so plain that even I and the other civilians could follow him easily. (I had no idea how varied and imaginative tank formations could be until De Gaulle educated me on the subject.)

It was then that his hauteur became annoying to the point of rudeness. De Gaulle's scheme required a feint that the Germans would not recognize as a counter bluff. He paused when he came to this point, and eyed me with what was almost a glare. I became infuriated. Of course, I was violently opposed to war, of course I had condemned the excesses of the military repeatedly (and justifiably), as had my supporters . . . but did he really believe I would fail my honor as a Frenchman and my duty as the President of the Ministry in a matter of this importance?

I assured him icily that mobilization orders of the requisite type would go forth at the appropriate time. I had the guarantee of the British that they would follow suit. De Gaulle accepted this assurance without comment, not even uttering a token apology for his unspoken doubts. Then he continued as briskly and brilliantly as before.

De Gaulle was brilliant. There is no question that he was the right man for the right occasion in this instance. But with that, I am done with compliments. Charles De Gaulle, later General De Gaulle, now Premier De Gaulle, is, in all other respects, made up completely of shit.

-

Interview with Premier Charles De Gaulle
Le Figaro
June 3, 1952

Sarraut was a typical socialist, surrounding himself with Communist pigs and Jewish dogs.

But I will give him due credit in the Rhineland affair. On this one occasion, he did his duty like a man, without regard to the political consequences.

-

Telegram
Windermere Castle
Windermere, Westmoreland
February 26, 1936

Leutnant Karl von Haydenreich
Berlin Germany

DEAR BEREFT HUSBAND STOP ELIZABETH MARTIN WILHELM
ARRIVED AND ENSCONCED SAFELY STOP CEASELESS NAGGING

FROM MATER ALREADY COMMENCED RE MY DUTY TO PRODUCE
GRANDCHILDREN STOP WHEN MAY WE EXPECT YOU? ALBERT

-

Excerpt from: My Life in Office
Stanley Baldwin
Houghton, Mifflin (1947)

The French response to the revelation of the Order was surprisingly long in forthcoming. But when it did arrive, its brilliance and acuity were apparent at once. Charles De Gaulle was the author, a name I did not recognize at the time. Everyone knows it now.

We had a chance to rebuke, even possibly destroy, Hitler, without bloodshed. I emphasized my continued support to Sarraut, and we laid our plans. By the first of March, all was in readiness.

-

Excerpt from: My Name is Ike - Reflections on Fifty Years of Service as
Soldier and Statesman
Dwight D. Eisenhower
Random House (1986)

. . . [S]o I had shot still another arrow into the air. Had this one landed? I hadn't the slightest idea. It was the same as always. Nothing happened. There were no events, there was no change, not a roar, not even the echo of a roar. Truth be told, I was not at all certain what my expectations were. I had never received a response from any of the material my source had provided. Even so, I had a sense of 'breathless hush', to give it a name . . . a feeling that a storm was about to break,

On the evening of March 1st, I had dinner with Karl, who was 'baching' it. Elizabeth and his sons had departed a week before to the Sommerville estates in England. He was in a sad, wistful mood; he missed his family keenly. I did my best to cheer him up, without mentioning the momentous events we both knew were imminent. Had I known then that this would be the last time I would ever see him, I don't know what I would have done.

It has preyed on me a bit over the years, that I never bid Karl a proper farewell, or told him directly how much I cared for him, not all that different from my own sons. I've never forgotten that. These days, no matter whom I'm with, it's always in the back of my mind that that meeting may be the last. I always try to find something to say at the end that will do for a proper farewell,

335

if it should turn out that way. That sounds foolish, I know. But I did not do that at that dinner with Karl. I'm determined that will never happen to me again.

-

Excerpt from: Eyewitness!
The True Story of the Fiasco on the Rhine and the Siege of the Reich
Chancellery
Oberfeldwebel (formerly) Victor H. Becker
Houghton, Mifflin (1950)

I didn't think I'd see any action. I was the General's driver, stuck like a horse in a mud pit at Headquarters. I certainly did not know the date.

But then on the afternoon of March 6th, General von Hammerstein called me to his offices. I felt my pulse quicken as he told me bluntly that the remilitarization of the Rhineland would occur the next day. He then told me that he was sending one of his staff, a Major Bergman, to observe and report directly to him. I was ordered to reconnoiter with the Major at 6:00 p.m., then join the main body of troops for the commencement of the march at dawn.

I met Major Bergman at the appointed hour. He seemed to be a solid, sensible officer. I liked him. We drove to the staging point, near Wutpal, when the troops had been called out to form up. This was about an hour before dawn. A colonel addressed them as a body. He shouted to them they were about to undertake the remilitarization of the Rhineland, the last step in freeing Germany from the shackles of Versailles. A huge shout of joy went up from the ranks. It was evident that the men had not been told of the actual plans until this very hour. The ranks were discharged to do the final assembly of the kit, and last minute adjustments. Then, just before dawn, the order came down to march, and we set off.

The sun came up and lit up the West in the direction of our march. As the cities and towns along the route came to life, the men began to sing, spontaneously, in ranks. Curious passersby came out of their homes to watch, first in ones and twos, then in numbers. Some asked where we were headed, and the men in the ranks told them it was the Rhineland. There were hurrahs and shouts of approval. Some of the citizens came up with flowers and fresh bread. Excitement buzzed along the way.

More than a few of the men were on bicycles, whether their own or provided by the Wehrmacht, I couldn't say. They wore their rifles slung over their shoulders, but otherwise no packs. They pedaled along smoothly by the side of the road, maintaining the pace. Other than that, the ranks were in good order and stepped out smartly, with heads high. We were German soldiers, and on the march! As we marched further westward, and the sun rose higher, there were more songs, more flowers, and more bread. The height of the good spirits was incredible.

Overhead, a few warplanes provided a lazy escort. But there was no armor, no artillery, and a minimum of military encumbrance. There were horsemen, and even horse-and-carriages. I kept our car towards the rear of the column so we could observe all. I remarked to the Major that the occasion seemed more like a holiday or festival than a military campaign. He answered that this was in accordance with Wehrmacht directives, to minimize the military significance of this movement, and thereby reduce as much as possible the chance of a response in force from the British and French.

There must have been drummers sent on ahead. As the morning progressed, more and more people appeared at the roadside. Loud throngs cheered and joined in our songs. There were still more flowers and foodstuffs. There was also an abundance of pretty girls, some of whom were not shy in shouting out to the soldiers. I myself caught the eye of one, then remembered myself and my fiancée, and broke off my gaze. This did not go unnoticed by the Major, who did not bother to conceal his amusement.

The march to Cologne was not a long one. I learned later that there were only 14,000 troops in the force. (Another 22,000 policemen were making their own way to civilian stations.) By 1:00 p.m. we were at the Hollenzollern Bridge. By then, the roadside was mobbed. Townspeople, mostly girls, strewed flowers in our path. Priests and ministers appeared and blessed us. Even Cardinal Schulte himself made himself known, and offered praise to Hitler for 'sending back our army'. The excitement resounded all along the highways and echoed through the city. For this day, anyway, no one had any doubts about the Fuhrer or the Nazis. We were all one, and all German – and on the march!

Then, shortly after we had arrived and reformed at the Bridge, everyone seemed to become distracted. We could hear whispers, and a stirring throughout the crowd on the street sides. Soon enough we learned the reason. The Fuhrer had begun an address to the Reichstag.

-

Excerpt from: Destiny Betrayed - A Chronicle of Treason
Harald Quandt
Franz Eher Nachfolger Gmbh (1952)

The high-water mark of the Third Reich was reached that seventh of March, when Adolf Hitler made his address to the Reichstag, announcing the final triumph over the Versailles Treaty and the November traitors. When he announced that Germany was resuming sovereignty of the Reich in all the Rhineland, the entire hall erupted in tumult. All 600 deputies joined in saluting him repeatedly, arms outstretched, hands raised high, in repeated joyous salutes. The shouts were so great and interrupted him so often, that his wise and generous proposals for a lasting European peace could barely be heard.

The 'heils' were echoed all over Germany by a jubilant people, in the schools and churches, in the beer halls and barracks, and along the street sides in Cologne and Dusseldorf.

And all over Europe and the world, Jews and Bolsheviks trembled.

-

Excerpt from: My Life in Office
Stanley Baldwin
Houghton, Mifflin (1947)

I received the report of Hitler's speech and its reception within minutes of its delivery. It had been broadcast by radio and all over Germany.

I knew then that my turn had come. I was under no illusion about the devastating effect the order would have on my career. Yet I had no misgivings, then or now.

At about 3:00 p.m., as I had promised Sarraut, the direction for a general mobilization went out. All over England, troops went on alert. Reservists were contacted and ordered to report.

-

March 7, 1936
Cavendish Square
London, England

Mr. A. A. Milne
Cotchford Farm,
Hartfield, East Sussex

Milne,

I dash this off in haste.

A young friend of mine, one Reginald Henry, a junior barrister and reservist, received a sudden notice to report to his military station by 6:00 p.m. tonight. Evidently the government is calling for a general mobilization in response to the German movement in the Rhine.

I am aghast. Has Baldwin lost all reason? The lessons of the Great War were so clear, so vivid, written in oceans of blood. How can they be so easily forgotten? Do they mean nothing to him? Absolutely nothing?

There must be an instant and dramatic response to this insanity, of the strongest possible nature.

Yours,

Cecil

\-

Excerpt from: A Twentieth Century Life
Albert Sommerville
Houghton, Mifflin (1959)

When the news of the Rhineland incursion flashed across the wireless that March 7th, I knew at once why Karl had sent his wife and children abroad, and why Karl had to remain. Elizabeth was in our garden, strolling with her older son, teaching him the English names of the things around them. She was radiantly happy. It seemed inhuman to bring any cloud into that sky. But I knew I must speak.

Her face turned ashen in a second. Karl had disclosed to her the imminence of the event, but not the precise date. She did her best to dissemble for the sake of Martin's state of mind. But her forebodings were instantly apparent to anyone of mature years.

Later that day, I learned that Baldwin had ordered a general mobilization. I was forced to share that news with her as well.

\-

Excerpt from: Ma Vie Publique, 1929-1940
Albert Sarraut
Editions du Cerf (1955)

In fact, I ordered a French mobilization about an hour before the English, within a moment or two after Hitler made his grandiose speech. I also contacted De Gaulle and gave him the formal authorization to initiate the plans we had discussed.

I knew the effect that these measures would have on my standing with the party. But it was an act that had to be done. A chance like this would not come twice. Baldwin at least had the consolation of knowing that he would be providing ammunition to his political enemies. I had to live with the knowledge that it was my friends who would do me in.

\-

With the cheers still ringing in our ears, and the whole city in celebration, we marched on, across the Hollenzollern Bridge, and onto the western bank of the Rhine. Our occupation was to begin with the smallest of forces, only three brigades, and only one at this site. Bergman's and my orders from General Hammerstein were to observe, not participate. So the Major and I watched them decamp, then re-crossed the bridge to the east side, before nightfall.

We had hoped to join in the celebrations we were sure were taking place in the city, and possibly meet some of the girls who had been making so merry. But as the afternoon became evening, the high spirits faded. A definite uneasiness took its place.

There were rumors everywhere that both the English and French had ordered general mobilizations.

I arrived at the Reich Chancellery promptly at 9:00 a.m. The letter in hand had been prepared well in advance. My French counterpart, M. Francois-Poncet, was only a minute late. (I was mildly surprised that there was no Italian representative. My briefing had been terse, and there had been no reference to this circumstance. But in view of the Ethiopian situation I understood immediately.)

We barely had time to greet each other before we were ushered in to von Neurath, the Nazi Foreign Minister himself. He was as composed as on every other occasion when I met him, the epitome of *sang froid.* But he was pale and his eyes hollow.

'*Gentlemen?*' he said.

With this, Francois-Poncet and I both presented our notes. They were in identical form, except for minor nuances in translation. Von Neurath read rapidly, I believe the English version first.

'*What is the meaning of this?*' he asked finally.

I explained briefly that he was receiving notice on behalf of his government that our two nations have become aware of the breach by Germany of its obligations as defined in the Treaty of Locarno, and of our intent to respond with appropriate military action. Francois-Poncet added that French troops, fortified by tanks and artillery, were entering the demilitarized zone as we spoke.

'*You cannot mean this!*' von Neurath exclaimed. '*You cannot bring war as the result of Germany deploying troops in its own land!*'

'*This is not at all a declaration of war,*' I answered. I will admit that the sight of his discomfiture gave me great pleasure. '*It is notification that our two nations intend to assert their rights under the Treaty. The proposed military action will go no further than that redress.*'

'*Whether war is to result is a question for your government,*' Francois-Poncet added. '*It is Germany that has provoked this situation by its deliberate breach of its treaty obligations. Your Fuhrer made that apparent in the speech yesterday, which, I must say, was remarkable in its arrogance and candor. If Germany acts promptly to restore the status quo, then all will be well. The Allies request nothing more than that restoration, and the military action has no further aim.*'

'*The military action has already begun?*' he said. '*Your nations began this before the delivery of this note?*'

The French ambassador shared an incredulous glance with me. '*The nation of Germany can hardly complain of a lack of fair warning,*' he said, finally, on behalf of us both, '*when it itself violated the treaty with no notice whatsoever.*'

Von Neurath went beet red. He stood up. '*There is no point in continuing this discussion,*' he said. '*I must share these communications with the Fuhrer and others. Good day.*' With that, he clicked his heels, turned, and left the room. Francois-Poncet and I were left to see ourselves to the door.

I felt breathless and confused by my own emotions. On the one hand, I was excited, even exhilarated. The Allies were way overdue in confronting Herr Adolf Hitler. But on the other hand . . . were we turning out the lights in Europe all over again? Would another continental war be the consequence?

I could only pray that the Almighty had guided our hand correctly.

-

Excerpt from: Eyewitness!
The True Story of the Fiasco on the Rhine and the Siege of the Reich

We first heard, rather than saw, the French force that arrived on the 8th. There was the distant sound of engines in mass, drumming, and – I could swear – faint bugles, though others say that was only my imaginings. At first, in the hour before dawn, there was not enough light to see anything in detail. But with the growing light, we could see French troops massing, with tanks and artillery. We knew then that the rumors of mobilization were true.

The Major had field glasses and was looking across the bridge. '*At least regimental strength,*' he murmured. '*Probably more than one.*' Then he mentioned tanks and artillery. This was how I became aware of them.

I heard then an artillery shot, from a cannon or tank, I could not tell which. Then there was another. I felt my breath becoming very short. Our forces had no artillery.

'*Powder only,*' the Major said. '*No shells or ordnance. Signals of some kind.*'

'*What do they mean?*' I asked. I will tell you I felt fear. My family comes from the Ruhr; I well-remembered the French occupation of a decade before; and I did not want to see anything like that again. Perhaps this was even war. The Great War started with less cause than we had given the day before. I worried in that moment for my kindred and all Germany.

'*I don't know,*' the Major answered. '*Warnings, I would suppose.*' His brow was furrowed with the same concern I had, I could tell. Then suddenly he redirected his glasses to the bridge. I looked in that direction, and did not need glasses to see.

The brigade that had proudly marched across the Hollenzollern bridge the day before was streaming across it, the men in small groups, some in twos and threes. Their kits had been packed with haste and sloppiness. Some were open, and some men kept dropping items. The trucks showed even more confusion. It was the most unmilitary scene I had ever witnessed. I felt ashamed.

The Major stopped one of the men running by, a sergeant by his insignia. '*What is the meaning of this?*' he demanded. His anger was visible.

'*We were ordered to retreat, Herr Major – by the Oberleutnant. He said our orders were to retreat if any Allied troops arrived. In obedience, we were packing up. But the French gave us only an hour. Then there were shots, and we made the most haste possible.'*

The Major stepped forward and slapped the sergeant, hard across the cheek. He looked back, astonished. *'You can retreat like soldiers!'* he barked. *'Not like a flock of frightened geese! Your orders did not mean a retreat like this! Now form up your men, and the other platoons. Rouse the sergeants, and send the Oberleutnant to me!'*

I was proud of my Major. That sergeant deserved that slap. He needed it – you always have to be a soldier! He wheeled and ran into the mass of men, barking orders. The effect was immediate. The troops ceased their pell-mell actions. The men with poorly packed kits stopped and repacked them, then came to formation. Others began to reorganize the trucks. Other sergeants met their own platoons. Then the sergeant we first encountered was back with the Oberleutnant.

'We were under orders to retreat,' he explained.

'I am aware of that,' the Major said icily. *'But like members of an army of proud soldiers, heads held high. Not like a mob of rabble.'*

'The men are formed up now,' the Oberleutnant said stiffly. Clearly, he was worried about what sort of report the Major might provide to the Staff.

'You have done well, Oberleutnant,' the Major said. *'Anyone can be surprised. My report will commend you for your poise in this matter.'*

'Thank you, sir,' the Oberleutnant said. I could see he was relieved. *Well done*, I thought. An officer has to be a stickler, but he doesn't have to be a shithead.

Then my attention was caught again by the roar of engines. At least one French regiment was crossing the bridge, with tanks and mobile artillery. It was a frightening sight, particularly for troops that had turned out more properly outfitted for a campout than military resistance. The French troops formed ranks, straddling the bridge on either side. The tanks pulled up in front of them, the sight of which would make an unarmed man wince. The turrets turned slowly in the direction of the retreat, with the first morning light glinting off their barrels.

My heart came to my mouth. My asshole shrank to the size of a pea. I'd seen firsthand in the Great War what those monsters could do to infantry. Did the French intend a massacre? Surely we had not done anything that deserved that sort of revenge. But facing us were those tanks. I had never before questioned orders, for a good soldier never does. But now doubts

343

flooded my mind. What could the Fuhrer have been thinking in ordering this venture? Why were our troops so ill equipped? The French and English had vastly superior forces to ours. Hadn't anyone considered how hopelessly we would be situated in the event of a military response? Apparently not. But now there were the bristling cannon and tanks, and no one knew what to do.

The streets should have been coming alive with the early morning commerce and traffic. But they were stone silent. The Cologners were no fools.

'*Continue the retreat, Oberleutnant,*' Major Bergman said calmly. He was not the Oberleutnant's commanding officer, but given the circumstances, and the disarray, it made sense for him to take command. My respect for him grew by the second. He was a real German officer!

Just then someone called out from the rear. '*Officer! Whoever is the commanding officer!*' We all turned around. A messenger was riding up on a bicycle. He came within a few feet, dismounted, and saluted.

'*The orders have changed, Herr Commandant,*' he said.

'*What change?*' a voice called out from the direction of the bridge. Striding up came Captain Schmidt, the actual commanding officer of the battalion.

'*You are ordered to entrench as best you can, and to fight to the last man,*' the messenger said. '*You are not to yield so much as a millimeter.*'

'*What?*' Major Bergman, the captain, the Oberleutnant, and me, the driver, said in a chorus – for I will tell you, none of us could believe our ears. This was not a military order, but an order to suicide and slaughter.

'*I cannot believe this order is correctly stated,*' the captain said.

'*It is from the Fuhrer himself,*' the messenger said. '*I was instructed to say that as well.*'

–

Excerpt from: A General Speaks - the Autobiography of Kurt von Hammerstein Equord
Major General Kurt von Hammerstein Equord
Reichswehr Press (1986)

From the moment that we received confirmation that the Allies were mobilizing, the corporal began to show his actual mettle – or, rather, the complete lack thereof. For an hour or so, he closeted himself in his office, with the cream of the Wehrmacht standing around in the Reich Chancellery, awaiting his word. We were all in a breathless and sleepless state.

344

Then suddenly, he emerged, in a furious rage, and hurled himself toward von Blomberg. Von Neurath, the coolest head in the Fuhrer's cabinet, tried to calm him, but the cause was hopeless. *How had this come about?!? Why had he been so poorly served by his generals?* He stormed about, becoming more hysterical by the second, damning everyone and everybody for creating the situation. One would never have guessed that Hitler himself had been the principal architect of the remilitarization, for political purposes of his own, against the more prudent advice of the General Staff.

Suddenly, abruptly, he was done, and stormed off again into his inner office, with the door slamming behind him. Two of his adjutants scuttled out immediately, and went to the phones. In a moment or two, Hess, the puppy dog, appeared and went into the inner office. Goebbels appeared a few moments later and also entered, Himmler a short while after that. Heydrich accompanied Himmler, but did not enter the office.

To what a sorry lot is entrusted the fate of Germany, I thought. But this was a sentiment I kept to myself, though I am sure others shared it. We could hear raised voices, shouts, and Hitler literally screaming from time to time. After about ten minutes, Hess emerged. His face was white and drawn.

'*It is the Fuhrer's order that the troops in the field stand their ground,*' he said. '*They must hold their position to the last man.*'

We all stared at him in disbelief. I myself could not believe my ears. We had sent to the extreme border the smallest possible force, of battalion strength, and lightly armed. They did not even have entrenching tools. They had no training, nor had any plans for the contingency of remaining in the field been made. Now they were expected to offer resistance to a force of regimental strength, equipped with tanks and artillery? I would say the order was madness, but it was in fact beyond madness. It had no relation whatsoever to any military thinking that ever was or ever will be.

There was a personal aspect to the matter as well. I had dispatched a Major Thomas Bergman to observe, the son of one of my oldest friends, and one of the finest young officers I knew. Becker, my driver, was with him. It had never crossed my mind that in sending him on such a simple mission I was recklessly endangering their lives. But apparently I had.

'*That is the Fuhrer's order,*' Hess repeated. '*See to it that it is dispatched to the field.*' He addressed von Blomberg, the most loyal and unthinking.

And, true to form, von Blomberg turned to an aide and saw to it that this direction to mass suicide was communicated immediately to the field commanders.

Until that moment, I had been well pleased with the way in which events had developed. A political fiasco loomed, and at little cost to the Wehrmacht. But when the corporal issued his incomprehensible 'no retreat' order, I was thunderstruck. I had never expected that men would be sent to needless, certain death. A good officer must reconcile himself to loss, but never waste. I knew at once that Hitler had erred, perhaps fatally, but at the time his error seemed the least of it . . .

-

Excerpt from: Eyewitness!
The True Story of the Fiasco on the Rhine and the Siege of the Reich
Chancellery
Oberfeldwebel (formerly) Victor H. Becker
Houghton, Mifflin (1950)

The captain turned to Major Bergman in desperation. '*This is insanity,*' he said.

'*I agree,*' the Major replied. '*But I am here as an observer, not a member of the General Staff. I can't countermand it.*' He addressed the messenger. '*Make haste back to headquarters and request with all urgency that the order be reviewed. The troops here do not have the numbers, equipment, or weapons to make any meaningful resistance possible.*'

The messenger saluted, mounted his bicycle, and pedaled away at top speed. The major then turned to the captain. '*Captain, I'm afraid you have no choice but to make the best job possible out of this order,*' he said.

'*God have mercy,*' the captain said, and set to it.

A paved road ran parallel to the river, and before that, a slight bluff, then a descent to the river bank. We had retreated further down the road. The captain called his troops to formation briefly, then ordered them to take up positions on the ridge behind the bluff, on either side of the road, midway between us and the French. They had of course no tools to dig in, and the angle of the ridge was too slight to afford any meaningful protection from shot or cannon fire. They were as exposed as one of Karl May's buffalo hunters on the American prairie. The captain urged them make shelter as best they could, but it was hopeless. And yet they set about the hopeless task with high spirits and unbroken will. Brave lads!

346

Meanwhile, the French troops continued to gather at the head of the bridge and behind it. The tank barrels lowered and raised. The troops separated; two additional field artillery pieces joined the tanks. We were not separated by more than 300 yards.

The Major turned to me then. '*Becker, go remind the captain he is not under orders to fire first,*' he said. I made haste to find the captain. I will tell you, I did not for one second enjoy being in the open under the eyes of those tanks and cannon! I found him, he acknowledged the advice, and then I returned.

Meanwhile, the French had done nothing. Bergman had his field glasses on them. '*The brass are all up there now,*' he muttered to himself. '*They don't know what to do. They can't believe their eyes. Where is that double damned messenger?*' I looked – there was still no sign of him, though I did see movement in the distance down the road.

Then several of the tank cannons lowered. The French brass had come to a decision. There was a moment of still silence, then a terrific blast as they all fired. The air seemed split in two by the sound. Wadding and power sailed by us. I don't mind telling you, dear reader, that I became scared. We were in the open and helpless, without so much as a haystack for shelter. I wondered if I would ever see my girl again. This was madness!

'*No shells,*' the Major muttered. '*Our final warning. Good. Sensible. There may still be time.*'

But then I heard rifle shots from our own troops. Someone – some one or two – must have panicked. The shots were ragged, useless, scattered, and from a distance where they could hit nothing, which they did not. I saw the captain stand up, clearly angered, to determine who had disobeyed orders. I turned wildly behind me. The movement in the distance had now resolved itself into someone moving toward us on a bicycle.

The French could draw only one conclusion from the shots. The tank barrels lowered again, including several that had not participated in the first volley.

'*May God have mercy,*' the Major said.

'*Look!*' I shouted. '*It is the messenger!*'

The cannons roared again, with the true sound of thunder, even louder than the first, for this time they were loaded with shells.

-

347

Excerpt from: *A General Speaks - the Autobiography of Kurt von Hammerstein Equord*
Major General Kurt von Hammerstein Equord
Reichswehr Press (1986)

I was drawn within myself, considering how to countermand this order for mass suicide, when at once von Neurath was by my side. He was, as always, unnaturally calm, but even his appearance was drawn and strained.

'*How will the Wehrmacht react to this?*' he asked quietly.

'*Do you have to ask?*' I responded. I did not add that Adolf Hitler had already made an indelibly bad impression. No one present would forget that hysterical voice.

'*But an oath was taken,*' he murmured. '*A personal oath to the Fuhrer. They would breach that?*'

'*All oaths are reciprocal,*' I answered. '*They can be broken by the oath-taker as well as the oath-giver.*'

Von Neurath nodded, but did not say anything. He was by far the most capable of the Nazi leadership, and one of the few who would stand up to the corporal. He walked towards the inner office, abruptly ordered the sentries out of the way, and without more notice went inside. In just a moment, Hess emerged, then the others. Von Neurath was alone with Hitler. It was not possible to make out the words, but we could hear Hitler's voice, loud and shouting, then von Neurath, quiet and unaffected by the shouting, then Hitler in fury, then von Neurath again, for a long, long time . . . then a silence. Finally, von Neurath emerged, alone.

'*The new order is rescinded,*' he said. '*The original retreat order is reinstated.*'

'*This is the Fuhrer's order?*' Hess asked, incredulity in his voice.

'*This is his order, yes,*' von Neurath answered. '*See to it that it is communicated as quickly as possible to the troops in the field.*' Von Blomberg reacted to this even more quickly than he had to the first, ludicrous revision earlier. His relief was evident.

'*I will need telephones,*' von Neurath said, '*and stenographers. It is necessary to transmit a formal note to the British and French embassies as soon as it can possibly be done.*'

-

Excerpt from: *Memoirs*
The Right Honourable Eric Phipps
Houghton, Mifflin 1946

I was in my office, so completely torn between hope and despair that I was engaged in prayer, for the first time since I was a child, when my assistant notified me that von Neurath was on the phone. I picked up the receiver with a final plea to the God who made us all.

He was abrupt to the point of rudeness. Without any formality, he informed me that the Reich had just then ordered the troops that had occupied the Rhineland the day before to withdraw beyond the line of the demilitarized zone, as defined by Locarno. He asked me whether the governments of France and Britain were prepared to undertake the reciprocal withdrawal of Allied troops, as we had indicated we would do in the formal notes that morning.

I did not need to consult my government to give him his reply. *'Without question,'* I answered. *'We will immediately undertake to withdraw to the Western bank and, when the German withdrawal is complete, end the mobilization.'*

Von Neurath indicated his satisfaction with that statement, informed me that the German movement had already begun, and rang off. It was apparent that this call had given him no pleasure, but that was of small moment to me.

The crisis was over. The merciful Lord had provided that there would be no war. I lifted my arms to the ceiling.

'Hallelujah!' I shouted, loud enough so that the entire office could hear me.

Excerpt from: Eyewitness!
The True Story of the Fiasco on the Rhine and the Siege of the Reich Chancellery
Oberfeldwebel (formerly) Victor H. Becker
Houghton, Mifflin (1950)

The discharge tore through the thin line of our troops. Some of the shot doubtless sailed high, but some hit the mark. I could hear cries and screaming from the ridge. I was seized with panic.

But then the messenger was with us. *'The order to fight has been withdrawn,'* he gasped, breathless. *'The original order to retreat has been reinstated.'*

'God in heaven,' Bergman said quietly. *'What a mess. You, go down to the ridge and ascertain the extent of the casualties,'* addressing the messenger. *'Becker,'* he said, turning to me. *'Come with me. I must work this out with the French. I will need a witness.'* Major Bergman was not in the chain

of command, there only as observer, but he took charge of the situation like a born general.

The messenger went off toward the ridge, as Bergman and I stepped out and onto the road. We had no flag of truce – we could only trust in the good sense of the French. I was more scared then than I had ever been before in my life. But the major went on firmly, with head high, and I tried my best to imitate him. As we approached the French line of tanks and artillery, one of the officers, I supposed the ranking officer, stepped forward. I tried as best I could to conceal my sigh of relief. We were not going to be blown up, after all.

Then we had come together. I had heard of the brotherhood of war, but never witnessed it before. But Major Bergman and his counterpart, a French colonel named De Gaulle, spoke with an understanding and professionalism that was quite beyond their different uniforms. I was there as witness; I made notes quickly later; and here is the what they said.

De Gaulle. '*Why have you sought this meeting?*'

Bergman. '*To request a cease fire. The orders to entrench are rescinded. Our original orders were to retreat have been reinstated.*'

De Gaulle. '*Ah, from Berlin, no doubt. Now I understand. Politicians. I could not believe my eyes when I saw your troops take up positions.*'

Bergman. '*Indeed. And your own orders as to the retreat?*'

De Gaulle. '*To hold this position. I wish I could take your word on the matter, but of course . . .*'

Bergman. '*Understood. We might be delayed. I think we have wounded.*'

De Gaulle. '*I did what I could. I fired a warning shot, and there was only one shell in the barrage. I knew this would not stand.*'

Just then the messenger approached. He reported four men wounded, one – the captain – hurt seriously. '*His right leg is mangled,*' the man said. '*We are stemming the bleeding with a tourniquet.*'

De Gaulle. '*Your captain should be treated as soon as possible. We have a field hospital.*'

Bergman. '*I have your word of honor he will not be treated as a prisoner?*'

De Gaulle. '*Of course. I have no such orders, and our nations are not at war. You have my word your captain will be released when medically sound.*'

'*We are agreed then,*' said Bergman, and extended his hand, which the French colonel took.

Bergman gave orders, so did De Gaulle, and the messenger went down, with two French medical officers and a stretcher. While they were down readying the captain for movement, another messenger arrived for Bergman. So did a French rider, for De Gaulle.

De Gaulle. '*My government has received an undertaking from yours, indicating its intent to abandon the occupation of the Rhineland.*'

Bergman. '*I have the same information.*'

De Gaulle. '*My orders now are to withdraw over the bridge, and take no further action, which we will do as soon as we have your wounded captain safe. When your movement is done, our mobilization will end.*'

Bergman. '*Understood.*' The two men shook hands again. By that time, the stretcher party was at the bridge. I could see the captain's face, pale as a fish, and what was left of his leg, even under the dressing. God, what havoc shells wreak! He looked up at Bergman and De Gaulle as he was carried by.

'*Thank you,*' he said to both.

'*It has been a pleasure,*' Bergman said to De Gaulle, after the wounded man passed. '*Au revoir,*' the colonel replied. '*I hope not,*' Bergman said, and both men laughed. Then we were done.

-

Excerpt from: Memoirs
The Right Honourable Eric Phipps
Houghton, Mifflin 1946

I sent off a cable to London. Then, throughout the office, one of the most spontaneous and uninhibited celebrations that I have ever witnessed or been a part of, took place. Corks were popped, wine flowed freely – no one worked or even tried to work the balance of the day. (I later learned there were similar scenes in Whitehall and the Quai d'Orsai.)

It was in this completely euphoric atmosphere that the seeds of tragedy were planted. I would rather not recount this, but a proper regard to historical accuracy insists that I must. Our military man, one William Keller, was always a bit unsound and something of a braggart. I had tried to have him replaced, but he had the support of someone in the military command structure. Under the influence of the wine, he was heard boasting that Baldwin and the French had always known the Germans would retreat, and that he himself had provided the critical information. He was immediately silenced, for we had German employees who had not yet left the building.

We all hoped that Keller had not been overheard, but alas! That was not the case . . .

-

Excerpt from: Eyewitness!
The True Story of the Fiasco on the Rhine and the Siege of the Reich
Chancellery
Oberfeldwebel (formerly) Victor H. Becker
Houghton, Mifflin (1950)

Now there was nothing for it, but retreat. With the captain gone, and no senior officer in sight, Bergman dropped the observer role completely. He found out that the two lightly wounded men were fit for travel. Then he ordered the troops into formation, announced the newly restored orders, and our retreat began.

We joined other troops on the road back. This day there were no songs, no cheering, no bystanders on the road, no girls. I did not even see any of the bicyclists who had ridden so cheerfully into the zone the day before. Everyone had wanted to join the success and the celebration. But they were now all behind closed doors, pretending this profound humiliation was not occurring.

It would have been a slow march in any case, but the Major insisted we keep company with the wounded men. He gave up his own place in the car to the wounded. It would have been better if the cabin of our car was large enough to accommodate all three, but there was only room for two passengers. So the three rotated as needed. They were able to step forward, but slowly, and needed frequent rest. It made for slow work. We were hours behind by the time we reached the border of the demilitarized zone.

Then it began. Someone in ranks proclaimed, '*Heil Hitler.*' Normally, others would answer back the same refrain. But that did not happen on this march. Instead, there was silence for a moment. Then some wit made a salute of his own – '*Heil Schicklgruber!*' Quiet, derisive laughter rippled through the ranks. Then another '*Heil Schicklgruber!*' Another followed, and still another.

Major Bergmann had been stoic until then. Now he turned to the men, and ordered a halt. '*Enough,*' he said, with quiet force. '*Do not disrespect the Fuhrer. A good soldier reacts to disappointment with the same face as he does success. Another day will come.'* The ranks quieted, and – it seemed to me – marched on with firmer step.

At last we approached the point of departure from the day before, a few hundred yards beyond the demilitarized zone. Beyond lay the Fatherland, as dark and sullen as one of the old Grimm's tales. We were marching home to defeat and disgrace. But then I was surprised to see an entire convoy of military cars and other vehicles, with lights on, and a dozen or so military policemen. I wondered what further trouble the Devil intended to bring to us that day.

As we neared the convoy, a man, apparently a ranking police officer, stepped forward. He confronted the Major.

'Are you Major Thomas Bergman?'

'Yes,' replied the Major.

'You are under arrest. For treason. You will come with us.'

—

Excerpt from: A General Speaks - the Autobiography of Kurt von Hammerstein Equord
Major General Kurt von Hammerstein Equord
Reichswehr Press (1986)

With the essential orders issued countermanding the descent into insanity, a numbness settled into the Chancery. We had suffered a fiasco, a humiliation, but it had hardly been a serious military undertaking. The task of regrouping and going forward would be unpleasant, but not unmanageable. These were the thoughts that occupied my mind.

I returned to Wehrmacht headquarters, to begin sorting out the botch of this affair. It was there that we received a report that shots had been exchanged near the Hollenzollern Bridge, including some artillery, and there had been casualties. This put a more serious cast on the matter. We could only hope that the conflict had been contained. The battalions in question were the ones to which I had assigned Bergman as observer, so I hoped for a direct report.

But before I could speak to Bergman, the phone rang. The speaker was Hess. Without even the pretense of formal courtesy, he informed me that I was summoned back to the Chancery, along with all the ranking members of the Wehrmacht, for a meeting 'of the highest urgency and importance'. It was now late afternoon. In all candor, I was more than a little irritated by still more commotion from the corporal. There was serious work to do. Nonetheless, I made my way to the Chancellor's office as soon as possible.

When I arrived, I found Hitler, Goebbels, Himmler, Heydrich, Hess, and a few other Nazi toadies arrayed around the corporal's desk, as stony-faced as Biblical judges. They said nothing as other members of the General Staff made their way into the room, and assembled. In some ways, it was a comic scene, with the two sides standing apart and facing each other, almost like chessmen arrayed for a game.

'*What is the meaning of this summons?*' I asked at last, after Wehrmacht staff were present in sufficient numbers. '*Why have you demanded our attendance so abruptly and rudely?*'

There was a moment's dramatic pause, then Heydrich, who had clearly been assigned as spokesman, spoke softly and clearly, merely a single word:

'*Treason.*'

The entire Wehrmacht staff erupted as one man, coming to attention and speaking or shouting – '*Outrageous!*' '*Slander!*' '*How dare you!*' and other such. Heydrich waited for the furor to subside, then went on as if no interruption had occurred.

'*We have reliable information from agents both here and in France that the Allies had complete knowledge of our plans for the Rhineland. In particular, they had knowledge of the order to our forces to retreat if confronted. This information was provided to them by an officer in the Wehrmacht.*'

Heydrich spoke in the flat tones of one stating a fact, an attitude calculated to stun us into acceptance of the assertion. We were indeed stunned and silent for a moment, me among others, until I collected my wits.

'*And on the basis of this rumor and tittle-tattle, you dare to insult the honor of German officers?*'

Hitler rose to his feet. '*The insult was done by the traitors, to the German Army, the German people, and to the Third Reich!*'

A captain – von Stauffenberg – spoke immediately. '*No, the insult was done by the leader who sent a small force of unarmed men, unprepared for combat, on a mission of pure bluff – who wagered the honor of the German Army on a roll of the die!*' In all my years of service, this was the most extraordinary scene I had ever witnessed. That a junior officer would dare to address the head of state in such fashion! That none of the seniors would see fit to reprove him! It did not happen, because he had given utterance to what we all thought. (Von Stauffenberg was adjutant to von Blomberg. Normally, he

354

could have expected discipline from his chief. But von Blomberg was not so stupid he couldn't feel which way the wind blew.)

Hitler's mouth literally dropped open. He and his coterie were all dumbfounded. They could not believe he had been addressed so. Perhaps only then did they begin to realize how much had been lost in the last two days.

Then the scene became even more extraordinary. Goebbels, Himmler, and the others began to shout that the Fuhrer was a man of genius, that the plan could not have failed without treachery. We Wehrmacht officers shouted back in turn that the fault lay in the leader who had been so reckless. I thought of two packs of schoolboys screaming insults at each other. The behavior was too unseemly to endure, and yet no means to end it.

Then the corporal threw a full-fledged fit. He became purple with rage. His voice became a shriek. He mounted a chair, then the desk, and began to scream curses at the staff, the Army, the English, the French, the Jews. The Wehrmacht was infested with cowards, traitors, and November criminals, it had betrayed the Reich before, and had done so again. The spectacle was both disgraceful and illuminating. So this was how the great Fuhrer reacted to crisis and disappointment! The 'Man of Destiny', as he liked to think of himself, had all the self-control and maturity of a small child – and it was to this creature the fate of Germany had been entrusted?!

I stole a glance at the other officers present. The same thought had intruded into many of their minds. I think even some of the corporal's supporters had the same realization, though they tried to deny it to themselves.

'*And the name of at least one traitor is already known!*' Hitler screamed. '*Who is the German officer who surrendered a German captain to the French?*'

'*A Major Thomas Bergman,*' Heydrich stated.

'*Ah, a Jew. I might have guessed.*'

'*He is not Jew –*' I began.

'*I knew it! Arrest him at once! Then shoot him!*' I could see the corporal was beginning to wind himself up again.

'*He is not Jewish,*' I repeated. '*And he did not surrender the officer, simply transferred him to a hospital. A medical necessity.*'

I might as well not have spoken. Hitler raged on. '*Nonsense!!*' he shrieked. '*A serving German officer, anyone who respected the Reich, would far rather accept an honorable death than go over to the care of the French – or yield them one inch!!*' A murmur of outraged support ran through the

355

numerous sycophants in the room. I looked to Blomberg for support in this matter, but he said nothing and would not meet my eyes. '*We have found the traitor. A Jew. He must be punished – as an example to all the other traitors!*'

'*Bergman is not Jewish,*' I said, summoning my powers of self-control, '*And he is no traitor. He will not be arrested, and he will not be shot.*'

Hitler stared at me. '*You have taken a personal oath to me,*' he said.

'*My oath does not extend to acquiesce in the arrest and punishment of a loyal officer, without proof, solely on your whim.*'

'*The Wehrmacht has already acquiesced,*' Heydrich said quietly.

'*What do you mean?*' I demanded.

'*General von Blomberg has already ordered the arrest of Major Bergman, by the S.S.*'

I spun around to confront Werner Blomberg, who was already known to be too much Hitler's man. '*Blomberg!? Is this true?*'

Von Blomberg is not a strong personality, then or now. Faced with the ranks of senior officers glowering at him, the approval shown to von Stauffenberg, and the open anger, he could only stammer out some feeble comments about the oath.

'*The order must be countermanded!*' I thundered. '*After all this controversy, I will concede that an inquiry is essential – though I will remind everyone present here that there would not have been any casualties had a battalion of lightly armed men not been ordered – against all military logic – to stand their ground against an artillery regiment – in an open field. But still, there must be an inquiry. But the detention will be made by the military police, and the matter conducted by the Wehrmacht. For Germany is not a sultanate – at least, not yet.*' I stared at von Blomberg.

'*Yes, of course,*' he muttered feebly. Hitler stared at him. '*My apologies, my Fuhrer, in the stress of these matters, I had overlooked the legalities that General von Hammerstein has called to my attention. Bergman will be arrested, but by the Army, not the S.S.*' Without attempting to meet anyone's eye, he left the room to adjust the order.

I faced Hitler's cohort squarely, and resumed. '*As for the other element in this nonsense, Bergman could not possibly have disclosed any plans to anyone. He was not in the chain of command, or in headquarters. He was not even assigned to the occupational force. He had no knowledge of the orders. I chose him as an observer for exactly that reason, that his neutrality would not be compromised by any personal motive of his own – that, and that Major Thomas Bergman is an officer of exceptional competence and loyalty.'*

Hitler began to redden, and another tirade was coming. But Heydrich put a hand on his shoulder. *'No, my Fuhrer,'* he said quietly. Hitler whirled around and stared at him, open mouthed in surprise.

To this point I have not written much about Reinhard Heydrich. I did not know of one man of honor who did not despise him, for he did not bother to conceal an unworthy tolerance for viciousness and an unlimited appetite for cruelty. Yet he was by far the most capable of the Nazi leaders, far more capable than the corporal he served. He had perceived, before anyone else in the room, the core of the crisis his Fuhrer now had to meet.

The ascendancy of Adolf Hitler and the Nazis now depended entirely on finding a traitor who had betrayed the plans of the reoccupation to the Allies – on demonstrating to the German people and to the Wehrmacht that the fiasco was not the fault of the Man of Destiny – that he had failed only because he had been the victim of treason. If the fault were to be laid at his door, the spell he had cast over all Germany would be broken, never again to be mended.

Thus, it was essential to find the traitor. And if there were no traitor? If there had been no treason? Then to create one, all the same. This, I knew, was the crux of Heydrich's insight – and in this, he was correct.

'No, my Fuhrer,' Heydrich repeated, unfazed, *'This Bergman, despicable though he is, may not have betrayed our plans to the French. But someone did. These weak, decadent, Jew-ridden democracies, with their passion for peace and their love of pleasure – they did not come to their iron resolutions unaided. Someone – or several someones – in the Wehrmacht betrayed us to our enemies, and specifically, our plans for prudent retreat. Someone betrayed his soldier's oath in its entirety, in the basest way possible.*

'I know these vermin,' he continued, *'this officer class, these arrogant snobs. I was one of them. I know their pretensions of honor, their snobbery, their overweening pride. They have never accepted the Nazi revolution. The notion that an ordinary man, an Austrian corporal, could be the destined savior of Germany, the Fuhrer – this they have never accepted, and never will. The Wehrmacht is honeycombed with treachery. I am as certain of that fact as that the sun is in the heavens.'*

He eyed the Wehrmacht staff present. *'And, my Fuhrer, I will find for you and for the German people, this someone, this group of someones, these Wehrmacht criminals – and when I do, we will have our reckoning, with this* traitor Bergman and with all the others. *We will demonstrate decisively to the world and to the people just what did occur in the Rhineland, and the contemptible depths to which our enemies – inside and out – will sink to destroy us. Leave this Bergman to the Wehrmacht today. His time will come, soon enough. I will find out everything.*'

He turned suddenly, and clicked his heels. '*My Fuhrer! Do I have your permission and authority to begin the investigation of the Wehrmacht at once?!*'

There was a momentary silence. Then Hitler shrieked '*Yes!!*' (I use the word 'shrieked' precisely.) '*Exactly! A conspiracy! We must root it out from top to the bottom!! From highest to lowest!! No one can believe himself safe!*'

'*No man will be safe,*' Heydrich stated emphatically. '*I will begin at once.*' He rose to his full height, gave an extravagant Hitler salute, glared once more at the assembled Wehrmacht officers in a manner calculated to inspire fear, then strode purposefully from the room.

And there *was* a wave of fear in the room. How could there not be? We could all see the inevitable. Scapegoats were to be sought, and of course scapegoats would be found. The actual question of guilt was secondary, if not irrelevant. We were all aware by that time of Nazi methods.

My own emotions were mixed. I was of course extremely satisfied with the events of the day, particularly that the political effect had been achieved with no loss of life. But I was also annoyed at my own stupidity. Of course, the corporal would not be able to accept responsibility for his own misjudgments. Of course, he would insist on a conspiracy, treason, betrayal. He had given too much evidence of the shallowness and childishness of his character for any other reaction to be possible. Of course, his flatterers would provide him with victims. I cursed myself for not foreseeing the inevitability of this reaction.

But to say I was unafraid . . . I would be untruthful if I said that. I knew then I was in terrible danger. We all were. My fear was not a fear of discovery. On that matter, I was quite confident. But this tiny tin pot of a man would never accept responsibility for his own blunders. He would find his scapegoats, guilty or not, aided by this icy devil Heydrich – he would find them among the Wehrmacht and their families. The thought that this thirst for revenge might extend to my wife and my children . . .

Meanwhile, the corporal had succeeded in working himself up to a new peak of rage and indignation. '*Treason!*' he shouted. '*Throughout the Wehrmacht! It will not go unpunished, gentlemen, that I promise you! There will be consequences! There WILL be consequences!!*'

I realized then how badly my group and I had misjudged Hitler. We had thought to give a simple bloody nose to the Nazi state, sufficient to reinvigorate the normal political processes and effect a change in Government. But we had not reckoned on the fragile personality of the corporal, that he would be unable to cope with failure of even the slightest sort. Now it was apparent that far more was at stake for me, for the persons close to me, and for the German people themselves. In the instant of that realization, I began to reconsider all my plans and objectives, and the different ways this game might end.

Oh, yes, I remember thinking, as Hitler raged on, *there will be consequences.* But of what kind? And to whom?

All that remained to be seen.

The Pen of My Uncle

March 9, 1936
Minutes of Emergency Meeting re: State Morale
Reich Chancellery
Subject: Events of March 7-8 (including Morale Report), presented by Joseph
Goebbels, Minister of Propaganda
Participants: Rudolf Hess (Secretary, NSDAP), Joseph Goebbels (Minister of
Propaganda), Wilhelm Frick (Minister of the Interior), Herman Goering
(Minister of the Interior for the Prussian State), Heinrich Himmler
(Reichsfuhrer, S.S.), Reinhard Heydrich (Chief of Police), Adjutant

An emergency meeting related to the aftermath of the Rhineland venture was held, commencing at 11:00 a.m. The Fuhrer, who was indisposed, did not attend.

Goebbels opened the meeting by describing the events of the preceding day. He noted that it was undeniable the Rhineland venture had taken an unfortunate turn. It had been a regrettable incident, but only an incident, and one which, with proper political management, should disappear in the annals of history soon enough. But management was required, lest the 'regrettable incident' magnify itself into an embarrassment or worse. Already, overnight, signs and slogans in the form 'Heil Schicklgruber!' – clearly intended to mock and ridicule the Fuhrer – had appeared on some Berlin walls. Immediate action was required.

Goering, speaking as the head of the Prussian police services, assured the Committee that his forces would find and punish these fomenters of deceit. He was confident the incidents would cease in a matter of days, if not hours.

Heydrich broached the matter of treason. He had no doubt that the Rhineland venture had failed because traitors within the Wehrmacht had betrayed the operation to the French and British, particularly the order to retreat if confronted. The Jew traitor Bergman was only the tip of the iceberg. He had denied any treason of his own or involvement in any plot, but unfortunately remained in the custody of the Wehrmacht, so that the circumstances of the questioning had been much more limited than the S.S. interrogators would have liked.

The Committee, particularly Goebbels, pressed on Heydrich the need for a speedy conclusion. Heydrich agreed. All leaves for S.S. officers had been cancelled, all files and orders were being reviewed continuously, the entire Wehrmacht staff had been notified of the investigation, every officer would be interrogated, and interrogated again, until the treason was found and uncovered. The Fuhrer had been clear that this 'monstrous backstabbing' (the Fuhrer's words, according to Heydrich) was an act akin to those of the November criminals of 1919. There would be no rest for anyone in the S.S., the Wehrmacht, or all of Germany, until the traitor(s) were found and the truth was known.

-

Excerpt from: My Life in Office
Stanley Baldwin
Houghton, Mifflin (1947)

The consequences of my decisions were not slow in arriving. Even during our joyous celebration, the office took calls from concerned members of Parliament. Had the Government really called for a general mobilization? Had we all gone mad? The members of my own party were alarmed and aghast. The members of the opposition were alarmed . . . and delighted.

That very evening the first of the rallies at Oxford occurred, small compared to what was to follow.

-

Excerpt from: Destiny Betrayed - A Chronicle of Treason
Harald Quandt
Franz Eher Nachfolger Gmbh (1952)

The traitors and malcontents wasted no time. Signs and slogans began to appear within a day after the Fuhrer ordered the sensible retreat. Shortly afterward, there were flyers, spread anonymously, containing the most disgraceful slanders of the Fuhrer and alleging he had given a preposterous order that in fact was never made!

The rumors spread like wildfire among all the doubters and faint of heart. Goering and his Prussian police were useless . . .

-

Excerpt from: My Name is Ike - Reflections on Fifty Years of Service as Soldier and Statesman

363

The month of March 1936, was the strangest month of my life, and no close second. Berlin was feverish. Everyone knew that the Rhineland adventure had gone badly, badly wrong. Everyone knew Hitler was desperately trying to shift the blame to someone else. Major Thomas Bergmann was at the center, with the Wehrmacht and the S.S. eyeball to eyeball, and neither giving an inch. Reinhard Heydrich was tearing the Wehrmacht apart, looking for the traitor, with the best (which is to say, the worst) of the S.S. working 24 hours, seven days, interviewing everybody remotely connected, endlessly reviewing and re-reviewing old files and dossiers. The fate of his party depended on it.

I saw the first '*Heil Schicklgruber*!' street sign on Monday, not even a day after the fiasco. A group of Brown Shirts was vigorously trying to erase it. Well, it was a useless labor. In the days that followed, '*Heil Schicklgruber*!' postings were everywhere, far too many to eradicate. I was not in contact with any of my normal military associates at that time, for obvious reasons – just too damned dangerous to be visible. (I didn't see Karl at all.)

Then flyers began to appear, everywhere, describing how Hitler had gone to pieces in the crisis and made an insane order that unarmed and untrained men sacrifice themselves to a French artillery regiment. These seemed to be all over Berlin in a matter of hours. The Brown Shirts and the S.S. did their best to scoop up all of those as well. Anyone caught holding one was in big trouble. Goebbels and the propaganda machine did their furious best to denounce the allegations as a lie. But the accusation more or less fit the image Hitler had projected, and I don't think the denials did much good. I sure didn't believe them.

Hitler was Humpty-Dumpty, and all the S.S. men, and Goebbels, and the other horses' asses were frantically trying to put him back together again . . . except that it wasn't working. Everything depended on Heydrich producing a real, live traitor to satisfy the public. From day to day, he redoubled his efforts. But he found nothing.

I was in a helluva position. There had been a spy, and I knew who he was, and I'd helped him. Karl was no traitor, for my money, but loyal to a better Germany. Of course, that nice distinction wouldn't make the slightest difference to the Nazis. I doubted very much Heydrich was even going to get close to us, let alone develop a case. But who knew for sure? And if they did by some miracle identify Karl and his anonymous friend, where did that leave me? The question that had gnawed at me from the start . . . how far would diplomatic immunity go? Assuming the State Department even asserted diplomatic immunity – it would be mad as hell at the extracurricular spying, and just might leave me on my own.

That was not exactly a pleasant thought.

March 12, 1936
34 Kantstrasse, Schoneberg District
Berlin, Germany

From the Journals of Karl von Haydenreich (Published 1986):

This morning at 10:00 a.m., my turn came. I was summoned before an S.S. panel to answer for myself. Heydrich was not present. I would suppose it was his turn to rest. They go on now 24 hours a day, in shifts, in the search for 'The Rhineland Traitor', with the consequence that some officers are roused in the dead of night and brought before the panel to justify themselves. I was one of the lucky ones whose sleep was not disturbed.

The interview was perfunctory enough – only 20 minutes in duration. My background is without flaw, and I was not that close to the Rhineland disaster. But even so, the intensity was fierce and unsettling. The goal of 'finding the Rhineland Traitor' has become all-consuming for the Nazis. In the importance of this, for once, they are not mistaken. The legitimacy of their claim to power depends on it. So the hunt goes on, with greater and greater fervor, and increasing desperation. Before my own session was done, I heard the clomping of boots in the hallway, and the next set of officers to be examined.

Then this afternoon at 3:00, summoned to von Blomberg's office, only six weeks after the last. But the times are extraordinary. The general was not content with a mere report. He cross-examined me closely about everyone of significance in my section of the Abwehr. But I could offer him nothing, for there was nothing to offer. Still he persisted, for nearly an hour, before he excused me. Only after I left did it occur to me that von Blomberg is frightened himself. He is fearful that if the 'traitor' is not found, suspicion will shift to him. No one is safe.

All of Berlin is a madhouse, with the Nazi fabric unraveling faster by the hour. There is talk of a general strike. I wrote to Elizabeth in the strongest terms, reminding her of my wishes in the matter. She would be enthralled by the spectacle, but Germany is simply too dangerous for her and my sons.

365

Heil Schicklgruber!

Excerpt from: Ma Vie Publique, 1929-1940
Albert Sarraut
Editions du Cerf (1955)

The success of our arms in the field gave me a bit more respite than poor Baldwin, the British Prime Minister. But not three days had passed before my colleagues in my own party were reminding themselves that we were the party of peace, not war, and taking their cues from the growing English protest movement.

Even the most loyal friend would find it hard to resist both the opportunity and the pressure – and I had next to no friends that loyal. I knew I would have to resign before the month was out.

Sic transit gloria mundi.

March 12, 1936
The Ballot Worker
News Story

25,000 at London March!

. . . [T]he march ended at Hyde Park, where the overflow crowd heard a series of speakers denounce the insane recklessness of Stanley Baldwin.

'*This was a simple matter of a movement of German troops within German borders,*' said Labour M.P. Clement Attlee, expressing the general sentiments of both the crowd and those that spoke. '*It was a simple act of national integrity, directed against a web of onerous treaties that every thinking person on the Continent knows to be unjust and inequitable. And for this foolish cause, this completely trivial cause, our Government ordered a general mobilization, allied itself with the French, and was prepared to dispatch troops to the Continent – in short, to repeat all the mistakes of the past generation! The question is legitimate; the question must be posed. Has Stanley Baldwin taken leave of his senses!!?*'

March 13, 1936
34 Kantstrasse, Schoneberg District
Berlin, Germany

Frau Elizabeth von Haydenreich
℅ Mister Albert Sommerville

Sommersby and Smith
London, England

My darling Elizabeth,

I know you have become aware of the shocking events in Germany, and the treachery that has damaged our cause. The weaklings among the German people now express their confusion in cowardly jokes and slogans painted at night on walls.

I know you, my love, well enough to be certain your instinct is to break off the Sommerville conference and return to Germany at once to give your utmost to our beloved Fuhrer. But I must insist that you remain at your post, like any loyal soldier. Now more than ever, it is imperative that our loyal friends and allies stand firm with the Fuhrer, and demonstrate in every possible way their loyalty to him and their solidarity against International Jewry. It is in this way we give our response to the doubters and traitors!

Be obedient to me in this, my love. Finish the good work you have begun so well in England. The highest and most noble cause relies on you. The time for our joyful reunion will come soon enough.

Your loving husband,

Karl

-

Excerpt from: A General Speaks - the Autobiography of Kurt von Hammerstein Equord
Major General Kurt von Hammerstein Equord
Reichswehr Press (1986)

L'affaire Bergman was in its sixth day, when I received one of the strangest phone calls of my life, from Joseph Goebbels.

By then, everyone in Berlin seemed to know that Bergman had been arrested for treason, without any real basis. As each day passed, with no formal announcement or charges, the German people became more cynical. Meanwhile, it had become known through Berlin, through flyers and word of mouth, that Hitler had issued an insane order requiring a needless sacrifice of life, and that Bergman had done his level-headed best on the battlefield to remedy the situation.

Goebbels phoned me to inform me that he had planned a major news story in the radio and the *Volkische Beobachter* denying that any such order had been given, and with numerous quotations from me to that effect. Hearing this, I was, in all candor, stupefied. Goebbels himself had been present when that

367

order was given. I said as much. He replied that the truth of the matter was unimportant, that what mattered was the political point, and restoring the faith of the People in their Fuhrer. These attitudes of his I had always known, but never had I believed he would speak so brazenly.

I then informed him that in no case would I consent. In fact, if he proceeded with his plans, I would dispatch Wehrmacht trucks with speakers and troops to proclaim the real truth of the matter. Goebbels then swore at me in the manner of a wharfman, and hung up the phone without another word.

I began then to understand how serious the crisis at the Chancellery had become . . .

-

Excerpt from: Destiny Betrayed - A Chronicle of Treason
Harald Quandt
Franz Eher Nachfolger Gmbh (1952)

. . . [O]f course, the Bolsheviks could be counted upon not to miss their chance . . .

-

Excerpt from: Memoirs
The Right Honourable Eric Phipps
Houghton, Mifflin (1946)

. . . [A]s the week passed, I began to hear and observe what were unmistakably signs of widespread street belligerence. There were reports, and not merely rumors, of young Socialists and Communists confronting and fighting S.A. men, apparently after the Schicklgruber insult had been made, and the police not making any arrests. I personally saw a group of men take on two Brown Shirts who were harassing a young Jewish couple, and send the Brown Shirts on their way. A regular police officer was nearby, but did not interfere with the group of men. Incidents of similar type were occurring everywhere. We were back to 1929, it seemed.

The indications were that the Nazi spell had been broken, and perhaps decisively. For this I thanked God.

-

March 15, 1936
Cavendish Square
London, England

Mr. A. A. Milne
Cotchford Farm
Hartfield, East Sussex

368

Milne,

Our success is extraordinary! 25,000 at Hyde Park, with next to no organization! We will have 100,000 Saturday night, by my word, and with torches! Baldwin, and all of them, must be shown that there are consequences to these mad acts. Britons will never again allow themselves to be led like sheep to slaughter. My friends in government tell me a rebellion in Baldwin's own ranks is brewing (for what sensible man would not be aghast at this recklessness?) and a vote of no confidence may take place before the month is out. Our leaders must know that these reckless actions will have savage consequences for their own careers.

I can't help taking pity on Herr Hitler. The poor man does nothing more than attempt to rectify one of the obvious injustices of the peace inflicted on Germany after the Great War, and finds the government of Great Britain siding with the oppressive French. The people of Great Britain long ago recognized the inequity of Versailles. Why can't the government?

I hear Sommerville's Imperial Party dispatched a telegram of support to Hitler. Perhaps we should do the same. We are, after all, all men of peace.

Cecil

-

March 15, 1936
Berlin, Germany

S.S. File No. 6842, 11088 (formerly SD: 20834)
Subject(s): Bergman, Thomas (Major - Wehrmacht)
Fourth Interrogation

Gruppenfuhrer Reinhard Heydrich,

I will make this summary of the latest interrogation of Major Bergman as succinct as possible, for there is nothing to add. Major Bergman continues to deny the existence of any conspiracy whatsoever, any knowledge of any orders with respect to the Rhineland other than those formally communicated to him, or any motive for the actions taken by him on March 7th other than the welfare of the wounded officer and the other troops. He is as stalwart as before.

We are getting nowhere.

Swartz

-

March 16, 1935
Minutes of Emergency Meeting re: State Morale
Reich Chancellery
Subject: Events of March 7-15 (including Morale Report), presented by

Joseph Goebbels, Minister of Propaganda
Participants: The Fuhrer, Rudolf Hess (Secretary for the Party), Joseph
Goebbels (Minister of Propaganda), Wilhelm Frick (Minister of the Interior),
Herman Goering (Minister of the Interior for the Prussian State), Heinrich
Himmler (Reichsfuhrer, S.S.), Reinhard Heydrich (Chief of Police, Adjutant)

The meeting began at 11:00. The Fuhrer was not present at the commencement, but joined approximately 15 minutes after Herr Goebbels began.

Goebbels reported the worsening situation with respect to State morale. Since the retreat from the Rhineland, there has been a marked upsurge in delinquent acts and behaviors in the German public, primarily in Berlin but also throughout Germany. The police do not seem interested in this situation. He reminded Goering that he had promised that the Berlin police would suppress such incidents within 24 hours. He reminded Heydrich that he had promised to expose the treason within days. Now eight days had passed, and nothing had happened.

Goering suggested to Goebbels that if he (Goebbels) was dissatisfied with the performance of the police, he might consider undertaking the task himself. Heydrich noted the problems of obtaining satisfactory information from Major Bergman, when all interrogations are conducted in Wehrmacht quarters with Wehrmacht observers. He placed the blame on the Minister of Propaganda, who had been unable to bestir the German people to indignation with the Army. Goebbels responded that he could not make bricks without straw. A successful propaganda campaign could not be mounted without an identified traitor, whom neither the Gestapo nor the S.S. had been able to provide. The meeting became heated and it was impossible to take notes.

At this point, we were joined by the Fuhrer. (Note: The Fuhrer was not in uniform, but in lounging clothing, and seemed to be only recently arisen.) Herr Goebbels attempted to repeat the gist of the report, but the Fuhrer interrupted. In the strongest terms, he denounced everyone responsible for their failures and declared the complete incompetence of all. He stated that he should have known that ultimately he could rely on no one but himself, that – as so often before – the task of explaining the Party and his own lofty goals to the German people could be undertaken only by himself.

He thereupon announced his intention to deliver a speech two days hence before the Reichstag, in which he would expose the treachery of the Wehrmacht and make all things clear to the German people. Goebbels urged him to wait until more was known of the plot. This drove the Fuhrer into even greater anger. He informed the Minister of Propaganda that the decision had been made, and forbade him to speak more of the matter.

Then the Fuhrer declared the meeting adjourned and left the room. The meeting was adjourned at that time.

-

March 19th, 1936
New York Times
Headline

Hitler Heckled, Jeered During Reichstag Speech; 36 Deputies Arrested

-

Excerpt from: Destiny Betrayed - A Chronicle of Treason
Harald Quandt
Franz Eher Nachfolger Gmbh (1952)

. . . [E]ven a man of genius will have his moment of weakness, particularly when beset by enemies from all sides. The Reichstag speech of March 18th was the greatest miscalculation of Hitler's career, even greater than the Rhineland . . .

-

March 19, 1936
34 Kantstrasse, Schoneberg District
Berlin, Germany

From the Journals of Karl von Haydenreich (Published 1986):

I lift my glass of champagne high, alone in my apartment, and toast my absent wife and my dear, lost brother-in-law. Today, I believe I have seen the beginning of the end. Today, I saw the first gleams of the morning light after the long, long darkness.

It would have been an eventful day, even if there had been no speech. Without warning, I was called before another S.S. panel and asked rude and brusque questions about my deceased uncle, about Martin, about my old friends at the Hochschule, with the insulting theme of shared interest in pederasty. But all of this was old stuff, which I had answered before. What was different was the brusque, pointed hostility with which these inquiries were put. I did not allow my composure to be disturbed, answered the trio of thugs as if they were gentlemen, and the session was over soon enough . . . but not before I had a sense of how desperate the Nazis have become.

371

But then the Speech. At about 2:00, all the staff officers gathered in a meeting room, with loudspeakers. The Fuhrer was to explain why the Rhineland disaster was not a disaster, or expose the treason that caused the disaster, something of that sort. He started well enough, in his usual manner of ordinary speech. But it was my impression that even from the beginning his tone was a bit edgier than normal, nervy and defensive. After all, this was the first occasion on which Hitler had come before the Reichstag with a decision of his own to defend. But not everyone agreed with my opinion on this.

Then he went on, with the familiar cadences and rhythms. About ten minutes after he began, Hitler's voice began to rise, with the usual denunciation of Bolshevists, Jews, and November criminals. But when he spoke the phrase 'November criminals', someone shouted out, loud enough for the radio to pick up – '*What about the March criminals? What about you?*'

Hitler stopped dead. He found himself speechless for a moment. He had always before managed to captivate his audiences. '*What about the March criminals?*' the shout repeated, only now it was a chorus of voices. '*Explain yourself, Schicklgruber!*' some others shouted, and there were so many then the cries were continuous. All this could be heard on the radio. There was a second or two of silence. Then the Fuhrer could be heard stammering a syllable or two, literally speechless.

Then – there is no other way to describe it – all hell broke out. Everyone began to shout. Some shouted at Hitler, others shouted at those shouting. The din became deafening. But above it all, Hitler could be heard, going to pieces. He descended into a frenzy of anger, shouting back at the deputies, sputtering incoherent threats, his voice as shrill as a magpie's. More and more deputies made their voices heard. Hitler continued to shriek, rabid and sputtering. The uproar became deafening.

Then, abruptly, all was silence. The broadcast ceased. After a few seconds, an announcer unctuously informed us that technical difficulties had interrupted the broadcast, which would resume when the problem had been solved. All at once, we were listening to a bad recording of Beethoven's Seventh. We listened to this for a few bars. Then, all at once, at the same time, we all burst into laughter. Even the most committed Nazis guffawed and roared. I do not think in my entire life I have heard more direct, natural laughter than I heard in that room. That day, the man with the Charlie Chaplin mustache had outdone Chaplin himself.

Later in the afternoon we learned from those who had been there that the pandemonium on the floor had been even greater than it seemed on the radio. Not all the shouters had been Social Democrats. Some Nazis, who felt more loyalty to the Army than they did to the Fuhrer, had also shouted at him. The sergeants-at-arms had tried to quell the disturbance. So had some of the more loyal Nazis. But there was resistance to this. Scuffles occurred, fist fights and wrestling matches broke out, shouts and curses, all over the Reichstag. The floor of the Reichstag became first a mob scene, then a riot, and all this in the nature of farce. Several newsreel companies had been present, and taken film, which Goebbels was now frantically trying to track down and censor. But there were probably too many of them to eradicate all record of the event. Adolf Hitler had played the fool, and was almost certainly going to have to live with the spectacle he made of himself.

Now I watch the streets of Berlin from my apartment window. One of the corners glows in the distance – almost certainly a bonfire. The police are out in force, but there is too much restlessness to quell completely. I think of Elizabeth – but then my heart goes to Martin, my poor brother-in-law. How he would have enjoyed this unintentional comedy! The mischief and jokes he could have made of this! I miss him this day more than most days.

[Editor's Note. This is the last entry in the Journals of Karl Haydenreich.]

March 19, 1936
Minutes of Emergency Meeting re: State Morale
Reich Chancellery
Subject: Events of March 18, Presented by Joseph Goebbels, Minister of Propaganda
Participants: Joseph Goebbels (Minister of Propaganda), Wilhelm Frick (Minister of the Interior), Heinrich Himmler (Reichsfuhrer, S.S.), Reinhard Heydrich (Chief of Police, Adjutant)

Goebbels convened an emergency meeting at 7:00 p.m. Neither the Fuhrer nor the Secretary of the Party were present, being indisposed. Frick inquired directly whether either had been notified of this meeting. Goebbels stated that they had not been. He said that the state of the nation and the Party had reached a stage of crisis that might best be resolved, at least in terms of preliminary solutions, in the absence of the Fuhrer and his principal deputy. He asked if any at the conference were in disagreement. No one voiced any opposition.

Goebbels then stated that the loss of confidence in the Fuhrer and the Party had now reached a point of crisis. After this afternoon's fiasco, who could blame the People for doubting the leadership? Himmler remarked that it was clear the Fuhrer was not himself, and had not been since the Rhineland adventure. With apologies for the observation, he commented that it might be necessary to formulate alternative plans for governance until the Fuhrer recovered from his indisposition.

Goebbels and Frick strongly disagreed. What was necessary, Goebbels said, was to identify the persons responsible for the Rhineland problems, and this as soon as possible. Frick concurred with this. Presenting the traitors to the public would both reassure the German people that the setback was not the fault of the Fuhrer, and present the Fuhrer himself with a platform from which he could reassert his authority. Even the Party structure itself was beginning to fray. He observed that Goering was not present, and stated his suspicion that the Reich Minister was already in touch with members of the opposition, with a view to deposing the Fuhrer and the Party. The traitors must be found and presented to the world, as quickly as possible. No task could be more urgent.

Heydrich reported on the status of the investigation. Though he remained certain Bergman was a traitor, obtaining a confession, when methods of forcible interrogation were not available, had proved impossible. The review of Wehrmacht officers had been ongoing, intense, and would become even more so. He had also had notices sent to all Party members to provide information about any suspicious person, particularly members of the Wehrmacht, who might be connected to the treason. Party members had responded with commendable zeal. The S.S. had received a huge quantity of information, which it was evaluating as rapidly as practically possible.

Goebbels told Heydrich that certainty was no longer essential. In fact, guilt had become irrelevant. For purposes of the Propaganda Ministry, what was essential was providing an individual to the German public who could be blamed for the Rhineland debacle. Plausibility was all that was required. Bergmann would no longer do, as he had been held too long without result and too much of this information had already come to public attention. Alerting the Wehrmacht to the accusation and the subject of the investigation had been a major mistake, one that should not be repeated. Heydrich replied that he understood this perfectly and completely agreed.

The meeting then adjourned.

-

March 20, 1936
NSDAP Headquarters
Directive

     . . . [A]ll Party members are directed to report any evidence or suspicion of disloyalty with respect to the Rhineland reoccupation, with special emphasis to persons with ties to the traitor Major Thomas Bergman, as soon as possible to his or her local Gauleiter, or directly to the S.S. . . .

/s/ Hess

Party Secretary

-

March 21, 1936
House of Commons
Parliamentary Debate
London, England

Mr. Attlee (Limehouse): I would request the Right Honorable Member answer the question directly. On what conceivable basis would His Majesty's Government order a general mobilization of troops, in response to a mere movement of German troops within the interior of Germany?

Mr. Baldwin (Prime Minister): I regret that considerations of policy and intelligence, which I am still bound to hold in confidence, prevent me from giving a more substantial reply to the question. [Interruptions]

Mr. Attlee (Limehouse): With all due respect to the Right Honorable Member, I would suggest that this answer was precisely the type in tone and substance that the late Mr. Asquith would have provided to this House, had it had the wisdom to pose such a question in 1914 [cheers] – and that that answer, then as now, is wholly inadequate. To those of us who participated in the Great War or suffered the grievous loss of loved ones, such a response to the prospect of another such conflagration simply will not do. [cheers] With regret, I must state to the Prime Minister that the time is coming when he must either provide a more satisfactory answer to this house and the people of this nation, or accept an inevitable consequence.

Mr. Baldwin (Prime Minister): I am prepared for that.

-

March 21, 1936
Letter to NSDAP Main Offices
Munich, Germany
[Hand-Delivered]

Herr Adolf Wagner,
Gauleiter, Munich - Upper Bavaria
NSDAP Headquarters, Brown House
Munich, Germany
Concerning: Information about Karl von Haydenreich

      Honorable Gauleiter Wagner,

      My duty as a loyal Party member requires I report certain information about Karl von Haydenreich as requested. The person of whom I write is now a Leutnant in the Wehrmacht assigned to intelligence duties, residing in Berlin. He is married to the former Elizabeth Golsing.

      For years Herr von Haydenreich has masqueraded as a loyal Party member. To my certain knowledge, he is not one. He is in fact an implacable opponent of the Party. He has a degraded, disgusting hatred for the Fuhrer, and is determined to destroy him by any means possible.

      His parentage does not tell his whole story. His natural mother died at his birth. My sister Rosamunde, who was the worst and most contemptible kind of retrograde Jew, attended the birth. She succeeded in seducing Heinrich von Haydenreich, the father of Karl, with an eye to her own betterment. During the Great War, it was she who was the principal influence on Karl, skillfully indoctrinating him in all sorts of strange, anti-German ways. This happened while his father was loyally serving the Kaiser at the front, and thus unaware of her pernicious influence. As a result, Karl von Haydenreich was raised with a diseased sympathy and affection for Jews, of the most backward nature possible.

      Leutnant von Haydenreich was enrolled in the National Socialist Party by his grandfather, Wilhelm-Mertz von Haydenreich, an ardent patriot and an early supporter of the Fuhrer. But the father Heinrich, under his Jewish wife's influence, came to despise and reject his father, and raised his son with the same disgraceful attitudes. The contributions made to the Party during the 1920s were in fact made by the trustees of the von Haydenreich estate, myself at first, before I resigned the position in disgust at his perfidy. Karl von Haydenreich had nothing to do with them, and expressed his extreme displeasure with my actions when he learned of them.

      Because my sister died childless in the plague of 1919, there are scant records of her life. It is therefore no surprise that Party investigators did not discover this blight on von Haydenreich's life. But he has never lost or renounced the perverted sympathies with which his stepmother infected him.

My sister and my mother lie in the graveyard at Neustrelitz, profaning the traditional resting place of the Haydenreich family. (My mother's affection for my sister outweighed her disapproval of my sister's unhealthy interest in the old traditions.)

His actual sympathy is further indicated by his marriage to Elizabeth von Golsing. The Party is aware that her brother, Martin, was briefly imprisoned at Dachau for political crimes, and thereafter demonstrated his weakness and cowardice by taking his own life. Subsequently, the older Golsing resigned his judicial office and emigrated to Zurich. What it might not have known is that these events were not isolated incidents, but thoroughly consistent with the anti-Party beliefs that Karl von Haydenreich has maintained since childhood.

I believe von Haydenreich was obligated to disclose these facts to the Party, but deliberately obscured them. He did not disclose them because he is the worst sort of Jew-loving, traitorous German. It is my belief that his intention was to trick the Fuhrer into inviting him into the most rarified and complete confidence, then do his worst to betray him as profoundly as possible. I know he is good friends with the American military attaché, and had the means to do treason.

I hope this information is useful to the Reich.

I am of Jewish descent, but a proud Bavarian Catholic of the modern kind, and holder of a *lebens erlaubnis*, based on my active support of the Party from 1923 on. I believe that Adolf Hitler is the best hope of the salvation of Germany and the world from Bolshevism.

Heil Hitler!

Fredrick Breslau

The Interview

Excerpt from: A General Speaks - the Autobiography of Kurt von Hammerstein Equord
Major General Kurt von Hammerstein Equord
Reichswehr Press (1986)

. . . [N]ews of the arrest of Karl von Haydenreich struck Wehrmacht headquarters like a thunderbolt. Haydenreich was seized by S.S. personnel as he arrived for duty at the Abwehr. We had no time to organize any type of protest or security, which was, of course, the reason for the secrecy.

I wondered if we had been betrayed. By that date, we had made contingent plans for armed resistance, but I knew that few of my colleagues would have the stomach for such measures in the case of a substantive accusation of treason. Even at that late date, we remained in a defensive, precautionary posture. As for myself personally, I found my sidearm, loaded it, and placed it beside me. I also retrieved a brief letter to my family, in the nature of a suicide note, that I had prepared for this circumstance. I had long before decided I would never submit to arrest.

But the morning wore on and nothing happened. I dispatched Becker, my driver, to Gestapo headquarters (which is also where the S.S. conducted operations) to find out what I could about von Haydenreich. I myself went to the Chancellery.

Excerpt from: My Name is Ike - Reflections on Fifty Years of Service as Soldier and Statesman
Dwight D. Eisenhower
Random House (1986)

Coincidentally, I had lunch plans with Karl on the day of his arrest. When he didn't show up on time, I knew something was wrong. He was unfailingly punctual. But I never thought of arrest, more like a traffic accident or some emergency at the Abwehr too critical to permit time for a message.

I returned to my offices at the Embassy. I was working at ordinary business when I received a call from the receptionist. Two S.S. officers were at the front desk, asking for me. I would have been within my rights to decline to meet them, but I was curious. I had them ushered into my office.

I knew immediately that this was no informal, background interview of the type I had had a few years ago. I steeled myself for the worst. These men were grim, purposeful, accusatory. It was all about Karl. How long had I known him? Why did we lunch together so often? What did we discuss? Did I know he had a Jewish stepmother? Had we ever discussed military matters? Did he ever pass information to me?

I didn't need any more cues than that. Karl was under a cloud of suspicion, and likely under arrest, which was why he hadn't shown up for lunch. The jumpiness I'd been living with for eighteen months took one final Olympian leap. I kept up the front of stoic nonchalance, but behind it I was sure this was it. The other shoe was finally about to drop. My heart beat sped up. I tried to steel myself for the worst. I did not succeed. Behind the front, my mind raced ahead on its own to imagine all the possible consequences in lurid detail. If I were arrested then and there, what exactly could I do? Who could I call? Who could I trust? If the worst happened, what would become of Mamie and my sons?

But then . . .but then . . . *what's this?*? My pulse rate slowed down. I gradually realized the questions being put to me by the interrogators were way, way off the mark, not at all threatening. None of them were about espionage, or documents that might have been passed, or the Order. Instead, they were about my long-term relationship with Karl, as family friend and godson, his attitudes, his beliefs, his loyalty to the Fuhrer and the German state. They weren't all that much different from the first interview. The apprehension vanished, replaced with bafflement. What the hell did this mean? If I wasn't going to be arrested . . . . if there was nothing new . . .then what *had* happened? Where was Karl?

I answered all their direct questions, but volunteered nothing. I did my best to recollect my answers in the earlier interview and conform to them. I denied emphatically that Karl and I had ever discussed anything militarily sensitive or even political, which was easy enough, because it was true as a matter of fact. I knew my answers matched the surveillance. When I told them to go ask Karl if they disbelieved me, they confirmed my worst fear, that Karl was under arrest. They grilled me for a while longer, but got nowhere.

Then they asked me if I were willing to go down to Gestapo headquarters. Hell no, I was unwilling. That wasn't a matter of physical courage, but simple common sense.

When they left, both my puzzlement and my alarm for Karl had reached gigantic proportions. I suppose in theory the realization that the shot had missed the mark — badly — should have been reassuring. But not hardly. In the privacy of my office, I found my entire body trembling uncontrollably. All I could think of was the promise I'd made his father. I decided to risk a phone call to England. Somehow I got through.

-

Excerpt from: A Twentieth Century Life
Albert Sommerville
Houghton, Mifflin (1959)

On that first dreadful day, I received the news of Karl's arrest by means of a phone call from Major Eisenhower. Ike, as he calls himself (though no Yid), told us of Karl's failure to show up for a lunch appointment, and then about an obnoxious session he'd had with the S.S. But he didn't know anything more than that Karl had been arrested.

My own heart turned to lead and my blood to ice. I was terribly, terribly afraid for my friend. But I knew I had to inform Elizabeth at once. I found her in the study, reading little Martin a child's story. I excused myself for interrupting, then gave her the news, in as neutral a tone as I could manage. I could see her swallow hard, as she somehow managed to compose herself. She found the presence of mind to send Martin to the kitchen in search of a treat. Then, once he had left, she buried her face in her hands and began to sob.

Elizabeth and I have a great fraternal affection, nothing more. But on this occasion, I did take her into my arms. She found a place on my shoulder, and continued to weep without restraint. I found tears coming to my own eyes. The world today knows Albert Sommerville, the head of the Imperial Party, and the dignified Mrs. Whittingham, QC, as two of the most composed and rational members of His Majesty's Parliament. But of course, we have endured our share of moments of public and private distress. On that day, in each other's arms, we were two inconsolable children.

-

March 23, 1936
Le Figaro
Headline

De Gaulle Awarded Croix de Guerre

The assembled deputies of the Parliament arose as one and stomped and cheered as Colonel Charles De Gaulle, the hero who frustrated the German attempt to breach the Treaty of Locarno by remilitarizing the Rhineland, yesterday was presented with the Croix de Guerre, the highest decoration of the French Armed Services, before a joint session of the Parliament at the Assemblée National. The medal was further embellished by an unprecedented gold star.

Meanwhile, opposition continued to mount against the President, primarily from the ranks of his own party. The first speaker to take the floor after the Chamber of Deputies reconvened, Deputy Reynaud, openly questioned the judgment of President Sarraut even as he applauded De Gaulle's achievements.

'*The remarkable feat of arms of Colonel De Gaulle,*' he said, '*in no way justifies the insane risk of continental war that the President in his questionable wisdom was willing to undertake.*'

\-

Excerpt from: My Life in Office
Stanley Baldwin
Houghton, Mifflin (1947)

It went on and on, day after day – protests, editorials, torchlight parades, and, of course, speeches and questions from the floor of Parliament. Three women, two mothers who had lost sons in the Great War and one who had been widowed, chained themselves to a post outside 10 Downing Street. It took hours to free them, during which time the newsreel cameras turned and they spoke freely to the press, politely damning me and everything I stood for – *no other women should have to experience their suffering* – and so forth.

In the face of all this, even the staunchest supporters of my own began to question their loyalty. My own conscience was not only clear, but stalwart – I knew I had acted in the interests of Peace, with next to near certainty, and I had succeeded. But to speak this aloud, let alone reveal the reasons why the actual risk of war was minimal to the point of non-existence, was beyond the pale of consideration. There were human lives at stake in the Third Reich, who were at far greater risk than the three misguided women chained near my front door. Endangering those lives for the sake of what amounted to my own moral vanity was out of the question.

So I endured. I have sometimes been asked whether I felt any sympathy with Herr Hitler, who was enduring his own trials in Germany at the same time. Good God, no! Hitler's dilemma and tortuous writhings were precisely the result we had hoped to achieve. His difficulties gave me the greatest possible satisfaction.

Of course, had I known the human cost that would ultimately be exacted from the Nazi predicament, I would have felt no satisfaction of any kind . . .

-

Excerpt from: Eyewitness!
The True Story of the Fiasco on the Rhine and the Siege of the Reich Chancellery
Oberfeldwebel (formerly) Victor H. Becker
Houghton, Mifflin (1950)

The day of Haydenreich's arrest started like any other. I drove the General to Headquarters, and went to my own station. But a half-hour into the day, the General called me to his office. He wasted no words.

'*There has been an arrest,*' he said, '*of a Wehrmacht officer in connection with the Rhineland Fiasco – on no basis whatsoever that I can understand. His name is Karl von Haydenreich, you may know of him.*' I told the General I did not know the name. He nodded.

'*In any case, he is a leutnant well known to me, and of impeccable loyalty. I am completely baffled by this event. The S.S. arrested him at Abwehr headquarters this morning. They were less than courteous. I am off to the Chancellery to find out what the reason is for this outrage, and see what I can do. I am dispatching you over to Gestapo headquarters*' – he saw my look – '*The S.S. has space and staff there. They either have him there, or know where he is. I have no staff to spare this morning, so you will be my emissary. You are to verify his location and, if possible, the conditions of his custody. You will make it known to his custodians that any mistreatment or physical indignity will be viewed by me and the Wehrmacht with the utmost seriousness. Do you understand?*'

I understood completely. I'd seen and heard enough about the S.S. to know they were the worst kind of thugs and bullies. We had managed to keep Bergmann from their clutches, but they already had their hands on this one. I didn't know this von Haydenreich, but I was already on his side.

384

The Gestapo headquarters were the same old Berlin Police headquarters. It was only about a quarter-hour away on foot, so I did not bother with transport. I was there before 10:00. I presented my credentials to the watch officers, and waited. I recognized and old chum, and we laughed and gossiped while my heels got cold. (The Gestapo wasn't a new agency. It was the name the Nazis gave to the revised organization, after they took power and Goering combined the regular police with the swine in the national security agency. I had many friends among the regulars, who were proud of being police officers, proud of enforcing the real law, and had no more patience with the security swine than most Germans.) Finally, the Chief of Police himself, Reinhard Heydrich, appeared. I had seen him often enough to know who he was. But it was clear he did not recollect me.

'*Yes*,' he said without more formality, '*I can confirm that Haydenreich is here, and below. He was arrested this morning.*'

'*I would like to see him*,' I said. '*I'm directed to make certain that he is receiving the courtesies due a Wehrmacht officer.*'

'*That is out of the question,* ' Heydrich snapped. '*Haydenreich is a traitor. He was arrested on the Fuhrer's orders. He will receive the treatment due any other traitor. I can assure General von Hammerstein that all the formalities of the law will be scrupulously respected.*' I knew what that meant, that the S.S. would do exactly as it liked.

I knew the General disliked Heydrich intensely. Now I found myself understanding and sharing that feeling. In fact, I realized in only a few seconds that I loathed him.

'*I always suspected him*,' he continued, '*from the first moment I met him. Did you know the Jew-loving swine played at my own wedding? Our first meeting. I knew even then, despite all the perfect credentials he'd managed to accumulate, that he was not what he seemed. And now there is proof.*'

'*Go back to your General*,' he finished. '*Tell him Haydenreich will get precisely the treatment he has deserved. Neither more nor less. There is nothing more to say, or for you to do. Good day.*' With that, he turned on his heel and left.

-

Excerpt from: A General Speaks - the Autobiography of Kurt von Hammerstein Equord
Major General Kurt von Hammerstein Equord
Reichswehr Press (1986)

After I dispatched my driver to Gestapo headquarters, I went myself over to the Chancellery. This was not a matter I wished to delegate. My sense was that a crisis was upon us.

Hitler was not available. I waited a quarter-hour before Hess appeared. During that time, I was summoned to the desk for a phone call from my adjutant. He reported that Oberfeldwebel Becker, my driver, had succeeded in contacting Heydrich, but had received no reassurance whatsoever about von Haydenreich's treatment. In fact, Heydrich had made a point of informing Becker that von Haydenreich would be handled no differently than any other accused traitor. This information did nothing to lessen either my apprehension or my anger.

Finally, Hess appeared. He seemed to know why I had come, which did not surprise me. I came immediately to the point about von Haydenreich, demanding to know the basis for this arrest. This, too, did not surprise Hess. He presented me with a dossier that had clearly been prepared to present to Wehrmacht officers. He seemed to me smug, even arrogant, attitudes he had been far too timid to display to me before.

I reviewed it quickly. An immense and contemptible feeling of relief swept over me (for which I still feel ashamed, even as I write these lines.) But it hardened almost at once into anger. I looked up, unable to conceal my astonishment and outrage. '*This is all? On this basis, you have arrested a serving Wehrmacht officer?*'

'*It is more than sufficient,*' Hess replied. '*The case is clear.*'

'*Case clear? The only new information here is that von Haydenreich had a Jewish stepmother, and that her brother believes he is an opponent of the Nazis. The fact that he had a brother-in-law imprisoned at Dachau, or that the American military attaché Eisenhower is a longtime family friend . . . all this is well known. You arrest a man for suspicion of treason on this showing?*'

'*It is more than sufficient,*' Hess repeated. '*The Fuhrer is devastated. Von Haydenreich's father was his commanding officer in the Great War. That the son would stray so far from his father's path . . .*'

'*This showing is absolutely worthless as a basis for arrest. There are all sorts of loyal officers with relatives with their own views, and even Jewish sympathies.*'

'*Oh?*' said Hess, raising an eyebrow. '*Really? Officers with Jewish sympathies? How interesting.*' I knew that my remark would find a place in my own dossier. '*But there are very few who have taken such pains to conceal this* aspect of their upbringing, this affection for the worst kind of Jew – her brother's words. There are very few with access to a foreign agent –'

'Of a neutral, New World nation. Every one of their meetings has been surveyed. Heydrich must know that.'

'– access to a foreign agent,' Hess continued as if I hadn't spoken. 'Access to the Rhineland plans, and the Order. This is more than enough cause for arrest. Heydrich is quite confident rigorous interrogation will produce more substantial and detailed information.' Hess did not even bother to hide his relish in the thought of 'rigorous interrogation'.

'This is outrageous!' I exclaimed. 'You insult the Wehrmacht, myself, every serving officer, when you make such accusations! I demand the immediate release of Leutnant von Haydenreich!'

'That will not happen,' Hess replied, completely unfazed. 'The Fuhrer himself is satisfied with the correctness of the action.' He leaned forward on his hands. 'We are going to find out exactly why the Rhineland operation failed, Herr General. We are going to find out the full scope of the treason, who the traitors are, and punish them. Then, and only then, will Germany become whole again.'

I could have told him why the Rhineland operation failed. It failed because it was undertaken, against all prudent military advice, by Adolf Hitler, who confounded his serious mistakes by issuing confusing and inhumane orders during the crisis. But this was not the time or place to remind the flunky Hess of these mundane facts. Instead, I eyed him as coldly as he had eyed me, bade him good day, turned on my heel, and left.

Those who have written the history of that time are sometimes of the opinion that Hitler sealed his fate and that of the Third Reich then and there, on that day. But that is not so. Even then, even as late as that, I hoped to avoid a putsch. I no longer believed the corporal fit for office, but I still hoped to avoid the seizure of the Government by force. The psyche of the German (and especially the Wehrmacht officer) is too orderly to consider revolution as the first alternative. Until three weeks before, Hitler had been widely admired in Germany, and many continued to revere him. I was not inclined to test the depths of this loyalty if the test could possibly be avoided.

But I did take additional precautions that night. Von Haydenreich remained in S.S. custody. Anything could happen. I remembered vividly how quickly and mercilessly Hitler and the Nazis had acted on the Night of the Long Knives. I remembered, too, how Schleicher and his poor wife had been callously murdered in their home on that occasion. Even though I doubted very much that the corporal would challenge the Wehrmacht until he had enough material to at least make a case in the press, I took no chances. I directed officers I thought might be endangered to alter sleeping arrangements. I instructed my own wife to take a room in a hotel that evening. For myself, I made my own plans to spend the night at headquarters. I took my pistol and the note with me.

I also made some discrete calls in the nature of a stand-by, or alert, to certain colleagues.

But even with all this, the die was not cast that night.

It was the next day that was decisive.

-

Excerpt from: *A Twentieth Century Life*
Albert Sommerville
Houghton, Mifflin (1959)

March 29th, 1936, became the longest day of my life. After the weeping ended, Elizabeth did her best to put on a brave front. When her sons were down for naps or otherwise, she went to her room and did her best to make progress on her studies. Then, a few moments later, she would emerge and pace, with her arms folded and her thoughts to herself. She never smoked, before or later. But on that day, when I offered her a cigarette, she accepted without comment. She would take a puff or two, then back to her room.

I could not remain passive with all this. I managed to contact our Berlin office by telegram and directed our Berlin counsel to send someone to Gestapo headquarters. I knew the Nazis had no respect for the niceties of legal process, but I hoped the show of some force, from abroad, from our prestigious counsel (for the Hengeler, Mueller law firm was known throughout Europe) might at least inhibit Karl's captors, and perhaps even turn the game around.

But the hours passed and we heard nothing. Elizabeth could barely touch a bite at dinner. Finally, at near midnight, the phone rang. The caller was Lawrence Whittingham, my father's junior partner and at that time the head of the Berlin office (and yes, the same man that the widowed Elizabeth von Haydenreich married a few years later). Elizabeth was instantly by my side at the receiver.

Lawrence informed us that, despite efforts that were in truth more considerable than we had requested, Karl remained in the custody of the S.S.

He expressed his personal and profound regrets for that, even though the situation was hardly of his making.

Then he told us of the worst development of all. One of the more loquacious guards had let slip that the Fuhrer himself had summoned Karl to the Chancellery the next morning, for the purpose of confronting him directly. Elizabeth turned even paler than her normal color, and put her hand to her mouth.

I was too dumbstruck to do more than stammer out my thanks to Whittingham for his effort. My hand shook when I replaced the receiver.

I had been frightened for my friend before. Now I was terrified.

March 29, 1936
Minutes of Emergency Meeting re: Rhineland Treason (Special Case)
Reich Chancellery
Subject: Investigation and Interrogation of Karl Haydenreich
Participants: The Fuhrer, Rudolf Hess (Secretary, NSDAP), Joseph Goebbels (Minister of Propaganda), Wilhelm Frick (Minister of the Interior), Herman Goering (Minister of the Interior for the Prussian State), Heinrich Himmler (Reichsfuhrer, S.S.), Reinhard Heydrich (Chief of Police)

The Fuhrer called this meeting on short notice. He began speaking the moment the last to arrive (Goering) entered the room. He said he had spent a great part of the day reviewing the dossier of Karl von Haydenreich. Sometimes he had been close to tears, sometimes he had shaken in fury. Von Haydenreich's father had been the commander of the unit in which the Fuhrer had served. He had known the elder Haydenreich as a good soldier and good German. He had even been gassed on the same occasion as the Fuhrer.

To witness now the shame and degradation to which the son had sunk! It was this thought that had moved him to the edge of tears. He had always known of the malice of Jews, but even now the depth of their cunning staggered him – that they would estrange a man from his own son, while the father served loyally on the battlefront! When he thought thus, he had shaken with anger. The von Haydenreich family was old and noble, a natural target for corruption. What a pity it had come to this!

The Fuhrer then inquired what progress had been made in the interrogation of Leutnant von Haydenreich. Gruppenfuhrer Heydrich reported that von Haydenreich had denied all accusations and added nothing to the dossier. The Fuhrer did not conceal his annoyance. He asked how this could be, and whether this traitor, too, was being sheltered by the Wehrmacht. Heydrich answered that von Haydenreich had been arrested by the S.S., and was in custody at the Gestapo headquarters. He had been subject to vigorous interrogation, with procedures appropriate to a traitor, but as of the time when Heydrich received the summons to this meeting, these had not been sufficient to break his resistance.

The Fuhrer became irate. He declared that von Haydenreich's treachery was self-evident, that obtaining the traitor's own confirmation of that fact should have been routine. The lack of new information made him wonder about treason in the S.S.

Goebbels asked if additional pressure could be brought to bear on members of the von Haydenreich family. Himmler said that was not possible. Von Haydenreich's wife and two sons were now in England, and his in-laws now lived in Zurich. These are his only living relatives. Goebbels remarked that this was all too much of a coincidence, and further evidence of treason.

Goering then asked about the uncle, the Jewish banker who had furnished the first report against Haydenreich. Heydrich answered that, though Frederick Breslau was a Jew, he had been loyal to the Party since its earliest days and an inestimable aid to its finances during the 20's. Goebbels stated that if one thing had been learned to date in this affair, it is that there is no limitation to the depths of Jewish cunning. This letter of Breslau's might easily be another subtle tactic. No one expressed any contrary view. The Fuhrer immediately ordered the arrest and interrogation of Frederick Breslau.

The Fuhrer then addressed the Committee again. His anger and frustration were so fiercely expressed that the door had to be securely closed, lest he be overheard. The Fuhrer accused Himmler, Heydrich, and all associated with the case of Karl Haydenreich, of incompetence or worse. He was infuriated that such a man had ever been allowed to reach a position of responsibility in the Abwehr. He was outraged that the investigation, to which the full resources of the Gestapo and the S.S. had been devoted, had not produced additional evidence of treason and conspiracy. He announced that he had lost all patience with these ineffectual measures. It was clear that this was still another matter with which the Fuhrer himself had to deal personally.

He ordered that Haydenreich be brought to the Chancellery on the morrow, to confront him personally. He also ordered that representatives of the Wehrmacht Staff, particularly Generals von Hammerstein and von Blomberg and representatives of their staffs, be present to witness the meeting. The

Fuhrer himself would obtain the admissions and the evidence necessary to make the full truth known to all. All would bear witness.

Both Heydrich and Goebbels rose to their feet to protest this plan, but the Fuhrer overruled them. He then declared the meeting over and left the room without another word.

-

Excerpt from: A General Speaks - the Autobiography of Kurt von Hammerstein Equord
Major General Kurt von Hammerstein Equord
Reichswehr Press (1986)

I received the summons to the Chancellery at my offices, by messenger. The sentry informed me there was a young Nazi to see me. I granted him entrance. Without formality, he told me that Leutnant Karl von Haydenreich was to be brought to the Chancellery the next morning, to answer for his treason to the Fuhrer himself. Von Blomberg and I and representative members of our staffs were ordered to attend. He then clicked his heels, bestowed the Hitler salute upon my household, and departed.

The announcement threw me into equal parts consternation, confusion, and excitement. On one hand, I was relieved that the young lieutenant was still in relatively good condition, for he would not be presentable otherwise. But on the other, the matter must have reached some sort of resolution, for Hitler to call for a public meeting of this sort. In this, I completely underestimated the corporal's hubris and vanity.

But I also felt a surge of the exhilaration that precedes combat. I knew then for a certainty that von Haydenreich had revealed nothing. The Nazis would have attempted my arrest if he had. Also, von Blomberg, the loyalist, was summoned. Thus, I made some more discreet calls before I departed. I knew the day would be historic, but I had no idea in what direction the history would go. Perhaps my instincts had run ahead of my conscious awareness.

-

Excerpt from: Destiny Betrayed - A Chronicle of Treason
Harald Quandt
Franz Eher Nachfolger Gmbh (1952)

The accounts by the traitor Becker (among others) of the meeting between the Fuhrer and Karl von Haydenreich, and the aftermath, are the grossest and basest of lies, distinguished only by their lurid psychopathy. In this instance, I have had the true account from my stepfather Joseph Goebbels. Here is the prosaic reality.

Haydenreich was brought to the Chancellery offices, unmarked and in good health. Confronted by the Fuhrer with stern, but civil, severity, with all the circumstances of guilt, his soul shrunk from the enormity of his lie. Haydenreich made a full confession of his treason. The Fuhrer then sentenced him to the harsh, but just, punishment his crimes deserved. The sentence was carried out by firing squad later that afternoon. And that is all.

Rather, that *should* be all – had not the traitors who were already intent on going forward with their plot seized on the occasion as their pretext. If Hitler had had enough time, he would have appeared before the German people, and made the wisdom of his efficient action apparent to the whole world, as he had in 1934.

But his enemies saw to it that he never had that opportunity.

-

Excerpt from: A General Speaks - the Autobiography of Kurt von Hammerstein Equord
Major General Kurt von Hammerstein Equord
Reichswehr Press (1986)

At the last moment, I decided to include my driver, Oberfeldwebel Becker, in my party, as a representative of the rank-and-file of the German Army. I had no awareness then that Becker was a gifted writer and historian. But he has proved to be such. I have read his account of that day more than once, never without losing my composure and finding my eyes moist with tears. It is accurate down to the last detail, lurid or not. I only wish these details were fiction.

I am also aware of the claims by Harold Quandt and others that Becker's account is completely fabricated. Readers should remember that before the fall Joseph Goebbels boasted of the value of the Big Lie and of his expertise in employing that tactic. There is no lie bigger than this.

It is Goebbels and Quandt who lie.

It is my driver Becker who reported the truth.

-

Excerpt from: Eyewitness!
The True Story of the Fiasco on the Rhine and the Siege of the Reich Chancellery
Oberfeldwebel (formerly) Victor H. Becker
Houghton, Mifflin (1950)

On that fateful day, I reported for duty as usual. Only when I arrived did I learn that Hitler had summoned General von Hammerstein and various members of his staff to the Chancellery, to bear witness to his interview with Karl von Haydenreich. I also learned that the General intended to include me, as a representative of the rank-and-file soldiery, in his party. Cold sweat went down my back. This was a different sort of fear than battlefield fear. I had never been in the Chancellery before. But now I was to be there, and in a short time possibly in front of the Fuhrer! Fortunately, I stored a formal uniform in a closet by my station at Headquarters. I barely had time to change into it, before it was time for us to leave.

There were three of us, the General, a Captain von Stauffenberg, and myself. Von Stauffenberg was formally von Blomberg's adjutant, but he went with us that day. I thought I was meant to drive, but the distance was short enough to walk, so we proceeded on foot. There was some frowning at me and my uniform when we reached the sentry, but the General told him curtly that I was with him, and so we passed.

If I had been nervous before we arrived, I found myself near frozen with fright in the large chamber itself. Hitler himself was not present, but there they all were, the Party bigwigs – Rudolf Hess, Goebbels (as short as a dwarf, to my surprise), Goering, Frick, men of whom I had heard and whose pictures I had seen in the newspapers. But I had never thought to be in the same room with them.

There were also a few S.S. officers, conspicuous in their shiny black uniforms and boots. I never cared for that look. The only other Wehrmacht officers were von Blomberg and two from his staff. Von Blomberg noticed me, and raised an eyebrow to von Hammerstein. '*A representative of the ranks*', my General said. Von Blomberg only nodded.

Then, at once, there was a commotion at the door, and two S.S. men entered, with Leutnant von Haydenreich between them. Heydrich trailed a step or two behind. The three men in front resembled three Norse gods, blonde and Aryan, and von Haydenreich, the man between, the tallest and blondest of the three. He was in handcuffs. I recognized him then. I had seen him from time to time when he paid visits on the General. I looked now to see if there was any evidence of rough handling by the Gestapo or the S.S. swine, but I did not see anything. (Of course, they would have taken due care to make certain their handiwork was invisible.) He did seem paler and somewhat wearier than I had known. But under all the circumstances, I was amazed at how remarkably calm and composed he appeared.

I did not notice it until the three of them entered, but a small chair, almost a stool, had been placed directly in front of the large desk near the window. The two S.S. men moved von Haydenreich to that chair and thrust him down roughly. I felt the General stir beside me. The seat on the other side of the desk had been elevated slightly, so the occupant would be staring down at von Haydenreich. Of course, we all knew who that occupant would be.

Then, suddenly, the S.S. personnel at the front of the room came to attention, heels clicked, and . . . there he was, resplendent in his best Fuhrer's uniform. I had never before been so near to him. I felt my spine turn to jelly. Ice formed in my stomach. His head was high, his gaze unwavering, his pace firm and steady. A wave of emotion swept over me, a mixture of fear, exhilaration, and awe; I could feel the wave spread through all those present in the room, in the manner of an electrical current in a chemical solution. This was the Fuhrer! The man who was himself the destiny of Germany! I understood at once how many who came before him spoke of a near religious experience . . . for this was the feeling in that room.

But he had business with only one that day. He ignored the men at attention and walked stiffly through the ranks toward his desk. Haydenreich regarded him calmly as he approached. Hitler came to the desk and seated himself on his own chair, with an air of stern formality. A hush fell over the room.

'*Haydenreich –*' he began.

'*Herr Hitler,*' von Haydenreich answered.

Without warning. Heydrich stepped forward and slapped von Haydenreich hard across his face. '*My Fuhrer,*' he said. '*You will show proper respect.*'

Von Haydenreich did not blink. '*Heydrich,*' he said, nodding.

Heydrich blanched in anger. He pulled his hand back to slap again, but someone grasped it – my General, von Hammerstein himself. '*You will not strike a Wehrmacht officer,*' he said.

'*He showed disrespect to the Fuhrer and myself,*' Heydrich snapped. '*He –*'

'*That may be grounds for reprimand,*' von Hammerstein snapped back, meeting his eye. '*But you will not strike a Wehrmacht officer.*' The two men glared at each other.

'*My General*,' von Haydenreich interrupted, '*my apologies. I did not mean to cause a scene. The Fuhrer omitted my honorific when he addressed me. I believed it was appropriate to answer in the same manner.*'

'*What is permitted for the Fuhrer is not permitted for you*,' Heydrich snapped.

'*I stand corrected then*,' von Haydenreich answered. His calm seemed utterly unruffled. There was a moment of tense silence, which Hitler broke.

'*I will <u>not</u> address a traitor by his honorable title*,' he said. '*I will not address a man who has betrayed his comrades, his father, his Fatherland, his Fuhrer, and all his sacred duties, in the fashion of an honorable man.* He had begun in a loud tone, and was becoming louder. '*I will not –*'

'*I am not a traitor*,' von Haydenreich interrupted. '*Not to my comrades or my duty or anyone. Least of all to my father.*'

'*You dare to speak of your father? I knew your father. I was proud to serve under him. He –*'

'*My father spoke to me of you, my Fuhrer*,' von Haydenreich interrupted again, '*on the train coming back from Munich. After the Putsch.*'

This second interruption threw Hitler back on his heels. Whatever his expectations had been, it was not this. '*He spoke of me?*' the Fuhrer stammered.

'*Yes. On the train. As we returned, after the Putsch. After I had seen you flee from your comrades when the shooting began.*'

Everyone in the room started at this, though the room remained silent – we were all dumbstruck. I could hardly believe my ears. Hitler . . . *fled?* Hitler reeled back, staring. It was obvious he could hardly believe his ears. A moment of dead silence followed, while the entire room took this amazing statement in.

'*You . . . you are . . . lying!*' he shouted. '*Liar! Traitor!*' I started. The Fuhrer was screaming, like a small child.

I saw Goebbels and Heydrich exchange glances. I was only a driver, but I knew why. This interview was not going as planned. The Leutnant was not the nervous, helpless victim they had expected. Yet to interrupt or interfere, or in any way come to the aid of the Fuhrer, was impossible. Hitler must triumph on his own, if he were to restore his position among these men. As I think back on it, it was probably already too late.

'*This is reprehensible!*' Goebbels said, temporizing, trying to restore order. '*I would not have believed a German youth could sink to such depths!*'

'*You are not making things easier for yourself, Haydenreich,*' Heydrich added.

'*I saw this with my own eyes, gentlemen.*' The Leutnant's calm voice was unchanged. He was no more intimidated than he had been before. '*I was there, at the head of the column.*' He glanced at Heydrich. '*You were not. Shots were fired, blood was shed, and the Fuhrer's comrades fell. Then he rushed into a big motorcar and raced away. He left them where they fell.*' Hitler was choking with fury, trying to find words. Goebbels gave him a nervous look. Young von Haydenreich remained completely calm. I began to admire him.

'*I was the youngest Party member then, I believe,*' he continued before Hitler could say a word. '*I admired you and your speeches back then. I was twelve. My grandfather brought me to the rally that morning to see history made. I marched beside him. He sang marching songs in a clear, bold tenor. I know you remember him.*'

And . . . I could see it . . . everyone in the room could see it . . . Hitler *did* remember the grandfather. He was too nonplussed to conceal his recollection.

'*These are all lies,*' he managed to choke out.

'*No, my Fuhrer, this is the truth. I was there and I saw what I saw. Later, when my father brought me home on the train, he spoke of you. The one and only time.*'

'*The father you have betrayed in betraying me!*' Hitler barked. He must have known by then what a poor impression he was making, but he could not help himself.

'*I have betrayed no one,*' von Haydenreich answered. '*I've committed no treason. And I am always my father's son in everything I do. He was no traitor to anything, any more than I am.*'

'*What of this!?!*' Hitler threw the dossier down in front of him, with a little *fwap* when it struck the desk. '*The meetings with the American military attaché. And the Jewish stepmother whom you so artfully concealed?*'

Von Haydenreich shrugged. '*Major Eisenhower is an old friend of my father. Shortly before his death, my father entrusted me to him. There is a letter to this effect, which I will produce, if the S.S. wishes me to do so. As for the rest, my stepmother died nearly 20 years ago, during the flu epidemic after the war. I am under no obligation to disclose such matters – and I do not choose to discuss my personal life with*' – he waved his hand – '*Heydrich. Or others of his kind.*'

396

Heydrich paled, stiffened, and took a step. He would have struck von Haydenreich again, if my General had not been there. For me, I was glad for the insult. Heydrich had played the bully and deserved it. I stole a glance at Hitler. Sweat now beaded in small drops over his mustache. His eyes were glittery with rage. His uniform was askew. I felt fearful of what was to follow, but – then – all at once – I wondered why I, or anyone, had been in awe of this man.

'*These personal matters are more important to you than your duty as a German officer,*' Hitler said stiffly, struggling to regain the upper hand. '*And you do not believe this is betrayal?*'

'*My Fuhrer, I have never confused the Nazi Party with the German nation,*' von Haydenreich answered. This, too, caused a stir. Goebbels started, as if he could not believe his ears, and looked about for others of the same view. There were a few. '*My father was a good soldier,*' Haydenreich continued. '*But he was a man of peace. When it was all over, all he wished to do was cultivate his own garden, with the woman he loved. He despised your Party, my Fuhrer. I am loyal to him in that.*'

'*He was my commanding officer,*' Hitler said. He was fighting for control again. '*My comrade in arms.*'

'*He spoke of you to me only once, my Fuhrer, as I said, on the train, as we were coming back from Munich after the Putsch.*' Von Haydenreich paid no attention to the mounting anger of the Fuhrer, the degree of which would have astonished me a few minutes earlier. Not anymore. '*But it was not about comradeship. He wished to explain you to me. He said you were a vacancy, a man without the ability to form the bonds that other men do – no sweetheart, no close friends, no family, all by yourself. He told me you were aware of this void, that it drove you to a bitter resentment, a hatred even, of all the others more fortunate than you – and of yourself, of course. I was too young then to understand what he meant. But I have come to share his opinion.*'

Now there was a huge uproar all over the room – a huge din, men shouting at one each other indecipherably, and not all in condemnation of von Haydenreich. I could hear Goebbels' voice – '*This is disgraceful! This is outrageous!*' Hitler tried to make himself heard above the noise, but for a few moments he was unable to do so. Meanwhile, the Leutnant sat in the small chair, as calmly as if he sat in church, indifferent to the furor around him.

'*Silence!*' Hitler screamed, once, then twice, then a third time. Finally, he was heard. The din subsided. He extended his hand towards von

Haydenreich. It shook. He was shaking with anger. '*You – you – you liar! You criminal! You speak nothing but filth and lies!!*'

'*You sought this interview, my Fuhrer,*' von Haydenreich responded in ordinary tones, as if he was speaking to a dinner companion. '*I am here at your command. I know what you expect. But I will not denounce my father, or my stepmother, or the Germany in which I believe. To do so would indeed be betrayal. True betrayal. True filth.*' I found my admiration growing. Surely others in the room had the same reaction, perhaps in spite of themselves.

'*These are lies,*' Hitler repeated, but not quite with conviction, feebly, as if he did not believe this himself.

'*My father said one more thing that day,*' von Haydenreich continued. '*It did not seem to matter much at that moment, but years later, when I read the book of your struggles, I was reminded of it. In Mein Kampf, you told the world of your battlefield gassing, and how you were blinded in the hospital when the war ended. But my father, who rescued you, told me different. He said you had suffered an attack of the nerves, a collapse of the spirit – that you were in a hospital for the nervously afflicted when the war came to its end.*'

If there had been an uproar before, now there was pandemonium. Everyone seemed to be shouting and gesturing, some at von Haydenreich, some at each other. Even the Wehrmacht officers broke ranks. The one exception was Hitler, who had gone ghostly pale and was stammering for words.

'*This miserable traitor piles one slander on another,*' an older man said – I did not know then who he was, but later learned he was Frick, the Minister of the Interior. '*He knew he would have the stage for this short moment. So he invented the grossest infamies he could imagine, and now he brays them aloud for all to hear. This is simply a tactic to distract us from his own crimes.*' A rush of approval followed this, from the true Nazis in the room.

'*I knew I was condemned before I entered this room, Herr Minister,*' von Haydenreich said calmly. '*I resolved on the full truth, whatever might befall me.*' Suddenly, without warning, he stood and pointed his finger at Hitler. His voice cracked like a whip through the din in the room, '*Tell me, my Fuhrer, answer me, was the commander you respected a liar? Do you dare tell me to my face that my father was lying to me!?*'

All eyes turned to Hitler. He knew it was essential he say something. But he was lost for words, hissing and sputtering. He reddened to the color of an apple. His hands clenched and unclenched. We could all see he would have torn von Haydenreich limb from limb, if he could.

But what we could all see, too, was that von Haydenreich's father was not a liar. It was true. The Fuhrer, the Man of Destiny, had suffered a nervous collapse at the end of the war. His account of his suffering was the lie, and not von Haydenreich's. It was too much for me to digest at that moment, too much to comprehend. But I knew it changed everything.

'*This is the Jewish woman speaking.*' Himmler spoke suddenly into the silence, because, I think, he understood that someone in his faction had to say something. '*Her influence, the source of all this nonsense. We see here how the cunning of the Jews can corrupt even the purest German blood, the noblest of families.*'

'*YES!*' Hitler agreed, seizing on the thought. '*Yes! One tries in vain to estimate correctly the malice and subtlety of these people. It is always greater! More subtle than one can imagine!*' A murmur of assent ran through the room. But then my eye was caught by von Haydenreich. He had resumed his seat. Now he was shaking his head slowly and smiling to himself.

'*Mummi,*' he said, softly, speaking to himself, lost in memory. '*That's what I called her when I was a small child. Her real name was Rosamunde Breslau. She came to attend my mother at the time of my birth. When my mother died, she never left. She cared too much for me and my sister to leave us. She was a city woman, and a Jew. The villagers had never seen the like. They were disposed by tradition to despise her. Instead she made herself the most beloved person in the history of our village – the best consolation of every widow, the warmest friend to every orphan. I loved her without reservation, as did my sister. As did my father. Malice? She was utterly, completely without malice. Cunning? Her only cunning was the habit of repaying spitefulness with kindness. We have all known such women.*' As indeed I had.

Von Haydenreich turned suddenly to Hitler. '*She would not even have disliked you, my Fuhrer, despite the violence of your hatred. She would have taken note of the gap between your ability and your pretensions. This would have made you an object of her concern. She would have taken pity on you.*'

Hitler digested this for a moment. Then, suddenly, he raised his head and shrieked, a dog's howl of hatred and outrage. In two large bounds, he moved to the large windows that overlooked the courtyard. With a maniac's strength, in an absolute fury, he ripped one of the large curtains down, then the other. They fell heavily onto the dark floor between his desk and the alcove. Still screaming, he began to jump up and down on the piled fabric, with his fists still clenched in complete rage.

I would have thought I could no longer be surprised, but I was wrong. I was once again stupefied. *THIS* was the man who proposed to lead all Germany? This Fuhrer, this Hitler, this Schicklgruber . . . this *infant*? My sister would not have tolerated such behavior in my three-year-old nephew.

Even the Nazi loyalists, who had been desperately hoping for better, realized how dreadful was the impression he made. Goebbels moved towards him. '*My Fuhrer –*' he began, putting his hand on Hitler's shoulder. But Hitler shook him off and continued in his frenzy. '*My Fuhrer*,' Goebbels practically begged, '*Please. Recollect yourself.*'

At this, Hitler finally stopped, sweating and panting. He had either heard Goebbels or – more likely – worn himself out. He pointed a shaking hand at Karl von Haydenreich.

'*Get him out of here!*' he screamed, now that it was much, much too late. The two S.S. men who had been standing nearby moved forward, seized von Haydenreich roughly by each arm, and stood him up.

'*I demand you treat him with courtesy!*' my General called out. Heydrich gave him a look of withering contempt and changed nothing in the handling. I started forward, enraged on behalf of my General. But the General himself stayed me with a hand on my arm. Von Haydenreich offered no resistance as the brutes dragged him through the door. Heydrich closed it behind them and turned back.

There was a brief silence. Then Hitler stood up. He began – there is no other word for it – to rant. *Was it for this he had suffered, had endured, had triumphed? Was it for this wretched generation of Germans, corrupted by Jews and November criminals? Was it for this he had formed the Nazi Party and fought with all his strength for a Germany free from the influence of Bolshevists and Internationalists?* And on, and on, and on.

I wasn't listening closely. I was digesting what I had just heard and seen. Pulling down curtains! Jumping about in the manner of a troll in a child's fable! And this screaming and shouting! This man was no man of destiny, I realized. He was a poser, a faker, whose only virtue was a cunning manner of donning the mask. What had von Haydenreich's father said? '*A vacancy, lacking the capacity of other men*?' Yes. That was it. And these lies in *Mein Kampf* about his war experience? I had seen enough that day to know the account of a nervous affliction was the truthful one.

Hitler ranted on, but I paid no attention. I would never hear him again without a feeling of contempt. I knew no one who had witnessed that scene that day would feel any different.

Finally, mercifully, he came to a halt, panting, catching his breath. Heydrich strode toward him

'*What shall we do with Haydenreich?*' he asked.

Hitler started. He had not thought of this. But he answered immediately. '*Do with him? That is obvious. He convicted himself out of his own mouth. He must suffer the consequences.*'

Nearly every Wehrmacht officer in the room reacted. Von Hammerstein spoke for all. '*Convicted? Of what? What consequences?*'

'*He has spoken treason,*' Heydrich said. '*He confessed his own traitorous thoughts and beliefs.*'

'*He made no confession of any kind,*' my General snapped. '*And even if he had, a court martial would be required. Consequences? Without a trial?*'

'*A trial?*' sneered Hitler. '*For what purpose? What more is there to say? Or know? He confessed his perfidy in his own words. He slandered me to my face, in front of all you as witnesses. What more is to be shown or proven?*'

My General was aghast. '*He expressed love for his stepmother and quoted his father about the Fuhrer. Neither is treason. Slander, if it is, would have to be proven at trial. This is appalling!*'

'*If the General believes that Haydenreich will be provided a forum in which to repeat and publicize his lies.*' Heydrich said smoothly, '*the General is very much mistaken.*'

'*There will be no trial!*' Hitler thundered. '*The Jew-loving traitor has said more than enough to condemn himself! And to suffer the gravest consequence! Gruppenfuhrer Heydrich! Reichsminister Goebbels! Hess! Please come into my office. I have orders for you. The rest of you, remain.*' The three of them strode into a small office. The door slammed, with an orderly outside.

The rest of us remained, no longer at attention, but largely silent, trying to digest somehow the extraordinary scene we had witnessed. After twenty minutes or so, the office door opened and out came Goebbels and Heydrich, who strode purposefully through the room and out the door. Hess followed a minute or so later.

'*The Fuhrer has no more need of your presence for the moment,*' he announced. '*You are dismissed.*'

401

My General, however, was not disposed to leave so easily.

-

:cerpt from: Service to the State - in War and Peace
!ajor General Werner von Blomberg
!eichswehr Press (1949)

I know I was present at the interview of Hitler and Karl von Haydenreich, for the Chancellery diary confirms it. But, in all honesty, I have no recollection of what happened. The event could not have been as sensational as some claim, or I would have a clearer memory.

What I do remember is that Hitler produced a disgraceful childish tantrum when questions of the wisdom of the Rhineland Fiasco were raised. I already had doubts about the fitness of Adolf Hitler to rule. That display of temper settled them. Von Haydenreich was only one of many, many junior officers over whose career I kept watch. He was neither more nor less important than any of the others.

-

Excerpt from: Eyewitness!
The True Story of the Fiasco on the Rhine and the Siege of the Reich
Chancellery
Oberfeldwebel (formerly) Victor H. Becker
Houghton, Mifflin (1950)

'*But what of von Haydenreich?*' von Hammerstein said, stepping toward Hess. He did not trouble to conceal his agitation.

'*The matter of Karl Haydenreich is now in the hands of the S.S. It is no longer a concern of the Wehrmacht. That is all you need to know at this time,*' Hess answered. '*Good day.*' He turned on his heel and left.

'*But where is he?*' von Hammerstein called out. There was no answer. '*What is to be done with him?*' Hess had vanished, and the General turned about, looking for someone. He noticed then the young Nazi who had been posted as sentry outside the door. The General instantly approached him.

'*Do you know where they have taken the young lieutenant who was just here?*' he asked.

'*I am not permitted to address you, Herr General,*' the young man responded in a soft voice. But he could not meet the General's eye.

'*You must tell me this,*' he said.

'*I cannot,*' the youth – hardly more than a boy – answered again. But he swallowed as he spoke and his hands trembling.

402

The General dropped his voice. '*See here, young man, the Nazi Party is not the only power in Germany. The Wehrmacht has a considerable amount to say, and often it has the last word. The day may come when you will need a friend in the Army. And you certainly do not wish to have an enemy. Now I repeat – where is Haydenreich? No one will ever know how I found out.*'

The young Nazi thought for only a moment. '*In the Gestapo basement,*' the other whispered. '*Sentence of death was pronounced. To be carried out in an hour.*'

The General paled slightly, and turned away. '*As I thought. Thank you. Stauffenberg!*' Blomberg's adjutant was suddenly there, coming from the corridor. I had not seen him leave. The two men conferred for several long minutes. I was not supposed to overhear, but I did.

'*Is it done?*' my General asked.

'*Yes,*' von Stauffenberg whispered, '*and no turning back. But we must find von Haydenreich. And we must bring my General.*'

'*Agreed on both counts,*' said my General. '*Go find von Blomberg. Bring him here.*'

'*Yes, sir,*' said von Stauffenberg, and moved back into the room.

'*Becker!*' my General said then, '*we are going to the Gestapo headquarters. I must try to prevent this outrage, and any other S.S. tactics, and I will need all the support available.*' He then noticed von Stauffenberg across the room with von Blomberg.

'*Blomberg! You must come with me to Gestapo headquarters!*'

Von Blomberg started. '*For what purpose?*'

'*Because this Fuhrer of yours, this corporal, intends to have Leutnant Haydenreich interrogated and shot in*' – he looked at his watch – '*less than an hour – and we must interfere with this, if we possibly can.*'

'*But the Leutnant was outrageously impertinent,*' von Blomberg sputtered. Back then I respected most generals, but everyone knew Werner von Blomberg was Hitler's toady and lickspittle. He looked like a schoolboy afraid to challenge the schoolmaster. I know what he wrote in his memoirs, but he is as much a jackal as his friend Goebbels, and it is all moonshine.

'*That might merit a court martial, but not a firing squad, not even in wartime,*' von Hammerstein snapped. '*Come. We represent the Wehrmacht. We must be off to the Gestapo headquarters, to prevent this, if at all possible.*'

Von Blomberg looked desperately to his own adjutant for support, but found none. '*General von Hammerstein is correct, my General,*' von

403

Stauffenberg said in a firm tone. '*You will have no standing in the Wehrmacht if you tolerate this.*'

With that, von Blomberg unhappily agreed. Von Stauffenberg then started towards the door. '*Where are you going?*' von Blomberg asked.

'*My General, there were some additional matters I overlooked in the hastiness of the summons,*' von Stauffenberg said, with a swift glance at my General. '*I will rejoin you in a moment.*'

'*Very well,*' von Blomberg answered, and von Stauffenberg hurried off. With that, the three of us were off to Gestapo headquarters.

A Dark Room Underground

Excerpt from: A General Speaks - the Autobiography of Kurt von
Hammerstein Equord
Major General Kurt von Hammerstein Equord
Reichswehr Press (1986)

Thus, the die was cast. The battle would be joined. There was no longer any choice or doubt. The incredible scene that we had just witnessed could neither be ignored nor forgotten. For his part, Hitler could not permit anyone who was there to bear witness to what he had seen. All my punctiliousness, my hesitation of the day and weeks before, was gone. We would either remove him, or be subjected to his version of justice, which we knew all too well. There was no middle ground, no room for compromise.

But it was not only a battle, but a race. What I knew, and what von Stauffenberg knew, and (most of all) what Reinhard Heydrich knew, was that the Nazi cause was not lost. Hitler's best chance, perhaps his only remaining chance, was to obtain some sort of statement or confession from Karl von Haydenreich, enough to spin some fantastic web of conspiracy, enough to placate the German people. That is why we were determined to find von Haydenreich and put a stop to these S.S. tactics.

What von Stauffenberg did *not* know – what only Major Eisenhower, myself, and Karl von Haydenreich knew – was that the real danger was not that Leutnant von Haydenreich would confess falsely. It was that he would tell the truth. I cursed the Devil's luck that had caused Heydrich's eye to fall at random on the very man most responsible for engineering the Rhineland Fiasco. Even at that late hour, revelations of the whole truth could be disastrous. I could not allow that to happen.

I also hoped to save a young man of whom I had grown exceedingly fond from becoming the victim of a horrific injustice. I had every hope that my presence at the scene as witness could prevent this barbarism.

Instead, what I witnessed was so incomprehensible, so monstrous . . . I have never written of it before. I will not write of it now. Read my driver's account, if you must.

-

Excerpt from: Eyewitness!
The True Story of the Fiasco on the Rhine and the Siege of the Reich Chancellery
Oberfeldwebel (formerly) Victor H. Becker
Houghton, Mifflin (1950)

The three of us made our way on foot to Gestapo headquarters, von Blomberg lagging, and attempting to make himself invisible. Midway through our trudge, von Stauffenberg caught up with us, and then we were four.

The officer at the desk was the old friend with whom I'd gossiped the day before, though we did not greet or otherwise acknowledge each other. He blanched when he saw us. At first, he was disposed to refuse admittance. But he did not have the hardihood to hold off the two ranking Wehrmacht generals. Then he came to another point.

'*I must insist that you surrender your firearms, Generals.*' This startled all of us. Von Stauffenberg protested fiercely. The police officer looked even more unhappy.

'*It is not a question of honor, gentlemen, but of security. All kinds of desperate gestures happen in jails, even to the most vigilant. Please. I must insist.*'

'*Very well,*' said my General. '*Becker? Major?*' I was not happy to give up my pistol, von Stauffenberg even less so. But we turned them over and received receipts. The relieved officer agreed to lead our party to the place where von Haydenreich was being held. It was not an ordinary cell.

We went two flights down a series of dreary corridors and stairs, illuminated by dim bulbs overhead. We passed small rooms with desks and chairs, some with doors ajar. But none were occupied. An eerie silence reigned throughout. It preyed on my nerves. Von Blomberg never left us. These days, he claims he was not present. But that is not true.

'*Did Heydrich order these small offices vacated?*' my General asked suddenly. I had been wondering the same thing. The Gestapo man did not speak, but nodded in affirmation. Von Stauffenberg and von Blomberg said nothing. We walked on. Two policeman in regular uniforms sat at a desk at the corner of two long, lonely corridors.

'*This is as far as far as I can take you,*' my old friend said. '*Police chief's orders. Only security personnel beyond this point. But I believe the person whom you seek is being held in a holding area down this corridor.*'

'*Thank you, officer*' my General said. '*We'll find our own way on. But please remain here. We'll need an escort out.*'

'*Yes, sir*' the officer replied.

The hall was so dimly lit it might as well have been dark. It was very long, and we went a long way down it. .Then, suddenly, von Stauffenberg stopped, before a door with a small window. '*I heard something,*' he said.

Inside were two small offices, and still another door, that stood open. Inside that was a large room, the size of a big classroom or small lecture hall. Sounds were coming from the interior, sounds of activity, men moving about, and voices. For some reason, an image of rats scurrying flashed across my mind.

General von Hammerstein pushed it open. Inside were Leutnant von Haydenreich and a young S.S. guard.

'*Who are you?*' the guard demanded. General von Hammerstein fixed him with the officer's glare that major generals seem to acquire with their commission.

'*Stand at attention!*' The guard stiffened at once. '*I am General Kurt von Hammerstein-Equord, the Commander-in-Chief of the Wehrmacht,*' the General said. '*You will behave appropriately.*'

'*But, General, I was ordered –*'

'*The orders are countermanded. You are excused. I wish to discuss this situation with Leutnant von Haydenreich.*'

'*But, General –*'

'*You are excused. Please remove yourself immediately. You can stand your guard down the hall, with the policemen. There is no risk of escape.*' He brought his right hand to his forehead. Reluctantly, the guard returned the salute. General von Hammerstein returned the salute crisply. The guard left, and the General and I were inside with von Haydenreich. Von Stauffenberg and von Blomberg were just outside.

I looked at von Haydenreich then for the first time. In the Chancellor's office, he had been cool and calm, in full possession of himself. But now he was pale and nervous. There were actual beads of sweat on his forehead, though the underground room was dark and cool. '*I am surprised to see you here, General,*' he said.

408

'I am surprised you are surprised, Leutnant,' the General said. *'Do you think I would permit a Wehrmacht officer to be judged and condemned in such a manner? After a travesty of that type?'*

'No, General, of course not,' von Haydenreich answered. *'My apologies. But there is no hope for this.'* Suddenly, improbably, he smiled. *'The great snowy owl flies black against the moon,'* he said, *'and I am soon to become a wild wolf in the wind.'* The General's puzzlement showed in his face. *'Something Mummi said to me long ago,'* von Haydenreich said with a faraway look, *'on a night as bad as is this day.'* He was speaking more to himself than to us.

'You must have known the consequences of showing up the corporal in that manner, my lad.' This informality astounded me; I had not known von Haydenreich and the General were on such terms. *'Inwardly, I applauded your performance, but you must have known the outcome.'*

'What was to take place in the Chancellor's office was a ritual. My fate was already decided. I could not change that, but I could see to it that the ceremony did not go in the way the Fuhrer planned. I hoped to show him the way he truly is, the way I know him. I hope I succeeded.'

'You did, Leutnant, you did, to a degree I would not have believed. What I witnessed – what we all witnessed . . .' he shook his head, as if the recollected spectacle was still before him.

'He undid himself,' von Stauffenberg added. *'No one present will forget it. And there were too many present to suppress it.'*

'Even so, Leutnant,' von Blomberg began, *'the outrageous effrontery you displayed –'* von Stauffenberg stared at him.

'Please be quiet, General,' von Hammerstein said. *'No amount of effrontery in peacetime justifies a firing squad – and without trial.'*

'It is not going to be a firing squad, General,' von Haydenreich answered. His voice quavered slightly. *'It is going to be much, much worse.'*

'What do you mean?'

Von Haydenreich didn't answer. He ran his hand down the back of his head. He spoke again mostly to himself. *'I always thought my last thoughts would be of Elizabeth. I hoped so. But all I can think of is the third song in the cycle I wrote at the Hochschule. I should have harmonized it in D minor. Why that thought? Why now?'*

Von Stauffenberg laughed at this. The General might have said more, but at that moment, Gruppenfuhrer Reinhard Heydrich pushed his way rudely into the small room. '*What is the meaning of this?*' he demanded of the General, without more preliminaries.

'*Show respect for the rank, Heydrich,*' the General said with iron in his voice. But Heydrich was not intimidated.

'*My S.S. rank is equal to yours, General. So, I repeat – what is the meaning of this? You have no right to be here. The orders were to detain you in the vestibule.*'

'*I am here to stop this travesty from proceeding any further. You have no right to impose any punishment on Leutnant von Haydenreich. There has been no trial, no court martial. Even you must see the madness of this.*'

'*The General's training in military matters extends to knowledge of law as well? In fact, the Reichstag Decrees give the Fuhrer more than sufficient authority to punish treason as he sees fit.*' Then he broke off. I could see him thinking, planning – I didn't like what I saw.

'*I expected you to come to the jail, General. But not you and your adjutant, General von Blomberg. You surprise me.*' He eyed von Blomberg and von Stauffenberg thoughtfully. '*Perhaps this is for the best. Additional witnesses. Perhaps more than witnesses.*' He looked straight at my General. '*Put your mind at ease, General. We do not contemplate an execution. We plan an interrogation.*'

'*An interrogation?*' The General was startled.

'*Yes. Come with me, if you will.*' He turned to the S.S. private now standing down the corridor. '*Truss the prisoner's hands and feet, hands behind his back. General?*' He opened the door into the larger room from which I had heard sound coming before.

We stepped inside. Von Stauffenberg gasped audibly. My blood froze at the sight. Affixed to a low wood beam near the wall was a meat hook, and dangling from that was a small noose, fashioned out of piano wire. The room was high ceilinged. The hook and noose were more than two-and-a-half meters off the floor. Underneath was a small stool. I could see both generals struggling to grasp the implications.

'*Heydrich,*' my General finally said, '*what do you intend to do here?*'

'*I intend,*' Heydrich responded evenly, '*to obtain the truth. There is a group of traitors in the Wehrmacht, gentlemen. I know for a fact as surely as I know I stand here. This fiasco at the Rhineland, these signs on the streets, this collapse – these events did not simply occur by chance. They were arranged.*'

410

Persons in this room either did the arrangement or have certain knowledge of who did.'

Only at that moment did it dawn on me what Heydrich's confidence that my General would come to von Haydenreich's defense might imply. He had not been dismayed at General von Hammerstein's presence. He had counted on it. Only von Blomberg and his adjutant had surprised him. Then I noticed that Heydrich's S.S. swine were armed, both with pistols and one with a rifle. Sweat of my own began to form on my spine.

'I will have the truth, Generals, either from Haydenreich or you. Officers!' He turned. *'Bring the prisoner in.'*

Karl von Haydenreich hobbled in, hands bound behind him and feet shackled together. He blanched when he saw the noose, but composed himself. *'As I thought,'* he murmured.

'You can spare yourself this, Leutnant,' Heydrich said coldly, *'if you are willing to tell me the truth.'*

'I have already told you the truth,' the Leutnant replied. Heydrich turned to the four of us.

'Gentlemen? Officers? Anything to say?' We were all silent. *'As you wish, then. We will have the truth, one way or the other.'* He turned to his thugs. *'Proceed.'*

They took von Haydenreich by the arms, but he threw them off and strode to the stool himself. I expected them to have him mount it, but instead one of the S.S. did, uncoiled a length of wire, pulled the noose down, and jumped off. Then they opened von Haydenreich's collar, and put the noose around his neck.

'Tighten it,' Heydrich said firmly – and so they did, twist by twist. The wire cut into von Haydenreich's throat, slightly at first, then deeper and deeper. Blood began to trickle. He turned white, then red, then purple.

'Do you have anything to say?' Heydrich asked our group.

'This is horrendous!' my General managed to choke out. He looked as sick as I felt.

'You are the cause of it, not I,' Heydrich answered. *'Give me the truth and this ends at once. No? Loosen the noose now. Haydenreich, have you anything to say?'*

'No. You have the truth already.'

'As you wish. Tighten the noose again. This time, lift him on to the stool – there.' He looked back at us again, then calmly pushed the stool out

411

from under von Haydenreich's feet. The noose tightened further as he struggled and kicked. The wire bit more deeply, and blood began to drip in quantity down von Haydenreich's chin and onto his shirt. I could see panic take hold of his features as he dangled in midair and the breath began to leave him. I wondered if I could loathe a human being more than I hated Reinhard Heydrich at that moment.

Then, with a gesture, he had his men pluck von Haydenreich out of midair, and he was seated again on the stool. Heydrich eyed our group coolly.

'*You are brave men,*' he said disdainfully, '*who let another suffer for your crimes. I know, General von Hammerstein, there is much you could tell me. Perhaps you could advise me how and why this man suddenly became so indispensable to your musical events. Or you, General von Blomberg, might let me know why you took it upon yourself to assist his family to safety in England. You might enlighten me as to what this has to do with the Rhineland treason, for I am certain there is a connection. But you keep silent. You let your leutnant pay the price.*'

Von Blomberg turned red, and was about to answer, when a movement at the back of the room distracted him. '*Who is that man??!*' he cried out, gesturing towards the opposite corner. We all turned. I had not noticed the man before, but there he was, an S.S. officer behind a motion-picture camera mounted on a tripod.

'*You are FILMING this!?*' Von Stauffenberg exclaimed. I could not believe it myself.

'*Yes,*' said Heydrich. '*For the Fuhrer. He wants to see for himself the traitor surrender and confess.*'

'*He would watch this with pleasure? With enjoyment?*' Von Hammerstein asked, incredulous.

'*Of course. As anyone would view the punishment for a traitor.*' Heydrich turned then to von Haydenreich. '*Do you wish more of this, Herr Leutnant? Are you willing to speak?*'

'*Yes.*' Von Haydenreich choked out the word, between gasps, with the blood oozing down his throat. '*I will speak truth to you.*' There was a sudden hush in the room. Perhaps it was my imagination, but I thought General von Hammerstein stiffened slightly.

'*Go on,*' said Heydrich, a note of excitement in his voice.

'*Yes,*' said von Haydenreich, gaining breath and strength. '*The truth is, Heydrich, you are a third-rate violinist. And the conservatory your father manages is a disgrace to German music.*' Heydrich reddened with anger. Then he wheeled around to von Blomberg.

'*This is the man you placed in the Abwehr? This is the man you believed was your loyal spy?*' Von Blomberg flushed beet red. He shook his head contemptuously. '*You utter fool. If all you are is fool.*' Then he turned to von Haydenreich again.

'*As you wish, Leutnant.*' He gestured again, and the same awful procedure – first the twisting, so tight I thought von Haydenreich's eyes might pop out of his head. Then he was hoisted up again. He tried to hold steady, but as with any human being, his legs began to flail, and his hands behind his back jerked, and jerked, and jerked again, as they reflexively tried to reach for his throat and end the pressure. But he made no sound. Then, suddenly, his mouth had reddened, grotesque with blood, and I realized he had bitten through his tongue. His tunic became a sloppy red mess. The scene was obscene, grotesque, unbearable to watch. Yet I was sure Heydrich was enjoying it – and the camera kept turning. I could hear it.

After an interminable time, he was lowered, gasping, totally out of breath, choking on his own breath, close to unconsciousness – close to death. The S.S. men expertly revived him, with water and slight slaps.

'*I will find out what I need to find out, gentlemen. One general thinks he is the general's spy, he plays music for another, his family escapes, the Order is stolen. All this is related, someone is responsible for this. You may admire your leutant's courage but there is a limit to any man's courage. This will continue until everything has come out. Only you can stop it.*' We all looked at each other, and it even seemed to me that the General was close to speaking. But then he thought better of it.

'*What ogres you all are,*' Heydrich murmured. '*Do you have anything to say, Herr Leutnant?*' From his agony, von Haydenreich looked up at him, too feeble even to shake his head. But the most incredible look of utter contempt passed over him. Somehow, he found the strength to spit out blood, which landed on Heydrich's shoes. Heydrich whitened with anger. He moved forward to strike the man. But then he forbore.

'*Twist it even tighter this time,*' he commanded. And then – more appalling than any before – von Haydenreich was hoisted again, off his feet, in greater agony now than he had been the first two times. The wire bit tighter, von Haydenreich writhed obscenely, his legs in a frantic dance now, his hands

413

beating a savage rhythm against his backside. Blood flowed more freely now, pouring down onto his discolored tunic. Then –

– the flow became a geyser, spurting high into the air and onto the floor. The wire had bitten its way too deep into the throat and severed the artery. Blood was everywhere.

'*No!*' shouted Heydrich.

Then, finally, Karl von Haydenreich squirmed upwards, one last, convulsive twitch . . . and then . . . suddenly . . . his body relaxed completely. His bowels released, and a brown river of shit flowed down his pants, over his shoes, and onto the floor. I had seen men die, but never like this. Yet I knew he was mercifully dead. His body swung lifelessly from the meat hook. The shit mixed with the blood on the floor, and made the most foul, disgusting inhuman stench I ever smelt in my life. I knew then what a slaughterhouse must smell like. Then they lowered the body off the hook.

Von Haydenreich had been grossly desecrated, his neck half-severed, close to decapitation. The corpse was covered with his own blood, his own filth, and his mouth a formless, bloody hole. He was popeyed, with one of his eyes protruding slightly from its socket. I felt the bile rise in my throat. There was a moment when I thought I might add to the insufferable odor with vomit of my own. For some absurd reason, this thought embarrassed me. All I wanted to do was leave that scene as soon as I possibly could, and get as far away as possible.

Meanwhile, the camera kept turning.

'*Heydrich, what have you done?*' my General asked with shaking voice.

'*Not enough,*' Heydrich said. He was shaken himself, but more by the failure of his plans than the gravity of his crime. I knew then we were facing a monster. '*He was not meant to die – at least, not yet.*' He wheeled around. '*You could have saved him, General. I know this plot centers on you. I know he was a major part of it. He did not live long enough to confess.*'

'*You know nothing,*' Von Stauffenberg snapped. He had recovered his composure before any of us. '*You have nothing. You tortured a German officer to death because he revered his stepmother. You accused senior generals of treason because of their comradeship in arms with him. And that's all.*'

'*It is not all,*' Heydrich retorted and eyed us all. I realized we were three floors down, in Gestapo headquarters, surrounded by the Gestapo, that Reinhard Heydrich headed, and his own S.S. men. It all came to me. He had

414

expected von Haydenreich to confess, or to say something, and then on that pretext he had intended to arrest as many of us as he could. But Karl von Haydenreich had defied him. Now I could see a note of uncertainty in his eyes. He had nothing. But we were still three floors underground, and in his power.

I clenched my fist. I would not go quietly.

'*He said nothing*,' von Stauffenberg insisted. '*You have no authority. The Fuhrer did not authorize this.*'

'*You must account for this, Heydrich*,' von Blomberg added. '*Otherwise, you will have no standing with anyone in the Party.*' He looked physically ill, but his voice was firm and he met Heydrich's eyes directly. I was as frightened as a child, but these two sounded as if they were speaking at drill. I had no use for von Blomberg, then or later, and I didn't know von Stauffenberg at all. But it takes a lot to unnerve a German officer, I'll tell you that!

Their remarks registered with Heydrich. He was in a state of confusion. He had expected the poor Leutnant, in his agony, to say something that he could use as a pretext for our arrests – or perhaps one general or the other would cry out to stop the horror. He could then bluff out the garrote as a necessary tactic to expose a stubborn traitor. But his brutes had botched it, it had ended in death, and no one had said anything. Now he did not know what to do next. His instinct was to go forward as planned and arrest some or all of us. I could see that thought trembling at the top of his brain. But my General and von Blomberg were the two ranking generals in the Wehrmacht. Moreover, von Blomberg and von Stauffenberg were committed Nazis (or so he thought) with important friends in the Party.

Thus, for the briefest moment, Heydrich was paralyzed with indecision. He was like a cat, uncertain whether to pounce or wait. But a moment's uncertainty was all my General needed. In that moment of hesitation, he stepped to the outer door and threw it open.

'*Officers!*' he shouted down the corridor. '*We will be going now! We need an escort!*' Heydrich started, but it was too late.

There was a second of silence. Then I heard one of the most welcome sounds of my entire life . . . the sound of footsteps coming down the hall. These were the three regular police officers, my friend and the two watch officers. The young S.S. guard was with them, but without a weapon. (My friend was no fool). To resist regular police by force of arms in the basement of the Berlin Police station was out of the question. Such an incident could never be

415

explained. I knew right then the circle of knowledge had become too great for Heydrich to control. He knew it, too. The grotesque, sickening carnage he had created could not be explained.

'*The officers will be here in a moment,*' von Hammerstein said. '*Do you wish them to report on —*'

An expression of criminal's panic flashed across Heydrich's countenance. I saw the same look on the faces of the S.S. men. They knew they had committed a horrible crime. A child could have seen the guilt written all over them! Heydrich barked out orders. One S.S. man stepped forward, and the others began moving about rapidly. I saw them produce a body bag and mops. Then the inner door slammed shut.

Von Hammerstein was not done. '*That is the body of a Wehrmacht officer. I expect it to be delivered to the military hospital in Berlin for autopsy and burial.*'

Heydrich stiffened. He knew perfectly well what even a slight examination of von Haydenreich's corpse would show. But he composed himself. '*Of course, General,*' he answered smoothly. I knew the body would never appear at the hospital. The officers were now quite near. The stench had followed us out into the corridor. I could see them wrinkling their noses in disgust and bafflement.

'*If you will excuse me, gentlemen,*' Heydrich said. The swine was already making new plans, that I could tell. Then he was gone into the larger room. The S.S. man who had come forward guarded the door. He directed the officers curtly to show us out. They knew there was something wrong, something very wrong, but they had no choice.

We did leave then, both generals walking stiffly with heads erect, Von Stauffenberg and I remaining wary. We retrieved our side arms like automatons, without thought. My hand remained close to my pistol the rest of the way, as we climbed the stairs, went back down the corridors, and finally reached the door, and out.

The sunlight and the street, with all its ordinary life, seemed to belong to a different universe.

-

Excerpt from: Destiny Betrayed - A Chronicle of Treason
Harald Quandt
Franz Eher Nachfolger Gmbh (1952)

If Haydenreich was subject to all these alleged indignities, where is the evidence? How is it that there is no evidence of his body? How is it that this supposed film has never appeared?

The true fact is that Leutnant Karl von Haydenreich suffered the proper punishment for an officer guilty of treason, death by firing squad, as duly authorized by the Fuhrer, after he had confessed his crimes to all in the Chancellery offices. There would be nothing more to say, and no controversy, had a group of vile conspirators not seized on this as a pretext for revolution.

-

Excerpt from: Service to the State - in War and Peace
Major General Werner von Blomberg
Reichswehr Press (1949)

I was not witness to the alleged mistreatment suffered by Karl von Haydenreich. I don't know whether any occurred. I did go to the Gestapo headquarters on the day this event supposedly happened. But my purpose was to consult with Rudolph Diels, the head of Berlin police, and secure his support for the plan I had in mind. Once he agreed, I knew the time had come.

I was aware that von Hammerstein was the center of a loose coterie of officers who had never approved of Hitler. I had permitted this liberty precisely to provide for the case that had now arisen. Now, with the time of action at hand, was the moment to make use of their attitudes.

So now I contacted him directly and told him that the time had come for bold action. There was in fact no time to lose. Von Hammerstein was taken aback by the suddenness and firmness with which I spoke. But he quickly decided to follow my lead. Perhaps if the scene at the Chancellery had been a first incident, and not the latest in a series of disquieting episodes – the Rhineland foolishness, the stand-firm order, the fiasco at the Reichstag – I might have sought less drastic alternatives. But the series of episodes made my duty to the Fatherland clear, and the also the need for immediate action.

Ignorant persons are still surprised at the speed at which events then moved. What they fail to realize is the extent to which the training of a German field officer emphasizes flexibility in battlefield situations. One must be ready to adapt to a change in the conditions of war in an instant.

Even as I mounted the Gestapo stairs, I had considered the dispositions that should be made, which troops we knew were loyal to the larger State and could be trusted. There was also simple good fortune. As it happened, a junior officer, von Stauffenberg, my adjutant, had planned and practiced exercises in the seizure of government buildings, as a war game, in the event of a Bolshevik seizure. We were all aware of the troop deployments around Berlin, some of whom were restive and demoralized because of the Rhineland and the premature arrest of a staff officer. It was the matter of a few moments to plan and staff our actions.

So the Wehrmacht Putsch of 1936 began.

-

Excerpt from: Eyewitness!
The True Story of the Fiasco on the Rhine and the Siege of the Reich
Chancellery
Oberfeldwebel (formerly) Victor H. Becker
Houghton, Mifflin (1950)

Many people are aware of the account Werner von Blomberg has given of these events. Well, I will tell you that what he wrote is a fairy tale. Enough time has now passed that I can write the plain, unvarnished truth. As much as von Blomberg would like the world to believe he played Prince Charming, here is what really happened.

We four came out into the sunlight, dazed and enfeebled in different ways. Myself, I felt a dizziness that made my head swim like a drunkard's. The stench of the slaughterhouse was still up my nose; I fancied it was on my clothing, in the wind, on the street, everywhere. The world seemed to tilt wildly on its axis. I thought I might fall or even collapse into an unmanly faint. Out of the corner of my eye, I saw von Blomberg, the cold-blooded warrior (as he would have it), stagger towards some shrubbery, and vomit, repeatedly, until he was throwing up bile, onto the ground. He did retain enough presence of mind to avoid soiling his clothing.

Somehow, I came to myself. When I did, I saw von Hammerstein and von Stauffenberg, in deep conversation. They both looked as pale as I felt, but they had retained their composure. I knew something important was taking place.

'*No compromise,*' von Stauffenberg said. '*No negotiation. A trial tonight. And sentence forthwith.*'

'*Agreed,*' said von Hammerstein, '*there is no longer a choice.*' At first, I did not understand, but then a cold electric thrill ran up my spine as I realized the subject. My vertigo disappeared. Von Blomberg joined them.

'*What are you discussing?*' he asked.

'*Blomberg,*' my General answered, '*there is going to be a putsch today. This is the last day of the Third Reich.*'

Trust me, to that very moment, von Blomberg was without a clue. You could see it on his face. He stared at von Hammerstein as if another head had just sprung from his neck.

'*The Fuhrer? A coup? You must be mad,*' he said.

'*Anything but mad. The shortcomings of this man have been evident for some time,*' von Hammerstein rejoined, '*But now? Today? You saw what we all saw. The man is a monster!*'

'*But – but – but – we have sworn an oath. We pledged fealty to –*'

'*Do you think he will allow anyone who was witness to this to live for long?*' Von Stauffenberg cut in. '*Or who witnessed that travesty in the Chancellery? Do you believe our oath compels us to wait like sheep for our own night of the Long Knives? Do you remember what he did to Rohm? Who was his comrade?*' These words made my stomach tighten, for I knew he was right.

'*But to succeed – my God! Do you seriously propose to improvise an –*' Von Blomberg began.

'*There is no improvisation,*' my General began. '*We have been developing these plans since the Rhineland. They were contingent plans, but after von Haydenreich was arrested, they became firm. And now? After this? It must be, Werner – this day! It has already begun.*'

Von Blomberg's jaw dropped. '*The Fuhrer was correct! There IS a circle of traitors!*'

'*No,*' von Stauffenberg answered impatiently, '*a circle of self-preservationists. Loyal to Germany.*'

'*I had von Stauffenberg transmit the orders by phone before we went to the Gestapo,*' von Hammerstein continued. '*It was obvious we had very little time. Perhaps only hours. You must realize how close we were to arrest down there, General? If von Haydenreich had broken in the slightest –*'

'*But why wasn't I informed? Haydenreich was my officer, too – he reported to me.*'

'*Because of your sycophancy, Werner,*' my General said. Perhaps there was a note of contempt in his voice. '*We all know you sponsored von Haydenreich because you thought he was another lackey.*'

'*Everyone thought you were the Fuhrer's pet dog,*' von Stauffenberg added. Von Blomberg stiffened. '*I do not wish to insult you, my General, but*

419

this is how you were perceived. The plan was to arrest you and keep you captive until the crisis had passed. Before today, the basic intention was to depose Hitler as Fuhrer and insist on a restoration of matters to a status quo ante, before he became Chancellor. Perhaps an election. But now – after this afternoon –'

'*Tolerating Hitler is out of the question,*' von Hammerstein interrupted. '*The corporal will receive a trial, tonight, and a better one than he gave poor von Haydenreich. We can all give evidence. If or when it passes judgment, then the sentence will be imposed then and there. Germany will go on without Adolf Hitler.*'

'*But – I don't know – I must think – this is too much –*'

'*Do you think you can go on as before, Werner?*' My General met von Blomberg's eye directly. '*You sponsored von Haydenreich, you had him report privately to you, you evidently obtained travel papers for his family –*'

'*But Himmler vouched for him!*' von Blomberg cried. '*The travel plans were to a conference of sympathizers –*'

'*Do you think that will make any difference to Hitler? Or Heydrich? Do you think any of us who were witness to the atrocity we just saw will be permitted to live? Heydrich lost his bearings there for a moment, but he will regain them soon enough.*' Von Blomberg opened his mouth to say something, then closed it and became thoughtful.

Von Hammerstein nodded towards von Stauffenberg, then continued. '*Your presence this afternoon is God's providence, General. You are the head of the Wehrmacht. You have the rank and status to address the entire Army, to disarm even the most devout Nazi loyalists. You will join us, willingly or –*' he directed General Blomberg's attention to his adjutant – '*not.*'

Von Blomberg turned. Von Stauffenberg had discretely unholstered his pistol and raised it. He pointed it directly at von Blomberg's head.

'*Von Stauffenberg!*' he cried. '*You too?*' The captain nodded.

'*It is your choice, General,*' my General continued. '*You can participate fully – or we will load you into the trunk of the car, dead or alive. Heydrich may have arrested you after all. So the world will be told.*'

'*Do your worst if it comes to that,*' von Blomberg said calmly. '*Do you think I value my life more than my honor?*' He did not lack courage, I'll say that for him.

'*It is your honor that must compel you, Werner. The pistol is only there in the event you misjudge it. You have witnessed the Fuhrer's behavior this last month – his rages, his inconsistency, his indifference to men – and now this horrible thing with Haydenreich. Adolf Hitler cannot be permitted to rule any longer. He must go. But after that? The Wehrmacht will need you, your nation will need you. Join us, take your position at the head, and do your duty as a German soldier.'* Von Hammerstein never let his eyes leave von Blomberg's.

Long moments passed while General von Blomberg took this in. Then, abruptly, he nodded. *'Yes. My duty. Where do I begin?'*

'With your own staff officers. Get them on the phone, beginning with the most senior, speak to them as I have spoken to you, and of what you have seen this day. Give them your orders, to have the serious Nazis and S.S. among them arrested (but no more), and to stand in readiness – above all, to disregard any orders from the Chancellery. Then, if and when all is done, come back and meet us at the Chancellery – for there will be a trial tonight, and best if you participate.'

'Yes. I understand all this. It will be done. But –' he held up one hand – *'I need your word of honor, you and Stauffenberg – that afterwards, there will be no mention of our discussion – nothing said of this pistol, or this conversation. If I am to be a rebel, on my honor, I will not have my honor questioned. Do I have your word?'*

'Yes,' said von Hammerstein. *'You have mine,'* said von Stauffenberg. (But stupid oaf that he was, von Blomberg did not even think to have me swear, so I made no oath, and was left free to recount the true story of how Werner von Blomberg was dragged into the Putsch much against his will. He may wish now it had all happened differently, but it didn't. I would have sworn if he had asked, but it did not cross his fool's mind. This was the level of the intelligence of the man who became the second Chancellor of the New State!)

'Then let us get on with it. Your car is nearby? May I borrow your driver?'

'Yes, of course. Becker? Good luck to you, Werner. I will see you at the Chancellery in a few hours.' Improbably, the two generals saluted. Without prompting, von Stauffenberg came with us in the direction of the car. His hand hovered near the handle of his pistol. Von Blomberg must have noticed this, but said nothing.

As we walked up the street, two automobiles filled with officers raced up from the other direction, and came to a halt near my General. To my great delight, out stepped Major Bergman.

421

'*How did it go?*' von Stauffenberg asked.

'*They sent four,*' Bergman replied. '*One dead, three prisoners, and now the prisoners are on the phone, furnishing the reports we dictate. Thank God your men arrived first. Ah, Becker*!' he said, noticing me, and it was my great pleasure to salute him as a soldier.

It had begun.

A Walk Across The Street

Excerpt from: A Twentieth Century Life
Albert Sommerville
Houghton, Mifflin (1959)

That second day became night, and we waited, and waited, and waited. The light under Elizabeth's door was not extinguished while I was awake. Periodically she arose from her bed and paced. I could hear her footsteps from my own room. Then all would be still, then she would pace again.

Morning came on the third day. The hours passed at the same glacial tempo. Elizabeth came to breakfast, did her best to be cheerful for her sons, then, quite unusually for her, left them in the care of the maid and went back to her room. We both knew Karl was to be taken to the Chancellery that morning. We had no idea what had happened at his meeting with Hitler. Of course, there was no realistic hope of news. There was nothing for it but to wait, and worry, and hope, and pray. The whole afternoon passed in this way.

Then, slightly after tea time, my butler came to me, with an air of excitement that he was not entirely able to subdue. '*Something is occurring in Germany, my lord,*' he said. '*The BBC just announced that several German radio stations have abruptly ceased broadcasting. There are rumors of military activity in Berlin and Munich. The commentator speculated that some sort of coup or revolution might be underway.*'

I leapt out of my chair, shook his hand fervently to his shocked surprise, raced upstairs, and knocked firmly on Elizabeth's door. When she opened it, I gave her the news as rapidly as breath would permit. My heart was bursting with exhilaration. But she did not react at all, only nodded her head dispassionately.

'*Don't you understand, Elizabeth? There is now every reason to hope.*'

'*For Germany, yes. Not for Karl. I have lost first my brother, and now my husband.*'

'*Karl is a much stronger person than Martin was, Elizabeth. You mustn't give up hope.*'

424

'Hope is exactly what I must surrender, if I am not to torture myself.
Karl is dead, Albert. These events would not be taking place if he were alive.'
And, of course, she was right.

-

Excerpt from: Eyewitness!
The True Story of the Fiasco on the Rhine and the Siege of the Reich
Chancellery
Oberfeldwebel (formerly) Victor H. Becker
Houghton, Mifflin (1950)

When we reached the Gestapo headquarters, von Blomberg began to bluster about commandeering an office. It was quite unnecessary bluster, since the police were completely cooperative. We found a space soon enough. Then the calls began, but von Blomberg seemed to develop a case of nerves between every call he placed. (I noticed he said next to nothing about the horror in the Gestapo basement. All he talked about was the Fuhrer disgracing himself in the Chancellery. I put it down to politics I didn't understand.) He hesitated and protested and complained about his fate. More than once, von Stauffenberg brought his hand to his holster.

Meanwhile, von Stauffenberg was on the phone himself, placing calls to influential military, junior and senior staff, and doing much more on that day than did von Blomberg. In flat, factual tones, he described what was taking place. He reassured one and all that the objectives of the operation were limited, and posed no threat whatsoever to the Wehrmacht as an institution. From what I overheard, nearly everyone pledged support. A few remained neutral. No one expressed opposition.

-

Excerpt from: Service to the State - in War and Peace
Major General Werner von Blomberg
Reichswehr Press (1949)

I found a desk and telephone, and began to communicate my orders to my staff and other units of the Wehrmacht. These were to the effect that matters between the Army and the Fuhrer had reached such a state that some reaction by the military was essential; that such an action was being undertaken by a few select Wehrmacht units; and that the balance of the Wehrmacht should stand down. I also ordered that Nazi political agents in the military, where identified, should be arrested and held incommunicado until the situation had been clarified.

425

Without exception, these commands were received, acknowledged, and obeyed. I was surprised at the time. But in retrospect, it is apparent that the fiasco on the Rhine and the 'suicide' orders had worked to alienate the loyalty of most of the Wehrmacht officers from Hitler. Also, without any false modesty, my own commanding presence, the firmness and authority of my manner, was also of great significance in conveying the moral force of these commands.

-

Excerpt from: My Name is Ike - Reflections on Fifty Years of Service as
Soldier and Statesman
Dwight D. Eisenhower
Random House (1986)

In the weeks that followed, I was somehow able to put aside my heart sickness and do my duty as a military attaché. The United States Army wanted to know exactly what had happened.

From what I learned, the Wehrmacht Putsch of 1936 was a textbook exercise in how to do a coup. German military planning at its best is a marvel of efficiency. The Putsch forces numbered no more than 5,000, but within an hour they had seized all the major communications points in Berlin. At the same time, chain phone calls (which had begun a few hours before) caused the Wehrmacht largely to remain neutral. A few trustworthy Army units, however, did make immediate arrests of hardcore S.S. units. Later in the day, as the Putsch gained momentum, the regular forces moved in to neutralize the rest of those thugs. The orders were no bloodshed or violence, and those orders were obeyed. The number of persons with a motive for retaliation or revenge was thus kept to a minimum. It was a beautifully clean affair.

Von Blomberg took all the credit, but I had a fair idea of who had truly done the planning. Years later, after we had become friends, I talked with Kurt von Hammerstein in considerable detail about the Putsch. I had some doubts about what von Blomberg had truly done. I pressed him on the point. But he told me he was honor-bound not to say more. On the day, he himself had spent the early afternoon in the Berlin Gestapo headquarters, with Rudolf Diels, the chief of Berlin police. He remarked that the cooperation of the police was essential to the success of such an undertaking. I hadn't even thought of that, but I saw at once that he was right.

In any case, I joked that if all the operations in the Great War had gone as well, the German Army would have won. He smiled a little at that. It wasn't much of a joke. But our meetings back then were burdened with so much mutual sadness and sense of loss that nothing seemed very funny.

Excerpt from: A General Speaks - the Autobiography of Kurt von Hammerstein Equord
Major General Kurt von Hammerstein Equord
Reichswehr Press (1986)

Rudolf Diels, the former chief of the Berlin Police had been a member of our group for some time. He was contemptuous of Goering and despised Heydrich. He was not political, simply a policeman who had been proud of his calling. To witness the depths to which the Berlin force was sinking as it became the Gestapo infuriated him. He had joined our cause with enthusiasm and without second thoughts. He had been making his own quiet calls.

When we arrived back at Gestapo headquarters, von Blomberg and von Stauffenberg went off to find an office. Diels arrived almost immediately afterward. I told him of the change in plan. This was no longer a matter of negotiating some limitation on Nazi power, but the complete deposition of Adolf Hitler. To my relief, he expressed even more enthusiasm for this proposal than the first. He had already had assembled as many ranking police officers as were available, and as many of the rank-and-file as could be found. Without fanfare, he assumed command of the station, and led the way to a podium in a large conference room, the one (I learned later) in which the police mustered daily.

Fervent applause greeted the appearance of Diels, for he had been wildly popular with rank-and-file police officers, and his replacement by Himmler bitterly resented. But when I introduced myself, there were gasps, then silence as I stood up, even though I knew many of them were aware of what I was about to say. I announced the Putsch and the plans that lay ahead. I did not know what the reaction would be. But in the middle of my remarks, someone burst in and notified the assembly that the radio stations had gone dead. We had attained our first goal, a fact not lost on my audience, and it seemed to approve. That reassured me. Then, the moment I was finished, there was a tumult of applause and enthusiasm, from all but the most committed Nazis. From then on, we had the police on our side. I learnt later there were similar scenes in Frankfurt and Munich.

I then turned to Diels. '*We must arrest Heydrich – now,*' I said.
'*Yes,*' he agreed.

427

But when we arrived at the place where he had performed his abominations, we found him gone. Not only had he vanished . . . every trace that anything untoward had happened in that room. The wire, the S.S. men, the odious cinematographer and his camera, and above all, the body of Karl von Haydenreich – all had disappeared. Even the blood was largely gone, only a stain or two. The only substantial evidence that remained was the overpowering stench.

'*How is this possible?*' I asked.

Diels shrugged. '*This is a large building. There are many ways out. He knew he was committing a crime. He came prepared for flight and concealment.*' Spoken like a true policeman.

I nodded my understanding and frustration. Just then, my driver Becker approached me, so briskly he was almost running. He saluted, then put his hand to his nose. '*Captain von Stauffenberg begs to inform you that Frick, the Minister of the Interior, has joined our cause, and is directing the Ministry police to cooperate. Also, the Captain has received a communication from the director at the radio station. He wishes to know if you have a statement.*'

I had indeed prepared notes for this purpose, but now was not the time to leave my post to deliver them. I pulled them out of my coat pocket, and handed them to Becker.

'*Here,*' I said, '*have von Blomberg deliver them. He is the more appropriate spokesman in any case.*'

Becker opened his mouth as if to say something, then (wisely) thought better of it. Then he saluted, clicked his heels, and was gone.

Since then, have I regretted that impulsive decision? The true answer is that sometimes I do, sometimes I do not.

But at that moment my sole attention had turned to the Chancellery – and Adolf Hitler.

-

Excerpt from: Service to the State - in War and Peace
Major General Werner von Blomberg
Reichswehr Press (1949)

Early in the afternoon, I was interrupted and summoned to the phone, to receive a call from Wilhelm Frick, then the Minister of the Interior. He expressed his unqualified support for the action taking place, and his own loss of confidence in the persons at the head of the Government. He asked if there was any way he could assist. Since as Minister of Interior he had authority over the regional police forces of the nation, I told him he could perform invaluable service by directing them to cooperate with the new direction Germany was about to take. This he was happy to do.

This was my first contact with Frick. Our rapport was instantaneous. In this meeting was the beginning of that political alliance that has since brought such huge dividends to the Republic.

-

Excerpt from: Eyewitness!
The True Story of the Fiasco on the Rhine and the Siege of the Reich Chancellery
Oberfeldwebel (formerly) Victor H. Becker
Houghton, Mifflin (1950)

Von Stauffenberg was engaged in a call, when a police officer entered with a message. The Captain turned to me. '*It's the radio people,*' he said. '*Citizens are alarmed that the radio is off the air. They are phoning the station and coming onto the streets. Someone must get on the air and make an announcement. Go seek out von Hammerstein, and bring him here.*'

I did that, and found my General, in the company of Diels. He did not want to leave the field of action, and believed duty required him to go to the Chancellery. To my dismay, he handed over his notes and bade me take them to von Blomberg. I knew this was a mistake, that he would be conferring on von Blomberg the status of spokesman. But it was not my place to give him advice. I saluted, and returned to von Blomberg and von Stauffenberg.

'*Well,*' said von Blomberg, when he understood the situation and had the notes, '*it seems it falls to me to explain to the German people the events of the day.*' He glanced at the notes. Von Stauffenberg rolled his eyes at me – quite informal for an officer, but we had developed a certain understanding that day. '*Find me a car.*' One of the policeman did just that, and von Blomberg was off to the radio station, and, as it happened, to a new career – alas.

Von Stauffenberg returned to his work on the phone, which he did as ably as before. I waited in case he needed a courier again. From his expression, and his occasional looks, I could see that all was going extremely well, even better than he and my General had hoped.

We continued with this until late in the afternoon, when another phone call summoned us to meet General von Hammerstein at the Chancellery.

It was there that the end occurred. I was there, too. There I was witness to the most courageous act, and the bravest man, I ever saw.

-

Excerpt from: A General Speaks - the Autobiography of Kurt von Hammerstein Equord
Major General Kurt von Hammerstein Equord
Reichswehr Press (1986)

We had known from the start that the last act would almost certainly take place at the Chancellery. By the time I arrived, it was apparent to all we would succeed. Party headquarters around Berlin and the other cities surrendered without protest. Police forces turned out to keep order. That meant the Communists and Socialists, who might have stirred up chaos for the sake of chaos, were completely neutralized.

The streets in Berlin began to fill with people, but not in protest. There were cheers from some; others gestured their support. We had known the public was disenchanted with the Nazis, but had no idea to what degree until that day. The sense of relief in the air was palpable.

The various reactions of the Nazi potentates also confirmed our imminent triumph. When Hess was arrested at his apartments, he burst into tears. (Having observed the man, I was not surprised.) As the whole world knows, Goering, with his survivor's instinct, made straight for the airport, boarded his plane, and flew directly to Denmark and then on to Sweden. Himmler had provided for this emergency by having a capsule of cyanide in a tooth. When our troops arrived, he pressed down on it and died. (On the day, I thought this was unduly melodramatic. But given the fate that awaited him when the full horrors of the behavior of the S.A. and S.S. in his concentration camps were revealed, he may have possessed the better wisdom.) Goebbels fortified himself in his newspaper offices, but these were surrounded, and he was without any power to intervene. That was sufficient.

So there only remained the Chancellery, Heydrich, and Hitler himself. I had not foreseen the exact roster, but I did know the last act would be played there. The handpicked troops we had assigned there, about 200 in all, had arrived. They were augmented by several dozen others, men who had completed their assigned tasks with an ease we had not anticipated. They milled about, awaiting orders. In addition, curious Berliners began appearing in numbers in the square outside. They had heard von Blomberg on the radio and wanted to see for themselves what was happening. Fortunately, they were

430

content to be eyewitnesses to history and not participants, and kept the distance we required. The German people are different than the French.

The corporal was not in the Chancellery. The emotions and exertions of the morning had tired him, so he had left his offices for the suite he maintained at the Kaiserhof Hotel. (Hitler was never a hard worker, and frequently left his office at an early hour.) The troops we had dispatched to arrest him had been stymied temporarily by his bodyguards. Even though these were completely outnumbered, a public display of force, particularly an exchange of gunfire, was out of the question in a residential hotel. But the Fuhrer could not be allowed sanctuary. At our request, the management had the hotel evacuated. Several hundred guests were suddenly out on their own in the street. That made a seizure of Hitler's person practicable. But we still wished to avoid an incident.

Then came the welcome news that Hitler himself had ordered his guards to stand down, and demanded to be taken to the Chancellery. It was apparent he still maintained the illusion that he had his erstwhile control over events. This was welcome news. Over the phone, I directed that his offer be accepted and that he be taken into custody, with pains taken to maintain his delusion as long as possible.

Meanwhile, events at the Chancellery took an unfortunate turn. We had located Heydrich. One of the office workers exiting the building informed a soldier that he was inside, with two dozen or so of the most loyal cadre of S.S. officers with him. He was preparing to make a stand.

This was not good. Heydrich did not have enough troops to contest possession of the building, but he did have enough to cause a very unpleasant scene. Unlike Hitler, he was under no illusions. The Nazi Reich was failing before his eyes. He could not prevent that, but he could attempt to see that the order that followed was baptized in as much blood and controversy as possible. Heydrich was that sort of person.

I assessed the situation. It was essential that Hitler not be permitted into the Chancellery while it was controlled by the S.S. But the means of achieving this goal were not clear. I was not sure how to proceed. It had to begin with forming up our troops. I gave those orders, meanwhile instructing our forces at the Kaiserhof to remain there with Hitler, regardless of how he ranted. Von Stauffenberg was by then on the scene, done with his calls. I dispatched him to the Kaiserhof to stiffen any weakening resolve.

431

Just then, Heydrich was sighted with his cadre of loyalists. They took up positions around the entrance to the Chancellery, using the columns as bulwarks. With our own troops formed and ready across the street, a stalemate had arisen not unlike the trenches of the last war. But I was determined that the battle not end as those had. I had the police move the bystanders several hundred yards away. The square became quiet and tense – our forces behind barriers outside, the S.S. men shielding themselves behind columns. Heydrich gave the command to level arms, and I had to reciprocate. Rifles were shouldered on both sides. German soldiers were aiming weapons at other German soldiers, with the possibility of killing each other. *This will not do,* I thought to myself.

Heydrich called out then. '*Drop your arms! In the name of the Fuhrer! You swore an oath*!'

I could see some of the rifles waver. Something had to be done. But what?

'*Maintain arms!*' I shouted, temporizing. '*This is an order from your General!*' And the rifles straightened.

'*I hesitated this afternoon, General,*' Heydrich shouted back. '*I will not make that mistake again. Drop your arms!*' The air now crackled with tension.

Then the only possible tactic occurred to me. Many since then have praised me for my action. In my opinion, the praise is overstated. There really was no choice for a German officer who valued his honor and loved his country.

-

Excerpt from: Eyewitness!
The True Story of the Fiasco on the Rhine and the Siege of the Reich Chancellery
Oberfeldwebel (formerly) Victor H. Becker
Houghton, Mifflin (1950)

What my General did then . . . I could not have believed a man could behave so remarkably if I had not seen it myself.

The rifles were leveled and Heydrich called out his demand to surrender. For a few moments, the outcome trembled in a void of indecision. Then, all at once, my General stood up, as tall as he could. He stepped out with firm strides into the middle of the street.

'*Shoulder arms!*' he called out to our troops. The rifles wavered for an instant, then our forces stood down, rifles on their shoulders. Then he turned to the dozen or so S.S. men with Heydrich, on the Chancellery front. '*You, too, as well!*' he commanded.

'*Ignore him! Stand ready!*' Heydrich shouted. My General paid him no attention.

'*German soldiers will not shed the blood of other German soldiers,*' he continued, addressing the S.S. '*We all served in the Great War. We are all brothers in arms. We have all seen too much blood of ours shed before. We will not commit crimes against each other.*' Now he had all their attention. I saw a few of the S.S. men put their rifles on their shoulders.

'*You all know the cause that brings us here – the Rhineland, the suicide order – there are other matters as well. It is time for Adolf Hitler to account for these, to justify himself, to the Wehrmacht and to the German people. You know the cause, and you know it is a rightful cause. You will not allow this man, this Austrian, to desecrate the sacred oath a soldier makes to his army and his country. You will not shame yourself in this manner. Now,*' he said, turning back to us, '*these men will walk with me into these offices – and you all will join us – for each and every one knows where your real duty lies, and it is with us. Gentlemen!*' he called and waved us all forward.

Bergman was the first that I saw with my own eyes. He walked, purposefully but without urgency, into the street and stopped beside the General. Then von Stauffenberg, then others, at first in ones and twos, but then in larger groups. One by one, our men stood up and joined the General. I cannot say I was the first, but I was by no means the last.

'*Shoot! Shoot!*' Heydrich shouted, but no one did. Instead, the rifles dropped. Two of the S.S. men even came out into the street and joined us.

'*We will go forward now, and into the building,*' von Hammerstein said. En masse, we moved forward. The S.S. men did nothing; one more joined our ranks. As one, we surged into the building. The remaining S.S. men scattered. I did not know where Heydrich had gone, but I did not see him.

Without opposition, we moved under the portico, through the doors, and down the corridor. Von Hammerstein led the way with von Stauffenberg at his side. Then, suddenly, Reinhard Heydrich made his reappearance. He stepped out suddenly from an alcove, almost an ambush, with four S.S. men beside him. These had their rifles leveled, and I could see at once that this time they could not be dissuaded by my General or any man.

433

'*In the name of the Fuhrer,*' Heydrich began, '*I arrest you —*'

Bergman was standing on the left, outside Heydrich's range of vision. In one quick, smooth, unhurried movement, he raised his arm, in which he held his pistol, and shot Heydrich twice in the forehead. No one had seen the gun before; he must have unholstered it quietly while we were mustering. It all happened too quickly for thought or reaction.

The queerest expression of surprise spread across Heydrich's face. Then, an instant later, he dropped to the floor like a felled ox. To this day, it pleases me to know that he knew he was dead before he died and went straight to Hell with that thought.

But the rifles were up and poised again, and a fight seemed very near. But my General spoke immediately. '*HALT! Stop! We will not shoot each other!*'

Then he turned to Bergman. '*Major, you are under arrest. You will face court martial for this,*' he said. '*Give me your weapon.*'

'*Yes, General,*' Bergman said immediately, and handed over the pistol. It was all so quick and smooth; I wonder even now if the two men had discussed this beforehand. If so, it was a good thing, for the instant arrest and surrender deprived the S.S. men of any pretext for action — that, and the fact that their demon-in-chief was now dead.

'*Do I have your word of honor you will not leave these premises or my presence until the police arrive? That you will make no attempt to escape?*'

'*You have my word, General.*'

'*Then we will proceed. Perhaps there will be two trials this evening. Gentleman, forward!*'

We moved forward again, in all our numbers, swelled now by the S.S. men themselves. We flooded the corridors and came to the central offices, where I had watched von Haydenreich stand up to Hitler just a few hours earlier. There von Hammerstein took charge again. He ordered that all the offices be cleared, the ministers and their secretaries sent home, and the building vacated. Cabinets and papers were to be secured. The General was emphatic that no papers or documents, government or not, be removed by some over-enthusiastic or over-loyal Nazi before a new government could examine them. Wehrmacht officers do not have the reputation they do for nothing. The junior officers were quick to organize the men into small task groups, and spread out throughout the building. About half our number remained.

'*Now it is time to prepare for the court martial,*' General von Hammerstein said then.

'*Of the officer, sir?*' someone asked from the ranks.

'*No,*' my General answered. '*Of a corporal.*' The set of his face was grimness itself. He had not forgotten the afternoon.

-

Excerpt from: Service to the State - in War and Peace
Major General Werner von Blomberg
Reichswehr Press (1949)

The question of whether justice was done to Adolf Hitler does not admit of a simple answer. On the one hand, there is no question he had committed grievous sins against the German state, and possibly against some German officers. On the other, there is little doubt that the trial he received lacked even the basic rudiments of fair procedure.

Therefore, I have always tried to avoid definite comment on this vexed subject.

-

Excerpt from: A General Speaks - the Autobiography of Kurt von Hammerstein Equord
Major General Kurt von Hammerstein Equord
Reichswehr Press (1986)

I was determined that justice be done to Adolf Hitler, and as expeditiously as possible. I had in mind the procedures applicable to a battlefield court martial. Those who have participated in these proceedings, as I have, know that they can be short, and summary, but not without fairness. The Fuhrer would be given a fair chance to defend himself, but not a public forum. My main concern was that the atrocities perpetrated against Leutnant von Haydenreich not become one more incident among many others in the Putsch. This I regarded as urgent.

I hoped von Blomberg, as head of the Army, would make himself available to conduct the trial. But he continued to busy himself with the press.

-

Excerpt from: Eyewitness!
The True Story of the Fiasco on the Rhine and the Siege of the Reich Chancellery
Oberfeldwebel (formerly) Victor H. Becker
Houghton, Mifflin (1950)

When von Blomberg opted out, my General was a picture of frustration. I think it was then he realized that the General had begun pursuing a different personal agenda.

'*Very well,*' he said grimly. '*I will preside. Where is Hitler?*'

'*En route, sir,*' someone said. '*We just heard from the Kaiserhof.*'

'*Good,*' said von Hammerstein. He looked about the room and selected four officers to serve as court. '*You will also sit on the case of Bergman, immediately afterward. Von Stauffenberg will serve as prosecutor to both. The accused will conduct their own defense. Do you understand?*'

Everyone agreed. I could name names here – I know who the officers were. But it is not my place to name the name of anyone who wishes to remain anonymous. So I will leave it at that.

'*Becker,*' my General said, '*you will give evidence as to what you saw this morning and afternoon. I will also testify, to those matters and others. Do you understand?*'

'*Yes, sir,*' I said. Then the room was rearranged, hastily, but appropriately, to conform to the conventions of a courtroom. The officers assigned to the panel took their seats.

'*He is here,*' someone reported, after a call from the desk at the entrance.

'*Becker, Clamper – go and escort the Fuhrer to this chamber.*' I left and went down the stairs.

The door opened and Hitler strutted in, between two soldiers. He did not seem aware these were custodians and not bodyguards. His head was high and his manner imperial. He stepped boldly down the hall. Then suddenly he stopped and stared. I moved forward to take charge of him.

'*What is that?*' he demanded.

'*The body of Reinhard Heydrich,*' I said. '*There has not been time to move it.*'

His eyes widened – and then he whitened with anger. '*There will be consequences for this!*' he said. '*Someone will pay! And you will address me as Fuhrer!*' He was already in a state.

'*Yes, my Fuhrer,*' I said – no point in making a fuss.

He led the way, by custom, down the corridor, up the stairs, and into the large conference room. He stopped short when he saw the arrangement in the room.

436

'*What is the meaning of this??*' Hitler demanded. '*Why has this room been altered from the form I ordered?*'

'*There is to be a trial,*' von Hammerstein answered. '*You are to answer for the murder of Karl von Haydenreich, and other crimes against the State.*'

'*Murder!!?*' Hitler screamed. '*Crimes??! You are the murderers!! YOU are the criminals!!*' – and with that, he was off, in a tirade about Jews, Bolsheviks, November criminals, and other persons who must be shot or hanged. He went on and on, barely pausing for breath, and not realizing he was not speaking in a beer hall or addressing the Reichstag. The room was dead silent, patiently waiting the end. But no end seemed forthcoming. Five, ten, fifteen minutes went by, as he worked himself into greater paroxysms of hysteria and fury.

Finally, General von Hammerstein had heard enough. He got out of his seat and moved forward to stand directly in front of Hitler. This did bring the tirade to a stop, mercifully. Hitler stopped and blinked, puzzled.

'*We have heard enough, Corporal,*' the General said. '*It is time for trial.*'

'*Corporal!!?*' Hitler reddened with anger, took a breath, and began to wind up again. But General von Hammerstein stopped him before he could start. '*Take your seat, and be quiet. Your trial is about to commence.*'

'*How dare you –*' Hitler began, but the General interrupted him. '*Take your seat. If you will not take your seat, you will be forcibly escorted to it.*'

Hitler tried to say more, but General von Hammerstein signaled. Two soldiers, one of whom was one of the S.S. men who had stood with Heydrich, took him by each arm, moved him to the small chair, and firmly forced him down onto it. His mouth fell open. I think it was only then that he realized how much had changed, and that he was no longer Fuhrer.

My General took his seat in the middle of the panel. '*I will preside, but, as I must give evidence, I will have no vote. The first witness will be my driver, Becker, for he is not an officer, and thus uncontaminated by ambition or envy.*' A few chuckled at that. I froze for a moment; I was suddenly the center of attention I never sought or wanted. Then I took the oath, and sat down.

I told my story then, as I have written it here for you, from the beginning of the day. Von Stauffenberg helped with a question or comment. The entire time, Hitler glared with fevered eyes at me, as if he could murder me with a look. A week before, even a day before, this would have made me

437

awestruck and dumb. But now I knew Schicklgruber for what he really was, and I didn't give a snap of the fingers what he did.

I was forced to stop several times when I described what had happened to poor von Haydenreich. Twice, I had to take a drink of water, once, I trembled at the brink of tears. Von Stauffenberg put a hand on my shoulder and steadied me.

When I spoke of the film camera, and told that all this was filmed for the corporal, there were audible gasps from around the room. Hitler himself did not flinch at all, but, as I continued, he looked away and would not meet my eye.

Finally, I was done. The room was silent.

'*Do you have any questions?*' General von Hammerstein asked Hitler.

'*These are lies, all lies,*' Hitler said. '*Haydenreich was a traitor, so I ordered him shot, and he was shot. This – enlisted man*' – he waved a dismissive hand at me – '*has made up this Grimm's fairy tale out of whole cloth.*' I felt myself flush, and began to rise to my feet. No man gives me the lie! But von Stauffenberg put a hand on my shoulder steadied me.

One of the officers on the panel stood and spoke at that time. '*I watched you, my Fuhrer, when the witness spoke of a cameraman. Others gasped and reacted. But you were calm. This did not come as a surprise to you. I wonder if you already knew this.*'

Hitler started. He tried to find words, but too late. '*No – this lie surprised me as much*' – then he found himself. '*Besides, where is the cameraman? Where is the body? Where is the proof?*' For a moment, he seemed triumphant. But he had forgotten himself.

'*How would you know that von Haydenreich's body is missing?*' von Stauffenberg asked. Hitler went pale. '*Or where the cameraman is? Did you speak to Heydrich? Did you give him orders to dispose of the corpse? Without even decent burial?*'

Hitler became even paler. He looked around, searching again for words. In that moment, his guilt became as evident as if the Apostle Peter himself had pronounced it. '*No – I had no – this was simply a fortunate guess – I knew –*'

'*I do not wish to let the larger question go,*' another officer interrupted. '*On what basis was Leutnant von Haydenreich executed, whatever the means? What proof was there of treason, without a trial or defense? And execution on the same day? What proof?*'

438

'*His stepmother was a Jew,*' Hitler answered. '*And he concealed the fact.*'

The room became silent. '*This is all?*' von Stauffenberg asked. '*You ordered a Wehrmacht officer executed on that basis? Without trial?*'

Hitler was now close to panic. '*No! There was other evidence! There were papers . . .*'

'*Well, they must all still be here. Nothing has been removed. Can you produce them? Or at least describe the content?*'

Hitler stood, and nervously wiped his mustache. He strode to a desk, opened a drawer, and paged rapidly through the files. Then he straightened up. '*No, they are not here. Hess must have removed them.*' He went back to his seat, then straightened up. '*But this was good evidence! Convincing evidence! I am too distressed by this mounting treason to recollect clearly!*'

'*I will submit to this panel that there was no other evidence. That this man had a German officer executed because he had a Jewish stepmother and did not wish to discuss the fact with the S.S.*'

'*No!*' Hitler shouted, '*There was more!*' But he was ignored.

'*I do not like Jews,*' said the officer who had stood first. '*Unpleasant people, generally. But they are not demons. There are good men among them.*'

'*What man would not revere the woman who raised him?*' another remarked. '*Of whatever race? This is human nature.*'

'*He was a traitor!*' Hitler shouted.

'*I would put it to you, Herr Hitler,*' von Stauffenberg said evenly, '*that there was no treason. That the real reason you ordered von Haydenreich's execution, and in such a savage manner, was that he was witness to your cowardice at the Beer Hall affair.*'

'*That is a lie!*' Hitler exclaimed.

'*Be that as it may, have you anything more to say on the matter?*'

'*I acted within the powers granted me under the Reichstag Acts,*' Hitler said. '*We are surrounded by Bolsheviks and Jews – severity is necessary!*'

'*I'm sure the panel will take that into account,*' von Stauffenberg said. '*But now we must take more evidence. General von Hammerstein?*'

My General left his seat, and came to the seat for witnessing. Before he seated himself, however, he took my hand and shook it. '*Before I move on to the other matters, I wish to say that I was with Oberfeldwebel Becker today. I confirm his testimony in every respect, including much I wish I could forget.*'

439

'*I, too, will confirm his account,*' said von Stauffenberg. '*I will answer whatever questions the panel has as witness.*' But there were no questions. The room was silent, even Hitler, muttering to himself.

'*Very well,*' said General Hammerstein, '*then I will pass on to the other charges – the suicide orders given during the Rhineland Fiasco, and the murder of General Schleicher during the Long Knives. This man took other innocent lives that night, but I will confine myself to Schleicher's case, which I know well.*' With that, he made his statement. I won't repeat it here, as the basics are known to all. What amazed me then was how much of it we all knew, even before my General spoke. Why had we been willing to tolerate and accept these crimes when Hitler was in the seat of power?

While this went on, Adolf Hitler writhed and squirmed in his chair. Twice, he tried to interrupt with a tirade, but was shushed directly by the panel. My General finished in a remarkably short time. The room was silent.

'*What is your response, Herr Hitler?*' von Stauffenberg asked.

'*Fuhrer! I am the Fuhrer! Address me by my title!*' Hitler shouted.

'*You have no rank now, Herr Hitler. What is your response?*'

Hitler stood, looked wildly around the room, then began – well, to rant. It was clear to me he really had no response. He spoke wildly (as always) of Jews and Bolsheviks, of how Schleicher was plotting against him – as if that were treason. He insisted on his power and right. His hair became disheveled. His eyes glittered maniacally, like one in an asylum. But he gave no answer.

'*What was the reason for the suicide order during the Rhineland?*'

'*It was not suicide!*' Hitler shouted. '*And there was a reason! The world – the West – all of the enemies – they had to see – to know – what Germans were capable of! The spirit that Germans possess! That we are indomitable, prepared to make whatever sacrifice is necessary for our destiny! And that was the reason!*'

The room was silent.

'*So,*' one of the panel asked, '*you were willing to send dozens of good men to their deaths to make an impression in the Western press?*'

'*No!*' he said. '*No! There was more than that!*'

But he was not able to say more. And that was the end of the evidence.

'*It is now up to you, gentlemen,*' General von Hammerstein said, addressing the five officers. '*Confer and consider your verdict. Do not be hasty, but do try to be expeditious. Time is of the essence.*'

'*This farce is no trial,*' Hitler snarled.

440

'*More than you gave von Haydenreich,*' the General answered. To this, Hitler could say nothing. The panel of five rose from their seats and went back to a desk at the corner of the room. There I could see them arguing and gesturing. It was not a lengthy process, but neither was it a rubberstamp. It was at least thirty minutes before they returned to their seats.

'*What is the result?*' General von Hammerstein said.

The first officer who had stood to speak now spoke for the group. '*We find Herr Adolf Hitler guilty on the first two charges. There is not enough known about Schleicher and his wife to say tonight. We also find that Leutnant Karl von Haydenreich was garroted in the manner described by Oberfeldwebel Becker.*'

'*Consider now the penalty,*' my General said.

'*We already have,*' the officer replied. '*For ordering the execution of a German officer out of personal vindictiveness? Death. We did not consider punishment for the other charges.*'

'*That is sufficient,*' said General von Hammerstein. He turned to Hitler. '*Do you have anything to say?*'

'*I will wait to make my statement until the appeal,*' Hitler said stiffly. '*I will not participate further in this farce.*'

The General stared at him as if he could not believe what he heard. Then he stepped forward, deliberately into Hitler's face. '*There is not going to be an appeal. Do you think you are going to be given another opportunity to turn a courtroom into your personal theater? Make another appeal to the worst elements of this nation? While a mass of followers parade about with torches outside? No, Corporal Hitler. Make your statement now. Because this verdict will be carried out within the hour, unless you can persuade us otherwise.*'

Hitler stared at him, then around the room. As amazing as it seems, I believe to that very moment he had counted on his destiny. But now he looked around at the silent room, the officers, the men at arms, all of whom – all of us – had heard enough to know him as he really was, without the trappings of office and power. He gulped then, and raised himself to his feet.

'*Officers – gentlemen,*' he said, softly, '*I – I – I never meant to be this. I was to be the drummer, the man who came before, John the Baptist to the man who came to redeem all Germany. I did not want this for myself. I only took up this burden because there was no other. And the Jews, the Bolsheviks – they were always on the prowl to destroy us. I did this because there was no other. I*

441

did my best. Please – I do not deserve this judgment. Spare me for a greater purpose.'

The room was silent. General von Hammerstein turned to the panel. *'Gentlemen, retire again and consider whether this plea of Hitler changes anything.'* The officers left to the same place, but were back very quickly. *'Our verdict is unchanged, Herr General.'*

'Very well,' the General said. He turned to von Stauffenberg. *'Organize a firing squad. Ten men. Two rifles without projectiles. Bergman must not participate.'*

'Yes, sir.' Von Stauffenberg went about the room, selecting men, ten for the squad, ten others to prepare the rifles. Two rifles would hold only power cartridges. In a moment, he was back, and saluted. *'We are ready, my General. Where should this take place?'*

'In the courtyard, of course.' He turned to Hitler. *'It is time, Herr Hitler. Stand up.'*

Hitler was as deathly pale as any man I have ever seen. *'No,'* he said, *'no! I will not! I am your Fuhrer! I order you to desist!'*

My General ignored him. He gestured to two S.S. men. *'Escort the prisoner to the courtyard.'*

The two men moved to Hitler, took him by the arms, and stood him up. But he would not stand. He went limp. His feet dragged underneath him.

'Take him out,' von Stauffenberg said, with complete contempt. *'And someone take the chair – you may yet need it.'* Still another man lifted the chair and carried it out behind Hitler, who was alternately squirming like a small child, and going limp. As they went through the door, he began to cry.

Von Stauffenberg turned to me. *'Take off your belt,'* he said, *'it may be needed.'* I started. *'Remember von Haydenreich,'* he whispered. I gave him the belt at once. He collected two or three more. As he did so, the sergeant von Stauffenberg had made head of the squad came through the door. *'He will not be still,'* he said, with disgust. *'He will not stand up, he will not seat himself. He keeps whining and crying.'*

'Here,' von Stauffenberg said, handing him the belts. *'Tie him into the chair. The farce must end.'*

Through the window, I saw two men hold Hitler firmly in place, while two others used my belt and the others to bind him to the chair. He was still weeping and pleading as they stepped back into place.

'*No!*' I heard him shout. '*I am the destiny of Germany! I must not die like this! I must –*'

But then the rifles fired, the shots rang out, and I could see the silhouette of the wretched little shithead who had styled himself Fuhrer, slumped in the chair, lifeless.

Thus ended the career and life of Adolf Schicklgruber.

The General slumped in his chair. I noticed then how exhausted he was. Then he found himself. '*Contact the hospital morgue. We must make provisions for the corpse. Someone phone the radio stations. Tell them Hitler is dead, and all the rest. Lock up the offices – we will leave it to the politicians to decide when and how to reopen them.*' Men moved to the phones and down the halls.

'*I wonder what comes next,*' I heard my General mutter to himself. '*I wonder what comes next.*' Then he straightened up, and looked at the officers who had served on the court martial panel. '*Ready yourselves, gentlemen. It is necessary now to conduct the court martial of Major Bergman.*'

Aftermath

Excerpt from: Memoirs
The Right Honourable Eric Phipps
Houghton, Mifflin (1946)

I was not in my offices ten minutes the next morning when my secretary bustled in. It was true, he said – Hitler, Himmler, Heydrich all dead – Goering in flight – Goebbels in hiding. Frick and others had joined the Wehrmacht faction. The Nazis had fallen. He did not conceal his jubilation.

I could not contain my own emotions. This was not a morning to remain in my offices. I cancelled my appointments, and went out and walked the streets. Others had the same notion. The streets were full of men and women, strolling and gawking, talking in small groups. Though no one shouted huzzahs or swung from the lamp posts, the feeling of relief and excitement – jubilation, if you will – was everywhere.

It occurred to me then, that though most of the aspects of the Nazi nightmare had been quite subtle, it was nonetheless a nightmare. As is the case with all nightmares, one was not aware of how pervasive it had been until it was over.

Excerpt from: My Name is Ike - Reflections on Fifty Years of Service as
Soldier and Statesman
Dwight D. Eisenhower
Random House (1986)

March 31st, 1936 should have been one of the most joyous days of my life. The streets of Berlin were like a festival. I was a little bothered that von Blomberg, whom I regarded as a pompous oaf, was going to be a big part of whatever was coming next. Von Hammerstein, whom I liked a lot, and who I suspected had a lot more to do with the events than von Blomberg, was nowhere to be seen. But that was small potatoes compared to Hitler and the other brutes being gone.

The big thing that preyed on my mind and cut me out of the general excitement was concern about Karl. I hadn't heard from him or anyone in a day. I couldn't reach him by phone or otherwise. Worry gnawed like a rat in my stomach. I feared the worst.

Excerpt from: A General Speaks - the Autobiography of Kurt von Hammerstein Equord
Major General Kurt von Hammerstein Equord
Reichswehr Press (1986)

After the acquittal of Bergman (a formality), I found myself completely exhausted. There was still much to do, of course, but I found myself unable to think or even move. It was unthinkable to leave my post, but I was literally incapable of movement. Becker sensed this, and somehow found me an unoccupied office. From somewhere he procured a cot. I laid down there, intending to refresh myself and proceed with vigor the next morning.

But I could not sleep. The horrors of the day, particularly in the Gestapo basement, were furies ravaging my soul. I knew there was one duty I had to perform the next day, the worst of all. As soon as staff was available the next morning, I procured the phone number of the Sommerville estate, where Elizabeth von Haydenreich was staying as a guest. I used my rank to procure a distance line and placed the call at the earliest moment. In my perplexity, I completely forgot the difference in time.

Excerpt from: A Twentieth Century Life
Albert Sommerville
Houghton, Mifflin (1959)

At a little after 7:00 a.m. on the morning of March 31st, the phone rang. The caller was none other than General Kurt von Hammerstein, head of Wehrmacht Staff. Normally, I would have been flattered and overwhelmed by a contact with such an important personage. But that day, I knew at once why he had placed the call. A lead weight sank in my stomach.

He asked for Elizabeth. I politely reminded him of the hour, which he had overlooked. He apologized at once for the early intrusion. I then asked if he had any message. He hesitated briefly, then remarked that perhaps it was better that the news be conveyed by a family friend.

'*Karl von Haydenreich is dead,*' he said. '*He was executed yesterday in the Gestapo headquarters. By order of Hitler.*'

447

Elizabeth had predicted this, but it was still a shock. I went completely numb. *'Did this have any connection with the coup?'* I asked.

'It had every connection,' the General answered. *'It was the triggering event. But not one that I would have wished. It was . . . was . . . an incomprehensible event.'*

'How was this done?' I asked numbly. *'By firing squad?'*

He paused for a long while. *'By order of Hitler,'* he said finally, *'and do not ask me more. That is all I am at liberty to say.'* His voice quavered.

I did not ask more. We rang off. I put down the receiver in a trance. For the first time in my life, I encountered the infinity of death. The fact overwhelmed me. I could not believe – I could not grasp – I could not comprehend – that I still inhabited a world in which Karl no longer lived. The Shakespearean formulation – *never, never, never, never, never!* – flashed through my consciousness. I understood it now, for the first time in my life.

I have no recollection of proceeding up the stairs. I only remember confronting Elizabeth, seated at the table in her room. She stood up. She knew at once, from my look and aspect, what I had come to tell her. Without a word, she embraced me, like the sister she has always been to me. Then – I do not know who began – for the second time in a week, we began to weep, like children, for the longest time. Then I heard her whisper. *'I will never forgive him'* or *'them,'* one or the other – whether she meant Hitler alone or all of the others, I have never been sure. I never asked what she meant. I was too far gone myself.

The next few days are utterly lost to me. I have no memory of any detail, only the fog of a numb, despairing, all-encompassing grief.

-

Excerpt from: A General Speaks - the Autobiography of Kurt von Hammerstein Equord
Major General Kurt von Hammerstein Equord
Reichswehr Press (1986)

When I completed the call to Sommerville, I once again found myself without energy. My limbs seemed to be made of lead. My heart barely beat in my breast. With some effort, I found Becker and had him drive me home.

There, I took to my bed. I can reveal now that I remained in this condition through the remainder of the year. I slept through most of the day, rarely went out, and found it impossible to take any interest in political or military affairs. I have been roundly criticized, I know, for not taking a greater part in the building of the New Germany.

But I had nothing more to offer my country at that time.

-

Excerpt from: Eyewitness!
The True Story of the Fiasco on the Rhine and the Siege of the Reich Chancellery
Oberfeldwebel (formerly) Victor H. Becker
Houghton, Mifflin (1950)

When I drove my General home that day, I knew he was finished. He was a shell of himself.

He was too good and decent a man to do all that God required him to do. But he did his duty. Many people wish he had played a greater role in the New Germany, but I do not think that was possible.

-

Excerpt from: My Name is Ike - Reflections on Fifty Years of Service as Soldier and Statesman
Dwight D. Eisenhower
Random House (1986)

It was two days before I could reach my contacts in the Wehrmacht. Then I managed to confirm what I knew in my heart was true, that Karl was dead. But the circumstances were murky and the details obscure. All that came to me was that there had been a dramatic meeting with Adolf Hitler, and that had led to his summary execution.

This was perhaps the most devastating news of my life. Karl, a wonderful young man, my godson – a person I had sworn to protect – dead!! Even though the causes were outside of anything I could have changed (the need of the Nazis for a scapegoat and the malice of the uncle who had never quite forgiven his father), I felt an overwhelming, deadening guilt. He should never have put himself that close to the Nazi apparatus. I should have said something.

It was days before I could eat, weeks before I slept normally. Even now, so many years later, the guilt has merely faded. It has not diminished.

-

March 15, 1936
Cavendish Square
London, England

449

Mr. A. A. Milne
Cotchford Farm
Hartfield, East Sussex

Milne,

. . . [T]he largest danger is that the fall of the Nazis as a result of the military success will placate the public, which will forget the horrific risk of continental war the great fool Baldwin ran to achieve this sordid result. The pressure must continue to be unrelenting. I have planned for a whole series of editorials and demonstrations.

Poor Hitler! Another martyr to the pretensions of France on the Continent and the severity of the Versailles Treaty. He will be keenly mourned in Germany . . .

Cecil

-

Excerpt from: *My Life in Office*
Stanley Baldwin
Houghton, Mifflin (1947)

I had thought I could manage the political repercussions. But they spiraled out of my control almost at once. The Peace Movement continued its campaign with increased fervor. To my surprise, however, a considerable portion of the Tories joined them in condemnation of me and my administration.

My colleagues and I then made one of those decisions that rarely, if ever, come to public attention, that reflect a commitment to the public welfare that transcends all political expediency. I claim no exceptional virtue in describing our acts in this way. There is more respect for high principle among public men of all parties than cynical historians are ever inclined to credit.

The particulars were these. We might have blunted or even dispelled the worst of the criticism had we revealed the full extent of the information available to us concerning the German remilitarization of the Rhineland. We were not quite the adventurists the most vocal of our opponents portrayed. But the German nation at that time was in a frenzied chaos as the State reformed itself. Nazi loyalists were among the most vocal in the first days, even without the spiritual force of their fallen leader. There was a strident insistence that Hitler had been undone by an inner cabal, not unlike the one that had undone the Kaiser at the end of the Great War. Of course, that earlier cabal had been a complete fiction. But this later one truly existed.

450

It was evident to me and the rest of the Cabinet that whatever political benefits might inure to us by full disclosure, were immeasurably outweighed by the credibility the revelations would grant the remaining Nazis. We decided therefore on a stoic silence. As the weeks passed and the revelations of the full extent of the brutality of Hitler's regime began to pour into a revitalized press in Germany, the erstwhile Nazis became silent themselves. Eventually, they drifted off into other political factions, most notably von Blomberg's and Goebbels' Military Conservative Party. But prudence still dictated silence. Even with that, the rumor and innuendo became so sustained that the American military attaché (none other than Dwight Eisenhower, now a Senator from Kansas) was forced to leave the country.

Only now, with the passage of many years, so much so that these revelations no longer have any political cogency, do I feel that my obligation to the demands of history outweigh the political consequences.

-

Excerpt from: Ma Vie Publique, 1929-1940
Albert Sarraut
Editions du Cerf (1955)

De Gaulle? What can I say of De Gaulle? He proved to be as adept at political intrigue as he was at military maneuvers. Somehow, with amazing deftness, he managed to portray himself as the military savior of France, while at the same time condemning me for my recklessness. My Socialist brethren had never been more than half-heartedly supportive. The Monarchist faction, Fascists themselves, were always ice cold. De Gaulle managed to rob me of any middle position.

Meanwhile, wave after wave of reaction came from the pacifists in England. My confrere Baldwin was under constant fire. They made a hero out of the fallen Hitler. This must have tempted Baldwin to divulge more. But in strictest confidence, I received notice from his government that it intended to continue to keep secret the full extent of the information it had available from persons inside the Wehrmacht, lest the remnant of the Nazi Party utilize that circumstance to renew its claim to power. I concurred with that, and to this day, without regret. But the decision left Baldwin and myself exposed to all the fire of our opponents, without the slightest shelter.

De Gaulle was merciless.

-

451

June 3, 1952
Le Figaro
Excerpt from interview with Premier Charles De Gaulle

. . . [B]efore that time, I had not considered politics as a career. But it became apparent to me that the Government was composed of a legion of imbeciles. What else could I do?

Excerpt from: My Name is Ike - Reflections on Fifty Years of Service as Soldier and Statesman
Dwight D. Eisenhower
Random House (1986)

Those days immediately after the fall of Hitler were strange days indeed, and not good ones for one Dwight David Eisenhower. The Army convened the Reichstag just long enough to call for new elections two months hence. That set off a political frenzy that in short order engulfed me.

For the Nazis may have been down, but they were not out. They hoped to regain power, if not absolute power as before, at least influence. It was then that the accusations of Karl von Haydenreich began, a campaign that has persisted to this day. For their own purposes, the Nazis insisted that Karl had in fact been a traitor and a British spy . . . that Hitler had been right. Never mind the absence of evidence. Little things like evidence never bothered Joseph Goebbels. Never mind, too, the arbitrary judgment that Adolf Hitler inflicted upon Karl. Goebbels denied that any such thing had ever happened. Karl von Haydenreich, despite the rumors, had suffered the fate he deserved at the hands of a firing squad. Hitler and the Nazis were the victims, and not Karl. That was the Goebbels view.

Inevitably, this came back to me. Goebbels had access to all the surveillance reports, all the accounts of the lunches I'd shared with Karl. Within days, he identified me in the newspapers and on the radio. Fevered speculation began about me. Who was I, what had I done? I was a friend of Karl's, and also a friend of British and French military men and diplomats. In short, I was the obvious suspect. I declined all interviews, and refused all comment, but it didn't end the wild fever. That got wilder every day.

Then, some Nazi dug up the fact that I'd received payments from the von Haydenreich estate, the trustee's fees I'd received in the 20's. So now I was not only a spy, but a venal, mercenary spy, who'd taken money from a traitor to undermine Hitler. Of course, the fact that the fees had ceased long before Hitler even took power made not the slightest difference to Goebbels' propaganda machine. All that meant is that we'd become more artful in our secrecy, aided (of course) by the cunning of our Jewish connections. Day by day, the heat became wilder. Of course, the United States papers picked up the story. *The Times, the Herald, the Washington Post*, all wanted interviews I declined to give.

The only saving grace is that there were other voices. Joseph Goebbels may have been the biggest loud-mouthed liar I ever encountered, but he was no longer the only game in town. Anyone with a printing press in the Reich seemed to be using it. That included many of the political opponents of the Nazis who had spent time in Dachau or the other concentration camps. They were not shy to tell everyone about what happened behind the barbed wire. There were others who raised the questions about Nazi murders, during the Night of the Long Knives and elsewhere, that should have been raised long before. That meant Goebbels had to play defense as well as offense. He didn't have a clear field as before. That took a little of the pressure off.

The one voice that was not heard, either by me or anyone else, was the one I wanted most to hear – the man in the Wehrmacht who'd been allied with Karl and myself, whose identity Karl had always been scrupulous to conceal from me. But there was no word, not even a hint in the newspapers. I never received so much as a scrap of paper. All was silent on that front.

The din and uproar went on and on. Within a few days, it all became too much. I was summoned to see the Ambassador.

-

Excerpt from: Service to the State - in War and Peace
Major General Werner von Blomberg
Reichswehr Press (1949)

Though the deposition of Adolf Hitler was a sad necessity, there was still much to be said for the National Socialism that he had represented. The German nation was beset by enemies, both foreign and domestic. Frick and I were concerned with the speed and vibrancy with which the Socialist press restored itself, like weeds sprouting after a rainfall. It was imperative that we react with all possible haste.

To that end, a few days after the coup, Frick brought Goebbels by to meet me. I must say I had never been on good terms with him. But the former Minister of Propaganda made an excellent impression. He confided in me that he, too, had had his doubts about the stability of Hitler as the month had

453

unfolded. As to some of the excesses of the S.A. and S.S., which were just then coming to light, Goebbels met my gaze directly and gave me his most solemn word that he had known nothing of these practices. I have never doubted his truthfulness.

He first put to me a rather delicate question. Rumors were circulating that the young Leutnant von Haydenreich had been treated with monstrous savagery by the S.S. It was also rumored that I was one of two generals who witnessed these events. I was able to reassure Herr Goebbels (as I have reassured all who have ever asked me) that I had no recollection of witnessing any such event. So far as I was concerned, the rumors were rumors only.

We then took up the more substantial issues concerning Karl von Haydenreich, to wit, whether he was in fact a traitor – whether Hitler had been right in fact, however deplorable his unseemly haste. The question of the truth of the accusation was critical to the credibility of the Nazi Party. He had brought with him the file on the matter. Collectively, we reviewed it in the cold light of day. Viewed objectively, evidence of guilt was overwhelming. Von Haydenreich as a Wehrmacht officer deserved a fair court martial, which Hitler was wrong to ignore. But in my view, a court martial would have come to the same conclusion

It was in this light that we then turned to the central question of Hitler. Goebbels candidly stated that the behavior of Adolf Hitler in the Rhineland crisis and after had caused Goebbels to wonder himself whether Hitler was indeed adequate to the leadership of the Nazi Party. But he emphasized that these personal failings should not be perceived by the public as a repudiation of the basic principles of National Socialism. It also did not change the fact that the Third Reich had fallen as a result of a coup organized by traitors and not as the result of any failings of its own.

I could not have agreed more with these sentiments. Thus, was the Military Conservative Party born. (We considered it imprudent to continue to identify our movement as Nazi.)

-

Excerpt from: My Name is Ike - Reflections on Fifty Years of Service as Soldier and Statesman
Dwight D. Eisenhower
Random House (1986)

Ambassador Dodd was not the sort of man to whom you could lie, or would want to lie. More than that, there were people in the Embassy, one in

454

particular, who had helped me in my little operation. There was no way I was going to let them be rolled up in a witch hunt.

But by that time, I had learned enough from the newspapers, from my contacts, from gossip, from the brute fact that no one had tried to arrest me, to know the whole wretched, farcical story. Karl hadn't been accused of anything that he or I had actually done. He'd been selected and murdered for no better reason than that the Nazis desperately needed a scapegoat. His uncle, my former co-trustee, acting purely out of ancient malice, had provided the pretext. I had become a target solely because of my association with Karl. It was only blind chance that had caused Heydrich's roving eye to fall on the very men who had brought about the Rhineland Fiasco.

The times in anyone's life when factual reality runs headlong into conflict with moral truth are rare indeed. But I knew this was one of them. If that vermin Goebbels ever got hold of the actual account of what had happened, that by purest chance Reinhard Heydrich happened on the right man, it would take him maybe fifteen minutes to pervert the injustice that his cronies had perpetrated against Karl into some righteous act of justice. There was no way in heaven or hell – *no way* – that I was ever going to see that happen.

So I admitted to espionage to the Ambassador, and took sole and full responsibility for everything. But I also told the Ambassador that I was not going to name my German contacts, not while they were still endangered. I was prepared to take the heat for what I'd done. But I was not naming anyone else.

Dodd understood at once. We Americans, one and all, high and low, have our standards about squealing. He thanked me for my candor, asked a few perfunctory questions, and that was all he wanted. I felt relieved for a moment. But then, in a gentle voice, he reminded me that the United States was firmly committed to neutrality, and told me that he had already received cables from the State Department and even some Congressmen demanding explanations. He was duty-bound to communicate my confession (his word) to them. I said I understood. But I felt sick to my stomach.

Of course, that wasn't the end of it. There were a couple of dozen reporters in the lobby, from both German and American newspapers. Someone, I don't remember who, counseled me it was better to take them on right then than put the confrontation off. That was good advice. Somehow, I recovered my composure and stepped into the lobby to meet the world.

It was in that instant, in that lobby, that my public life began. In the very same instant began the Great Camouflage. I had already made my choice for moral truth. I wasn't going to retreat. I admitted my own role. But I refused to give any more details. I wouldn't name anyone. As to Karl, I obfuscated, I equivocated, I spoke half-truths . . . and when I was pressed to the mat, I lied outright and directly. *I won't tell you who my contact was, but I will tell you that it was not Karl von Haydenreich.* That was my slogan, from then and the rest of my life, until the publication of these memoirs. I left Goebbels, and von Blomberg, and all the rest, to struggle endlessly justifying the ridiculously flimsy case they had against Karl. It became a constant anchor on their cause and their pretentions. I hope by the date this appears, it has sunk them permanently.

I would do the same thing all over again if it came to that. I was not going to throw the name, and the honor, and the decency, and the human reality, of my godson Karl and my best friend Heinrich von Haydenreich, into the cesspool of German politics. Truth hadn't mattered to the Nazi scum of the earth when they murdered my godson. They weren't going to get it from me now. They could keep wallowing in their self-serving justifications for the rest of time for all I cared. To be candid, I didn't care much more for the reporters. The more aggressive types were vermin. The callous ones who just wanted a story did not do much for me, either.

Of course, I knew even as I spoke, that there was at least one person (maybe persons) who could blow up everything I said. That was the mysterious, silent person in the Wehrmacht who had allied himself with Karl and myself. But my instinct was that that man, whoever he was, was very much on our side. Even if he was not, however, I'd reached a point where negative consequences didn't matter much to me. In the words of the hero of the novel that was so popular that year, *frankly, my dear reporters, I didn't give a damn.*

-

April 18, 1936
Volkische Beobachter
Editorial

. . . [T]he spy Eisenhower would like to persuade the world that he had dinner with Karl Haydenreich one evening, and by complete coincidence, a copy of the Order that betrayed Adolf Hitler and the Nazi cause to its foulest Jewish enemies appeared on his doorstep a few hours later.

Anyone who believes this is living in Cloud-Cuckoo-Land.

-

Excerpt from: My Name is Ike - Reflections on Fifty Years of Service as Soldier and Statesman
Dwight D. Eisenhower
Random House (1986)

My story, and my photograph, and all of it, made headlines around the world – particularly in the U.S. I had hoped the whole storm would end in the Ambassador's office. But now I knew it was just beginning. At the end of the day, I was summoned back to the Ambassador the next morning.

The Ambassador was a straight shooter, and he gave me all the bad news straight from the shoulder. The State Department and the War Department had heard enough. I was being recalled. I felt like I'd been punched in the stomach. I also received a hand-delivered letter from MacArthur, signed with his usual flourish, informing me in blunt language that I was a disgrace to the uniform, the tradition, all the rest. I knew then that my military career was completely kaput, without the slightest prayer of revival.

But worse was coming. Ambassador Dodd told me that the Senate was busy organizing a committee to inquire into my behavior. There was even talk of criminal charges. At that point, he looked up and noticed my expression. He got up and came around his desk. He sat on the front edge and looked down at me.

'*Ike,*' he said, '*for my two cents, you did the right thing. I will absolutely do my best for you.*'

He took my hand and shook it as warmly as anyone ever has in my life. His words were comforting and encouraging, but they were only words. Meanwhile, my career in the Army had disappeared like smoke, and I had to confront a mess of angry Senators. I had known the risks when I began with Karl. But knowing something in the abstract and confronting it in the flesh are two different things. To realize my entire career in public service had come to an end . . . the realization was devastating.

I went back to my quarters to pack. The next day I boarded the train for Calais, and from there, the long voyage home. I still had not heard from my 'friend' in the Wehrmacht. I still had no idea who he was. I was certain of three things as the train pulled out of the station. First, I would never return to Germany again. Second, I was never going to find out who the spy in the Wehrmacht was. Third, the future held nothing for me but shoveling manure on some farm in Kansas.

I was wrong three times.

457

Excerpt from: Eyewitness!
The True Story of the Fiasco on the Rhine and the Siege of the Reich
Chancellery
Oberfeldwebel (formerly) Victor H. Becker
Houghton, Mifflin (1950)

I served out my enlistment and left the Army the very day it was up. I had a little inheritance and I set up my own repair shop in Dusseldorf, where I am to this very day. For all these years, I've kept my peace. I knew I'd never be believed, any more than any of the others. But I'm not going to live forever, and people have to know these things. That's the reason I have told it all. All sorts of persons are going to call me liar, but I don't care.

You might think after all that service I'd support the Military Conservative Party. But I don't. I saw enough of those pig farts to know who they really are. Von Blomberg is the worst. If he admitted the truth, that he thought von Haydenreich was a spy for him, and that Heydrich accused him of treason, his own crowd would have nothing to do with him. If he admitted what a wretched fool he made of himself during the Putsch, no one would vote for him. If he admitted he saw what the Nazis actually did to von Haydenreich, no one would vote for *them*. So von Blomberg pretends he doesn't remember anything, and lies about everything. I've got no use for him or any of them.

I vote Center these days or Social Democrat. I even vote Communist every once in a while, if the girl handing out leaflets gives me a nice smile.

Excerpt from: Ma Vie Publique, 1929 -1940
Albert Sarraut
Editions du Cerf (1955)

So as events played out, I had traded Hitler for De Gaulle. Sometimes I am asked my opinion of that bargain, for France and for the world.

What a foolish thing to ask, I reply. I would endure a thousand Hitlers before one De Gaulle!

History played the cruelest of jokes on myself and France.

Excerpt from: A Twentieth Century Life
Albert Sommerville
Houghton, Mifflin (1959)

458

Elizabeth made no plans to leave, nor did we expect her to. (Always the best of house guests, she made repeated offers of reimbursement, all of which were instantly and firmly refused.) We were adrift and aimless in those numb, dead days. But then one day in late April, the maid delivered a note of Elizabeth's to me, that in crisp language inquired if she could join me at tea to discuss some business of an urgent, personal nature. Naturally I accepted, curious as to what the business was.

It proved to be momentous. Elizabeth told me of her pregnancy, of which Karl had never known. She had not been certain enough of her condition to inform him before she left Berlin. Then she gave me more news, almost as significant, of her family's plans to relocate to England. She had already applied to Oxford to finish her legal studies. She had also been in touch with her parents in Zurich. With Hitler gone, there was nothing to obstruct their return to Germany. But her father was revolted by that thought. He and his wife preferred to join her and their grandchildren in Great Britain. The decision had been made, final and irrevocable. She had sought the meeting to ask my help in finding suitable quarters in England for her sons and her parents, and with the other arrangements.

The announcement of a new baby helped to dispel the gloom that had enveloped the household. As to the rest, I was eager to provide all the aid I could, to be of some service to Karl's widow. A change of location as complete as she contemplated for a family as well established as hers would be of great practical difficulty for a woman in her condition. An agent in Germany would be required.

I suggested William Whittingham for the role, our agent in Berlin, little realizing I was playing Cupid. William was not at all the sort of man I would have thought matched up well with Elizabeth – twenty-five years her senior, and the type all his close associates thought might be euphemistically described as a confirmed bachelor. But his kindness and gentleness appealed to her, and perhaps provided a welcome change from the perturbations of her first married life. Three years later, they married. He is a good, decent man who has made a good, decent home for Elizabeth and her children.

So that is how I came to sponsor in this country my closest personal friend, and my bitterest political enemy, the Honorable Elizabeth Whittingham, Q.C., M.P., and leading light of the Universalist Party. I do have an unusual relationship with her. We are united by mutual affection for the memory of Karl and separated almost as completely by principle as two public figures can be. The rumors that we exchange glasses of wine at dinner in the evening, after exchanging insults all the living day, are true.

-

Excerpt from: My Life in Office
Stanley Baldwin
Houghton, Mifflin (1947)

I was able to delay the inevitable vote of no confidence for several months, until the King had sorted out his relationship with Wallis Simpson and come to the disgraceful decision that he did. But the outcome was inevitable. University opinion, labor opinion, middle class opinion, even Tory opinion – all united in decrying the decisions I had made with regard to Hitler, and in opposition to me.

That was the end, and no hope of redemption, either. These were not the sorts of issues that would ever be forgotten or forgiven. My career, which I had cherished, was over.

Biographers and historians sometimes approach me with the question – would I do it again? Was the candle worth the game? Was Hitler that dangerous? I do become impatient with some of the sentimentalizing about Hitler and his party, for they were bad, bad men. That basic fact is too often overlooked. But the basic inquiry – was the ruination of my career worth it?

I will provide a truthful answer to that question.

I don't know.

-

November 8th, 1936
London Times,
Birth Announcement

Born, to Elizabeth Golsing-von Haydenreich and the late Karl von Haydenreich, a daughter, Magdalena Charlotte Rosamunde Golsing-von Haydenreich, November 3rd, 1936. 7lbs, 1 oz.

-

Excerpt from: My Name is Ike - Reflections on Fifty Years of Service as
Soldier and Statesman
Dwight D. Eisenhower
Random House (1986)

. . . [I] was flayed alive at the Senate hearing. Newspaper reporters were there, magazine photographers, even newsreels. The Senators with large German and Irish constituencies were particularly brutal. How could I, an American officer serving on behalf of a neutral country, allow myself to be

460

involved in espionage for the British and French? Then there were the believers in isolationism. Senator Borah said he only wished there were a statute I could be charged under, so I could serve as a good example to anyone else with the same bright ideas. About the only good thing was they accepted my refusal to divulge the names of my associates. I told the Senators bluntly they were still in danger in Germany, and I wouldn't do that. They were American enough not to press, and I think even respected me for that.

My only friend was Mamie. She sat in one corner, with the same encouraging smile, while my career went up in flames and our lives collapsed in ruins. Her own opinions were blunt. *'If those high and mighty know-it-alls had seen what I saw in Berlin, that poor girl and that mob, they'd sing a different tune!'* It was nice to have my wife on my side, but of course it didn't count for much with the Senate.

It all ended with a round of ferocious denunciations of yours truly, each more vehement than the last. But it was only that. They took no other action. Finally, after everlasting fulminations, they were done. I left then with Mamie, both of us shaken to the core, and wondering what on earth we were going to do next. We were back in our hotel room to change for dinner, when the phone rang. The front desk phoned to inform me that I had visitors in the lobby. Mamie was dressing, so I went down by myself to find out who had business with me.

There were a half-dozen men there, one in rabbinical garb. One of the others I recognized as Felix Frankfurter, the aide to Roosevelt, and another as Bernard Baruch. To say I was amazed would be to put it mildly. What did men of this eminence want with a discredited major, a farm boy from Kansas?

The rabbi introduced himself as Rabbi Stephen Wise of the American Jewish Congress. Although he was not nearly as well known as the others, he was in charge. He took my hand and pumped my arm vigorously. Tears glistened in his eyes.

'Thank you, thank you, thank you,' he said, *'may God bless you, for what you have done, for Jewish people everywhere. For all the men of goodwill in the world.'* I recalled then some of the sickening incidents I had witnessed in Germany, and some that I had read about in the press. My attention had been so long focused on the political and military repercussions of the Nazi fall that I had scarcely thought of that. But now, at once, the veil fell. All these implications rushed upon me. I was speechless, and embarrassed, completely discomfited. I could only stammer out my thanks.

461

The men understood, I think. Baruch suggested we all have a drink in the lounge, where they could all hear more of my story. We did that, and I told them pretty much what I have written here – a much shorter version, of course.

Then Baruch looked at me and said seven words that changed my life.

'*Major,*' he said, '*have you considered running for Congress?*'

-

Excerpt from: Destiny Betrayed - A Chronicle of Treason
Harald Quandt
Franz Eher Nachfolger Gmbh (1952)

Thus, it was that Germany lost its best chance to restore its glory and regain its rightful place in the sun, and resigned itself to another decade of slavery to Versailles. The denials of the British and French governments that treason lay behind the fall of Hitler would not have fooled a child of six, had not the same Jewish traitors and Socialists against whom the Fuhrer had warned, arisen again almost instantaneously the moment he passed. How quickly the weeds infest the garden!

Within days, or even minutes (so it seemed), the eye of the public had shifted from grief at the fate of the Fuhrer, to the alleged misbehavior of S.A. and S.S. officers in the so-called concentration camps. Crocodile tears in abundance were shed for Kurt von Schleicher, Frau Schleicher, von Bredow, and von Kahr, and others such, even though these cases had long been closed.

Worst of all was the whitewashing of Karl von Haydenreich, the 'innocent' Wehrmacht officer who had been rightfully condemned by Hitler. Outrageous lies were spread about the manner in which he died, his corpse having conveniently been spirited off by von Hammerstein's friends in the Wehrmacht, so that no denial was possible. Even after proof emerged of his connection to the American military attaché, and the certainty that he was a spy for the British, the public could not be aroused. The most the new Government would do was the expulsion of Eisenhower, which did no good at all.

Then, years later, the useless gossip of a chauffeur emerged to reignite these scandalous insults. The truth is that von Blomberg, Frick, Joseph Goebbels (my stepfather), and others, have attempted to keep the principles of National Socialism alive in the new State. But the repugnant amorality and cynicism of the others makes their task a difficult one. Try as they might, the voice of the Military Conservative Party is too often lost in the wilderness.

462

The best days, and the holiest of chances, have passed forever. They died with Adolf Hitler and the coup. May all who betrayed the Third Reich fry in Hell.

Excerpt from: My Name is Ike - Reflections on Fifty Years of Service as
Soldier and Statesman
Dwight D. Eisenhower
Random House (1986)

I did not have contact with Elizabeth von Haydenreich until the fall of 1938. She was just back from the one and only visit she made to Germany, where she had completed the liquidation of her family's estates. She had taken the opportunity to retrieve her husband's journals, well concealed in a hidden compartment in the baby's nursery (and a good thing for that)! She was planning marriage to William Whittingham the following spring. But before moving on to that life, she wanted the truth from me about Karl.

She got it. Before the publication of this memoir, she was the only one who did. We had an exchange of letters, in which she was as forthright about her own attitudes as I was with her. She has always asked me to respect their confidentiality, and I always have. When, if ever, she chooses to make her own views known is her business.

-

Excerpt from: A Twentieth Century Life
Albert Sommerville
Houghton, Mifflin (1959)

As to the central controversy of Karl's life, his role as spy in the overthrow of Hitler, I have always been forthright. If my friend did help bring about the fall, all the better for him – it was a good work that he did. I never had any use for Hitler or his Party. They seemed to me at best to be an encumbrance. At worst, they were frightening human beings.

Perhaps this is an apt point to consider the effects the Nazis had on the world. Since my Imperial Party has much in common with the German Conservatives, one might assume I have the same lingering sympathy for Hitler that they sometimes exhibit.

Nothing could be further from the truth. In my opinion, the Fuhrer and his Nazis did incalculable damage to causes and principles of utmost importance to the world. His repugnant brutality and coarseness slandered us, one and all. Nowadays, the influence of the Yid and the Bolshevik spread in ever widening circles through all our society and institutions. But those who wish to speak out against these ominous trends must contend with the same inevitable allusions to Hitler, and his thugs, and his camps, and his barbarities, as if we were all criminals.

But we are not.

Racial solidarity has never been more important than now. The world is shrinking more every day. Sooner rather than later, some of these promising experiments with jet propulsion will be practical enough to utilize in aircraft. There is also the disturbing prospect of uranium-fueled super weapons. Already physicists in some American universities are attempting to create small atomic reactions (as they are called). It is not futuristic to expect these efforts to succeed by the turn of the century. In short, the White Man's Burden is becoming greater, not lesser. The Anglo-Saxon and Teutonic peoples of the earth must stand together.

As much as I admire her personally, Elizabeth's Universalism is as dangerous to Western civilization as any ideology ever promulgated. In her Party's endless insistence on equality and independence for Irish, Indians, Egyptians, niggers, and wogs of all kinds, she ignores the plain lessons of history, to the effect that these peoples are incapable of order, discipline, and self-government. She ignores, too, the endless opportunity for intrigue and subversion these campaigns grant to the Yid. The British Empire stands as it always has, as the one great bulwark in the world of orderly law and enlightened progress.

Adolf Hitler, in his hatred and cruelty, did incalculable damage to a clear understanding of these basic truths. One need not abandon law and all standards of decency in insisting on an appropriate social and racial order.

-

Excerpt from: My Name is Ike - Reflections on Fifty Years of Service as Soldier and Statesman
Dwight D. Eisenhower
Random House (1986)

I did return to Berlin, in 1943, not seven years after I thought I'd left for good. So much for predictions. I was on a Congressional committee examining our trade agreements with Germany. An uncharitable person might call it a junket. We were staying in the Adlon Hotel, a bittersweet experience for me. One night, shortly before dinner, I was crossing the lobby when an elderly gentleman accosted me. I did not recognize him at first.

'*General von Hammerstein,*' I said after a moment. It was no wonder I had been bewildered for a second. Not only was he out of uniform, but he had lost a great deal of weight and aged considerably.

'*Congressman Eisenhower,*' he said. '*I should like to talk to you. Perhaps over dinner.*'

'*It would be an honor, General,*' I answered, '*but I am invited on this evening –*'

'*I would like to talk to you,*' he interrupted, '*about a mutual friend of ours. Who did not end well.*'

In one moment of transcendent clairvoyance, I understood everything. My plans for the evening changed instantaneously. '*It was you,*' I said.

'*Yes,*' he answered, '*me.*'

Our dinner that night in a private room lasted past midnight. The General had just completed his memoirs. But he found himself reluctant to furnish them to the publisher, for precisely the same reason I had stonewalled in 1936 and after. His sense of responsibility to the truth was at odds with his sense of moral outrage. I knew that I, too, would have to address the same issue again and again, throughout my career and eventually in my own autobiography. By the end of the dinner, we had reached the understanding that you, the reader, see reflected here. We would both defer the publication of our books until March of 1986, when they would be published simultaneously. That was soon enough to be of value to historians, but long enough (we hoped) to be without political significance.

(A few months later, I mentioned in passing the meeting and agreement to Elizabeth. She informed me then that she was in possession of her late husband's journals, which she had retrieved from their hiding place on her one visit to Berlin. She decided on the instant to join us in the plan of publication. In 1947, we three met in London to confirm our mutual understanding. It was never more than a handshake agreement, and I am beyond the grave now and not in a position to know. But I would be amazed if all three of us did not honor it.)

'*They shot him out of expedience without trial and for nothing to do with anything he actually did,*' I said. '*Reason enough to deny them the benefit of the actual facts.*'

Von Hammerstein was quiet for a long moment. '*You believe he was shot?*' he said at last.

465

I felt a sick feeling in my stomach. Elizabeth had never believed in a firing squad. *'You heard different?'* I asked.

'I know different,' von Hammerstein replied. He took a big swallow of cognac. *'I bore witness. I must swear you to secrecy because I am honor-bound myself. But give me your word, and I will tell you everything. I promise you it will not weaken your resolution.'* I did so, and he gave me pretty much the same account that his chauffeur Becker published a few years later, the one that destroyed that bastard von Blomberg's career. I listened, not wanting to believe, but believing. Then we bid a shaky *auf wiedersehen*.

I stumbled into the bar, and got drunker that night then I have ever been before or since.

-

Excerpt from: A General Speaks - the Autobiography of Kurt von Hammerstein Equord
Major General Kurt von Hammerstein Equord
Reichswehr Press (1986)

Thus, fifty years after the fact, I will at last put an end to all the conjecture, rumors, controversy, the furious arguments pro and con. There was a cadre of resistance among the officers of the Reichswehr (later Wehrmacht), recruited by me personally after the Night of the Long Knives and organized by von Stauffenberg. Contingency plans were drawn up, various schemes discussed, though no action was undertaken until after Karl von Haydenreich's interview with the corporal. The numbers of officers in this group swelled after the Rhineland Fiasco, and again after the Coup began. All this is well known.

But who played the dubious role of spy? Who was it who provided the information and the Order itself to the British? Numerous supporters and well-wishers have defended me from the implication, pointing out how absurd it is that the head of the Reichswehr himself would take on the ignoble task of espionage. I regret I must disappoint them all. The one and only person who selected and prepared the material to the British was I myself, Kurt von Hammerstein-Equord, Major-General in the Reichswehr. I had seen enough of the corporal to perceive a grave threat both to the German nation and the German Army if his true plans and character were not exposed. I was uniquely positioned to distinguish between information that would be harmful to Hitler, and that which might damage the military. My objective was to provide the West with a plentiful amount of the first, and none of the second. History will judge whether my judgment was correct, but I believe it was. I acted alone. The

466

involvement of any other persons, no matter how committed, would have expanded the risk to unacceptable degrees. As to whether espionage is too disreputable an activity for the dignity of a general officer, in my view there is no action too undignified for a general, once a duty and a need to act on it has been perceived.

There were thus only two German officers involved – myself, who chose the information, and Karl von Haydenreich, who was the courier. I trusted Leutnant von Haydenreich completely. He was in fact more committed than I. I had my moments of irresolution, but he never did. '*I have seen enough of Hitler myself*', he once said, '*to know the necessity of this.*'

The copy of the Order that was furnished to the British was my own copy, marked for destruction until my young colleague spoke up. The idea of providing the actual Order to the British was his, though it had my enthusiastic approval. That is the historical fact.

I hope these disclosures end all controversy

I will now venture my opinion on another controversial matter. There is great disagreement as to whether Karl von Haydenreich was hero or villain with respect to the German nation. I witnessed him endure unimaginable cruelties with unflinching fortitude and grace. Not only his fate, but mine, and our other comrades, and possibly the fate of countless others, rested on his resolution. But he never wavered, and exhibited a degree of valorousness equal to any I have ever encountered on the battlefield.

In my opinion, Karl von Haydenreich was one of the great heroes of German history. Others will have their own opinions, but this is the perspective I wish to leave to history.

March 31, 1946
The Advocate (formerly: The Ballot Worker)
Editorial

On this, the tenth anniversary of the travesty that Great Britain and France managed to inflict on Germany, let us at least console ourselves that the advocates of peace were able to exact a political accounting from Stanley Baldwin and all the other believers in war and national revenge. We may hope that never again will raw, national power be the sole motive for the action of His Majesty's Government. But we will more than hope, we will guarantee, that similar consequences will be visited upon any and all statesmen who abuse the trust of this nation's people in like manner in the future.

Finally, let us wish a restful peace to Adolf Hitler, the true victim of Baldwin's machinations. His only crime was to devote himself to a renewed, more vigorous Germany. For this he paid with his life. May he find the eternal rest granted to all those martyred in the just causes of history.

-

Excerpt from: A History of Europe in the Twentieth Century
Giacomo Benedetti
Houghton, Mifflin (1957)

. . . [A]pplication of the most elementary principles of Marxism-Leninism easily demonstrates that by the spring of 1936 Adolf Hitler and the Third Reich were doomed. He had lost the allegiance of the petit bourgeoisie in German society, owing to the frustration of their consumerist desires. He no longer had the unfaltering support of the military nationalist elements. Of course, he had never had the loyalty of the proletarian mass, who despised him from the beginning due to his absurdist anti-Bolshevik rhetoric. Finally, he had challenged the super-imperialist hegemony of the Western powers by the denunciation of the Versailles Treaty.

Even a novice historical scholar could have predicted the outcome with confidence. The Third Reich was bound to collapse as a matter of historical science. The discussion of personalities, the search for heroes and villains, only demonstrates the strength of the delusions under which conventional historiography still labors . . .

-

Excerpt from: A Twentieth Century Life
Albert Sommerville
Houghton, Mifflin (1959)

Elizabeth made one trip back to Berlin and Munich, shortly after her daughter was born, to settle her family's affairs. She has never since returned to Germany. But I still make my way to Neustrelitz with family every July. This might sound cloddishly insensitive, but I do not go for the recreation. With Elizabeth and now her children's, permission, I always have leave to visit the gravesites. They are as peaceful and tranquil as ever.

It is my fancy that Karl's spirit communes there. I like to think when I visit that I am once more in the presence of my best friend. Then my mind rolls back to that day in 1925, when I learned that Karl had a far higher opinion of me than I had of myself – in fact, a far higher opinion of me than anyone else did. It was a day that changed my life. God knows we had different views of the world. But I know we would have remained friends. That is what is important.

This to me is the ultimate value in life, comradeship and the mutual respect of honorable men. Ideas, values, particularly politics – all those are secondary in the last analysis. At the end of the day, good will trumps everything.

Fresh flowers still decorate the grave of Rosamunde Breslau, even now, nearly forty years after her death. I had thought that might simply reflect the inertia of custom, but not so. It is the conscious act of the children and grandchildren of the people she befriended in her time. The young man she helped emigrate did well in America; his family has endowed a fund. Others have added to it.

The effects of her deeds ripple on, like a stone thrown in the lake her resting place overlooks.

Coda

2006

-

March 31, 2006
London Times
Four Letters Published Post-Mortem at the Direction of Dame Elizabeth
Whittingham, GCB, OBE, QC, LL.D. (Oxford, 1938)

To Whom It May Concern:

Our late, celebrated mother spoke frequently of the father none of us ever met. She loved to recall the summer of their courtship, the good times and high spirits she shared with our father and her brother Martin. Her eyes shone with laughter, and her voice was alive with merriment. These were the happiest days of her life, and she loved reliving them. But she never spoke of the central controversy of our father's life. From an early age, we all understood that questions about that were not to be put to her. The subject was one she refused to discuss, even with her children.

The historical controversy was largely resolved 20 years ago, by the simultaneous publications of the memoirs of Senator Dwight Eisenhower and General Kurt von Hammerstein-Equord. However, our mother did not wish to pass from this life without giving expression to the effect these events had on her personally. Accordingly, in her last will and testament, she directed us, her children and executors, to publish the four letters appended here on the next March 31st following her death. If the publication appears as intended, that would be this date, March 31, 2006, the 70th anniversary of the Wehrmacht Putsch and the fall of the Third Reich. The many admirers of our late mother who believe that she viewed these distant events with some sort of Olympian detachment will find their eyes opened wide by these letters.

From a larger historical perspective, this correspondence was the beginning of the long and profitable partnership of Elizabeth Whittingham and Dwight Eisenhower in the Universalist and Progressive causes that have done so much to undo the dismal effects of Western colonialism and racism. As

472

before, the family would request that, in lieu of remembrances, donations be made either to the British Universalist or Republican Progressive Parties (respectively)

Memorials should be made in the form of contributions to the Universal Party, which she led for so many years. Our mother does not have a gravesite. It was her testamentary wish that she be cremated and her ashes scattered over the Spree River in Berlin, where she believed our father's remains were discarded.

The Honorable Martin von Haydenreich, MP, QC
Commodore William von Haydenreich, RN
Mrs. Magdalena C.R. Smithson, CBE
(first oboist, London Philharmonic)

-

October 1, 1938
London, England

Dear Ike,

I had hoped to put the past behind me, and make my new life in England. But that has not happened. After two and one-half years, I am still mired in loss and anguish. I must know what truly happened, what Karl did or didn't do. His name is kicked about Germany like a football, and I know no more of the matter than anyone else.

I know you admitted spying before you left Berlin, but denied Karl was involved. Was that the truth, Ike? Or were you concealing something to protect Karl's reputation, or for some diplomatic purpose? My ignorance of the real facts torments me. Perhaps if I knew them, I could make sense of all that happened. So please oblige me in this, Ike, if you possibly can.

The United States is not so far from Great Britain that we get no news of your elections. I am aware you are running for Congress, and that you have a fine chance to win. No news of you could please me more, after the indignities you experienced with your Senate. You will make a splendid Congressman.

Sincerely,
Elizabeth Golsing-von Haydenreich

-

October 14, 1938
Olathe, Kansas

Dearest Elizabeth,

I had been wondering about you, and worrying about you, for a couple of years now. It was a great pleasure, and a relief, finally to hear from you. I

473

think about Karl all the time and miss him every day. I know it is worse for you. There are some stories that never entirely end. I think this is one of them.

As to what you asked, your question deserves the full, unvarnished truth and that is what I will give you. You have a moral right that belongs to no one else.

The truth is that Karl was the man who provided me with the copy of the Order that I gave in turn to the British. Karl obtained the Order from someone whose name I don't know, of high rank in the Wehrmacht. In the eighteen months before that, we had been systematically providing information to the Western powers, about who Adolf Hitler really was and what he intended. It started after the Night of the Long Knives. I can give you more details, and I will, if you ask. But let's leave it at that.

That's the truth. I hope puts you on the road to peace with yourself. You can do whatever you want with it. I'll keep to my story to the rest of the world. The ones who make the loudest demands for the truth are the ones who deserve it least. I'm not going to help them out. I hope you'll keep quiet, too, for the same reason. But that's entirely up to you.

I thought I was completely washed up when I left Berlin, but indeed I am running for Congress. Those newspapers of yours are right, too; I'm probably going to win. If I do, I'll be going to Washington with a lot I learned in Berlin, from Karl and even more from you. I'll never forget any of it. There's a lot more to say about all that, but maybe it can wait until we meet again.

Because we *will* meet again. Karl's memory, and you, and all of it, are too important to let go.

Sincerely,

Dwight D. Eisenhower

-

October 30, 1938
London, England

Dear Ike,

Thank you for the speed and candor of your reply. I realized as I read it that I did not need your confirmation. I realized I knew without it. I always knew. I was too much my mother's daughter, the dutiful German frau, to call Karl to account. I loved it when he was the hero for me. But I knew. I should never have pretended to myself that I did not.

I wanted to die in those first awful days. Perhaps I would have, were it not for my sons and the child I bore. That passed. It left in its place an aching grief from which I cannot free myself. Martin was old enough to ask about his father. What could I say to him? I finally gave Karl the daughter he wanted so badly, but he was not there to name her with me. Lena is a little beauty, but my beloved will never see her.

Why were we abandoned? Why did Karl do this? Adolf Hitler was a cruel, wicked man. I hated and feared him. I hope he writhes in hell fire for all eternity, for Martin and my father, and so many, many others. But though his crimes were huge, he himself was a small, feeble person. His misdeeds were the spiteful revenge a petty man takes on those he considers his betters. Karl once told me his father regarded Hitler as a person of infinite vacancy, and that is right. He did not come to power by brilliant stratagem or seize it by personal force. Von Papen handed him his chance in a moment of foolish weakness. He was no Napoleon. He lacked grandeur. Natural force would have brought him down, as surely as a dead leaf falls from a tree. My brother Martin made a joke about Hitler the day before he was arrested. *He is just a small flea near the arsehole of history*, he said, *and a loud fart will destroy him.* That is right, too. Hitler was already failing in 1936. There was no reason for Karl to take it upon himself to bring about his downfall. He did not have to do this.

Sometimes I become so angry I could howl at the moon. I become angry at all of us – his father, Mummi, myself, you, too, Ike – all of us. Then I remember that no one wanted this fate for him. Karl chose this path himself, all by himself. His mother, who died giving him life – how horrified she would be. Rosamunde, Mummi, would be in agonies of grief if she had lived to see this. You may believe in firing squads and military order, Ike, but I do not. The swine mutilated my beloved so badly they were ashamed to show his body. I cannot even bury him with the people he loved, where I hoped to lie beside him one day, when our allotted days were done. This unbearable thought torments me, but I cannot rid myself of it.

Millions of women lost husbands or sweethearts in the Great War, yet found another, and renewed themselves. Two of my mother's best friends were among them. For a time, I hoped I might be another such. But it was always a forlorn hope. There is another type, that lights only one candle. I knew in my heart I was one of those. After a suitable time, Albert introduced me to some of his eligible friends. They were all kind and decent, some quite attractive. But none was Karl. I was at dinner one evening, when I heard a saxophone in the

475

band play a certain way. I was at once as uncontrollably in tears as my baby daughter. My escort was sweet and understanding. But he was not Karl. I knew I must go another way.

You have heard or will hear I am engaged to a Mr. William Whittingham. But it is not a real marriage, Ike. It is an accommodation, nothing more. William is nearly 50, a sweet, decent man, who will make a good home for me and my children. I respect him enormously, and I will be a good, loyal wife to him. But William has made it clear he has no interest in troubling my bed, nor am I to ask where he sometimes spends his nights apart from me. He will have his wife, and I will have his name and a refuge from more ardent suitors. It is not the way I want to live, or ever thought I would live. But it is the way I will live.

I have at least found my calling. It was not the arsehole flea who murdered my brother, robbed my father of all his belief in life, and corrupted my husband's sense of himself. It was the cobwebs of prejudice, suspicion, and ancient distrust, which we refuse to brush away from our modern thoughts and institutions. It was those that provided the wretched, ridiculous little man with the opportunity to wreak the havoc that he did in the brief time granted to him. Thus, I have found my path. I will raise Karl's and my children as best I can, and I will use my little broom to brush away what muck I can. It is not possible to cleanse it all, but the house can be made cleaner. That will be my life's work.

By this time, your election is over. I am certain you won. I hope so; you will make a wonderful Congressman! Do you remember the conversation we had after the Nuremberg laws? I am embarrassed even now with the recollection of my youthful rudeness and beg your pardon again. But I hope you remember. I hope you remember, too, when you are in Congress. You live in the most wonderful country, Ike, founded on the most wonderful principles. It should not endure the stains on its character that it does. Albert Sommerville, Karl's friend, could not be a finer, more honorable man. He does not realize how he belittles himself with his 'Yids' and 'wogs' and 'niggers'. I hope someday he sees this.

As for Karl and Hitler and all of that, I know now I must bid adieu to these subjects, Ike, and forever. I cannot accomplish anything if I remain paralyzed in this confusion of grief and anger. So there will be no more of this. My wonderful Martin is as lively and precocious as the uncle he was named after, and little William no less so. But I must teach them that there are questions they must not ask, and answers I will not give. It must be the same

476

with Albert and Goldberg and all the others, who are naturally curious about what happened to a man they knew well, admired, and may have loved. I am sorry to frustrate them, but I will not speak of these matters to any of them. How the Wehrmacht Putsch happened, what Karl thought and did, what Hitler thought and did, who your friend in the Wehrmacht really was . . . all that is for others. I have just written all I am ever going to write or say on the subject.

Such must be, and will be, my public face. But it is only a mask, Ike. I am sure you knew that already. Behind the mask, my heart is uncontrollable. The least little thing – the sound of certain jazz chords, a familiar turn of phrase, an unexpected kindness – and at once the pain of loss is with me again. I keep the mask on, as best I can, but behind it, I go to pieces. Later, when I am alone, I find myself overcome by sorrow, and anger, and longing, and tears that cascade without end. The anguish is the same as it was on that first awful day. I know now it will always be thus – I cannot escape my own heart. All I can do is my best to confine my grief to the deepest, most private recesses of my soul. Perhaps there, someday, somehow, I might find a way to forgive Karl – for looking directly into my eyes and lying to me – for heeding his father's advice and not listening to me – for forgetting all he meant to me, to his children, to Albert, to you, to everyone, and waging meaningless war on a pipsqueak.

Perhaps, someday, somehow, I might even find the strength to forgive him for breaking my heart. I hope so.

For I will never, ever, ever, ever stop loving him.

Write to me, please, as soon as you are able, but never again on these subjects. I am done with them.

Your friend.

Elizabeth

-

November 20, 1938
Olathe, Kansas

Dear Elizabeth,

That letter of yours knocked me for a loop. All I can say is that I'm sorry, so sorry. I felt the loss of Karl so keenly myself, I didn't realize how tremendously greater the personal shock and sorrow must have been to you. I have to ask your forgiveness, which I never realized I needed, but which I can see now I need badly. It's an odd thing when the apology comes so belatedly, but that's the way it happens sometimes.

But enough of that. You're right, we must move on. We will indeed be friends, and allies as well. We both know something about the world not everybody else has found out. You predicted right —I did win the election. Now I'm Representative Dwight D. Eisenhower, Kansas, Third District. Mamie and I will be going off to Washington in a month or two. She's thrilled to be going back to the Capitol. So am I.

Of course, I remember what you said to me that evening. You weren't rude. You were appropriately emphatic. You lit into me about American hypocrisy when I tried to condemn Germany for the Nuremberg laws. It made me realize how much my own nation shoots itself in the foot by not even trying to live up to its principles. I'm going to be bringing that little pearl of insight with me to Washington. Mind you, I'm way ahead of my constituents on that point, probably 50 years. But it is a cause I am going to push, and soon as I can.

One of these fine days you're going to be a member of Parliament yourself. I'm certain of it. And then we'll see what we can make happen!

I'm enclosing your letter to me. I don't need to keep it, and I don't think you want it seen by anyone else. I understand what you wrote about closing the door. You're right about no one wanting that fate for Karl, though I sure hope you're wrong about firing squads being a fairy tale. You made me laugh with that word 'pipsqueak'. It sure describes the way I see Adolf Hitler now – a funny, silly man who would have been pathetic if he hadn't hurt so many people so badly. His regime unraveled so fast when it did unravel, that in hindsight he seems ridiculously small. I understand how infuriated you must become when you make the comparison between the magnitude of the loss you suffered, and the wretched little clown who was its cause. I feel a little bit of that myself.

And yet . . . and yet . . .

That wasn't the way we saw it at that time, was it? You, or me, or anyone? If I put my mind to it, I remember well enough what a political storm he threw up back then. I can remember how frightening Berlin was in those days. I remember those street scenes of Jews being harassed, and how no one said 'boo' after the Long Knives', even though it was clear he'd had innocent men murdered. Those Nuremberg rallies with the massed chanting —Lord, how that chilled my blood! I remember, too, the torch lights and the Black Shirts and Brown Shirts, and everyone listening on the radio to those speeches, with the same feverish blood.

478

When I think like that, I wonder how it might have turned out otherwise. Suppose Hitler'd gotten away with it in the Rhineland? Quieted down the Wehrmacht? Suppose he'd managed to parlay that into some additional successes? It might have turned out bad, far worse than anything we could possibly imagine now.

We will never know, because none of it ever happened. It's all in the world of might-have-been. They say a prophet is without honor in his own land. In the world we do live in, Karl's end seems sad and unnecessary, a 'useless waste', as you put it. But maybe in that other land, it's different. Maybe there he's the hero who saved the world. History — human reality— isn't as easy as we sometimes like to think. We never really know, do we? I mean this thought to be a consolation to you in those recurring moments of agonizing grief. Maybe, despite all the evidence, Karl had more wisdom than the rest of us.

It's a consolation I need for myself. There's another forgiveness besides yours I'm going to need one of these days. Somehow, somewhere, I'm going to meet up with my old, best friend Heinrich von Haydenreich — him, and Rosamunde, Charlotte, Karl's sister Lena, Frau Schallert, all of them. They will demand an explanation of the care I took of my godson. I don't know how I'm going to answer. I don't know what I'm going to say. I hope for myself, that somehow, somewhere, in some way, maybe in that land of might-have-been, it all means more than it seems to.

But now I, too, am done. I will never return to the subject again. You have my word on that. Let us by all means be friends. Let us be the strongest of allies. Let us do great things together in the memory, if not specifically the name, of my late godson and your late husband, Karl von Haydenreich!

Your friend,

Ike

P.S. 'Arsehole flea'? My God, Elizabeth. You Germans, even you women, are the most vulgar people on earth. But let's meet up as soon as we can. Let's make history!

End

Author's End Note

I hope you enjoyed reading *'A Prophet Without Honor'*. Some readers might be interested in learning more about the actual career paths taken by some of the more notable non-fiction characters who appeared in the story.

Dwight D Eisenhower did not go either to France with the American Expeditionary Force during World War I, or to Berlin in 1933. He did not refuse to participate in the Army's campaign against the Washington Hooverville. He remained a protégé of MacArthur and served on his staff in the Philippines during most of the 30's. He was very much a 'go-along, get-along' career officer during the years in which this narrative is set. His sterling qualities of leadership and moral sense did not assert themselves until he was chosen in 1942, over more than 300 senior officers, to head the Allied forces in Europe.

Kurt von Hammerstein-Equord was a German officer of exceptional intelligence and great intellectual scope. (Two of his daughters were active members of the German Communist Party.) He did become the Commander in Chief of the Reichswehr in 1930. However, rather than confronting the rising tide of Nazi influence in the German Army, he resigned out his position in January 1934, performing what the poet Dante in a different context contemptuously termed 'il gran rifiuto' – the refusal of a person in a position of authority to use his power for a good (perhaps necessary) purpose. He died of natural causes in 1943. The story grants him a few more years

Stanley Baldwin was very much a business-as-usual Prime Minister, often compared to the American Presidents Coolidge and Hoover. He was indifferent to the increasingly ominous pattern of German aggression.

Charles De Gaulle was, in fact, the author of a book on tank tactics and would have been a logical choice to command the relatively small military force required to oppose the Rhineland reoccupation.

That the **Reichswehr** (later, **Wehrmacht**) was the last and most resilient line of resistance to the Nazification of Germany may come as a surprise to many readers. But the military was honeycombed with plots and resistance throughout the entire duration of the Third Reich. Similarly, during the time span of the story, the **Gestapo** contained in its ranks any number of ordinary policemen who were in no way committed Nazis. It was not the instrument of political terror it later became.

481

Finally, the antics of **Adolf Hitler** described in the story, no matter how apparently excessive or bizarre, are all drawn from actual behaviors that he exhibited at various moments during his career. The case that Hitler suffered a breakdown at the end of World War I, that the blinding he recounted in Mein Kampf was actually a psychological break of some sort, was persuasively made by Thomas Weber in his book, *Hitler's First War,* which appeared in 2010.

The baseline portrayal of 'the corporal' in *A Prophet Without Honor* reflects my own view that Hitler was in fact a fragile, disordered personality, prone to hysteria and emotional fits. He was successful as an orator because he learned how to utilize these traits to transport himself into wildly emotional states that resonated with a mass audience (just as a well-struck tuning fork causes everything in the vicinity to vibrate on that wave length). Hitler had diabolical luck from 1928 on. During his vulnerable years, it shielded him from any crisis that would have caused his unstable character to crack or disintegrate. At the end, he was able to escape the reckoning his deeds and delusions deserved, by means of an orderly suicide on his own terms. His luck held.

The gruesome execution of Karl von Haydenreich is based on the executions of the July 20th conspirators. Hitler apparently did have the death agonies filmed for his own edification.

*

The Harvard professor and polymath Stephen Pinsker, in his fascinating book '*The Better Angels of Our Nature',* describes a growing consensus of historians who regard World War II as the product of a single individual. There was no drift towards war among European nations during the 30's. The pacifism engendered by the nightmares of the Great War was firmly rooted in the culture, even in military circles. There was only one person who actively sought a general European war. Unfortunately for Germany, Europe, and history, that person happened to be the son of Alois Schicklgruber, the man who occupied the position of Chancellor of the Third Reich. There is not that much to be gained from recognition of that depressing fact these days, in connection with events that happened so long ago and are so calcified in time.

It is, however, a good place to start a novel.

Other Works by the Author

I hope you enjoyed '*A Prophet Without Honor'* and the brief excursion into the land-of-might-have-been.

I am the author of three short novellas, all written under the name 'Joseph Wurtenbaugh', (or the alternative, 'Josephine', in the case of my one excursion into the romance genre). The first novella '*The Old Soul'*, is based on a unique concept of reincarnation and the phenomenon of *déjà vu*, centered on one of the most unusual protagonists in all fiction. The story was an Editor's Choice selection of Kindle Select in 2012.

The second, '*Warm Moonlight'*, is a supernatural tale of iintergenerational conflict and resolution. It has been translated into German by Amazon and added to its German catalog.

The third, '*Newton in the New Age,*' is a comic story in the mode of American domestic comedy of yesteryear. Readers who detest thrill rides will find it particularly appealing.

Finally, I am the author of the novel '*Thursday's Child',* which is an attempt to infuse a conventional 'Harlequin style' romance, with a novel of ideas and resonance. I believe the attempt was successful, but that is for the reader to decide. In any case, the novel has an epic, ,heroic quality that is almost entirely absent from most contemporary romances. (I feminized my normal writing name in that case, since a female writing name is all but required in that genre.)

All four works contain the same lively play of ideas which characterizes '*A Prophet Without Honor'*. All are uniquely voiced; I never repeat myself. I hope readers who enjoyed this novel will take a look at the others.

My Amazon author's site, with reviews and other commentary, is located here.

Thanks again for your interest in this book. Good reading to you.

Made in the USA
Las Vegas, NV
10 December 2021

36960972R00288